CHRONICLES
OF
ÆTHEL

BY: WESLEY A OLSON

DEDICATION & ACKNOWLEDGEMENTS

To the tireless dreamers, the relentless storytellers, and the unwavering believers in the power of myth and the magic woven within the fabric of reality. This tale, a tapestry spun from shadows and starlight, is dedicated to you. For it is you who inspire the creation of worlds beyond our own, who breathe life into the characters that walk the tightrope between light and darkness, and who seek the answers to life's most profound questions within the intricate patterns of narratives, both ancient and new.

This book is a testament to the human capacity for both immense cruelty and breathtaking compassion, a reflection of the duality that exists within each of us, mirroring the battles fought within the heart of the protagonist. His journey—a relentless confrontation with internal demons and cosmic forces—is a metaphor for the perpetual struggle between the shadow self and the aspiration towards a higher ideal. It is a journey that echoes across millennia, a testament to the enduring human experience of overcoming adversity, finding meaning in chaos, and seeking the light even when surrounded by the deepest darkness.

This dedication is also an acknowledgement of the rich tapestry of mythologies that have inspired its creation. From the ancient whispers of forgotten gods to the epic struggles of heroes long gone, these narratives have provided the fertile ground from which this story has sprung. It is a tribute to the power of storytelling to transcend time and space, to connect us to our shared human experience across generations and cultures. May this book serve as a small token of appreciation for the endless well of inspiration that these stories have provided. May it inspire you to continue to seek the fantastical, the mystical, and the awe-inspiring within yourselves, within the world around you, and within the realms beyond. For within these realms reside not only darkness and despair, but also an endless capacity for hope, redemption, and the creation of paradise from the ashes of hell. May this story inspire you to explore the boundless potential within both yourselves and the universe.

TABLE OF CONTENTS

1

The Whispers of Xalzar

The air hung thick and cold, a damp chill clinging to the skin like a shroud. Mist, thick as a woolen blanket, clung to the gnarled, ancient trees surrounding the village of Oakhaven, swallowing the rough-hewn houses in its ethereal embrace. It was a village untouched by time, or so it seemed, its existence a relic from a forgotten age, a place where whispers of forgotten gods mingled with the creak of ancient wood and the rustle of unseen things in the undergrowth. This was the place of my birth, a place etched forever in the tapestry of my memory, a place forever stained with the crimson hues of horror.

I remember the night vividly, though the years have blurred the edges of other memories, leaving only fragments and half-formed images. The moon, a malevolent eye in the inky sky, cast long, skeletal shadows that danced and writhed like the limbs of some unseen beast. The villagers, their faces contorted in a mixture of fear and grim determination, gathered around a crudely constructed altar. It was built from weathered stones, slick with an unnatural sheen, and the air thrummed with a palpable energy, a sickening sweetness that masked a deeper, more primordial stench.

At the center of the altar lay a young child – me. I was no older than five, my memory clouded by the terror and the ritual's unholy power. I can recall the piercing cold that numbed my body, a chilling wind that seemed to originate not from the outside world but from a dreadful abyss within myself. My screams, muffled and choked, were swallowed by the mist and the chanting voices of the villagers.

The chanting was a discordant symphony of pain and supplication, a terrifying incantation that scraped against my very soul. It spoke of ancient pacts and forgotten deities, of a being named Xalzar, a name that even now sends shivers down my spine. Xalzar, they said, was a being of immense power, an entity that dwelled in the shadows between worlds, a creature of darkness and despair. They sought his favor, his power, his unholy blessing.

The ritual itself remains a fragmented nightmare, a series of disjointed images that haunt my waking hours and plague my dreams. I see the glint of steel, the flash of wickedly sharp obsidian blades, the searing pain as the incisions were made across my flesh. These were not mere cuts, but ritualistic markings, symbols of power and servitude etched deep into my skin, scars that run far deeper than the surface of my being. They carved into the very fabric of my soul, tethering me to Xalzar, binding me to his will, making me a conduit for his hellish energies.

The smell of burning incense, acrid and suffocating, still lingers in my memory, a constant reminder of the horrific ordeal. The taste of blood, metallic and bitter, stains my tongue even now. The chilling touch of the demonic entity, cold as the grave and yet burning like the fires of hell, a sensation that remains imprinted on my soul. Xalzar's essence clung to me like a parasitic vine, entwining itself within my being, twisting and contorting my very essence.

The ritual ended with a shuddering groan that seemed to tear the very fabric of reality. The mist roiled and churned, the air crackled with unholy energy, and a wave of overwhelming darkness washed over me. I collapsed, unconscious, my body wracked with pain, my spirit broken. The villagers, their faces pale and drawn, scattered, leaving me alone in the chilling aftermath.

I awoke to a world that felt utterly different. The familiar warmth of Oakhaven was replaced by a pervasive chill that settled deep within my bones. The comforting embrace of my mother was replaced by an overwhelming sense of isolation, a profound loneliness that mirrored the darkness that had settled within me. The physical scars were evident, gruesome marks that would forever serve as a reminder of the nightmarish ritual. But the true scars were unseen, etched deeply into my psyche, into my very being.

Xalzar's influence was insidious, a creeping darkness that twisted my thoughts and clouded my perception. Nightmares plagued my sleep, vivid and terrifying visions of a world writhing in pain and consumed by shadows. During the day, a dull ache resided within my very core, a constant reminder of the demonic entity that had taken root within me. I experienced strange sensations, phantom touches, whispers in the silence, visions that blurred the lines between reality and delusion.

The villagers, once kind and familiar, now seemed to recoil from me, their eyes filled with a mixture of fear and apprehension. They whispered about my strange behavior, the dark aura that clung to me, the unsettling visions that occasionally escaped my lips. They spoke in hushed tones of Xalzar's curse, of the darkness that resided within me. I was ostracized, isolated, a pariah in my own village.

My childhood was one of solitude, of pain, and of the ever-present dread of Xalzar's growing influence. I learned to suppress my fear, to hide the monstrous entity that festered within. I learned to control, or at least to manage, the visions and the whispers, the unsettling sensations that wracked my body. But the darkness never truly left me. It was a constant companion, a lurking predator, a sinister presence that shaped my life and determined my destiny.

The mists of Oakhaven, the shadows of the ancient trees, the chilling memories of the ritual – all served as constant reminders of the demonic entity that had become a part of me. It was a burden I carried, a weight that pressed down upon my shoulders, threatening to crush me beneath its immeasurable darkness. But even in the face of such overwhelming horror, a faint spark of defiance ignited within me, a flicker of hope that whispered of a future where I might finally break free from Xalzar's grasp, a future where I might ultimately transcend the hell within and forge my own destiny. This hope, faint as it was, would become my guiding light, leading me on a perilous journey into the heart of darkness, a quest for redemption and the mastery of the very magic that had cursed me. It was a journey that would eventually lead me to confront not just the forces of darkness but also the daunting and terrifying powers that resided far beyond the mortal plane, powers that manipulated the fabric of reality itself. The whispers of Xalzar had set me on this path, but it was my own will that would ultimately determine my fate.

The obsidian city of Xylos, capital of the Crimson Scale tribe, was a monument to both terrifying power and breathtaking artistry. Jagged spires of black glass, polished to a mirror sheen, clawed at the perpetually twilight sky. Buildings, seemingly carved from the very heart of a volcano, rose in layers of unsettling symmetry, each a testament to the reptilian architects' mastery of shadow and light. Crimson banners, adorned with symbols that seemed to writhe and shift before my eyes, snapped in a wind that felt less like air and more like the breath of some colossal, slumbering beast. This was the heart of the Crimson Scales, the most powerful of the seven reptilian tribes, their winged rulers a chilling blend of majesty and menace.

These seven tribes—the Crimson Scales, the Emerald Fang, the Azure Claw, the Obsidian Heart, the Jade Wing, the Amber Eye, and the Shadow Scale—were not merely nations; they were interwoven threads in the tapestry of existence, their influence subtly shaping the very fabric of reality on the mortal plane. Their winged rulers, beings of terrifying grace and immense magical power, governed their respective tribes with an iron fist, their authority unquestioned, their whims the law. They did not rule openly; instead, they manipulated from the shadows, their machinations extending far beyond the boundaries of their obsidian cities and emerald jungles, their influence slithering into the hearts of nations and the minds of men.

Each tribe possessed unique magical abilities, their powers honed over millennia. The Crimson Scales, masters of blood magic, wielded the life force itself as a weapon, capable of summoning infernal flames and weaving enchantments of unimaginable power. The Emerald Fang, gifted with the manipulation of plant life and venomous toxins, controlled the very growth and decay of the natural world. The Azure Claw commanded the storms and tides, their power over the elements unmatched. The Obsidian Heart, dwelling in the deepest caverns, held sway over earth and stone, capable of manipulating the very bedrock of reality. The Jade Wing, masters of illusion and deception, manipulated minds and perceptions with terrifying finesse. The Amber Eye, gifted with precognitive visions and prophetic dreams, saw into the past, present, and future. And the Shadow Scale, their magic hidden in the deepest darkness, controlled fear itself, their very presence a chilling reminder of the abyss.

My journey to Xylos was arduous, a perilous trek across treacherous landscapes and through territories haunted by creatures born of nightmares. I had to navigate treacherous mountain passes, where the very air crackled with latent magical energies, and dense, primordial forests teeming with monstrous flora and fauna— creatures crafted from the nightmares of a thousand sleepless nights. The journey was fraught with encounters with the tribes themselves, with chance encounters shaping my understanding of this ancient and powerful race and their role in the intricate tapestry of my world.

I witnessed the intricate societal structure of these tribes firsthand. Their cities, built from materials that defied description, were marvels of engineering, intricate labyrinths of corridors and chambers that reflected the complexity of their culture. The winged rulers, towering figures draped in opulent finery, maintained their authority through a complex system of rituals, traditions, and unspoken agreements, their influence weaving through every aspect of their society, from the lowest scuttling servant to the highest-ranking sorcerer. Theirs was a rigid hierarchy, with strict codes of conduct and severe punishments for any perceived infraction.

But there were whispers, murmurs in the dark corners of the cities, hints of dissent and unrest. Not all within the tribes were content with the rule of the winged ones. Some sought to overthrow the established order, while others simply yearned for a different way of life, a world free from the subtle manipulations of their masters. These whispers, faint as they were, spoke of a growing unease, a simmering resentment that threatened to boil over and reshape the power dynamics of the entire world.

The Crimson Scales, in particular, fascinated me. Their obsidian city, Xylos, pulsed with an unsettling energy, a tangible sense of power that hummed in the air. Their magic, fueled by the very essence of life, was both terrifying and captivating, its potential both creative and destructive. I learned of their ancient rituals, their bloody sacrifices, and the terrible price they paid for their power. I learned of their alliances and betrayals, their complex relationships with the other tribes, and their interwoven history stretching back to the dawn of time.

The obsidian city itself was a character in this unfolding saga. Its towering spires, intricate carvings, and labyrinthine corridors reflected the tribal structure. Each district bore witness to a facet of the tribe's existence, from the grand palaces of the rulers to the squalid slums where the less fortunate toiled, fueling the city's engine with their sweat and blood. Even the city's layout seemed designed to reinforce the hierarchical nature of the Crimson Scale society, with the rulers dwelling at the apex, overlooking their subjects from their lofty positions.

I encountered individuals within the Crimson Scale tribe who defied the typical stereotype of cold, heartless reptilian rulers. There was a certain grace to them, a regal bearing, but beneath that veneer, hints of compassion, loyalty, and even love occasionally surfaced. This dichotomy further fueled my intrigue, challenging my preconceived notions about these ancient and powerful beings.

The city's defenses were formidable, a testament to their understanding of both mundane and magical warfare. Giant obsidian walls, carved with intricate runes, encircled the city, a formidable barrier against any would-be invaders. Powerful magical wards protected the city from unwanted intrusions, a web of unseen energies that shielded it from outside attacks. And the Crimson Scales themselves were fierce warriors, their prowess in combat legendary.

But the true power of the Crimson Scales lay not in their military might but in their mastery of magic, their ability to control the life force itself. They were able to manipulate the flow of energy through their bodies, summoning flames from their very being, healing grievous wounds with a touch, and unleashing devastating spells that could obliterate entire armies. They possessed a deep understanding of the underlying principles of magic, a knowledge passed down through generations, honed and perfected over millennia.

My time in Xylos was a dangerous dance with destiny. I learned of their long-standing manipulation of the mortal world, their insidious influence on events that shaped the very destiny of humanity. I saw how they used their power for their own gain, how they controlled the flow of magic to maintain their dominance over the mortal realm. This knowledge, both terrifying and revelatory, was a crucial step on my journey to conquer the hell within and ultimately reshape the destiny of our world. The echoes of the Seven Tribes, especially the chilling power of the Crimson Scales, resonated deeply, shaping my understanding of the cosmic horror that lay at the heart of our reality. This was far more than a simple struggle against a personal demon; it was a battle for the very soul of existence.

The obsidian spires of Xylos receded behind me, swallowed by the encroaching twilight. The journey had been brutal, a crucible forging my resolve, hardening my spirit against the chilling realities of this world. But the memories of Xylos, of the Crimson Scales and their terrifying grace, were not all that lingered. A more profound impression, a vision far more vivid and terrifying than any earthly encounter, haunted my waking hours and pierced even my deepest sleep.

It began as a tremor, a ripple in the fabric of reality, a sensation more felt than seen. Then, a blinding flash, a kaleidoscope of impossible colors erupted in my mind, a symphony of light and sound that transcended the limitations of human perception. I was swept away on a tide of pure energy, flung across vast gulfs of space and time, until I found myself... there.

The Celestial Court.

The words themselves felt inadequate, a pathetic attempt to capture the overwhelming grandeur of what I witnessed. It was not a place, not in the conventional sense. It existed outside of space and time, a realm of pure energy and consciousness, a shimmering tapestry woven from starlight and dreams. Beings of unimaginable power, entities that dwarfed even the winged rulers of the Seven Tribes, moved through this ethereal landscape.

They were not gods in the human sense – benevolent rulers dispensing blessings and punishments. These were something... older. More fundamental. They were the architects of reality, the weavers of fate, their very existence an embodiment of the cosmic forces that shaped the universe. Some resembled humanoid figures, though their forms shifted and changed, their bodies a kaleidoscope of light and shadow. Others were amorphous entities, swirling nebulae of consciousness, their thoughts rippling across the fabric of the Court like waves across an ocean.

One, in particular, captured my attention. It was a colossal entity, radiating an aura of unimaginable power, its form a swirling vortex of cosmic energies. Tendrils of light and shadow stretched out from its core, reaching into every corner of the Court, manipulating the very fabric of reality with effortless grace. Its presence filled me with both awe and terror, a profound understanding of my insignificance in the face of such immeasurable power.

I saw fragments of the mortal world reflected in the Court, miniature replicas of cities and landscapes, manipulated like pawns on a gigantic cosmic chessboard. The Seven Tribes were not merely powerful; they were pieces in a far grander game, their actions orchestrated by these unseen entities. Their manipulation of the mortal plane was not an act of random cruelty, but a calculated strategy, a means to an end that was far beyond my comprehension.

The colors were impossible, defying any earthly description. Imagine a sunset on a thousand suns, the iridescent shimmer of a nebula, the electric glow of a thousand thunderstorms, all woven together in a breathtaking spectacle. The very air thrummed with energy, a potent cocktail of power that vibrated in my bones, resonating deep within my soul.

I saw glimpses of the future, fragments of destinies unfolding across the mortal world. Battles raged, empires rose and fell, and the fates of mortals played out like a grim theatre. Yet, beneath this chaotic dance of events, a pattern emerged – a subtle manipulation orchestrated by the entities of the Celestial Court, a grand design that unfolded across millennia.

The beings in the Court did not communicate through words, but through emotions, thoughts, and pure energy. Their intentions were difficult to discern, a mix of apathy, amusement, and a chilling indifference to the suffering of mortals. They were not inherently malevolent, nor were they benevolent. They were simply... powerful. And their actions, however seemingly random or cruel, served a purpose beyond human understanding.

My vision ended as abruptly as it had begun. I was flung back into the mortal realm, the blinding light fading to leave behind only a lingering echo of the Court's overwhelming power. The experience was both transformative and terrifying. The memory of the Celestial Court lingered, a burning brand in my mind, a source of both immense fascination and dread.

This vision, this fleeting glimpse into the machinery of existence, ignited something within me. A thirst for power, a yearning for understanding, a desperate need to comprehend the forces that shaped my world, and my place within them. The whispers of Xalzar, the childhood ritual that had unleashed the demonic forces within, now felt insignificant compared to the cosmic horror I had witnessed. The battle was no longer merely a personal one; it was a struggle against the very architecture of reality, against the indifferent gods that manipulated the lives of mortals.

The knowledge I gained was a terrifying burden, a responsibility I could not ignore. I was no longer simply a man haunted by demons; I was a pawn in a cosmic game, and if I hoped to survive, let alone triumph, I needed to understand the rules of the game. I needed power. The power to comprehend the machinations of the Celestial Court, the power to defy their manipulation, and ultimately, the power to reshape the world in my own image.

The journey to Xylos had been a test, a prelude to the true challenge that lay ahead. I had glimpsed the reality beyond the mortal plane, a chilling reality of cosmic manipulation and indifferent power. Now, armed with this unsettling knowledge, I would embark on a new quest, a journey into the heart of darkness, a battle against the forces that sought to control my destiny. This wasn't simply about conquering the hell within; it was about confronting the hell that lay at the heart of existence itself, a battle that would transcend the mortal realm and pit me against forces older than time itself. The memory of the Celestial Court was a constant reminder of the scale of the challenge, the overwhelming power of my adversaries, and the potentially catastrophic consequences of failure. The path ahead was perilous, but my resolve was hardened, my spirit tempered in the fires of revelation. I would not be a pawn; I would be a player. I would carve my own destiny, even if it meant challenging the very architects of reality.

The obsidian shards of the Celestial Court's vision still glittered at the edges of my mind, a painful, beautiful reminder of the terrifying indifference of cosmic forces. My journey, I realized, was far from over. The whispers of Xalzar, the demonic echoes of my childhood ritual, were now a distant hum compared to the deafening roar of cosmic power I had witnessed. That power, that terrifying indifference, held a strange allure, a perverse invitation to grapple with forces beyond human comprehension. And then, it came. The summons.

It wasn't a voice, not in the conventional sense. It was a sensation, a subtle shift in the very fabric of reality, a tremor that resonated deep within my soul. It was a feeling of being watched, observed, assessed by something… ancient. Something powerful. It emanated from the forbidden forest, a place whispered about in hushed tones, a place shunned by even the bravest of adventurers. A place known as the Shadowwood.

The whispers spoke of Xylos, a being of immense power, a creature shrouded in mystery and rumor. Some spoke of Xylos as a benevolent guardian, a protector of the ancient secrets held within the Shadowwood. Others whispered of a malevolent entity, a twisted creature who fed on the fears and despair of those who dared to enter its domain. The truth, I suspected, lay somewhere in the shadowy space between these two extremes. Xylos was not simply good or evil; it was something… more.

The summons was not a command, but an invitation, veiled in ambiguity and laced with a chilling sense of foreboding. It spoke not of promises of reward or threats of punishment, but of a destiny yet to be unveiled, a path that beckoned me toward the unknown, toward a confrontation with forces that dwarfed even the terrifying entities of the Celestial Court.

The Shadowwood itself was a living entity, a place of immense power and unsettling beauty. Twisted, gnarled trees clawed at the sky, their branches intertwined like skeletal fingers reaching for the heavens. The air hung heavy with the scent of decay and damp earth, a perfume of ancient secrets and forgotten magic. Strange, luminous fungi pulsed with an inner light, casting an ethereal glow on the forest floor. Creatures both beautiful and terrifying lurked in the shadows – ethereal sprites with eyes like burning coals, monstrous spiders with legs that spanned the width of a man, and shadowy beasts that moved with unnerving silence.

The deeper I ventured, the more profound the sense of unease. The very trees seemed to watch me, their ancient eyes following my every move. The whispers of the wind carried with them not just the rustling of leaves but the unsettling murmurs of forgotten tongues, the echoes of ancient rituals, and the chilling laughter of unseen things.

The journey was a test, not just of physical endurance, but of the strength of my spirit, a trial designed to push me to the very limits of my sanity. The constant pressure, the pervasive sense of being watched, the constant threat of unseen dangers, all chipped away at my resolve. But I pressed on, driven by an irresistible force, a destiny I couldn't comprehend, yet could not ignore.

I encountered beings born of the Shadowwood's darkness, creatures of myth and legend brought to terrifying life. There were the Dryads, ancient tree spirits with bark-like skin and branches for limbs, their movements as slow and deliberate as the growth of the trees themselves. They watched me with ancient eyes, their silence far more menacing than any spoken threat. I also encountered the Shadow Wolves, creatures formed from the very darkness of the forest, their eyes burning with malevolent intelligence. Their howls echoed through the woods, a chilling symphony of fear and despair.

My path was strewn with obstacles, each more terrifying than the last. I navigated treacherous ravines, crossed rushing streams that pulsed with unnatural energy, and fought off creatures whose very existence challenged the boundaries of reality. The forest itself seemed to fight back, the trees themselves twisting and contorting to impede my progress.

But I persevered, driven by a primal instinct, a deep-seated need to understand the summons, to unravel the mystery of Xylos, and to confront whatever destiny awaited me. Each challenge tested my mettle, honed my skills, and pushed me closer to the brink of madness.

As I journeyed deeper, I began to notice subtle changes in the forest. The air grew colder, the darkness more profound. The whispers intensified, becoming more coherent, more insistent. They spoke of power, of knowledge, of a destiny intertwined with the very fate of the world.

Finally, after what felt like an eternity, I arrived. Before me stood Xylos.

It was not what I expected. It was not a towering beast, nor a magnificent god-like being. Xylos was... different. It was a being of pure energy, a swirling vortex of darkness and light, a creature that defied easy categorization. Its form shifted and changed, its essence fluid and elusive, making it difficult to perceive its true nature.

Xylos emanated a power so immense it was almost unbearable, a force that resonated deep within my very being. Yet, despite this overwhelming power, there was also a sense of vulnerability, a hint of uncertainty, almost as if Xylos itself was struggling with some hidden conflict. The entity's motives were as opaque as its form, a mixture of chilling indifference and unsettling curiosity.

Xylos did not speak in words, but in images, sensations, and pure energy, a language far beyond the capacity of human comprehension. Yet, somehow, I understood. Xylos spoke of the machinations of the Celestial Court, of the cosmic game being played out across the universe. It spoke of destinies woven and unwoven, of a grand design that encompassed all of existence.

The entity's message was ambiguous, a mixture of warnings and invitations. Xylos spoke of a coming conflict, a battle for the very soul of reality itself. The being offered no guarantees, no promises of victory, only a chance, a desperate gamble against impossible odds. The choice was mine.

The experience left me shaken, the weight of Xylos's revelations pressing down upon me. The forest, the creatures, the journey itself – all part of a grand design, a carefully orchestrated test to prepare me for something far greater. The summons from Xylos was not merely an invitation; it was an initiation. A ritual, as ancient and terrifying as the one that unleashed the demonic forces within me, was designed to forge me into the instrument of cosmic change. My destiny was no longer mine alone; it was intertwined with the fate of the cosmos, a terrifying and exhilarating prospect. The whispers of Xalzar were silenced, finally eclipsed by the immensity of the cosmic horror and the inescapable weight of my destiny. The path ahead remained shrouded in darkness, but for the first time, I felt not fear, but a chilling anticipation. The game had begun.

The Shadowwood's influence lingered, a clinging chill despite the warmth of the midday sun now climbing the eastern peaks. My journey continued, not into deeper woods, but upwards, into the jagged teeth of the Dragon's Tooth mountains. The range was infamous, a barrier of obsidian peaks and treacherous passes, a place where the wind howled with the voices of the dead and the earth itself seemed to writhe in silent agony. But this ascent was not a random choice; it felt... ordained, guided by an unseen hand, a continuation of the cryptic summons from Xylos.

The ascent was brutal. The air thinned with each gained elevation, the sun's warmth replaced by a biting wind that sought to tear me from the mountain's face. The path, barely a trail in places, wound precariously around sheer drops and across crumbling ledges. My boots, already worn from the Shadowwood's relentless undergrowth, struggled to find purchase on the loose scree and ice that coated the higher slopes. But the physical hardship was nothing compared to the inner battle raging within me.

The whispers of Xalzar, though subdued, were still present, a persistent undercurrent of malice that threatened to consume me. They were not mere auditory hallucinations; they were a manifestation of the demonic power still festering within my soul, a constant reminder of the ritual that had irrevocably altered my life. These whispers were accompanied by visions, fleeting images of swirling darkness and unimaginable horrors, a glimpse into the abyss from which Xalzar had emerged. I fought against these visions, against the insidious creep of despair, drawing upon the newfound strength and resilience forged in the crucible of the Shadowwood.

The struggle was not just physical; it was metaphysical. I was battling not only the elements and the demons of the Dragon's Tooth, but also the remnants of my former self, the man haunted by fear and plagued by self-doubt. I was learning to channel the cosmic energy that coursed through my veins, to mold it, to weaponized it against the darkness within and without. This was a slow, painful process, a constant dance between self-destruction and self-discovery. Each breath, each step, was a victory hard-won.

I began to notice subtle changes in my own perception. My senses sharpened, becoming more attuned to the subtle energies that permeated the world. I could sense the hum of the earth, the flow of magic in the wind, and the faint whispers of forgotten spirits trapped within the mountain's heart. My body, too, was undergoing a transformation. I felt stronger, faster, and more resilient. My skin seemed to shimmer with an otherworldly glow, a testament to the cosmic energy that now flowed through me.

The mountain itself seemed to test me. I encountered treacherous ice bridges that spanned yawning chasms, navigating them with a newfound grace and balance. I scaled sheer rock faces, using my growing magical abilities to create handholds and footholds where none existed. I endured blizzards that threatened to bury me alive, using my will alone to fight back against the relentless onslaught of snow and ice. Each challenge pushed me further, testing the limits of my physical and mental endurance, shaping me into something... more.

During one particularly harrowing ascent, a monstrous Gryphon, its plumage the color of a stormy sky, attacked. Its talons, sharper than any blade, tore at the fabric of my clothes, and its beak, strong enough to cleave stone, lashed out at my face. The fight was ferocious, a dance of death high amongst the peaks. I used my newfound magical abilities to deflect its attacks, summoning bolts of pure energy that seared its flesh. Yet, even as I fought, I felt a strange kinship with the creature, a recognition of the wild, untamed power that resided within both of us. It was a fight not of pure hate, but of a struggle for dominance, for survival, in the harsh landscape of the Dragon's Tooth.

The Gryphon, finally defeated, crashed down into the abyss below, leaving behind only a lingering sense of sorrow and awe. I was left contemplating the violence I had unleashed and the fragility of existence in this unforgiving world. Was I merely a tool of cosmic forces, or was this journey a matter of choice? Doubt plagued me, but soon the need for survival overcame my philosophical introspection.

The higher I climbed, the more ethereal the landscape became. The air grew thinner, the wind more ferocious, the land transformed into a tapestry of ice and snow, punctuated by jagged peaks that pierced the clouds. The flora and fauna of the lower slopes gave way to a barren, otherworldly landscape, seemingly untouched by life, a world of pure rock and ice. The silence was immense, a deafening hush that emphasized the isolation of my solitary ascent.

One evening, as the sun dipped below the horizon, painting the sky in hues of blood orange and bruised purple, I stumbled upon a hidden cave. Its entrance, barely visible beneath a shroud of ice and snow, concealed a space bathed in a strange, ethereal glow. Inside, I discovered ancient runes carved into the cave walls, symbols that resonated with a power I hadn't previously encountered. They spoke of a forgotten civilization, of beings who possessed a mastery of magic far surpassing my own, beings who had once walked these very peaks.

These ancient runes, I realized, were not merely inscriptions; they were a guide, a roadmap leading towards something... greater. They were a repository of forgotten knowledge, revealing a hidden history and offering a glimpse into the power that lay dormant within me. As I touched the runes, a surge of energy coursed through my body, invigorating me, strengthening my already heightened senses and magical abilities.

The whispers of Xalzar intensified, now laced with a frantic desperation, as if the demonic entity sensed the growing power within me. I countered them with a newfound confidence, channeling the cosmic energy flowing through my veins, using it to push back against the darkness that clung to my soul. The struggle continued, a relentless internal war between light and shadow.

The mountain's peak was finally within sight. It loomed before me, a pinnacle of rock and ice that seemed to reach toward the heavens, a place of immense power and untold mystery. As I approached, I felt an undeniable sense of destiny, a feeling that I was nearing a turning point, a place where my path would diverge, leading me towards a destiny I couldn't yet comprehend.

The path to the summit was the most perilous yet. I navigated icy slopes that threatened to send me tumbling into the abyss, traversed narrow ridges that seemed to defy gravity, and fought against winds that felt capable of ripping my very soul from my body. But with each challenge overcome, I felt my strength grow, my will hardening, my understanding of my own power expanding. The final ascent was a testament to my physical and spiritual fortitude, a journey of self-discovery and self-acceptance.

As I stood upon the summit, the world stretched out before me like an epic tapestry of mountains, forests, and valleys bathed in the golden rays of the setting sun. I had conquered not just a mountain, but a part of myself, silencing the whispers of Xalzar, and laying claim to the destiny that awaited me. The path ahead remained uncertain, yet I faced it with a chilling sense of anticipation, a warrior ready for the battles to come. The journey had just begun.

2

Trials of Xylos

The wind howled a mournful dirge as I stepped from the Dragon's Tooth summit onto a plateau of shimmering obsidian. Before me, the landscape twisted and reformed, a kaleidoscope of impossible angles and shifting shadows. This was Xylos's Labyrinth, a place not merely of physical challenge, but of psychological torment, a reflection of the chaotic battle raging within my own soul.

The air itself thrummed with a palpable energy, a chaotic symphony of magical currents that tugged at my senses, threatening to disorient and overwhelm. The obsidian ground beneath my feet was not solid; it shifted and flowed like dark water, threatening to swallow me whole. Each step required intense concentration, a careful negotiation between my will and the labyrinth's capricious nature. Ahead, the path, or what appeared to be a path, vanished and reappeared, a mocking mirage in the swirling mists.

My first trial was not a physical confrontation, but a test of perception. The labyrinth played tricks on my senses, creating illusions of familiar faces, long-dead friends and family, their voices whispering promises of comfort and escape. These weren't mere hallucinations; they were carefully constructed illusions, designed to exploit my deepest vulnerabilities, to tempt me toward despair and self-doubt.

I battled these phantoms with the newfound strength of my spirit, summoning the cosmic energy within me to shield my mind against their insidious influence. I focused on the breath within my lungs, the beat of my heart, anchoring myself to the present moment, refusing to be drawn into the vortex of the past. I would not succumb to the seductive whispers of grief and regret. The illusions eventually faded, replaced by a chilling silence, a testament to my resilience and unwavering resolve.

The next trial was a physical one. The landscape transformed into a treacherous maze of razor-sharp obsidian shards, each one imbued with a dark energy that threatened to consume me. I navigated the maze with caution, my movements precise and deliberate, my senses honed to the keenest edge. A false step would mean impalement, a careless touch, a searing burn that would leave me crippled. The labyrinth tested my physical prowess, my agility, and my reflexes.

As I moved deeper into the labyrinth, the trials became increasingly complex, each one a metaphor for a specific internal conflict. One trial presented me with a series of mirrors reflecting distorted versions of myself – arrogance, doubt, fear, rage – each one a different facet of the inner turmoil I sought to conquer. I had to confront these reflections, to acknowledge the shadows within myself without succumbing to them. I saw the boy who had unleashed Xalzar, haunted by the horrors of the ritual, terrified of the power that coursed through his veins. But I also saw the warrior, the survivor, the man who had stared into the abyss and refused to yield. The mirrors shattered as I embraced both the light and the darkness within.

Another trial was a series of riddles posed by spectral guardians, entities composed of pure shadow and malevolent energy. Their questions were not mere puzzles; they delved into the deepest recesses of my consciousness, probing my motivations, my beliefs, my very understanding of existence. Each answer required a deep and honest self-assessment, a confrontation with my own moral ambiguities.

One riddle, in particular, stood out. "What is the difference between power and dominion?" the spectral guardian asked, its voice a chilling echo in the labyrinth's heart. It was a question that spoke to the very core of my journey, forcing me to confront the potential for corruption inherent in my newfound power. My answer was born not from intellect alone, but from a hard-won wisdom forged in the crucible of my struggles: "Power is the capacity for action; dominion is the control of the will of others. One can be wielded for good or ill; the other corrupts inevitably."

The guardian, after a long pause, seemed to contemplate my answer. The shifting ground solidified for a moment, a hint of approval in this place of perpetual flux. The riddle was resolved not by a simple answer, but by a deeper understanding.

As I progressed, I realized that the labyrinth was not merely a place of trials, but a mirror reflecting my own inner landscape. The shifting terrain mirrored the instability of my own emotions, the shadows and illusions reflected my own self-doubt, and the trials themselves were symbolic representations of the internal conflicts I was striving to resolve.

The final trial was a confrontation with a manifestation of Xalzar himself, not as the physical entity I had previously encountered, but as a powerful psychic projection, a manifestation of the demonic power that still clung to my soul. This wasn't a physical battle, but a war of wills, a struggle for control over my own being. Xalzar attempted to overwhelm me with visions of despair, to sow doubt and self-loathing, to tempt me into succumbing to the darkness.

But I was prepared. I channeled the cosmic energy flowing through me, weaving a shield of pure light around my consciousness, resisting Xalzar's onslaught. I fought not with violence, but with the unwavering strength of my spirit, with the clarity of my purpose, with the unwavering conviction that I had the power to overcome this final obstacle.

The confrontation reached a fever pitch, a violent clash of wills that threatened to tear my soul apart. But slowly, steadily, I gained the upper hand, pushing back against Xalzar's influence, eroding the demonic power that had held me captive for so long. Finally, with a final, agonizing surge of energy, I shattered the illusion, freeing myself from the demonic grip that had plagued me for years.

The labyrinth dissolved around me, the shifting landscape solidifying into a tranquil garden, bathed in the warm light of dawn. The trials were over, but the journey had only just begun. I stepped out of the labyrinth, transformed, a being of immense power, yet humbled by the challenges I had faced. The path ahead remained uncertain, but I was ready, prepared to face whatever destiny awaited me. The seeds of a new world, a new pantheon, now rested within me.

The obsidian plateau gave way to a descending path, carved into the very heart of the earth. The shimmering surface dissolved into rough-hewn stone, the air growing heavy, thick with the scent of damp earth and something else... something ancient and unsettling. The mournful wind from above was replaced by a low, guttural hum that vibrated in my bones, a sound that seemed to emanate from the very fabric of the earth itself. This was no mere labyrinth; it was a descent into the underworld, a journey into the forgotten depths of Xylos.

The path twisted and turned, leading me through a series of subterranean caverns, their vastness dwarfing my own insignificance. Gigantic stalactites hung like petrified icicles from the high, shadowy ceilings, their surfaces slick with moisture, reflecting the feeble light of my own inner luminescence. The air was still, heavy with a sense of expectation, of lurking secrets. The silence was broken only by the occasional drip of water, each drop echoing through the cavernous spaces like a mournful knell.

As I ventured deeper, the walls began to shift and writhe, the stone itself seeming to breathe. Strange, bioluminescent fungi illuminated pockets of the cavern, casting an eerie, otherworldly glow on the surroundings. Their phosphorescent light revealed carvings on the cavern walls, intricate and disturbing, depicting scenes of cosmic horror, of beings beyond human comprehension, their forms twisting and shifting in a never-ending dance of chaos and destruction. These weren't mere decorations; they were warnings, glimpses into the true nature of the labyrinth and the horrors it contained.

Then, I heard them – whispers, faint at first, like the rustling of leaves in a distant forest, growing steadily louder, more insistent, until they filled the caverns with their cacophony. The whispers were not human; they were ancient, echoing with the weight of millennia, laden with the knowledge of forgotten ages. They spoke of the creation of the world, of the rise and fall of civilizations, of the gods and monsters that had walked the earth before. They spoke of Xalzar.

Not as a simple demon, but as something far older, far more terrifying. The whispers painted a picture of Xalzar not as a singular entity but as a fragment, a shard of a cosmic horror, a being of pure, unadulterated chaos that had been imprisoned within the world, its essence splintering across time and space, infecting the hearts of men and fueling their darkest desires. The whispers revealed that the ritual I had performed as a child had not merely unleashed Xalzar, but had awakened him, providing him with a vessel, a conduit to the mortal plane.

The entities themselves remained unseen, their whispers emanating from the very stones, from the shadows that clung to the cavern walls. But I sensed their presence, a palpable weight in the air, a chilling sense of being watched, judged. They were monstrous in their power, in their ancient wisdom, in their utter indifference to my plight. They were keepers of secrets, guardians of forgotten truths, and they chose to reveal these truths to me, not out of benevolence, but because I had somehow earned the right, or perhaps the misfortune, to know.

One whisper, clearer than the rest, spoke of a prophecy, a prophecy of a savior, a being who would unite the mortal and cosmic realms, who would harness the power of Xalzar and use it to forge a new reality. The prophecy was veiled in riddles, its meaning obscured by layers of symbolism and allegory, but I understood its core message: I was that savior, or at least, I had the potential to be.

The whispers also revealed the true nature of the Labyrinth of Xylos. It was not merely a test of strength and willpower, but a pilgrimage, a journey into the heart of darkness, a confrontation with the deepest recesses of my own soul. The trials were not arbitrary; they were designed to reveal my true nature, to expose my weaknesses, and to test my resolve. The Labyrinth was a mirror, reflecting my own internal conflicts, forcing me to confront the shadows within myself, to embrace both the light and the darkness that coexisted within my being.

As the whispers continued, the caverns deepened, the passages twisting into a maze of ever-increasing complexity. I began to lose all sense of direction, swallowed by the labyrinth's relentless, suffocating embrace. The bioluminescent fungi cast grotesque shadows, twisting familiar shapes into monstrous parodies, adding to the unsettling atmosphere. The air grew colder, a chilling dampness seeping into my clothes, clinging to my skin.

I encountered more carvings, deeper into the caverns, depicting not just cosmic horrors, but also scenes of ritualistic sacrifice, of ancient gods being appeased with the blood of mortals. The images were visceral, unsettling, leaving a lingering sense of dread that chilled me to the bone. These weren't mere historical depictions; they were active, pulsing with a dark energy, a malevolent aura that threatened to corrupt my very being.

The whispers intensified, morphing into a chorus of voices, a symphony of ancient hatred and cosmic despair. They pressed against my mind, attempting to overwhelm my senses, to shatter my resolve. They showed me visions of a future consumed by darkness, a world ruled by Xalzar, where humanity was enslaved, its spirit crushed under the heel of the demonic tyrant.

But I resisted. I drew upon the cosmic energy within me, creating a shield of light around my mind, protecting myself from the insidious whispers. I focused on my purpose, on my mission to conquer Xalzar, to save humanity, and to forge a new world.

The whispers retreated, temporarily silenced, but only for a moment. They would return, stronger, more persistent. My journey through the depths of Xylos was far from over. The ancient entities, unseen but ever-present, continued to watch, to judge, to test my resolve. The deeper I went, the more I realized that the true battle was not against Xalzar himself, but against the darkness within my own soul. The subterranean caverns, the whispering entities, the terrifying visions, they were all tests designed to push me to my limits, to see if I had the strength, the willpower, the very essence of divinity within me, to succeed where others had failed. The path ahead was uncertain, fraught with peril, but I knew, with a growing certainty, that I had to continue. For the fate of the world, and perhaps even the cosmos, rested upon my shoulders. The whispers from the depths were not just a warning; they were a challenge. A challenge I was determined to meet.

The air grew colder, a palpable shift that went beyond the natural chill of the subterranean depths. It was a cold that seeped into my very being, a cold born not of ice, but of dread, of pure, unadulterated terror. The whispers ceased, replaced by a silence even more unnerving than the cacophony that had preceded it. The labyrinth seemed to hold its breath, the very stones themselves seeming to anticipate something momentous.

Then, it began, not with a bang, not with a scream, but with a subtle shift in the air, a distortion in the perceived reality around me. The cavern walls rippled, their surfaces dissolving into a swirling vortex of shadow and light. The bioluminescent fungi pulsed with an unnatural rhythm, their phosphorescent glow intensifying, casting grotesque, elongated shadows that danced and writhed like sentient beings.

I was no longer in the labyrinth of Xylos, not entirely. The physical reality around me had become a reflection of my inner world, a nightmarish landscape sculpted from the deepest recesses of my subconscious. It was a hellscape of twisted forms and unsettling imagery, a reflection of the Xalzar within, the demon I had unwittingly unleashed years ago.

Before me, a vast, desolate plain stretched to an impossible horizon. The ground was cracked and parched, the earth itself seemingly bleeding a viscous, black ichor. Twisted, skeletal trees clawed at the sky, their branches adorned with grotesque, parasitic growths that pulsed with a sickly, internal light. The sky was a swirling vortex of crimson and black, devoid of stars, a perpetual twilight that hinted at an eternal night.

And then I saw him. Or, rather, I saw *it.* It wasn't the Xalzar of the whispers, the cosmic horror hinted at in the ancient carvings. This was something... different. This was Xalzar as a manifestation of my own inner demons, a reflection of my deepest fears and insecurities, given form and substance within this twisted reflection of my soul.

It was a monstrous amalgamation of shadow and flame, a being of pure malevolence, its form shifting and changing constantly, defying any attempt at concrete definition. Sometimes it resembled a serpentine creature, its scales shimmering with infernal light, its multiple heads hissing with venom. Other times, it took the form of a towering, skeletal figure, its bony fingers reaching out, clawing at the air, its empty sockets burning with an inner fire. And at other times, it was simply a formless entity of pure darkness, its presence felt more than seen, a suffocating weight that pressed down on me, threatening to crush my very being.

This was not a physical battle; it was a war within my own mind, a struggle for dominance between the light and the darkness that coexisted within my soul. The Xalzar before me was not simply an external threat; it was a part of me, a festering wound that had lain dormant for years, now awakened and demanding recognition.

The battle began with a torrent of psychic attacks. Waves of pure hatred and despair washed over me, threatening to drown me in their suffocating embrace. The entity twisted my memories, presenting them in a distorted, nightmarish light, amplifying my past failures, magnifying my deepest regrets. It fed on my doubts, my fears, my insecurities, seeking to break my spirit and consume my soul.

But I resisted. I drew upon the cosmic energy within me, the same power that had guided me through the labyrinth, the same force that had allowed me to survive the whispers. I created a shield of light, a bastion of hope against the encroaching darkness. I focused on my purpose, on my mission to save humanity, to conquer not only the external Xalzar but also the demon within.

The battle raged for what felt like an eternity. I fought back with everything I had, drawing upon reserves of strength and willpower I didn't know I possessed. I confronted my deepest fears, acknowledged my past mistakes, and forgave myself for the sins I had committed. With each blow I parried, each psychic attack I deflected, I felt myself growing stronger, more resolute. The darkness within me began to recede, slowly, but surely.

The landscape of my subconscious began to change. The desolate plain slowly transformed into a fertile valley, the cracked earth giving way to lush greenery. The twisted trees became majestic oaks, their branches reaching towards a sky that gradually shifted from crimson to a hopeful blue. The parasitic growths withered and died, replaced by vibrant flowers and lush vegetation. The black ichor transformed into crystal-clear streams, feeding life back into the parched land.

As the landscape changed, so too did the form of Xalzar. Its monstrous form began to shrink, its menacing presence growing weaker. The shadow and flame that constituted its being slowly faded, leaving behind only a faint whisper of its former power. It was a slow, agonizing death, not of physical annihilation, but of spiritual dissolution.

Finally, after what seemed like a lifetime of struggle, the last vestiges of Xalzar vanished, dissolving into nothingness. The nightmarish landscape around me transformed completely. The valley flourished, bursting with life and vibrant color. A sense of peace and serenity washed over me, a feeling of profound release and liberation.

I stood in the midst of this newfound paradise, feeling lighter than I had ever felt before. The darkness within me was gone, replaced by a newfound understanding of myself, my strengths, and my weaknesses. The battle had been brutal, but I had emerged victorious. I had confronted the beast within and emerged triumphant. The path ahead was still uncertain, but I knew, with unwavering certainty, that I was ready. The trials of Xylos had not broken me; they had forged me anew, transforming me into something greater, something stronger, something ready to face whatever challenges lay ahead. The journey to defeat Xalzar was far from over, but this internal victory was a critical turning point, a testament to the resilience of the human spirit, and the indomitable power of self-belief. I was ready for the next challenge, for the next trial, for the next step on the path to saving the world.

The silence that followed Xalzar's annihilation was profound, a stark contrast to the cacophony of the psychic battle. It wasn't an empty silence, though. It was a silence pregnant with possibility, brimming with the quiet hum of nascent power. The landscape of my reformed subconscious shimmered, the vibrant colors intensifying, the air thick with an almost tangible energy. Then, from the heart of the valley, a light bloomed, a radiant orb of pure, unadulterated energy that pulsed with a life of its own. It expanded, growing until it filled my vision, a celestial sun in miniature.

As I approached, the light resolved itself into a form, solidifying into a structure of breathtaking beauty. It was a crystalline obelisk, approximately five feet tall, its facets shimmering with an ethereal, internal light. Runes, unlike any I had ever seen, pulsed across its surface, glowing with a soft, celestial radiance. They seemed to shift and change, their meaning elusive, yet somehow instantly understandable. They were a language of pure energy, speaking not to the intellect but to the soul. The obelisk itself was cool to the touch, but radiated an intense heat that permeated my very being, a warmth that was both invigorating and soothing.

A voice, not spoken but felt, resonated within the crystalline structure. It wasn't a voice in the conventional sense, but rather a direct transmission of thought, a communion between my mind and the obelisk itself.

"The Gift of Xylos," it echoed, the words reverberating within my very essence. *"A fragment of the cosmos, a vessel of power, a key to unlocking your true potential."*

The obelisk pulsed again, its internal light intensifying, and a wave of knowledge washed over me. It wasn't the simple accumulation of facts, but a deeper understanding, a profound insight into the nature of reality, of magic, and of my own place within the grand cosmic tapestry. I understood the underlying principles of the universe, the delicate balance between chaos and order, and the intricate web of connections that bound everything together. I saw the flow of cosmic energy, the ebb and flow of creation and destruction, the endless cycle of birth, death, and rebirth.

The knowledge was overwhelming, yet exhilarating. It was a feeling of empowerment, of potential unleashed. The Gift of Xylos was not just an object; it was an extension of myself, a part of me, a reflection of my own innate power. The obelisk contained a vast reservoir of cosmic energy, subtly influencing my consciousness, amplifying my abilities, enhancing my already formidable gifts. I felt a surge of power, the sort of power that could rewrite the very laws of nature.

As the initial surge of knowledge subsided, I began to comprehend the full extent of the obelisk's powers. It wasn't just a source of raw magic, it was a conduit to the cosmos, a connection to the very fabric of existence. Through it, I could manipulate the elements, harness the energies of the universe, and even affect the flow of time itself. Its power was subtle yet profound, capable of the most delicate manipulation as well as acts of unimaginable creation.

The runes on its surface revealed themselves to be keys to its power. Each rune represented a different aspect of the cosmos, a different facet of reality. By understanding and manipulating these runes, I could unlock specific aspects of the obelisk's power, granting me access to a vast array of abilities. I sensed an almost limitless potential within the obelisk, a power that was both awe-inspiring and terrifying. With its power, the lines between creation and destruction blurred. The balance of cosmic energies could shift, to a point of unimaginable power, or utter destruction.

With a newfound understanding of my abilities, I felt a sense of responsibility. This power was not to be wielded lightly; it was a gift, but it was also a burden. It was a responsibility that I now bore the weight of, and that weight felt immense, yet strangely exhilarating.

The landscape around me shifted once more, the ethereal valley transforming into a vast, subterranean chamber. The walls of the chamber were formed from an obsidian-like material, polished to a mirror-like sheen, reflecting the light of the obelisk in an infinite array of shimmering reflections. The chamber was circular, immense in size, and utterly silent, except for the faint hum of the obelisk itself.

In the center of the chamber, a pedestal of polished black stone stood silently awaiting. Upon it, rested a second artifact – a circlet of twisted silver, inlaid with what looked like tiny, pulsating stars. These stars glowed with a faint, ethereal light, their luminescence synchronized with the obelisk's own internal radiance. As I drew closer, the circlet hummed in response, resonating with the energy of the obelisk.

The Gift of Xylos resonated with an unknown power, amplifying the faint pulse of the circlet. The obelisk's internal light surged, illuminating the chamber, throwing long, distorted shadows across the obsidian walls. The circlet's stars brightened, their light intensifying until they burned with a brilliant, almost blinding, radiance. Another wave of knowledge washed over me. This was the Circlet of Xylos, an amplifier for the obelisk's power, a focusing lens for the cosmic energy it contained. It was designed to magnify and direct my abilities, channeling the raw power of the obelisk into focused beams of energy, allowing for precise and controlled manipulation of reality. It was a tool of immense power, but it was also extremely dangerous if used carelessly.

The circlet pulsed once more, a silent invitation. I reached out, my fingers trembling slightly, and gently touched its surface. A surge of energy flowed into me, a connection forged between the obelisk, the circlet, and myself. I felt a strange, almost symbiotic connection with the artifacts, a sense of unity that transcended the boundaries of my own being. The power was intoxicating, overwhelming, yet I felt a newfound sense of control, a mastery of the immense energy flowing through me. I was no longer merely a conduit; I had become one with the power itself.

The obsidian walls of the chamber seemed to pulse, their polished surfaces rippling with unseen energy. The air crackled with power, the silence punctuated by the faint hum of the obelisk and the rhythmic pulse of the circlet. The very fabric of reality seemed to tremble beneath the weight of the power that flowed through me. The trials of Xylos were far from over, but with the Gift and the Circlet, I felt an unwavering sense of purpose. I was ready. The journey to confront the true threat of Xalzar had truly begun. My internal demons conquered, and I felt ready to face the horrors to come. I possessed the power to alter reality itself; the fate of humanity rested upon my shoulders. The path ahead would be fraught with peril, with impossible odds, but I would not waver. I had faced my own darkness and emerged triumphant. The journey to conquer the external darkness had only just begun. The weight of the cosmos rested upon my shoulders, and I felt ready to bear it. The time to save humanity had arrived.

The obsidian walls dissolved, not with a bang or a crackle of energy, but with a slow, almost imperceptible shimmer. One moment, I was surrounded by the cold, polished surface; the next, I stood in a vast, open cavern bathed in the ethereal glow of a thousand unseen stars. The air here was different, lighter, carrying the scent of ozone and something else, something ancient and indescribably alien. The labyrinth had been a crucible, forging me anew in its heart of darkness. I emerged not as the man who entered, but as something... more.

My reflection in a nearby pool of still, crystalline water confirmed the transformation. My eyes, once a commonplace brown, now burned with an inner fire, radiating a faint, celestial glow. My skin, once pale and unremarkable, now possessed a subtle luminescence, as if infused with starlight. The lines etched on my face by years of hardship seemed to have softened, replaced by a newfound confidence, a serene power that emanated from within. Even my physique seemed altered; leaner, more defined, imbued with an almost unnatural grace and strength. The demonic energy that had once haunted me, that had threatened to consume me entirely, was now a subdued current, a faint tremor beneath a sea of cosmic power. The hellish torment within was not vanquished entirely, merely tamed, a subdued energy now harnessed and controlled.

I looked at my hands, studying them carefully. The subtle pulse of the Circlet of Xylos thrummed beneath my skin, a faint vibration resonating with the power of the obelisk. I could feel the raw cosmic energy flowing through me, a ceaseless river of pure power, potent and exhilarating. It was a power that both thrilled and terrified me, a burden and a gift inextricably entwined. The weight of the cosmos felt less like a crushing burden and more like a thrilling responsibility.

The cavern itself was a marvel of nature, or perhaps something beyond nature. Gigantic stalactites, shimmering with an inner light, descended from an unseen ceiling, their surfaces intricately carved with symbols that echoed the runes on the obelisk. Strange, bioluminescent flora illuminated the cavern floor, casting an otherworldly glow on the landscape. The air hummed with an unseen energy, a symphony of vibrations that resonated deep within my bones. The feeling of immense power, the awareness of potential, was overwhelming. I had to control it, focus it.

As I walked deeper into the cavern, I noticed strange, geometrical structures scattered throughout the space. They appeared to be some form of ancient technology, crafted from a dark, metallic substance that seemed to absorb light rather than reflect it. Runes similar to those on the obelisk were etched upon their surfaces, pulsing faintly with an internal light. These structures seemed to be resonating with the energy emanating from me, their surfaces humming softly in response to the power flowing through the Circlet.

I felt a pull, a subtle guidance, drawing me towards the largest of these structures. As I approached, its surface began to glow more intensely, and a wave of knowledge washed over me, revealing its purpose. It was a gateway, a portal to another plane of existence, a conduit to the realm where the true threat, the entity that had orchestrated the events of the past few weeks, resided. This was the next trial.

The gateway was not a simple opening, but a complex, multifaceted structure, pulsating with an energy that seemed to defy the laws of physics. It shimmered and shifted, its form constantly in flux, its surface a kaleidoscope of colors and impossible geometries. The knowledge I received revealed that this wasn't just a portal to another location, but a journey through time and space itself. I would not merely travel to another realm; I would traverse the very fabric of existence.

The gateway pulsed once more, beckoning me forward. Hesitation, a flicker of doubt, danced at the edge of my consciousness. The weight of the cosmos was immense, the responsibility immense, and the potential for failure enormous. The possibility of failure loomed, sharp and unforgiving. Yet, I knew I could not hesitate. The fate of humanity, of countless lives, rested upon my shoulders. I had faced my inner demons and emerged victorious; now, I had to confront the darkness that threatened from beyond.

With a deep breath, I steeled my resolve. The power flowing through me felt like a torrent of liquid light, exhilarating and terrifying in equal measure. I channeled this power, focusing it through the Circlet, readying myself for the journey. The gateway pulsed again, its energy intensifying. I stepped forward, into the heart of its swirling vortex.

The journey was unlike anything I could have imagined. Time and space became meaningless concepts, lost in a sea of chaotic energy. I was flung through dimensions, witnessing landscapes that defied description – swirling nebulae, fractal dimensions, and landscapes crafted from pure thought. I saw glimpses of alternate realities, possibilities both beautiful and horrifying. The sheer scale of the cosmos, its boundless vastness and infinite possibilities, both awed and terrified me. I glimpsed past, present, and future, all converging in a breathtaking kaleidoscope of existence.

The journey tested my sanity and my resolve. The sheer power of the cosmic energies buffeting me threatened to overwhelm my senses, to unravel the very fabric of my being. But the power within me, the power of the obelisk and the Circlet, was my shield, my guiding light in the overwhelming darkness. I clung to the threads of my consciousness, focusing on my purpose, the reason for this perilous undertaking.

Finally, the chaos subsided. The kaleidoscopic vision faded, replaced by a landscape of stark, alien beauty. I stood upon a desolate plain, under a sky filled with swirling nebulas of vibrant crimson and emerald. Giant, crystalline structures pierced the sky, their surfaces etched with symbols that resonated with the runes on the obelisk. This was the realm of the entity that had manipulated events from the shadows.

The silence here was different from the silence of the labyrinth. It was not a silence of peace, but a silence of anticipation, a pregnant pause before the storm. I felt the presence of something vast, something ancient, something profoundly evil. My journey had led me to the heart of the darkness. This was the final trial; my destiny awaited. The power resonating within me was a beacon, the light that would pierce the darkness of the coming trials. The trials ahead would be a test of my strength, my resolve, my very being. The labyrinth was but a precursor. This was the real test. I was ready. My transformation was complete. The final battle, the ultimate showdown, was imminent. The fate of worlds hung in the balance.

3

The Sevenfold Alliance

The obsidian city of Xylos, capital of the Crimson Scale tribe, rose from the volcanic plains like a petrified nightmare. Jagged spires of black glass, reflecting the crimson sunset in fractured shards of light, pierced the smoke-choked sky. The air thrummed with a low, resonant hum, a symphony of arcane energy woven into the very fabric of the city. It was a place of breathtaking beauty and terrifying power, a testament to the Crimson Scale's mastery of dark magic.

My arrival was met with a chilling silence. No welcoming committee, no fanfare. Only the obsidian walls themselves, seemingly watching with ancient, knowing eyes. The city felt less like a place inhabited by living beings and more like a colossal obsidian monument to an extinct god. Then, from the shadows of a colossal obsidian ziggurat, a figure emerged.

He was Xalzar, the Crimson Scale's leader, a being of terrifying majesty. His scales shimmered like polished onyx, his eyes burned with the cold fire of a dying star. Two immense, leathery wings, folded tight against his back, hinted at the power he commanded. He moved with the fluid grace of a predator, his every step measured, deliberate.

"You are the one who shattered the Labyrinth," Xalzar's voice resonated, a deep rumble that seemed to shake the very foundations of the city. "The one who wields the power of the Circlet." It wasn't a question, but a statement of fact, imbued with an unnerving certainty. The air crackled with anticipation, heavy with unspoken power.

"I am," I replied, my voice steady despite the overwhelming presence of the Crimson Scale leader. The cosmic power flowing through me served as a counterpoint to his raw, demonic energy, a silent assertion of my own strength. "And I seek your alliance."

Xalzar chuckled, a sound like grinding stones. "An alliance? With the Crimson Scale? You speak boldly, mortal." He circled me slowly, his gaze sharp and assessing. "What makes you think we would aid you? What benefit is there for us in your... crusade?"

"The entity that threatens us all," I began, my words measured, "resides beyond the gateway. Its power is vast, its influence insidious. To defeat it, we need strength in numbers. Your tribe's mastery of shadow magic, its control over the very earth itself... It's a vital component in this fight."

Xalzar stopped circling, his gaze piercing. "You speak of a great threat, yet offer little proof. The Crimson Scale does not act on whims or empty promises. Show me your worth."

His challenge was not verbal; it was a tangible force, a pressure emanating from him, pushing against my very being, testing the limits of my newly acquired power. I met his gaze unflinchingly. The cosmic energy within me surged, pushing back against his formidable pressure, a silent clash of titans in the heart of his obsidian city.

"The proof lies in my actions," I replied, the words laced with the force of my will. "I have faced the darkness within myself, and emerged victorious. The power I wield is not of this world. I offer you not only a chance to defeat a common enemy, but the potential to ascend beyond your current limitations, to harness a power unlike anything you have ever known."

My words seemed to pierce through his defenses, causing a ripple in the almost palpable tension of the air. A flicker of something akin to curiosity, or perhaps intrigue, crossed his face. This was my chance. "The other tribes," I continued, "they are hesitant, divided by ancient grudges and petty ambitions. But we can forge a sevenfold alliance, a force powerful enough to overcome even the most ancient evils. Will you join us, Xalzar? Will you stand against the darkness?"

The negotiation with the remaining tribes followed a similar pattern: each possessed unique strengths and weaknesses, and each leader was driven by their own ambitions and fears. The Emerald Scales, masters of illusion and deception, demanded proof of my control over the demonic energy that still pulsed within me, forcing me to perform a display of controlled chaos. They sought to gauge my true allegiance. The Obsidian Scales, guardians of ancient knowledge, demanded access to the knowledge within the Circlet, pushing me to reveal a part of myself that I had only just begun to understand.

The Amber Scales, masters of healing and life magic, were the most reluctant, deeply distrustful of all forms of magic deemed unholy. They demanded a demonstration of my commitment to their values—a commitment they could never fully understand. The Sapphire Scales, renowned for their mastery of the wind and storms, challenged me to control the very elements, while the Topaz Scales, manipulators of earth and stone, tested my ability to command the very ground under our feet. Lastly, the Jade Scales, masters of water and illusion, played a game of riddles and deception, pushing me to my limits of comprehension and strategy.

Each negotiation was a dance of power, a careful balancing act of threats, promises, and demonstrations of strength. I offered them not only salvation from a common enemy, but the promise of a new era, an era where the seven tribes could unite and rule the world in harmony. I painted a vision of unprecedented power, a future forged in the fires of cosmic energy. The vision was potent, and it resonated with each of them, for each of them yearned for power and control, an ambition I would leverage to bind them together.

The process was arduous, fraught with peril. I had to navigate treacherous political landscapes, overcome deep-seated distrust, and outmaneuver cunning and ambitious leaders. There were moments where I was on the brink of failure, moments where the alliances crumbled under the weight of ancient feuds and personal desires. But my own strength, my resolve, and the sheer force of the cosmic energy I commanded proved to be potent bargaining chips. Ultimately, I succeeded. Each leader, drawn to my power and enticed by the promise of a new era, agreed to join the Sevenfold Alliance.

The obsidian city of Xylos, once a symbol of isolation and terrifying power, now stood as a testament to the newly formed alliance. The seven tribes, their differences set aside, stood united against the looming darkness. The weight of their combined power was palpable, a force that promised to shake the very foundations of the world. The coming conflict would test not only my abilities but also the strength of the alliance I had so painstakingly forged. The fate of the world, indeed the fate of existence itself, now rested on the precarious balance of this uneasy pact. The true trial was yet to come.

The final pact was forged not amidst the obsidian spires of Xylos but high atop Mount Cinderfang, a volcanic peak that pierced the clouds, its summit perpetually shrouded in a swirling vortex of ash and lightning. Here, in the aerie of the Sky-Born, the winged rulers of the seven tribes convened, their forms magnificent against the backdrop of a tempestuous sky. The air crackled with arcane energy, a tangible manifestation of their combined power.

Xalzar, his onyx scales gleaming, presided over the gathering. Beside him perched the other leaders: Lysandra of the Emerald Scales, her eyes shimmering with an unsettling green light; Orgoth of the Obsidian Scales, his ancient gaze filled with the wisdom – and weariness – of centuries; Anya of the Amber Scales, her presence radiating warmth and life; Zephyr of the Sapphire Scales, her form almost indistinguishable from the swirling winds around her; Terra of the Topaz Scales, her very essence seeming to be woven from the earth itself; and finally, Ondine of the Jade Scales, her movements fluid and deceptive as the water she commanded.

Each leader, before agreeing to the pact, demanded specific concessions. Lysandra, ever the pragmatist, requested the ability to influence my dreams, a subtle form of control that could, at a whim, turn my greatest strengths into crippling weaknesses. Orgoth, in exchange for the vast knowledge contained within the Circlet, sought a deep dive into the Circlet's secrets, a chance to comprehend its workings on a fundamental level, a level beyond mortal understanding. He coveted access to the very language of creation that pulsed within it.

Anya, ever wary of the darkness that still pulsed within me, demanded a ritual of purification, a ceremony designed to cleanse me of the demonic influence, a task that would challenge not only my physical and magical endurance but also the very core of my being. Zephyr, in turn, requested the mastery of a new, chaotic form of wind magic, one that would harness the raw energy of the storms that perpetually raged around Mount Cinderfang, an ability that would bind her loyalty to me and the Alliance.

Terra, grounded and pragmatic, wished to explore the relationship between the Circlet's power and the earth itself. She craved an understanding of the tectonic shifts and the very flow of the planet's energy, seeking to use the Circlet's power to manipulate the land itself, to reshape the landscape according to the Alliance's desires. Ondine, her eyes like shimmering sapphires, desired the ability to manipulate and control time and perception itself, weaving illusions so potent they could rewrite history. Her request was the most insidious; it challenged my own grasp of reality itself.

The concessions were not mere symbolic gestures; each held immense power, the potential for both immense good and devastating evil. Granting these requests placed me in a precarious position; I was granting the very rulers I was seeking to ally with significant leverage over my being. Each concession opened doors to potential betrayal. Yet, the alternative—a fractured world, ravaged by the entity beyond the gateway—was far more terrifying.

The pact itself was inscribed not on parchment or stone, but on a shimmering, ethereal tapestry woven from moonlight and starlight, its threads infused with arcane energies. Each ruler touched the tapestry, their essence merging with its intricate design, sealing their oaths with the very fabric of their being. The contract itself was less a legal document and more a living entity, its power pulsating with the combined wills of the seven leaders and my own. It was a dance between darkness and light, a delicate balance of power that would only grow more precarious as the conflict intensified.

The terms, etched in cryptic symbols that pulsed with inner light, were far more complex than simple alliances. It was a system of checks and balances, each leader's power carefully calibrated against the others, preventing any single faction from becoming too dominant. A council of seven would govern, with decisions made through a complex system of voting and negotiation, designed to avoid internal conflict. The pact included a clause for the sharing of resources, a system to prevent hoarding and ensure fair distribution of goods among the tribes.

The risks were immense. The seven tribes, despite their shared enemy, were deeply divided by centuries-old hatreds and conflicting ambitions. Any one of them could break the pact at any moment, plunging the Alliance into chaos. And the power I granted them was substantial, placing their well-being, their continued power, very much in my hands. Their loyalty wasn't entirely certain. The act of binding oneself to a pact was an act of faith.

But the potential rewards were even greater. United, the seven tribes represented an unstoppable force, a power capable of confronting and defeating even the most ancient evils. Their combined mastery of magic, their diverse strengths, represented a synergy greater than the sum of their parts. It was a fragile pact, built on a foundation of mutual benefit and shared necessity, but it was a foundation upon which I hoped to build a world free from the encroaching darkness.

As the sun dipped below the horizon, casting long shadows across the volcanic peaks, the ceremony concluded. The air vibrated with a palpable sense of power, a testament to the uneasy alliance that had been forged. The seven-winged leaders, their gaze fixed on the horizon, appeared as a united force. Their differences remained, their distrust lingered, but a common thread now united them: the shared threat that lurked beyond the gateway and the possibility of a future ruled by the Sevenfold Alliance. The mountaintop, once a sanctuary for the Sky-Born, now symbolized a turning point in the fate of the world. The future remained unwritten, filled with the potential for glorious triumph and devastating failure. The coming conflict would determine whether this pact was the dawn of a new era or simply a prelude to an even more catastrophic end. The weight of this responsibility rested heavily on my shoulders. The pact was signed. The game had begun.

The pact, though signed, was far from a guarantee of unity. The seven tribes, each with its unique culture, history, and power dynamics, harbored deep-seated resentments and rivalries that centuries of conflict had only exacerbated. My journey to unite them was far from over; it was merely the beginning of a far more arduous task. The immediate challenge lay in translating the abstract agreement forged on Mount Cinderfang into tangible cooperation across vastly different territories.

The Emerald Scales, residing in the lush rainforests of Xylos, were renowned for their cunning and mastery of illusion magic. Lysandra, their queen, while outwardly supportive, held a deep suspicion of the other tribes, particularly the Obsidian Scales, with whom they had a history of bitter conflict dating back millennia. Their rainforest city, a labyrinthine network of interconnected vines and shimmering waterfalls, pulsed with a life force that both fascinated and unnerved. Gaining their complete trust required more than just a signed pact; it demanded a demonstration of my power, a tangible proof of my ability to protect their interests. This meant confronting the shadow guilds operating within Xylos, groups who thrived on the chaos and sought to undermine any semblance of order.

The Obsidian Scales, dwelling in the desolate volcanic regions of Cinderfang, were a tribe steeped in ancient wisdom and powerful necromantic arts. Orgoth, their stoic leader, valued knowledge above all else. His skepticism was palpable, a stark contrast to the more outwardly enthusiastic leaders. The task of gaining his trust involved not just granting access to the Circlet's secrets, but demonstrating my understanding of their culture, their history, their complex relationship with death and the afterlife. This meant navigating their intricate network of underground catacombs and confronting the ancient evils that lurked within their sacred grounds, entities tied directly to their necromantic practices and integral to their culture. It demanded a level of respect for their ways of life and a demonstration of my ability to navigate the dangerous spiritual currents flowing through the region.

The Amber Scales, inhabiting the sun-drenched plains of Aethel, were renowned for their potent healing magic and their deep connection to the land. Anya, their benevolent queen, harbored a genuine concern for the well-being of her people, a concern that extended to the other tribes. Nevertheless, past injustices and broken alliances weighed heavily on her. Uniting the Amber Scales required demonstrating a commitment to their principles, a commitment to healing not just the physical wounds of the land, but also the emotional scars of centuries of conflict. This involved establishing a network of healing sanctuaries across the plains, places of peace and reconciliation where the diverse factions could meet and begin to heal their wounds. It demanded diplomacy, compassion, and the ability to show tangible results, a visible demonstration of my commitment to improving the lives of everyone across the seven tribes.

The Sapphire Scales, masters of wind and storm magic, resided in the treacherous mountain passes of Aerilon. Zephyr, their leader, was a whirlwind of chaotic energy, her loyalty difficult to secure. Earning her trust required a mastery of the very elements she commanded, a demonstration of my ability to harness the unpredictable forces of nature. This meant traversing the perilous mountain passes, braving the unpredictable storms that raged through the peaks, and ultimately mastering a new form of wind magic that only she could teach – a volatile, unpredictable magic as unpredictable as Zephyr herself. The trials to gain her trust were not merely tests of skill, but also tests of courage and adaptability, mirroring the unpredictable nature of the storms and Zephyr herself.

The Topaz Scales, the tribe closest to the earth, lived within the vast caverns of Terra's Embrace, a network of underground tunnels and subterranean cities. Terra, their pragmatic leader, focused on tangible results and the security of her people. Uniting them necessitated a tangible demonstration of my commitment to their safety, a guarantee of protection against outside threats, and a plan to address their concerns about resource allocation. This involved exploring the deep caverns, mapping out the intricate network of tunnels and subterranean cities, and establishing a secure trade route between Terra's Embrace and the other tribes, establishing a sense of security and mutual cooperation. It meant confronting the creatures that lurked in the darkness and demonstrating an understanding of their close relationship with the planet's natural energies.

The Jade Scales, masters of water and illusion, dwelled in the vast, shimmering oceans of Serenith. Ondine, their enigmatic queen, possessed a mastery over time and perception itself. Her trust was the most elusive, requiring not merely a display of power but a deep understanding of the subtle currents of manipulation and deception that shaped the world. This involved navigating the treacherous currents of the Serenith ocean, facing illusions and deceptions orchestrated by Ondine herself, and demonstrating my mastery over subtle manipulations of time, weaving illusions to counteract her own. It was a test of understanding, not just a show of force. The goal was to understand her manipulation of time and perception and to use that understanding to prove my loyalty and commitment to the alliance.

Finally, uniting the factions of the Obsidian Scales required a delicate balance of diplomacy and force. The internal power struggles were not limited to disagreements between the tribes; significant factions within the Obsidian Scales themselves actively sought to undermine Orgoth's authority. The solution was not a simple military conquest, but a gradual, strategic dismantling of the opposition's power base, a campaign of calculated moves that strengthened Orgoth's authority while minimizing casualties and fostering a sense of unity within his own tribe. This involved subtle maneuvering, strategic alliances, and displays of judicious mercy.

The process of uniting the seven tribes was not a single, decisive battle, but a series of smaller, more subtle conflicts. Each tribe presented a unique challenge, demanding a different approach, a unique combination of diplomacy, force, and understanding. The success of the Sevenfold Alliance rested not just on my ability to negotiate pacts and forge alliances, but on my understanding of each tribe's unique culture, history, and internal dynamics. The path to unity was fraught with peril, demanding a profound level of diplomatic skill, strategic thinking, and an understanding of the power dynamics at play in a world teetering on the brink of chaos. The creation of the Sevenfold Alliance was not just a political accomplishment, but a testament to the power of understanding, compromise, and the ability to forge a common purpose amidst centuries of conflict and ingrained distrust. The true test lay not in the initial signing of the pact, but in the long, arduous journey of transforming that fragile alliance into a truly unified force capable of facing the looming threat that lay beyond the gateway.

The air, once thick with the heady scent of Xylos's rainforest, now carried a whisper of something else – a chill that seeped into the bones, a dissonance in the vibrant symphony of nature. It was a subtle shift, almost imperceptible to the untrained senses, yet it resonated deeply within me, a premonition of a gathering storm. The pact, the forging of the Sevenfold Alliance, felt less like a victory and more like a temporary reprieve, a fragile truce before a far greater conflict. This wasn't just about unifying seven warring tribes; it was about preparing for something far larger, something that threatened not only the mortal realm but the celestial spheres as well.

The whispers started subtly. An unusual stillness in the usually boisterous avian life of Xylos, a tremor beneath the earth in the volcanic heart of Cinderfang, a sudden, unnatural drought in the sun-drenched plains of Aethel. These were not isolated incidents; they were tremors in the fabric of reality, subtle warnings of a cataclysm to come. The nature of this looming threat remained shrouded in mystery, a chilling enigma that added a layer of urgency to my task. The unity of the Sevenfold Alliance, previously a complex political challenge, now became a matter of survival, a desperate race against time.

Lysandra, Queen of the Emerald Scales, sensed the shift as keenly as I did. Her usually sharp eyes, often flickering with amusement or suspicion, now held a deeper concern, a shadowed apprehension that mirrored my own. "The old gods stir," she murmured one evening, her voice barely a whisper amidst the rustling leaves of her rainforest palace. "A darkness rises, one older and more profound than any we've faced before." She offered no further explanation, leaving the ominous words to hang in the air like a poisonous mist.

My efforts to solidify the alliance continued, each interaction a delicate dance between diplomacy and demonstration of power. With the Obsidian Scales, I delved deeper into the catacombs beneath Cinderfang, confronting not only the ancient evils bound to their necromantic practices but also the lingering echoes of forgotten gods, their power weakened but not entirely extinguished. The air within these tunnels vibrated with a dark energy, a palpable sense of ancient malevolence. Orgoth, though stoic, revealed a flicker of unease during our explorations, his usually impassive face etched with a grim determination. The threat was something that transcended even the ancient grudges and rivalries within the tribes.

In Aethel, the Amber Scales' connection to the land manifested as a visible withering, a slow, creeping blight that mirrored the subtle decay I sensed in the world around me. Anya, her normally radiant face clouded with worry, pleaded for my aid, not just to restore the land's fertility but to understand the nature of the creeping blight. The healing sanctuaries I'd established became not just places of reconciliation, but also centers of observation, places where we monitored the strange phenomena impacting the land. The blight wasn't merely a natural disaster; it was a symptom of a deeper cosmic disturbance.

The Sapphire Scales, perched high in the treacherous peaks of Aerilon, were buffeted by storms unlike any Zephyr had ever witnessed. These weren't mere weather patterns; they were chaotic expressions of the unfolding cosmic disturbance, violent and unpredictable. The wind magic Zephyr taught me was not merely a means to navigate the storms, but a key to understanding their strange, chaotic nature. They weren't natural storms; they were manifestations of the encroaching darkness, distorted expressions of elemental power warped by an outside force.

The Topaz Scales, within their subterranean city of Terra's Embrace, felt the tremors more intensely than the other tribes. The earth groaned beneath our feet, cracks spreading through the cavern walls, revealing strange, pulsating veins of energy that resonated with the premonitions I was feeling. Terra, pragmatic as ever, demanded concrete assurances, not just promises of protection but a demonstrable understanding of the growing threat, a plan to counter it. The creatures dwelling in the deepest caverns, usually docile, grew restless, mirroring the rising unease within the other tribes.

The Jade Scales, in the shimmering depths of Serenith, faced not only illusions orchestrated by Ondine but also glimpses of a reality warped and distorted by the encroaching darkness. Ondine's mastery over time and perception became not just a tool of manipulation but a window into the unfolding cosmic horror, glimpses of futures ravaged by the encroaching darkness, alternate timelines corrupted beyond recognition. The illusions she weaved weren't mere distractions; they were warnings, showing possible futures should the alliance fail to confront this new threat.

Even within the Obsidian Scales, the internal struggle intensified. The factions vying for power within Orgoth's tribe were now driven not by mere ambition but by the fear of the looming cosmic threat. The threat galvanized them into action, forcing them to confront the divisions that weakened them, the past conflicts forgotten in the face of an enemy that threatened their very existence. My strategy shifted from subtle manipulation to forging a stronger, unified front within the Obsidian tribe, a single, powerful force to face the coming storm.

The unification of the seven tribes wasn't complete; it was a work in progress, a fragile alliance struggling to find its footing amidst a changing world. The individual challenges of each tribe were now intertwined, their fate inextricably linked to the unfolding cosmic horror. The threat, however, was not simply a physical one; it was a philosophical one as well, a challenge to the very fabric of reality, a threat that questioned the nature of existence itself. The old gods stirred, their slumber broken by the emergence of a force far older and more terrifying than any previously imagined. The Sevenfold Alliance was not merely a political pact; it was a desperate plea for survival against forces far beyond our comprehension. The true battle, the one for which we were preparing, had only just begun. The whispers of the coming storm were growing louder, the premonitions more insistent, leaving no room for doubt that the world was on the brink of a cataclysmic event. The journey toward unity was far from over. It had only just begun.

The forging of the Sevenfold Alliance was far from a celebratory occasion. The air crackled with unspoken anxieties, a palpable tension that hung heavier than the humid breath of Xylos's rainforest. While the treaties were signed, the seals impressed, and the oaths sworn, a deep unease persisted, a shared premonition that the true battle had yet to begin. The unity was a fragile thing, a delicate tapestry woven from threads of ancient grudges, simmering resentments, and the shared terror of an unseen enemy.

My role shifted from mediator to architect. I was no longer simply uniting warring factions; I was building a bulwark against the encroaching darkness, a fortress of seven tribes against a cosmic tide. This required more than diplomacy; it demanded a display of overwhelming power, a demonstration of the strength this alliance represented.

My first task was to solidify the alliance within each tribe. Within the Obsidian Scales, the internal power struggles, usually veiled in subtle maneuvers, exploded into the open. Two powerful factions, the Shadowfang and the Nightspire, had long clashed for dominance. Their rivalry, fueled by ancient blood feuds and conflicting interpretations of necromantic arts, threatened to shatter the fragile unity. Orgoth, their stoic leader, while outwardly supportive of the alliance, walked a tightrope, his authority tested by the simmering conflict.

I didn't impose a solution; instead, I presented a shared enemy – the looming cosmic horror that threatened to consume them all. I showed them not through words, but through actions. I led them deeper into the catacombs beneath Cinderfang, where the echoes of forgotten gods were not just whispers, but tangible forces. We faced not only the animated dead but also the remnants of forgotten deities, their power fractured but still terrifyingly potent. We fought alongside each other, a united front against these ancient evils, their shared struggle forging a new, stronger bond. The victories, though hard-won, were spectacular, demonstrating the power they could wield together. The Shadowfang and Nightspire, facing such a formidable threat together, found their old rivalry dwarfed by the immensity of the external danger. They began to cooperate, their combined necromantic expertise proving far more potent than either could muster alone. The alliance within the

Obsidian Scales solidified not through force, but through shared sacrifice and undeniable victory.

The Amber Scales, custodians of Aethel's fertile plains, were grappling with a different kind of horror. The creeping blight, a manifestation of the cosmic disturbance, was not only ravaging the land but also eroding their connection to it. Anya, their queen, a woman whose radiance usually illuminated the land, was now beset by despair. The healing sanctuaries I had helped establish became hubs of research, places where we studied the blight, not just to cure it, but to understand its origins. We discovered that it was not merely a disease, but a distortion of the very life-force of the land, a twisting of nature's fundamental energies. Anya, working with the other tribes' mages, developed potent counter-spells, drawing upon the collective magical strength of the alliance. We channeled not just healing magic but also a protective force, creating a barrier against the encroaching blight. The revitalization of Aethel became a symbol of the alliance's power, a testament to their ability to overcome seemingly insurmountable challenges.

The challenge with the Sapphire Scales, the masters of the winds atop Aerilon's treacherous peaks, was far more tempestuous. Zephyr, their leader, faced increasingly violent and unpredictable storms, chaotic expressions of the cosmic unrest. These weren't simply natural phenomena; they were warped manifestations of elemental power, reflections of the cosmic chaos that threatened to engulf the world. Zephyr, working alongside my apprentices, developed powerful wind magic techniques designed not just to weather the storms but to understand and even manipulate their unnatural forces. They learned to channel the chaotic energies, using them as tools rather than as weapons of destruction, creating a fascinating and dangerous display of coordinated elemental manipulation. The mastery over these chaotic storms became a powerful symbol of the alliance's ability to control even the most destructive forces.

The Topaz Scales, dwelling within their subterranean city of Terra's Embrace, faced the brunt of the cosmic unrest's physical manifestations. The earth itself groaned beneath their feet, the very foundation of their city threatened by tremors and fissures that revealed veins of pulsating energy. Terra, a pragmatic ruler who valued stability and order above all else, demanded tangible proof of the alliance's effectiveness. The tremors provided that proof; they showed that working together they could dampen their effects and stave off the threat of catastrophic collapse. Their combined knowledge of geomancy and their collective strength allowed them to reinforce the city's foundations, stabilize the earth, and even begin to harness the strange energies pulsating beneath the surface, converting a threat into a potential source of power.

The Jade Scales, within Serenith's shimmering depths, faced a more insidious threat. Ondine, their queen, was a mistress of illusion and time manipulation; her power, however, was being warped by the encroaching cosmic horror. Her illusions weren't merely deceptive; they were glimpses of potential futures, terrifying visions of worlds ravaged by the darkness. She showed us not what we hoped to avoid, but what we were fighting to prevent, galvanizing the alliance with the stark reality of failure. Her visions, though harrowing, provided vital information. We saw the patterns of the encroaching darkness, the points of vulnerability in their strategy, the weaknesses in our defenses. We used these glimpses of potential futures to hone our strategies, reinforcing our alliances and preparing for the inevitable confrontation.

The unification of the Sevenfold Alliance was far from complete, but it was a formidable force. The unity, born from necessity and forged in the fires of a cosmic threat, was not just a political agreement; it was a shared understanding of their fate, a commitment to survival. The task was still immense, the threat vast and unknowable, but for the first time, they stood united, not as individual tribes, but as a single, powerful entity prepared to confront the darkness that threatened to consume them all. The whispers of the old gods were growing into a roar, the tremors were intensifying, and the battle for the very fabric of reality was about to begin.

4

War of the Heavens

The first assault came not as a thunderous roar, but as a whisper on the wind – a chilling dissonance that vibrated through the very bones of the world. It started subtly, a creeping unease that permeated the air, a distortion in the light that made shadows seem to writhe and twist. Then came the tremors, more violent than any experienced before, rending the earth and shattering the illusion of stability. The very fabric of reality seemed to fray at the edges, unraveling into a chaotic tapestry of warped space and time.

The battlefield was Xylos itself, a sprawling canvas of destruction painted in shades of fire and shadow. The emerald rainforest, once a sanctuary of life, was now a scarred and ravaged landscape, choked by the tendrils of a malevolent purple vine that pulsed with an unnatural energy. Twisted, skeletal trees clawed at the sky, their branches adorned with shimmering, obsidian crystals that dripped with a viscous, black ichor. The air itself hummed with a discordant energy, a symphony of screams and crackling magic.

The vanguard of the invading forces consisted of creatures ripped from nightmares – grotesque amalgamations of flesh and shadow, their forms shifting and contorting with each passing moment. There were the Gloom Stalkers, hulking behemoths wreathed in shadow, their eyes burning with malevolent intelligence. Their movements were unnervingly fluid, their bodies seeming to melt and reform as they stalked through the battlefield. Their weapons were as terrifying as their forms – jagged obsidian blades that dripped with a venom that dissolved flesh and bone. They were followed by the Screeching Harpies, winged creatures of pure shadow, their wails capable of shattering sanity and rending the very air itself. Their claws were as sharp as shattered glass, and their beaks capable of tearing through even the toughest armor.

The forces of the Sevenfold Alliance met this onslaught with a ferocity that mirrored the enemy's own brutality. The Obsidian Scales, masters of necromantic arts, unleashed legions of animated dead, a terrifying army of skeletal warriors and shadowy wraiths that clashed with the invading horrors. Orgoth, their leader, stood at the forefront, a figure carved from obsidian and shadow, his blade a whirlwind of death that cut through the Gloom Stalkers' ranks. The Nightspire and Shadowfang fought side-by-side, their combined necromantic power creating a vortex of death and shadow that swallowed the enemy whole.

The Amber Scales, guardians of Aethel's plains, responded with a torrent of nature magic. Anya, their queen, her radiance now tempered with a fierce determination, unleashed waves of healing magic that repaired the ravaged landscape while simultaneously bolstering the allied forces. Her mages wove intricate spells, summoning towering vines that ensnared the invading creatures and unleashing torrents of fire that consumed them in searing flames. The blight itself, a manifestation of the cosmic horror, proved a double-edged sword – for every tendril that ravaged the land, a counter-spell was woven, a wave of pure lifeforce that pushed back against the encroaching darkness.

The Sapphire Scales, masters of the wind, unleashed a tempest of their own, a furious maelstrom of wind and lightning that tore through the ranks of the invading forces. Zephyr, their leader, rode the storm's eye, his mastery of the wind allowing him to navigate the chaotic maelstrom and deliver devastating blows. His warriors, armed with enchanted wind blades, sliced through the enemy, their movements as swift and unpredictable as the wind itself. They turned the very elements against their adversaries, shaping the storm into a weapon of terrible beauty.

The Topaz Scales, guardians of Terra's Embrace, fought a brutal, subterranean war. Terra, their pragmatic leader, unleashed earth-shattering tremors that swallowed the invaders whole. Her warriors, armed with earth-forged weapons and imbued with the very essence of the earth's might, fought with a relentless tenacity. They channeled the pulsating energy from the fissures in the earth, using it to power their attacks, turning the threat of catastrophic collapse into a weapon of unimaginable power.

The Jade Scales, masters of illusion and time, fought a more subtle, but no less deadly, war. Ondine, their queen, wove illusions that not only deceived the enemy but also revealed their strategies and weaknesses. Her mages manipulated time itself, slowing the invaders' attacks and accelerating their own, turning the tide of battle with carefully placed spells of temporal disruption. They used their understanding of the future glimpsed in Ondine's visions to anticipate the enemy's moves, striking with precision and deadly efficiency.

The battle raged for days, a chaotic maelstrom of magic and bloodshed. The air vibrated with the clash of steel, the shriek of dying creatures, and the roar of magic unleashed. The ground trembled beneath the weight of the conflict, scarred and rent by the furious exchange of power. The very landscape reflected the cosmic horror that threatened to consume the world, a terrifying testament to the scale and intensity of the conflict.

Amidst the chaos, a new kind of unity emerged. The seven tribes, bound by a shared destiny and forged in the fires of war, fought not as individual entities but as a single, powerful force. They learned from each other, adapting their strategies and techniques, sharing their knowledge and skills to overcome the seemingly insurmountable odds. The lines between their unique magical styles blurred, as they discovered synergies and new techniques from their cooperation, creating a unified battle-style as powerful and flexible as the myriad individual approaches they once employed.

The first assault was a brutal test, a chilling preview of the horrors to come. But despite the devastating losses, the Sevenfold Alliance stood firm, their resolve unshaken. They had faced the darkness and lived to fight another day. The war had begun, and the fate of the world hung precariously in the balance. The whispers of the ancient gods had grown into a deafening roar, a terrifying promise of the epic battles to come, a promise that would test not only their strength but their very souls. The true war of the heavens was just beginning.

The initial onslaught had served as a brutal awakening, a stark reminder of the cosmic horror that threatened to engulf their world. But the Sevenfold Alliance, far from being broken, had adapted. They had learned to leverage the unique strengths of each tribe, weaving their disparate magical styles into a tapestry of coordinated defense and devastating offense. The protagonist, having witnessed the scale of the conflict and the horrifying power of the invading forces, understood that brute force alone would not suffice. He needed a strategy, a plan that would exploit the enemy's weaknesses while minimizing their own losses.

His first move was a calculated deception. While the main force of the Sevenfold Alliance held the line against the relentless assault on Xylos, he secretly dispatched a smaller, highly mobile task force to the Obsidian Peaks, a seemingly impenetrable fortress believed to be invulnerable to attack. The enemy, focused on the main battlefield, had overlooked this strategic location, a crucial oversight that would prove fatal. This diversionary force, composed primarily of the Jade Scales' illusionists and the Sapphire Scales' wind mages, was tasked with creating a devastating illusionary display—a mirage of immense scale and power. They conjured a colossal replica of the protagonist, an image that radiated overwhelming power and menace, positioned in a way that would mimic an imminent devastating counter-attack against the enemy's main lines of advance.

This illusionary attack was more than mere spectacle. It was a psychological weapon designed to sow chaos and disarray within the ranks of the invaders. The Gloom Stalkers, normally unflappable, hesitated, their movements becoming hesitant and uncoordinated as they questioned the sudden appearance of such a formidable foe. The Screeching Harpies, creatures easily manipulated by fear and uncertainty, became disoriented, their chilling wails faltering as they turned their attention to the seemingly impenetrable threat. The invading forces, already battered and bruised from the initial assault, were plunged into a state of confusion, a critical vulnerability exploited by the protagonist's next move.

Simultaneously, a second force, consisting of the Topaz and Amber Scales, launched a devastating two-pronged attack. The Topaz Scales, burrowing deep into the earth, unleashed a series of meticulously planned subterranean earthquakes, targeting the enemy's supply lines and communication networks. The carefully calibrated tremors caused widespread destruction, cutting off the invaders from their reinforcements and resources. The earth itself became a weapon, shifting and fracturing under the Topaz Scales' precise control, causing landslides and collapsing caverns that swallowed entire legions of the enemy. Their efforts were synchronized with the Amber Scales, who used their mastery of nature to unleash devastating attacks, funneling the molten earth from the quakes into raging torrents of fire that engulfed entire units of the enemy army. The twin assaults, one from above and one from below, effectively shattered the enemy's coherent formation, turning their organized invasion into a chaotic rout.

Having sown confusion and disrupted the enemy's supply lines, the protagonist shifted his focus to the main battlefield. Utilizing his knowledge of celestial warfare, gained through his union with the cosmic entities, he performed a ritual that harnessed the energy of the stars themselves. This spell, a symphony of light and power, created a celestial shield that deflected the incoming attacks and even neutralized some of the invading force's magical weaponry. The Obsidian Scales, initially struggling to maintain their defenses, now found themselves supported by this celestial barrier, allowing them to unleash more potent counterattacks. The celestial energy revitalized their necromantic armies, lending them unprecedented strength and agility.

The battlefield shifted once more to the Whispering Woods, an ancient forest steeped in forgotten magic. The invaders' advance had reached the edge of this sacred grove, unaware of the dangers lurking within. The protagonist, understanding the potential of the enchanted flora and fauna, orchestrated a cunning ambush. The Jade Scales, masters of illusion, created a massive illusion, masking the true strength and numbers of the defenders. The Sapphire Scales, meanwhile, manipulated the winds to create a vortex of blinding sand and swirling leaves, obscuring vision and disorienting the enemy. This chaotic scene was then punctuated by the sudden appearance of the Amber Scales, who unleashed a swarm of magically enhanced insects and beasts, creatures both terrifying and immensely effective in close-quarters combat. The forest itself seemed to rise up against the invaders, its trees becoming animated and attacking with an almost supernatural ferocity.

The combined efforts of the Alliance forces, expertly orchestrated by the protagonist's strategic brilliance, began to turn the tide of the war. The initial shock and fear that had gripped the Sevenfold Alliance faded, replaced by a growing sense of confidence and resolve. The invaders, once seemingly unstoppable, were now struggling against the coordinated might of a unified force, their well-laid plans crumbling under the weight of skillfully executed counter-strategies. The battlefield became a chaotic ballet of magic and combat, a breathtaking display of skill and determination. Each move made was a testament to the cunning and strategic mastery of the protagonist, a dance between offense and defense, chaos and order, reflecting the protagonist's growing mastery of both mortal and celestial warfare. The war of the heavens raged on, but the tide was beginning to turn. The protagonist's strategic maneuvers had not only saved the Sevenfold Alliance from utter annihilation but had paved the way for a decisive counter-offensive, a bold step towards reclaiming their world from the clutches of the encroaching cosmic horror. The war, however, was far from over. The cost of victory remained to be tallied, and the true extent of the cosmic horror's power remained to be revealed. But for now, a glimmer of hope had emerged from the ashes of devastation, a testament to the power of unity and the cunning of a single, extraordinary man.

The Whispering Woods, once a sanctuary of serene beauty, now echoed with the screams of dying men and the roars of monstrous beasts. The ambush, while initially successful, had come at a cost. Several members of the Amber Scales, their bodies riddled with the venomous stings of the Gloom Stalkers' grotesque insects, lay lifeless amongst the tangled roots. The Jade Scales, though their illusions had bought precious time, had suffered significant losses as well, their ranks thinned by the invaders' desperate counterattacks. Even the Sapphire Scales, with their mastery of wind and weather, were not immune to the brutal reality of war; several of their most skilled mages were lost in the maelstrom of their own creation.

But amidst the carnage, victory tasted bittersweet. The invaders, their ranks decimated and their morale shattered, were forced to retreat from the Whispering Woods, leaving behind a trail of broken weapons and shattered bodies. The protagonist, witnessing the heavy toll of the battle, felt the weight of command pressing down upon him. He knew that this was only a temporary reprieve, a fleeting moment of respite in a war that would continue to claim lives and demand sacrifice. The losses, both human and spiritual, were profound. The Whispering Woods, once a place of tranquility, was now scarred, its beauty marred by the brutality of war.

The next battle raged in the desolate plains of Xantus, a vast expanse where the wind carried whispers of forgotten empires and the ghosts of long-dead warriors. Here, the Obsidian Scales, their necromantic powers amplified by the celestial energy harnessed by the protagonist, faced the full might of the Screeching Harpies. The Harpies, creatures of pure chaos and unbridled fury, attacked in a relentless wave, their piercing cries shattering the silence and tearing at the very fabric of reality. The Obsidian Scales, however, stood their ground, their undead legions fighting with a ferocity born of the netherworld, their bony hands grasping at the Harpies' ethereal forms.

In the midst of the chaos, a figure emerged—Xalzar, the leader of the Obsidian Scales, a powerful necromancer whose mastery over life and death was unmatched. He wielded a scythe forged from solidified shadow, its blade shimmering with an unholy light. He was a towering figure of immense power, his very presence exuding an aura of death and decay. But even his formidable skills were tested as he faced the sheer number of the Harpies. Xalzar fought with the grim determination of a warrior facing his final battle. His every strike was precise, each movement calculated to maximize his destructive power. Yet, even his incredible strength was tested to its limits. He cut a bloody swathe through the Harpies, yet their numbers seemed endless, their cries never ceasing.

His victory, however, was short-lived. As Xalzar vanquished the last of the Harpies, a gigantic shadow descended upon the battlefield. A monstrous creature, described only in whispered legends, emerged from the twilight sky: The Gloombringer, a behemoth of pure darkness, its eyes burning with malevolent energy. The creature was a physical manifestation of the cosmic horror that threatened their world, a horrifying being that surpassed even the most nightmarish visions. Xalzar, despite his power, was no match for this monstrous being. The Gloombringer unleashed a torrent of shadow energy, engulfing Xalzar in a wave of darkness that extinguished his life force in an instant. The loss of Xalzar was a devastating blow, a reminder that even the mightiest warriors could fall before the immense power of the cosmic horror.

The war shifted again to the sky, to the celestial battleground where the gods themselves clashed. The protagonist, his powers enhanced by his union with the cosmic entities, confronted the leader of the invaders, a being known only as the Shadow Lord. The Shadow Lord was a figure of immense power, his aura radiating a chilling coldness that froze the very air around him. His command over darkness was absolute, his legions of demons and shadow creatures appearing at his will.

The battle between the protagonist and the Shadow Lord was a clash of titans, a cosmic ballet of light and shadow. The sky crackled with energy as they exchanged devastating blows, their magical attacks shattering the clouds and leaving trails of burning light in their wake. The protagonist, drawing upon the power of the stars, countered the Shadow Lord's attacks with celestial energy, his light banishing the darkness. The battle raged for what seemed like an eternity, each blow threatening to end the conflict or the world itself.

Finally, after a long and brutal struggle, the protagonist prevailed. He did not vanquish the Shadow Lord through brute force, but through a masterful display of strategy and cunning. He discovered a weakness in the Shadow Lord's power – a vulnerability to the power of creation, the life force that pulsed through all living things. The protagonist, drawing on his own connection to the cosmic entities, unleashed a wave of pure creation, overwhelming the Shadow Lord's darkness and shattering his power. The Shadow Lord, defeated, vanished into the nothingness from which he came.

But the victory was not without its sacrifices. Countless members of the Sevenfold Alliance had fallen during the war, their deaths a testament to the brutality of the conflict. The protagonist, looking over the ravaged landscape, knew that the war was over, but the true cost of victory remained. The world was saved, but the scars of war would forever remain, a reminder of the price of freedom and the endless struggle against the cosmic horror that lurked just beyond the veil of reality. The heavens had been shaken, and though order was restored, the peace was a fragile one, secured at immense cost. The protagonist's victory was complete, yet he knew this was merely one battle in an ongoing war, a war that might one day require even greater sacrifices. The seeds of a new world had been sown, but their growth would depend on the choices made in the coming years, choices that would determine whether peace would truly prevail or if the shadow of cosmic horror would one day return to test the resilience of the world once more.

The crimson sun bled across the obsidian peaks of Mount Cinderfang, casting long, skeletal shadows across the battlefield. This wasn't a clash in the whispering woods or the desolate plains; this was the heart of the conflict, the final stand at the very precipice of the world. Mount Cinderfang, a dormant volcano whose slopes were now littered with the wreckage of a thousand battles, became the stage for a turning point in the war against the Shadow Lord.

Here, the Emerald Scales, masters of earth and stone, made their final, desperate stand.

The air itself crackled with volatile energy. The ground, churned and scarred by previous conflicts, trembled under the weight of the approaching armies. The Emerald Scales, outnumbered but not outmatched, formed a phalanx of hardened warriors, their shields a shimmering wall of jade, reflecting the dying light. Their leader, a grizzled veteran named Lyra, a woman whose eyes held the wisdom of centuries and the fierce determination of a cornered lioness, surveyed the battlefield. She knew this was their last chance.

The enemy, the vanguard of the Shadow Lord's forces, surged forward – a tide of obsidian-armored warriors, their weapons dripping with a viscous, black ichor. These were not mere soldiers; they were the elite, the most hardened and ruthless of the Shadow Lord's legions, beings twisted by dark magic into something barely human. They were beings of pure shadow, fueled by hatred and malice. Their movements were unsettling, their eyes burning with malevolent fire. They were a manifestation of the Shadow Lord's will, a mirror to the darkness that threatened to engulf their world.

The battle began with a thunderous roar. The Emerald Scales met the onslaught with a wall of unwavering resistance, their earth magic reinforcing their defenses. Lyra, her jade staff humming with power, directed her troops with chilling efficiency. Massive earth tremors shook the mountainside, toppling the advancing legions into chasm-like crevasses, swallowing them whole. The air filled with the clash of steel, the screams of dying men, and the guttural roars of the Shadow Lord's monstrous creations.

But the enemy's numbers were overwhelming. As the battle raged, the Emerald Scales began to falter. Their ranks thinned, their defenses weakened. One by one, the valiant warriors fell, their bodies adding to the growing pile of casualties that stained the mountainside red. Yet, they fought on, fueled by a desperate hope, a flickering flame of defiance against the encroaching darkness.

Amidst the chaos, the protagonist, drawing upon his newly honed abilities, arrived on the battlefield. His presence was immediately felt. A wave of celestial energy radiated from him, bolstering the morale of the Emerald Scales and striking fear into the hearts of their enemies. He moved with a grace that belied his immense power, his every movement a calculated strike, a precise maneuver designed to inflict maximum damage.

His appearance wasn't just a boost in morale. It was a beacon of hope in the encroaching darkness. He did not simply fight; he orchestrated the battle, manipulating the battlefield itself. He summoned earth tremors of incredible magnitude to further break the enemy lines. He raised mountains of earth as obstacles, slowing their advance and funneling them into pre-determined kill zones. He fought not merely as a warrior, but as a conductor of war, directing the flow of the conflict, turning the tide in favor of the Emerald Scales.

His actions were a marvel to behold. He bent the earth to his will, creating formidable barriers and weapons from the very ground itself. The air crackled with his power as he unleashed devastating blasts of energy, tearing through the enemy ranks. His mastery of magic transcended the mere utilization of spells; he had become one with the elements, a force of nature itself.

But even with the protagonist's intervention, the battle remained a brutal struggle. The Shadow Lord's forces were relentless, their numbers seemingly endless. Lyra, though wounded, fought with the ferocity of a cornered beast, her jade staff a blur of motion, deflecting blows and shattering the enemy's formations.

The turning point arrived not through a final, devastating blow, but through a strategic maneuver of breathtaking brilliance. The protagonist, recognizing the enemy's reliance on the volcanic energy coursing through Mount Cinderfang, channeled his power to disrupt the flow of this very energy. A colossal tremor, unlike any seen before, ripped through the mountain, causing a massive fissure to open up, engulfing a significant portion of the Shadow Lord's army. This wasn't just a tactical advantage; it was a strategic masterpiece, disrupting the enemy's power source and crippling their ability to sustain their offensive.

The collapse of the mountainside, a cataclysmic event of immense scale, shifted the balance of power irreversibly. The remaining Shadow Lord's forces, disoriented and demoralized, retreated in disarray. The victory at Mount Cinderfang was hard-won, purchased with the blood and sacrifice of many valiant warriors. Yet, it was a victory nonetheless – a victory that shattered the enemy's momentum, a victory that heralded the beginning of the end.

The mountain itself bore witness to the carnage. The volcanic rock, stained crimson with blood and blackened by the shadow energy, became a monument to the resilience of the Sevenfold Alliance and the power of the protagonist. The battle at Mount Cinderfang was not merely a military victory; it was a symbolic triumph, a resounding rejection of the encroaching darkness, a testament to the enduring power of hope and courage in the face of overwhelming odds. The turning point had arrived, marking a shift in the war, a decisive step toward the ultimate confrontation with the Shadow Lord himself. The road ahead remained treacherous, but the path toward victory had been forged in the fires of Mount Cinderfang, a beacon of hope illuminating the darkness that had threatened to consume their world. The heavens themselves seemed to sigh in relief, the clouds parting to reveal a sliver of the moon, a quiet promise of a future reclaimed from the grip of unending night.

The aftermath of the battle at Mount Cinderfang was a scene of grim beauty. The obsidian peaks, once sharp and imposing, were now scarred and fractured, a testament to the earth-shattering conflict. The air, thick with the scent of smoke and blood, still hummed with residual magic, a ghostly echo of the titanic struggle that had just transpired. Lyra, her face streaked with grime and blood, leaned heavily on her jade staff, her gaze sweeping across the ravaged landscape. The victory was hard-won, a pyrrhic triumph purchased with the lives of countless brave warriors. But it was a victory nonetheless, a critical turning point in the seemingly endless war against the Shadow Lord.

As the Emerald Scales began to tend to their wounded, a low rumble echoed from the distant canyons. The ground vibrated, not with the earth-shaking tremors of the battle, but with a deeper, more resonant hum. A wave of shimmering heat radiated across the plains, illuminating the approaching figures. They were unlike anything Lyra, or any of her people, had ever encountered.

From the heart of the Whispering Canyons, a legion emerged – a breathtaking spectacle of living light and shadow. They were the Lumina, beings of pure energy, their forms shifting and shimmering like heat haze on a summer's day. They moved with an ethereal grace, their movements fluid and silent, their presence both awe-inspiring and unsettling. Their bodies seemed woven from starlight, their eyes burning with an inner radiance that could pierce the deepest darkness. Their very essence pulsed with a power that dwarfed even the most potent earth magic.

Trailing behind the Lumina were the Sylvani, beings of the ancient forests, their forms entwined with the very flora and fauna of their home. Towering trees walked beside them, their branches laden with phosphorescent blossoms. Giant, feathered serpents slithered through their ranks, their scales shimmering with iridescent colors. The air around them thrummed with the energy of the forest, a symphony of rustling leaves and whispering winds. They were creatures of immense power, guardians of the ancient groves, beings who commanded the life force itself.

Lyra, her mind reeling from the unexpected sight, could only watch in stunned silence as these incredible beings approached. Their arrival was both a shock and a potential turning point, a glimmer of hope in the relentless darkness that had threatened to engulf their world. She had heard whispers of these legendary beings, tales of their power and their aloofness, their existence relegated to legend and myth. Yet, here they were, a tangible force on the battlefield, ready to lend their aid.

Their leader, a Lumina named Aella, whose form shifted and shimmered like liquid light, approached Lyra. Her voice, though soft, resonated with a power that could shake the very mountains. "We have witnessed your courage, your unwavering resolve in the face of overwhelming odds," she said, her words echoing in Lyra's mind. "The Shadow Lord's darkness threatens not only your world, but the balance of all existence. We have come to offer our aid."

The Sylvani leader, a massive, ancient oak tree named Elderwood, whose voice was a low rumble that seemed to emanate from the very earth itself, added, "The forests weep for the encroachment of darkness. We will not stand idly by while the Shadow Lord defiles the sanctity of nature."

Lyra, still struggling to comprehend the scale of this unexpected alliance, could only nod. She knew their aid would change the course of the war, tipping the balance irrevocably in favor of the Sevenfold Alliance. But the reasons behind their intervention remained shrouded in mystery. Why would these beings, renowned for their detachment from mortal affairs, choose to involve themselves in this conflict? Their motives, Lyra suspected, were more profound and complex than mere benevolence.

The arrival of the Lumina and the Sylvani drastically altered the war's dynamics. Their powers were unlike anything the Shadow Lord's forces had encountered before. The Lumina unleashed waves of pure energy, obliterating swathes of the enemy ranks with blinding flashes of light. Their attacks were precise and devastating, leaving behind only wisps of smoke and the faint scent of ozone.

The Sylvani, on the other hand, wielded the power of nature itself. Giant vines snaked out from the ground, ensnaring the enemy soldiers and dragging them into the earth. Massive trees erupted from the ground, crushing the enemy under their weight. The forest itself became a weapon, a living, breathing force that overwhelmed and consumed the Shadow Lord's legions.

The combination of the Lumina's raw power and the Sylvani's mastery of nature proved to be utterly devastating. The Shadow Lord's forces, accustomed to facing brute force and dark magic, were ill-equipped to deal with such unconventional and overwhelming power. Their formations crumbled, their ranks shattered. Their retreat became a chaotic rout, a desperate scramble for survival.

The protagonist, witnessing the combined might of these unexpected allies, felt a surge of hope. He had fought valiantly at Mount Cinderfang, but even his power seemed insignificant compared to the might of the Lumina and the Sylvani. Their intervention was more than just a turning point; it was a paradigm shift in the war, a testament to the interconnectedness of all existence.

The Lumina and Sylvani led a sweeping offensive across the battlefield, routing the remaining Shadow Lord's forces. Their combined efforts pushed the enemy back towards their shadowy fortress, a dark citadel shrouded in perpetual night. The combined forces of the Sevenfold Alliance, bolstered by the might of their unexpected allies, pressed their advantage, driving the enemy back to their dark stronghold, initiating a siege that promised to be the culmination of this epic struggle.

However, the reasons behind the Lumina and Sylvani's involvement remained a mystery. Their initial reticence, followed by their sudden, decisive intervention, hinted at a larger, more complex narrative. Was there a hidden prophecy? A cosmic threat only these beings could perceive? The very fabric of reality seemed to shift, subtly hinting at forces far beyond the mortal plane. The protagonist sensed a deeper, more sinister power lurking in the shadows, a presence far older and more powerful than even the Shadow Lord.

The war was far from over. The victory at Mount Cinderfang, though momentous, was merely a prelude to a far greater conflict, a cosmic struggle that threatened the very existence of their world. The unexpected alliance, while a crucial turning point, raised more questions than it answered, adding layers of intrigue to the unfolding narrative and promising a climax that would determine not only the fate of this world but perhaps the fate of countless others beyond the veil of mortal understanding. The coming battles promised to be even more harrowing, the stakes immeasurably higher, and the path to victory fraught with peril and uncertainty.

Yet, with the Lumina and the Sylvani at their side, the Sevenfold Alliance faced the future with a newfound sense of hope, a hope tempered by the knowledge that they were now participants in a cosmic game of immense proportions. The true war, the war for the very fabric of existence, had only just begun.

5

The Cosmic Confluence

The air crackled, the very ground beneath their feet vibrating with a power that transcended mere magic. It was a hum, a thrumming resonance that resonated deep within the bones, a prelude to something immense, something...other. The swirling vortex, initially a barely perceptible distortion in the fabric of reality, expanded rapidly, growing into a colossal, shimmering gateway. It wasn't a simple opening, a hole in the sky, but a maelstrom of impossible colors, a chaotic ballet of light and shadow that defied comprehension. Crimson bled into sapphire, emerald spiraled into amethyst, and gold blazed with an incandescent fury that threatened to scorch the very landscape. Within the vortex, shapes flickered, fleeting glimpses of impossible geometries, colossal beings hinted at rather than revealed, their presence felt more than seen.

This wasn't just an opening to another realm; it was a tear in the very tapestry of existence, a glimpse into the raw, unfiltered power of the cosmos itself. The air thrummed with a symphony of unseen energies, a chaotic orchestra of power that both terrified and captivated. The very ground seemed to writhe beneath this celestial intrusion, the earth itself reacting to the sheer force emanating from the gateway. The Lumina and the Sylvani, powerful as they were, seemed to recoil slightly, their radiant forms dimming momentarily under the sheer might of this cosmic event. Even the victorious air of the recent battle was overshadowed by a profound sense of awe and unease.

Lyra, ever pragmatic despite the wonder before her, felt a shiver run down her spine. This wasn't simply the arrival of powerful allies; it was something far grander, something that spoke of destinies long foretold, of prophecies whispered on the wind. The gateway pulsed, radiating an energy that felt both ancient and profoundly alien, an echo of a creation far older than her world, far older than the gods themselves. It was a power that spoke of cosmic indifference, a vast, unconcerned entity that held the fate of worlds in its grasp. The silence that followed was profound, a tangible thing pressing down on them, broken only by the rhythmic pulse of the gateway.

Aella, the leader of the Lumina, stepped forward, her form shimmering and reforming as if woven from liquid starlight. Her voice, when she spoke, carried a resonance that was not just audible but felt, a vibration that permeated the very core of being. "This," she said, her words echoing not just in their ears but in their very souls, "is the Celestial Confluence. A gateway to the realms beyond." Her eyes, twin galaxies blazing with starlight, held a depth of knowledge that suggested she had traversed those realms, witnessed the wonders and horrors that lay beyond the veil of mortal perception.

Elderwood, the ancient oak, his voice a low rumble that shook the earth, added, his leaves rustling like whispers of forgotten ages, "The veil is thin here. The energies are...unbalanced. This is more than a simple passage; it is a confluence of realities, a nexus of power that could reshape the very fabric of existence." His words painted a picture of cosmic implications, far beyond the immediate conflict with the Shadow Lord. This wasn't just a war for a single world; it was a struggle that echoed through the cosmos, a battle for the balance of countless realities.

The gateway pulsed again, brighter this time, the colors intensifying into a blinding radiance. From within the vortex, figures began to emerge, beings that defied description. They were not simply entities of light and shadow, like the Lumina, or living embodiments of nature, like the Sylvani. They were...something else entirely. They moved with a fluidity that suggested they were not bound by the laws of physics, their forms shifting and reforming, their essence radiating an overwhelming sense of power and ancient wisdom. Their very presence suggested eons spent traversing the cosmic tapestry, witnessing the birth and death of stars and the rise and fall of civilizations.

These beings, they realized, were the architects of the cosmos, entities beyond the comprehension of mortal minds. They were the gods of the gods, the weavers of reality itself. Their arrival was not a mere intervention; it was a cosmic event of the highest order. The silence stretched, broken only by the whispering wind and the rhythmic pulse of the gateway. The air hummed with anticipation, a palpable tension that held the entire landscape captive.

One of the cosmic entities, taller than any mountain, its form a shifting kaleidoscope of nebulae and starlight, extended a hand towards the gateway. Its touch, though unseen, was felt as a ripple through the fabric of existence itself. A torrent of cosmic energy poured forth, a river of pure power that flowed through the gateway and into their world. The very essence of the world seemed to quiver under the sheer weight of this cosmic influx.

The effect was immediate and profound. The air vibrated with an almost unbearable energy. The ground beneath them pulsed, as if the earth itself were breathing in time with the cosmic heartbeat. A sense of awe washed over them, a profound reverence in the face of such unimaginable power. The conflict with the Shadow Lord, suddenly, seemed insignificant, a mere skirmish in a cosmic war that dwarfed any earthly conflict.

As the cosmic energy surged, the gateway pulsed violently, then with a final, earth-shattering roar, it began to close. The brilliant colors faded, the impossible geometries dissolved, and the celestial music faded into silence. The entities, having delivered their message and having unveiled the cosmic scope of the conflict, retreated back into the void from whence they came. Only the residual hum, the aftershock of their presence, remained, a palpable reminder of the cosmic forces at play. The ground, still shimmering faintly with residual energy, was now imbued with a power far greater than anything they had witnessed before.

The silence that followed was filled with a profound sense of responsibility. The war against the Shadow Lord had suddenly taken on a new, cosmic dimension. They were not just fighting for their world; they were fighting for the balance of existence itself. The intervention of these beings had revealed the stakes to be immeasurably higher than they had ever imagined. The future remained uncertain, shrouded in the mystery of cosmic design, but one thing was clear: their battle was far from over. The true fight, the fight for the very fabric of existence, had truly begun. The gateway was closed, but the cosmos itself had opened its eyes upon their world. And within those cosmic eyes, they saw not just judgment, but a profound, if incomprehensible, purpose. The path forward was uncertain, but their resolve, forged in the fires of cosmic wonder and terror, was unbreakable.

The air throbbed, a living thing vibrating with the power of a thousand suns. The ground beneath their feet pulsed with a rhythm that mirrored the heartbeat of the cosmos, a palpable connection to something ancient and immense. The gateway, though closed, left behind a lingering aura of raw, untamed energy, a tangible testament to the cosmic entities that had briefly graced their world. The scent of ozone hung heavy in the air, mixed with the earthy fragrance of the ancient forest, a strange and unsettling combination that reflected the surreal nature of their situation.

The protagonist, his face etched with a mixture of awe and apprehension, approached the heart of the residual energy field. He felt a pull, a magnetic force drawing him towards the epicenter of the cosmic aftershock. He wasn't afraid, not in the traditional sense.

The fear he once knew, the gnawing terror of the demonic forces within him, had been replaced by a different kind of dread—a profound awareness of his own insignificance in the face of cosmic power. This was not the fear of death but the humbling recognition of his place within the grand design.

The Lumina and Sylvani, their forms shimmering with residual cosmic energy, gathered around him, their eyes filled with a mixture of respect and trepidation. They understood the gravity of the moment; they had witnessed the power of the entities firsthand. They knew that the negotiation, if it could even be called that, would not be a simple exchange of favors. This was an interaction with forces that operated on a scale far beyond their comprehension.

The protagonist, drawing upon the newfound power surging within him, the culmination of his trials and tribulations, spoke. His voice, though barely a whisper, carried a resonance that matched the humming of the earth, a testament to the power he now wielded. He didn't demand or plead; he offered a proposition, a bargain forged in the crucible of cosmic conflict.

He spoke of the Shadow Lord, of his dominion over the mortal plane, and of his insidious corruption of the world. He described the shadow-lands he commanded, the unending night that threatened to swallow everything. He spoke of the war, the endless cycle of violence and destruction. But more importantly, he spoke of the potential for peace, for a world free from the grasp of darkness. He spoke of a new order, a new dawn, a world where balance and harmony would reign.

His words, amplified by the lingering cosmic energy, resonated through the land. The trees seemed to listen, their leaves rustling in silent agreement. The very air pulsed in time with his words, amplifying their meaning, conveying their intent to something far beyond the mortal realm.

The response wasn't a voice or a physical manifestation. It was a feeling, a subtle shift in the energy around them. The residual energy pulsed stronger, faster, as if responding to his words. It was a communication not of words, but of concepts, of ideas exchanged on a level far beyond human understanding. It was a dialogue of pure energy, a conversation between the mortal plane and the boundless cosmos.

He offered the entities a solution, a chance to shape the future. He didn't attempt to dictate terms; he presented a vision, a potential outcome, a possible reality. He offered them not submission, but partnership. He suggested a collaboration that would not just eliminate the Shadow Lord's influence but transform the world itself. He proposed a metamorphosis, a fundamental alteration of existence, guided by a collaborative vision between the mortal and the cosmic.

The entities, he realized, were not benevolent gods or omnipotent rulers. Their motives were not simple, their goals not readily apparent. They were forces of creation and destruction, arbiters of balance, and indifferent observers of cosmic cycles. Their involvement wasn't necessarily altruistic; their presence hinted at a grand design, a universal pattern that humanity had only glimpsed at the edges.

The energy shifted again, a wave of pure potential washing over them. This time, the shift wasn't just a reaction; it was a suggestion, an indication of approval. It wasn't a clear-cut "yes," but a subtle nudge in the right direction, a confirmation that their proposal was feasible. It was a subtle manipulation of probability, a subtle shaping of fate.

The protagonist, strengthened by the cosmic affirmation, felt the potential shift within him. The demonic forces that had once haunted him now served as a powerful wellspring of energy. This dark energy, once a source of torment, now fueled his transformation, acting as a catalyst for change. He began to understand the entities' indifference not as cruelty, but as a detachment stemming from a vastness of experience beyond mortal comprehension. Their focus was on the grand design, the overall cosmic balance.

The air crackled with anticipation as the residual cosmic energy began to reshape itself. Slowly, it started to flow, to organize, to take form. It wasn't a chaotic surge; it was a deliberate, controlled transformation. The land around them began to change, subtly at first, then more dramatically. The forest grew, new forms of life emerged, and the very landscape seemed to shift and rearrange itself.

The transformation wasn't merely physical; it was a fundamental shift in the fabric of reality. The world was changing, evolving, and adapting to the cosmic influence. The energies were reorganizing themselves, aligning to a new pattern, a new design. The protagonist felt a sense of responsibility, not just for his world but for the grander cosmic order itself. He knew he was walking a tightrope, balancing between the forces of creation and destruction, guided by the cosmic whispers and the echoes of ancient prophecies.

The negotiations weren't over. This was only the beginning of a long, intricate dance, a delicate balancing act between the mortal and the cosmic. The protagonist knew that the conflict was far from over; the true challenge lay ahead. He had gained powerful allies, but he also bore the burden of a cosmic responsibility. He stood at the precipice of a new era, a new beginning, armed with the power of the cosmos and the unwavering conviction that his vision for a world of peace and harmony was not merely a dream but a potential reality. The transformation was underway, a symphony of cosmic energies weaving a new tapestry of existence, a testament to the potential for cooperation between mortal will and cosmic design. The future was still unwritten, but the path had been laid, forged in the fires of cosmic negotiation, bathed in the brilliance of a shared vision.

The residual energy pulsed, a heartbeat of creation and destruction echoing in the very core of the world. The air shimmered, not with heat, but with the weight of untold possibilities, a tangible manifestation of cosmic indifference and boundless power. The Lumina and Sylvani, their ethereal forms flickering like candle flames in a gale, remained silent, their eyes fixed on the protagonist. They had witnessed his strength, his resilience, and his unwavering commitment to a future free from the Shadow Lord's tyranny. But this was not simply a matter of providing aid; the cosmos demanded a price, a toll for its intervention in the affairs of mortals.

Silence stretched, heavy and expectant. The protagonist, his heart pounding a rhythm against the cosmic pulse, waited. He had anticipated a demand, a request for sacrifice, perhaps even a soul-rending bargain. Yet, the entities' silence was far more unnerving, a void filled with the unspoken weight of eons. It was a silence that spoke volumes, a silence that hinted at a price far beyond anything he could have foreseen. He felt the pull of the cosmic energy, a force both seductive and terrifying, whispering promises of power and threatening annihilation in the same breath.

Finally, a shift, subtle yet profound, occurred in the energy field. It wasn't a voice, not a sound, but a feeling—a chilling understanding that penetrated his very being. The price wasn't a physical offering nor a material sacrifice. It was a demand far more insidious, a price etched not in blood or tears, but in the very fabric of his soul. It was a test of his resolve, a challenge to his very essence. The cosmic entities, it seemed, weren't interested in simple bargains; they sought to evaluate the very core of his being, his moral fiber, and his capacity for sacrifice.

The weight of the demand pressed upon him, an invisible burden that threatened to crush him. He felt the allure of the power swirling around him, the seductive whisper promising unimaginable strength, but coupled with a chilling knowledge of the cost. It was a Faustian bargain, a pact with forces beyond mortal comprehension, where the reward came at the price of his soul's integrity. This was not a simple transaction but a profound transformation, a metamorphosis that would alter his very essence, shaping him into something more, yet leaving him forever changed.

The understanding of the price resonated within him, a deep and unsettling truth. It was not a specific demand but a shifting reality, a manipulation of probabilities. The cosmic entities were not demanding a specific action; they were manipulating his very being, testing his resolve, and probing the depths of his morality. They were seeking a change, a sacrifice in the essence of who he was, a reshaping of his very being to fit their cosmic design.

He sensed the implications, the potential consequences that extended far beyond the immediate. This was a price not just for himself, but for his family, his world, and perhaps even the very fabric of reality. The weight of this responsibility, the magnitude of the decision he faced, pressed upon him like a physical force. His earlier victories, his triumphs over inner demons and external foes, felt insignificant now, dwarfed by the immensity of the cosmic price.

He envisioned possible outcomes, scenarios that unfolded before him like threads of a cosmic tapestry. He saw himself transformed into a being of immense power, his actions shaping the destiny of worlds. But with this power came isolation, a detachment from his humanity. He saw the potential for corruption, the allure of absolute power twisting his very being. He saw the possibility of sacrificing his humanity, losing the very essence that had driven him on his journey. The price, he realized, was a choice between becoming an instrument of cosmic will, sacrificing his humanity in the process, or rejecting the offer and accepting the consequence of failure.

The Lumina and Sylvani remained impassive, their silent observation amplifying the pressure. They didn't offer guidance or consolation. They simply waited, observing the internal struggle, the agonizing process of choosing between the overwhelming temptation of cosmic power and the preservation of his own soul. Their silence was a deafening affirmation of the price's immensity, a stark reminder of the cosmic forces at play.

He delved deep within, confronting the shadows within his soul. He recalled his past, his struggles, and the demonic influence he had overcome. These experiences, once sources of pain, now served as a guide, shaping his understanding of the cost. He considered the potential for redemption, the possibility of using the cosmic power not for personal gain but for the benefit of all beings. The price, he slowly realized, wasn't just about his transformation; it was about his purpose.

The energy around him pulsed with intensity, the cosmic entities subtly manipulating the probabilities, guiding his thoughts, and nudging him towards a decision. He felt the weight of their presence, the vastness of their indifference, but he also detected something else: a hint of anticipation, a sense that they were waiting not merely for a decision, but for a transformation, a reflection of their cosmic will in a mortal shell. He was being molded, shaped by forces beyond his comprehension, but he wasn't entirely passive. He still possessed a choice, a sliver of free will in the grand cosmic scheme.

The silence continued, broken only by the rhythmic pulse of the cosmic energy. The price remained unspoken, yet profoundly felt, a crucible in which his very being was being tested, refined. The decision wasn't simply a yes or no; it was a surrender, a transformation, an acceptance of the cosmic bargain, a fusion of mortal will and cosmic design. He looked at the Lumina and Sylvani, not with fear, but with a newfound understanding. He understood the price, and he was prepared to pay it, but on his own terms, shaping the transformation, not succumbing to it.

The air crackled with anticipation, the unspoken agreement hanging heavy between them. The gateway, though closed, remained a potent symbol of the cosmic influence. The price was paid, not in sacrifice, but in a profound change, a transformation of his very essence, a metamorphosis that would reshape his future, and perhaps the destiny of the world. The true test of the price would not be the act of payment, but the enduring struggle to maintain his humanity amid the boundless power he was about to wield. The journey had just begun.

The understanding solidified, not as a sudden revelation, but as a slow dawning. It wasn't a specific demand, a list of sacrifices. The price was a reshaping, a molding of his very being, a fusion of his mortal essence with the cosmic energy. He felt the shift, not as a violent disruption, but as a subtle alteration, a gradual merging of his consciousness with the pulsating energy of the gateway. It was a merging, a symbiotic relationship, not a domination. He wasn't being consumed but rather expanded, enhanced, and transformed.

The Lumina and Sylvani, their forms shimmering, seemed to intensify, their essence intertwining with the changing energy field. They were not passive observers but active participants in this cosmic alchemy, guiding the transformation, ensuring its success. Their presence felt less like external entities and more like extensions of the cosmic energy itself, weaving the threads of his metamorphosis. He felt their touch, not as a physical sensation but as an understanding, a merging of wills.

The gateway pulsed, its energy intensifying, as if mirroring the changes within him. It wasn't simply a portal but a conduit, a living entity that served as a bridge between the mortal realm and the cosmic expanse. The air crackled with energy, vibrating with the rhythm of creation and destruction, a symphony of cosmic forces playing out in the heart of the gateway. He was becoming a part of this symphony, a note in the grand cosmic composition.

A wave of intense energy washed over him, not a shock, but a surge of power that resonated deep within his very being. He felt the expansion, a stretching, a breaking down of his limitations. His senses sharpened, extending beyond the boundaries of his physical form. He saw the intricate tapestry of reality, the interwoven threads of existence, and the subtle dance of energy that governed the universe.

His understanding expanded exponentially. The whispers of the cosmos, previously muffled and distant, now resonated clearly, offering insights into the universe's intricate workings. He saw the connections, the interplay between seemingly disparate events, the threads of destiny that wove through time and space. The knowledge wasn't simply imparted; it was woven into the fabric of his being, becoming an integral part of his consciousness.

The transformation was not painless. It was a crucible, a refining fire that tested his will, his resolve. He felt the push and pull of cosmic forces, the subtle manipulations of probabilities, and the constant reshaping of his very essence. But he didn't resist. He understood the necessity, the cosmic design. He was not a passive recipient but an active participant, collaborating with the Lumina and Sylvani, shaping the transformation to suit his own will.

The merging continued, his physical form subtly altered. His skin shimmered with energy, radiating a faint glow. His senses expanded beyond the limits of human perception. He felt the pulsations of the cosmos, the rhythm of the universe, and the echoes of creation and destruction. He saw the interplay of forces, the dance of energies, and the intricate balance that held the universe in place.

The gateway began to shift, its energy intensifying, swirling around him like a cosmic vortex. The Lumina and Sylvani faded, not disappearing, but becoming one with the energy field, their essence dissolving into the gateway's swirling heart. He felt their presence within him, not as separate entities, but as a part of his being, as a guide, an assurance.

With a final surge of energy, the gateway expanded, revealing a vista beyond comprehension. It wasn't a physical location but a realm of pure energy, a plane of existence beyond the constraints of space and time. He stepped through, not physically, but through a shifting of consciousness, leaving behind his former self, his mortal limitations, and entering into a realm of boundless potential.

The higher plane was a kaleidoscope of colors, a symphony of energies. It was a world of pure energy, shimmering with iridescent light, swirling with cosmic currents. There were no fixed forms, no solid objects, only energy, vibrant and pulsating, a living entity that breathed, shifted, and changed with the ebb and flow of the cosmos. He felt a sense of vastness, an understanding of the insignificance of his former existence. Yet, he also felt a sense of empowerment, a sense of belonging.

He saw other entities, beings of pure energy, swirling through this higher plane, their forms shifting, their energies intertwining. They were not hostile, not indifferent. They were part of the cosmic tapestry, each playing a role in the grand design. He felt their presence, their understanding, and their acceptance.

The pact was forged, not in blood or ink, but in the transformation of his being. It was a merger, a fusion of mortal will and cosmic energy, a symbiotic relationship that bound him to the cosmos. He had paid the price, not with sacrifice, but with change, with transformation, with a profound alteration of his very essence.

His new existence was not devoid of challenges. The power he wielded was immense, the responsibility daunting. But he was prepared. He had faced his inner demons, conquered his fears, and now he stood on the precipice of a new beginning, a new destiny. The journey had been long, arduous, and filled with sacrifice. But now, the ultimate test lay ahead: not merely the possession of cosmic power, but the ability to wield it responsibly, ethically, for the betterment of all. The fate of worlds rested on his shoulders, a burden he bore not with trepidation but with a newfound understanding of his place within the grand scheme of the cosmos. He was ready. The transformation was complete. The pact was sealed. The next phase of his journey had begun.

The world, once vibrant with the clashing hues of seven reptilian tribes and the ethereal glow of fairy settlements, began to shimmer. It wasn't a chaotic upheaval but a deliberate, almost artistic, reshaping. The very fabric of reality seemed to bend to his will, guided by the lingering echoes of the Lumina and Sylvani, now woven into the very essence of his being. Mountains rose and fell, not with the slow, geological processes of eons, but with the speed of thought. Valleys deepened, rivers rerouted, forming intricate patterns that mirrored the constellations above. Forests bloomed in impossible colors, their leaves shimmering with an inner light, each tree a testament to the power he now commanded.

The transformation wasn't limited to the physical landscape. The very air hummed with a newfound energy, a cosmic resonance that permeated everything. Magic, once a scarce resource, now flowed freely, a river of pure potential coursing through the veins of the world. The demonic energies that had once plagued the land, the lingering echoes of the ritual that had scarred his childhood, were not eradicated but transmuted. They were not destroyed but woven into the tapestry of creation, serving as a counterpoint to the light, a necessary shadow in the dance of existence. The darkness was not vanquished; it was understood, embraced, and integrated into a new, more balanced reality.

He walked across continents, his steps leaving trails of shimmering light, his presence altering the very structure of the land. The seven reptilian tribes, initially wary, gradually found themselves drawn to the newfound harmony. Their scales shimmered with iridescent hues reflecting the new cosmic energy, their winged rulers no longer symbols of fearsome authority but benevolent guides, their wisdom integrated into the fabric of this new world. The fairies, once confined to secluded groves, now danced freely across the transformed landscapes, their wings glittering like a thousand tiny stars, their songs weaving new enchantments into the world. Even the gods and goddesses, initially resistant, eventually bowed before the transformative power he wielded, acknowledging the new order.

The process was not without its challenges. There were moments of doubt, moments when the sheer magnitude of the task threatened to overwhelm him. He felt the weight of responsibility, the daunting task of balancing cosmic forces, of shaping a world free from the tyranny of darkness yet retaining the necessary elements of shadow and light. He experienced moments of intense pressure, the very fabric of reality threatening to unravel under the strain of his power. Yet, each time, he persevered, guided by the remnants of the Lumina and Sylvani within, their wisdom and guidance a constant source of strength.

He sculpted the skies, painting them with celestial wonders, creating constellations that told stories of his journey, of his struggles, and of his ultimate triumph. He imbued the stars with new energies, transforming their light into beacons of hope, guiding lights for lost souls. The sun and moon, once mere celestial bodies, became vibrant expressions of cosmic energy, pulsating with life and power. The oceans responded to his touch, their waters glowing with an ethereal luminescence, their depths teeming with creatures born of the new, transformed reality.

His family, once ordinary mortals, were transformed alongside him. Their bodies glowed with the same ethereal light that radiated from him, their minds expanded to encompass the infinite. They became not merely his companions but co-creators, helping him shape the new world, sharing the burden of responsibility, and contributing their unique perspectives and talents to the creation of a harmonious reality. His family, now imbued with cosmic energy, became a new pantheon, symbols of strength, wisdom, and compassion, embodying the ideals of this newly created world.

This wasn't a world of perfect harmony, a utopia devoid of challenge. Instead, it was a world of balance, a world where light and shadow coexisted, where strength and vulnerability were intertwined, a world that reflected the complexity of his own journey. He had faced the darkness within, integrated it into his being, and used that understanding to forge a reality where darkness wasn't banished but understood, controlled, and ultimately, transformed.

The reshaping wasn't merely physical; it was also spiritual and emotional. The world's inhabitants felt a profound shift in their consciousness, a heightened awareness of their interconnectedness, and a deeper understanding of their place in the grand cosmic tapestry. Fear and prejudice lessened, replaced by a sense of shared purpose, a collective understanding that they were all part of something greater, something magnificent. The very essence of existence shifted; the world wasn't merely populated by mortals, but by beings touched by the divine, connected to the cosmos.

He stood on a mountain peak, overlooking the transformed world. It stretched before him, a testament to his power, his sacrifice, and his unwavering will. The world below was not perfect, yet it was whole, a reflection of the complex harmony between opposing forces. It was a world born from the ashes of his inner torment, a world imbued with the wisdom of the cosmos, a world where humanity, in its newfound connection to the cosmic energies, had the potential to reach its full potential.

The transformation continued, evolving, adapting, guided by his intuition and the cosmic energy that flowed through him. It was a continuous process, a never-ending dance between creation and refinement, a reflection of the ever-changing nature of existence itself. He had reshaped the world, not to impose his will, but to create a space where all beings, from the smallest insect to the most powerful god, could find their place, could thrive, and could evolve. The hellish torment within him had been transmuted into a heavenly paradise, a testament to the possibility of redemption, the potential for transformation, and the boundless power of the human spirit when aligned with the cosmos. The path ahead remained uncertain, filled with potential challenges, yet his heart was filled with a sense of peace and purpose. He was not merely a god; he was a guardian, a shepherd, leading his people toward a future of unimaginable potential, a future where the cosmos and humanity danced together in an eternal waltz of creation.

6

The New Pantheon

The celestial realm shimmered, a kaleidoscope of nebulae and swirling cosmic dust, born from the very essence of his being. It wasn't a mere imitation of the heavens he'd known, but a new creation, reflecting the complex tapestry of his journey. Here, amidst the swirling galaxies and constellations that mirrored the transformed world below, he began the task of establishing a new pantheon, a divine order that would guide and protect his people. His family, transformed beyond recognition, stood beside him, their forms radiating an ethereal light, their eyes mirroring the endless expanse of the cosmos.

His wife, Elara, once a gentle healer, now possessed the power to mend not only flesh but also the fabric of reality itself. Her touch could soothe the tormented souls, calming the echoes of past traumas and ushering in an era of peace and understanding. She was the Goddess of Healing and Reconciliation, her presence a balm to the wounds of a world that had known much suffering. Her compassion, amplified a thousandfold by the cosmic energy flowing through her, would be a cornerstone of the new divine order.

His son, Orion, with a spirit as vast as the cosmos itself, had inherited his father's strategic mind and tactical prowess, but tempered by an unwavering compassion. He became the God of Strategy and Protection, his gaze encompassing the entire realm, ever-vigilant against any potential threat. His power wasn't brute force but a keen intellect, a profound understanding of cosmic energies, and the ability to anticipate and avert danger before it could manifest.

His daughter, Lyra, with a heart as bright as the stars, possessed an innate ability to connect with the deepest emotions of all beings. She became the Goddess of Empathy and Inspiration, her songs capable of soothing even the most tormented souls, her words weaving a tapestry of hope and understanding. Her power was not in raw might but in the ability to connect with others on a fundamental level, forging bonds of unity and compassion.

These were not simply titles; they were reflections of their transformed natures, their powers interwoven with the very fabric of the newly created cosmos. But the pantheon was not limited to his immediate family. Among the newly ascended were the representatives of the seven reptilian tribes, their wisdom and leadership now imbued with cosmic power. Each held a unique place in the new divine order, reflecting their tribal heritage and their transformed understanding of their place in the greater scheme of things.

Xalzar, the elder of the Crimson tribe, became the God of War and Justice, his formidable power tempered by an understanding of the delicate balance between strength and compassion. He represented the warrior spirit, not as an instrument of aggression, but as a protector of the innocent, a champion of fairness, and a guardian of the newly established harmony.

Zylara, the matriarch of the Azure tribe, became the Goddess of Wisdom and Guidance, her keen intellect and profound understanding of the cosmos providing counsel and direction to those in need. Her wisdom wasn't confined to abstract knowledge; it was the embodiment of experience, insight, and an ability to navigate the complexities of existence.

The other five tribes, each with their unique attributes and strengths, were similarly integrated into the new pantheon. Their leaders, transformed by the same cosmic energy, now occupied positions of authority and responsibility, their powers reflecting their unique tribal heritage, yet united under a shared vision of harmony and cooperation.

Beyond his family and the reptilian tribes, the pantheon extended to include beings from across the spectrum of existence. The fairies, once enigmatic and elusive, now embraced their role as messengers and weavers of enchantment, their magic intertwined with the very fabric of the celestial realm. They became the Celestial Chorus, their songs shaping the emotions and energies of the cosmos, ensuring that the realm remained balanced and harmonious.

Even some of the former gods and goddesses, humbled by the sheer magnitude of the transformation, found a place within this new divine order. Those who had once opposed him, who had doubted his power, now embraced his vision, realizing that the new pantheon offered a chance for redemption and a future of unprecedented peace and prosperity. They were not merely integrated but re-evaluated, their roles redefined to reflect the new values and priorities of the transformed world.

The establishment of the new pantheon was not a mere act of power but a carefully orchestrated process. It involved a delicate balance of authority and collaboration, a weaving together of disparate elements into a unified whole. He didn't impose his will; he guided, encouraged, and collaborated. His family played a vital role in this, ensuring that all members felt valued, heard, and empowered.

The celestial realm served not just as the dwelling place of the new pantheon but also as a bridge between the mortal and cosmic realms. It was a place of learning, contemplation, and growth, where the gods and goddesses could draw strength and inspiration from the endless expanse of the cosmos. It wasn't a static structure but a dynamic entity, constantly evolving and adapting to the ever-changing needs of the mortal world below.

The creation of the Pantheon was a monumental task, a testament to the protagonist's unwavering determination and the boundless capacity of the human spirit. It was a reflection of his journey, a symbolic representation of his triumph over inner demons and his embrace of the cosmos. It was a bold, ambitious undertaking, a commitment to a future where humanity could thrive, protected and guided by a divine order that reflected its own aspirations for harmony and understanding. The challenge now lay in guiding this new order, ensuring its stability, and ensuring that its powers were wielded for the good of all beings.

The new pantheon wasn't just a collection of powerful beings; it was a living, breathing entity, constantly adapting to the needs of the transformed world. It was a reflection of the intricate balance between the forces of light and shadow, a testament to the fact that even in a world of profound transformation, challenges would persist, requiring the constant vigilance and cooperation of the pantheon. It was a constant process of refinement, of adjustments made in response to the evolving needs of the realm. The new world, still in its nascent stages, needed constant care and guidance. The pantheon, therefore, would not stand as a static entity but as an ever-evolving reflection of the cosmic dance of creation and destruction.

The protagonist understood that the success of the new pantheon wouldn't rely solely on his power but on the cooperation and understanding of his fellow gods and goddesses. He had learned, through his own journey, the importance of collaboration and the shared responsibility that came with wielding such profound power. He established a council, a gathering place for the pantheon members to discuss matters of importance and collectively address any challenges facing the world. This wasn't a system of top-down control but a cooperative effort, where every member's voice was heard and valued.

The celestial realm itself reflected this ethos of collaboration. It was designed not as a fortress or a sanctuary but as a place where the divine and mortal realms could interact and exchange knowledge. Paths of shimmering light connected the celestial realm to different points across the transformed world, allowing for swift communication and intervention where needed.

The establishment of the new pantheon marked not an end but a new beginning. The work was far from over. The task of guiding humanity towards a brighter future required constant effort, unwavering commitment, and the unwavering cooperation of the new divine order. Yet, as the protagonist surveyed his creation, the celestial realm teeming with life and energy, he felt a sense of profound satisfaction. The hell within him had indeed been transmuted into a heavenly paradise, a testament to the enduring power of hope, resilience, and the transformative power of the human spirit. He had not only remade the world; he had remade himself, becoming a beacon of hope, a guardian of a world poised on the brink of an extraordinary future. The eternal waltz of creation had just begun.

The task of dividing the realms was not a simple allocation of territory but a complex tapestry woven from the unique strengths and abilities of each member of the new pantheon. It required a deep understanding of the interconnectedness of all things, a recognition that each realm was intimately tied to the others, and a delicate balance that needed to be maintained. He began with the mortal realm, the foundation upon which the entire cosmos rested. This realm, still bearing the scars of past conflicts, needed nurturing and guidance, a gentle hand to heal its wounds and foster growth. Elara, the Goddess of Healing and Reconciliation, was the natural choice to oversee this crucial realm. Her influence wasn't just about physical healing; it extended to the emotional and spiritual well-being of humanity. She would weave a tapestry of understanding, mending broken hearts and fostering unity among the diverse populations. Her touch would inspire forgiveness, empathy, and collaboration, healing the wounds of the past and paving the way for a more harmonious future.

Orion, the God of Strategy and Protection, took on the responsibility of the ethereal plane, the realm of spirits and dreams. This was a vital realm, influencing the subconscious minds of mortals and subtly shaping their destinies. Orion's keen intellect and strategic mind were perfectly suited to navigating the complexities of this ethereal realm, anticipating potential threats, and guiding the flow of spiritual energy to ensure a balance of light and shadow. His watchful eye would prevent the incursion of malevolent spirits and guide lost souls toward enlightenment, ensuring that the ethereal plane remained a source of inspiration and guidance for the mortals below.

Lyra, the Goddess of Empathy and Inspiration, was entrusted with the realm of the Feywild, a magical place of enchantment and wonder. Her innate ability to connect with the deepest emotions of beings, both human and fae, made her the ideal guardian of this realm. She would nurture the connection between mortals and the Feywild, ensuring a harmonious relationship between these two worlds. Her songs would weave enchantments, her words inspiring creativity and wonder, protecting the delicate balance of the Feywild while fostering its mystical gifts for the benefit of the mortal world. She would ensure that the magic of the Feywild was used for the betterment of all, preventing its misuse and guiding its potent energies for the growth and prosperity of the world.

The seven reptilian tribes, now elevated to godhood, each took responsibility for a unique aspect of the newly formed cosmos. Xalzar, the God of War and Justice, oversaw the elemental plane, the realm of fire, water, earth, and air. His formidable power, now tempered with wisdom and compassion, ensured the balance of these fundamental forces. He wouldn't simply control the elements; he would act as a guardian, ensuring that their power was used responsibly, preventing natural disasters and harnessing their energies for the benefit of all. His leadership would be one of judicious restraint and calculated action, ensuring that elemental forces remained a source of life and prosperity rather than destruction.

Zylara, the Goddess of Wisdom and Guidance, took on the mantle of the celestial archives, the repository of all knowledge, past, present, and future. Her profound understanding of the cosmos allowed her to safeguard this invaluable resource and make it accessible to those who sought enlightenment. She would not hoard knowledge but ensure that it was used for the betterment of all, guiding those seeking wisdom and knowledge and preventing its misuse for selfish ends. She would be the custodian of cosmic truths, ensuring their preservation and understanding by the new pantheon and the mortal realm.

The remaining five tribal leaders, each imbued with unique cosmic powers reflecting their ancestral heritage, assumed stewardship of different cosmic planes, each intricately woven into the fabric of the newly created reality. One became the Guardian of the Netherworld, ensuring that the realm of shadows remained in balance; another governed the Astral Sea, ensuring safe passage for wandering souls; another oversaw the plane of dreams, ensuring the flow of inspiration and avoiding nightmares; another governed the realm of time, ensuring its steady passage and preventing paradoxes; the final leader held dominion over the plane of creation, ensuring the continual genesis of life and the renewal of the world.

The integration of these new gods into the cosmic hierarchy wasn't forced, but a carefully choreographed dance of power and cooperation. The protagonist, in his newfound role as the supreme god, acted as a facilitator, a guide, not a dictator. He ensured that the realms were divided not by arbitrary power plays, but by a thoughtful consideration of each god's unique strengths and the interconnectedness of the realms. The result was a cosmic balance, a carefully constructed ecosystem where each realm influenced the others, creating a vibrant, dynamic whole.

The process was not without its challenges. There were disagreements, moments of tension, and even some subtle power struggles. But through careful negotiation, mutual respect, and a shared vision of a harmonious cosmos, the conflicts were resolved. The new pantheon was not a monolithic entity but a tapestry of diverse personalities, abilities, and perspectives working in concert to maintain cosmic balance. It was a reflection of the world itself, a microcosm of its complexity and beauty, its strength born not from uniformity but from unity in diversity.

The establishment of the realms was not merely a symbolic gesture. Each realm responded to the energy of its assigned god, changing and evolving in accordance with its influence. The mortal realm, under Elara's nurturing touch, began to heal. The scars of war began to fade, replaced by a burgeoning sense of hope and unity. The ethereal plane, guided by Orion's strategic mind, became a realm of greater clarity and balance, where spiritual energy flowed freely, aiding mortals in their spiritual journeys.

The Feywild, under Lyra's stewardship, flourished, its magic becoming a source of inspiration and wonder for the mortal realm. The elemental plane, under Xalzar's watchful eye, became a source of life-giving energy, its power harnessed for the benefit of all. The celestial archives, guided by Zylara's wisdom, became a beacon of knowledge, guiding the mortals and the gods toward a deeper understanding of the universe. The cosmic planes, under the stewardship of the remaining tribal leaders, flourished, each contributing to the overall harmony and balance of the cosmos.

This wasn't merely a division of realms; it was a rebirth, a transformative process that reshaped the cosmos in the image of the new pantheon. It was a reflection of the protagonist's journey, a testament to his ability to forge unity from chaos, to create harmony from discord. His victory was not simply a conquest of his inner demons; it was a testament to the human spirit's capacity for growth, adaptation, and the creation of a better world. This newly established order wasn't a static entity; it was a living, breathing system, constantly evolving and adapting to the changing needs of the cosmos, ensuring a perpetual cycle of creation, destruction, and renewal. The celestial realm, the home of the pantheon, became a nexus of cosmic energy, a vibrant hub that connected all realms, a symbol of the interconnectedness of all things. The protagonist, having forged a new pantheon, now stood at the precipice of a new era, a future shaped by his actions, a future brimming with both promise and peril. The true test would lie not in the establishment of this new order, but in its preservation and the ongoing challenge of maintaining the fragile balance of the cosmos. The eternal waltz of creation, a constant dance of life and death, light and shadow, continued, guided by the new pantheon, a testament to the resilience and transformative power of the human spirit.

The establishment of the new pantheon wasn't merely a redistribution of power; it was the dawn of a new era, governed by principles forged in the crucible of the protagonist's journey. These weren't laws etched in stone, but living principles, adaptable and evolving with the cosmos itself, reflecting the dynamic nature of existence. The first and most fundamental law, the cornerstone of this new reality, was the Principle of Interconnectedness. It recognized that all realms, from the mortal plane to the farthest reaches of the cosmos, were inextricably linked. Actions in one realm rippled outwards, affecting others in unforeseen ways. This principle encouraged empathy, understanding, and collaboration, fostering a sense of shared responsibility for the well-being of the entire cosmos. It was a departure from the old ways, where realms often warred with each other, fueled by self-interest and a lack of understanding.

The second principle, the Principle of Balance, emphasized the delicate equilibrium between opposing forces. Light and shadow, creation and destruction, order and chaos—these weren't enemies but complementary forces, necessary for the dynamic growth of the cosmos. This principle rejected the notion of absolute good or evil, embracing the complexities of existence. It encouraged the gods to understand and manage these opposing forces, preventing one from overwhelming the other, maintaining a harmonious flow of cosmic energy. This was particularly important in the elemental plane, where Xalzar's judicious governance was crucial to preventing catastrophic imbalances. He didn't suppress the raw power of the elements but guided and channeled them, ensuring their creative potential was harnessed for the benefit of all.

The Principle of Growth and Renewal emphasized the cyclical nature of existence. Death wasn't an end but a transition, a necessary part of the cycle of creation and renewal. This principle encouraged the gods to embrace change, adapt to the ever-shifting dynamics of the cosmos, and foster the growth and evolution of all beings. This was exemplified in Elara's nurturing touch on the mortal realm, where she not only healed physical wounds but also fostered spiritual growth, encouraging humanity to learn from the past and embrace the future with hope and resilience. Her influence wasn't limited to healing; it extended to fostering a culture of learning, encouraging exploration, and promoting understanding between different cultures.

The principle of compassion and empathy guided the interactions between the gods and mortals. It recognized the inherent value of all life, regardless of form or origin. This principle promoted understanding, tolerance, and mutual respect, encouraging the gods to act as benevolent guides rather than tyrannical rulers. Lyra, in her stewardship of the Feywild, embodied this principle perfectly. She fostered a harmonious relationship between mortals and the Fey folk, ensuring that the magic of the Feywild was used for the betterment of all, preventing its misuse, and promoting a deep understanding between different magical beings. Her influence wasn't simply limited to the Feywild; it extended to all of creation, promoting tolerance and understanding between different races and beings.

The Principle of Justice and Accountability held the gods accountable for their actions. It established a system of checks and balances, ensuring that no single god or realm held excessive power. Xalzar, despite his dominion over the elemental plane, was not above the law. His power was tempered with wisdom and compassion, ensuring that his actions were always guided by justice and fairness. This principle promoted transparency and responsibility, preventing the abuse of power and ensuring that the cosmos remained a fair and equitable place for all. This system was not only for the gods; it extended to mortals as well, instituting a system of law based on fairness and compassion, aiming to foster a just and equitable society for all.

The Principle of Knowledge and Wisdom emphasized the importance of learning and understanding. Zylara, as guardian of the celestial archives, played a pivotal role in ensuring the accessibility of knowledge to all. Her stewardship wasn't about hoarding information; it was about ensuring its dissemination and responsible use. This wasn't merely the preservation of facts; it was the promotion of critical thinking, encouraging everyone—gods and mortals alike—to seek knowledge, question assumptions, and strive for a deeper understanding of the universe. This encouraged a culture of learning, fostering scientific advancements and technological innovations that would benefit all of creation.

These principles, interwoven into the fabric of the new reality, created a cosmos where cooperation replaced conflict, understanding replaced prejudice, and harmony reigned supreme. The realms themselves reflected this new order. The mortal realm, once scarred by war, flourished under Elara's gentle guidance. Cities rose from the ashes, agriculture flourished, and a new era of peace and prosperity dawned. The ethereal plane, under Orion's watchful eye, became a sanctuary for spirits, a realm of inspiration and guidance. Dreams flowed more freely, nightmares lessened, and the connection between mortals and the spiritual world deepened.

The Feywild, under Lyra's influence, continued its magic, but it was a gentler, more harmonious magic. The relationship between mortals and the Fey folk blossomed, bringing a unique magical prosperity to the mortal realm. The elemental plane, under Xalzar's wise stewardship, became a source of life-giving energy, powering civilization without causing chaos. The celestial archives, under Zylara's care, became a beacon of knowledge, guiding all toward wisdom and understanding. The Netherworld, the Astral Sea, the plane of dreams, the realm of time, and the plane of creation each thrived under the responsible guidance of the remaining tribal leaders, their actions in accordance with the new principles of the pantheon. The cosmos, once a tapestry of warring realms, was now a symphony of interwoven energies, a testament to the power of cooperation and the enduring human capacity for change and creation.

The protagonist, now the supreme god, didn't rule with an iron fist but with a gentle hand, guiding and fostering the growth of the new pantheon. His role wasn't about dictating laws but about ensuring that the principles were understood and upheld. He acted as a mediator, resolving disputes and guiding the gods towards a shared vision of harmony. His reign wasn't about absolute power but about shared responsibility, a testament to his understanding that true power lies not in domination but in collaboration and the fostering of a thriving cosmos. He understood that the new laws weren't static; they were fluid, constantly evolving and adapting to the ever-changing dynamics of the cosmos. He established councils and assemblies where the gods could discuss, debate, and collaborate on issues affecting the different realms. This encouraged a sense of shared governance, preventing the concentration of power and fostering a more equitable distribution of responsibility.

The establishment of this new order didn't eliminate challenges. Conflicts still arose, disagreements persisted, and the delicate balance of the cosmos occasionally teetered. But the new principles, ingrained in the hearts of the gods, provided a framework for resolving conflicts, fostering understanding, and maintaining the delicate balance. The new pantheon wasn't a static entity but a dynamic system, constantly adapting and evolving, reflecting the vibrant and ever-changing nature of the cosmos itself. The protagonist, in his new role, understood this fluidity, constantly adapting his approach to meet the ever-evolving needs of the cosmos. His triumph wasn't a final victory but a continuous process, a constant striving for harmony and balance, a testament to the enduring struggle between chaos and order, and a reflection of the human spirit's capacity for both destruction and creation. The new era was one of perpetual creation, a dynamic dance of life and death, light and shadow, forever shaped and reshaped by the collective will of the new pantheon and the ever-evolving nature of the cosmos.

The transition was not immediate, nor was it without its challenges. The echoes of the old wars, the ingrained prejudices, and the lingering anxieties of a world teetering on the brink of annihilation didn't vanish overnight. Yet, under the watchful guidance of the new pantheon, a palpable shift occurred. The air itself seemed to hum with a newfound energy, a vibrant pulse of creation and renewal that resonated across all realms.

In the mortal realm, Elara's influence was profoundly felt. Cities, once ravaged by conflict, blossomed into vibrant hubs of culture and innovation. Ancient ruins, monuments to past wars, were slowly repurposed, integrated into new structures as reminders of a hard-won peace. Architectural styles evolved, reflecting the newfound harmony; soaring spires reached towards the heavens, not as symbols of dominance, but as expressions of aspiration and unity. Grand libraries, filled with scrolls from across the realms, became centers of learning, fostering a culture of inquiry and shared knowledge. The arts flourished. Musicians composed symphonies that echoed the cosmic harmony, while artists painted vibrant murals depicting the intertwined fates of gods and mortals. New technologies emerged, fueled by the wisdom gleaned from Zylara's celestial archives, harnessing the elemental energies under Xalzar's careful guidance to power cities and improve the quality of life for all.

Agriculture, once disrupted by war, experienced a golden age. Innovative farming techniques, inspired by the wisdom of the Feywild, led to abundant harvests. Fields once scarred by battle were transformed into fertile landscapes, yielding crops of unimaginable bounty. Food became a symbol of shared prosperity, a reminder of the interconnectedness of all beings. Feasts and celebrations became commonplace, bringing communities together to share in their newfound abundance. The emphasis on growth and renewal, instilled by the new pantheon, permeated every aspect of mortal society. A deep respect for nature emerged, fostering a harmonious relationship between humans and the environment. Forests were no longer viewed as sources of resources to be exploited but as sacred spaces, vital to the health of the world. Rivers flowed freely, their waters unpolluted, providing life-giving sustenance.

The Feywild, under Lyra's gentle rule, became a source of wonder and inspiration. The relationship between mortals and the Fey folk, once fraught with distrust and conflict, blossomed into one of mutual respect and understanding. The magic of the Feywild, once wielded for capricious purposes, was now channeled for the benefit of all. Magical creatures, once feared and hunted, were now protected and revered. The Feywild's enchantment spread to the mortal realm, enriching it with vibrant colors, enchanting melodies, and a renewed appreciation for the beauty of the natural world. Mortals and Fey folk collaborated on creative projects, weaving together their unique skills and perspectives to create breathtaking works of art and ingenuity. The vibrant tapestry of their shared creations was a testament to the power of collaboration and mutual understanding.

The elemental plane, under Xalzar's careful stewardship, became a source of sustainable energy. Volcanoes, once symbols of destructive power, were harnessed to provide geothermal energy. Rivers and oceans, carefully managed, generate hydroelectric power. The very winds themselves were used to power wind turbines, creating a clean and sustainable energy source for the entire world. The balance between the elements was meticulously maintained, preventing natural disasters and ensuring the well-being of all realms. Xalzar's wisdom ensured that this power was used responsibly, preventing its misuse and promoting sustainable development.

The celestial archives, under Zylara's guidance, became a beacon of knowledge for all beings. Scholars from across the realms flocked to the archives, seeking wisdom and understanding. The archives weren't just a repository of information; they were a place of learning and discovery, fostering a culture of intellectual curiosity and critical thinking. Knowledge was freely shared, encouraging innovation and progress in all realms. The archives themselves evolved, incorporating new discoveries and perspectives, reflecting the ever-changing nature of the cosmos. The focus on knowledge and wisdom extended beyond scholarly pursuits. It inspired a renewed interest in education and learning, making knowledge accessible to all beings, regardless of their origin or social standing.

The Netherworld, the Astral Sea, the plane of dreams, the realm of time, and the plane of creation each experienced a similar transformation. The tribal leaders, guided by the principles of the new pantheon, ensured that each realm thrived in harmony with the others. The old conflicts and prejudices gradually faded, replaced by a sense of shared purpose and mutual respect.

However, the Era of Harmony was not a utopian fantasy without its challenges. Minor conflicts still arose, disagreements persisted, and the delicate balance of the cosmos occasionally teetered. But the principles of the new pantheon provided a framework for resolving these conflicts, fostering understanding, and maintaining the delicate balance. The protagonist, in his role as supreme god, acted not as a ruler but as a guide, a mediator who helped navigate these disputes, ensuring that the principles of interconnectedness, balance, growth, compassion, justice, and knowledge continued to shape the cosmos.

The system of governance he established was fluid and adaptable, constantly evolving to meet the needs of a constantly changing cosmos. Regular councils and assemblies of the gods allowed for open dialogue and collaborative decision-making. This system prevented the concentration of power, fostering a more equitable distribution of responsibility. The gods, once isolated and self-interested, were now interconnected, their fates interwoven, their collective actions shaping the destiny of the entire cosmos.

The Era of Harmony was not a static state but a dynamic process, a perpetual dance between order and chaos, creation and destruction. It was a testament to the enduring human capacity for change, a reflection of the cosmos's inherent dynamism. It was a hopeful beginning, a promise of a future where cooperation replaced conflict, understanding replaced prejudice, and harmony reigned supreme—a future yet to be fully written, a future that held both incredible promise and the subtle whisper of unforeseen challenges. The newly formed pantheon, with the weight of this future upon its shoulders, stood ready to meet whatever lay ahead.

The wind carried the scent of blooming jasmine and ripening grapes across the plains, a fragrant testament to the bountiful harvests that now characterized the land. Gone were the scarred battlefields, replaced by rolling hills of emerald green, punctuated by vibrant wildflowers that painted the landscape in a kaleidoscope of colors. Villages, once huddled in fear behind crumbling walls, now sprawled outwards, their houses adorned with intricate carvings and cheerful murals depicting scenes of prosperity and peace. The laughter of children echoed through the streets, a melody that had been absent for generations. The very air seemed to hum with a quiet contentment, a palpable sense of security that permeated every corner of the mortal realm.

This transformation wasn't merely cosmetic; it was a profound shift in the consciousness of the people. Generations scarred by war had learned to value peace, understanding that true strength wasn't measured in the ability to inflict pain but in the capacity for empathy and cooperation. The old tribal rivalries, once fueled by fear and prejudice, had faded into distant memories, replaced by a shared sense of identity and purpose. The people now saw themselves not as separate entities, but as interconnected parts of a larger whole, bound together by their shared experiences and their collective aspiration for a better future.

This new unity extended beyond mere coexistence; it manifested in collaborative projects that enriched the lives of everyone. Farmers shared their knowledge and techniques, ensuring that every field yielded its most abundant harvest. Artisans collaborated on breathtaking works of art, their creations reflecting the diverse cultures and traditions that once existed in isolation. Scholars from across the land met regularly to exchange ideas, fostering a vibrant intellectual atmosphere that sparked innovation in every field of human endeavor.

The legacy of the new pantheon wasn't limited to the mortal realm. Across the Feywild, the once-fragile truce between mortals and the Fey folk had blossomed into a vibrant partnership. Fey magic, once wielded capriciously, now served as a catalyst for growth and renewal, enriching the land with its enchanting power. Mortals and Fey folk worked side by side, their skills complementing each other, creating a breathtaking fusion of artistry and ingenuity. The forests, once seen as potential sources of conflict and danger, were now revered as sacred groves, brimming with life and teeming with magical creatures that lived in harmony with their human neighbors.

In the celestial archives, Zylara had overseen the creation of a vast network of interconnected libraries, accessible to all beings, regardless of their origin or social standing. This vast repository of knowledge became a beacon of learning, empowering people to shape their own futures through education and self-improvement. The old emphasis on secrecy and control was replaced by a culture of open sharing, where knowledge was freely exchanged and used to propel progress across all realms. The archives, however, were not simply repositories of accumulated information; they were living, evolving entities, constantly expanding and refining their collections, reflecting the ever-shifting landscape of knowledge and understanding.

Xalzar, master of the elements, had not merely prevented natural disasters but had also overseen the creation of sustainable energy sources, transforming the elemental plane into a wellspring of power. Volcanoes, once feared for their destructive potential, now provide geothermal energy, powering cities and improving the quality of life for all. Rivers and oceans were carefully managed, providing hydroelectric power without harming their delicate ecosystems. The winds were harnessed, creating a clean and sustainable source of energy, demonstrating the potential for harmony between human progress and environmental stewardship.

The influence of the new pantheon reached into every corner of the cosmos. In the Netherworld, the Astral Sea, the plane of dreams, the realm of time, and the plane of creation, similar transformations took place, fostering unity and cooperation among disparate beings. Ancient rivalries and conflicts were resolved, not through force, but through understanding and mutual respect. Each realm flourished, its unique characteristics enhanced, and its potential maximized through collaboration and cooperation with the other realms.

The protagonist, in his role as supreme god, did not exert absolute control; instead, he acted as a guide, a mediator, ensuring that the principles of balance, growth, compassion, justice, and knowledge guided the actions of the pantheon and its subjects. He established a fluid system of governance that was adaptive and responsive to the ever-changing needs of the cosmos. Regular councils and assemblies allowed for open dialogue and collaborative decision-making, ensuring that power was not concentrated in any single entity or realm.

His legacy extended beyond tangible achievements; it was rooted in a profound shift in consciousness, a change in the very fabric of being. People learned to value cooperation, understanding, and empathy, fostering a culture of mutual respect and shared responsibility. The old systems of oppression and control were dismantled, replaced by a society that celebrated diversity and valued individual potential. The emphasis on growth and renewal permeated every aspect of life, fostering a harmonious relationship between humanity and the environment.

Centuries passed, and the Era of Harmony continued, not as a static state, but as an ongoing process of evolution and adaptation. Minor conflicts arose, disagreements persisted, but the principles established by the new pantheon provided a framework for resolving these conflicts, preventing them from escalating into larger-scale upheavals. The institutions established under the protagonist's guidance evolved, adapting to changing circumstances and ensuring that the system remained responsive to the needs of all its inhabitants.

The world that the protagonist helped create wasn't a utopian paradise devoid of challenge. It was a world characterized by ongoing growth, development, and evolution. New cultures emerged, new technologies were developed, and new ideas were explored. The cosmos continued its eternal dance between creation and destruction, order and chaos, but this dance was now tempered by a newfound sense of balance and understanding.

The protagonist's children, grandchildren, and their descendants continued the work he began, ensuring that the principles of the new pantheon endured through generations. Their reign marked not an end, but a beginning, a testament to the human capacity for change, progress, and the enduring hope for a better future. Their legacy was not simply a peaceful world; it was a world that continually strived for improvement, a world that learned from its past mistakes, and a world that consistently sought to create a future worthy of its inhabitants. The echoes of their actions reverberated through the cosmos, a beacon of hope that shone brightly into the future, inspiring generations to come to strive for harmony and understanding. The story of their achievements was a testament to the power of hope, the resilience of the human spirit, and the enduring capacity for good in a world forever grappling with the forces of chaos and the whispers of cosmic horror.

7

The Afterglow

The air thrummed, not with the boisterous energy of creation, but with a deep, resonant hum that vibrated in the very marrow of his bones. He stood within the Sanctuary of Echoes, a place he'd crafted not of stone or metal, but of solidified memories, a shimmering, ethereal structure that pulsed with the light of a thousand sunsets. Here, amidst the spectral forms of those he'd lost and those he'd saved, his transformation reached its final, glorious crescendo.

His skin, once marked by the scars of countless battles—physical and spiritual—now glowed with an inner light, a celestial luminescence that shifted subtly with his emotions. It wasn't the harsh brilliance of a sun, but the gentle radiance of a thousand stars, a constellation mapped onto his very being. The demonic taint, once a festering wound, was gone, replaced by a purity that felt both ancient and utterly new. His eyes, once pools of shadowed intensity, now shimmered with the wisdom of ages, reflecting the cosmos themselves. They held the gentle gravity of a black hole and the explosive energy of a supernova, a paradoxical balance of power and peace.

The physical changes were but a prelude to the metamorphosis within. He felt the weight of the cosmos settle upon him, not as a burden, but as an embrace. Each breath he took pulsed with the rhythm of the universe, a symphony of creation and destruction, harmony and chaos. He was no longer merely a man, nor even simply a god, but a nexus, a point where the infinite streams of existence converged and flowed, a living embodiment of the cosmic tapestry.

He could perceive the delicate threads of causality stretching across time and space, weaving a narrative that both encompassed and transcended his own existence. He understood the subtle dance between entropy and order, the delicate balance that held the universe in its precarious equilibrium. He could feel the pulse of other realms, the subtle whispers of forgotten gods and slumbering cosmic entities, all connected through the intricate web of existence. This was not merely knowledge, but a visceral understanding, an innate awareness that permeated his very being. He was both observer and participant, a conscious node within the grand design.

His connection to the mortal realm remained, but it was transformed. He no longer saw the world from a distance, as an observer, but from within, a part of its very fabric. He felt the joy of a child's laughter, the sorrow of a grieving parent, and the hopes and dreams of countless individuals, all interwoven into the vibrant tapestry of life. This empathy was not simply compassion but a profound understanding of the interconnectedness of all things. He was not separate from them but a part of their collective existence.

The transformation wasn't solely a matter of power or perception; it was a radical shift in his consciousness. He had spent years battling the demons within, not just to eradicate the evil, but to understand its origins, its purpose, its place within the grand design. He now understood that darkness was not simply the absence of light, but its complement, a necessary counterpoint in the cosmic ballet of creation. The duality that had once tormented him was now embraced as a source of strength, a testament to the complex and multifaceted nature of existence. He had transcended the duality, not by rejecting one side, but by integrating both into a harmonious whole, a synthesis that reflected the very nature of the cosmos itself.

Within the Sanctuary of Echoes, surrounded by the spectral remnants of his past, he felt a profound sense of closure. The ghosts of his former selves—the scared boy haunted by childhood trauma, the rebellious youth wrestling with his newfound power, the warrior battling the demonic forces within, the weary traveler searching for redemption—all coalesced into a singular, unified consciousness. He had become the summation of his experiences, the culmination of his journey, and the embodiment of his destiny.

The transformation complete, he looked out across the landscape of his recreated world. The gentle hills, the sparkling rivers, and the vibrant forests all bore the imprint of his own essence, a testament to his power and his compassion. He had not simply remade the world; he had infused it with his own being, transforming it into a reflection of his own newly achieved harmony.

But his reign was not one of absolute power but one of guidance and stewardship. He understood the fragility of balance, the delicate dance between chaos and order. His role was not to impose his will upon the cosmos, but to facilitate its natural evolution, to guide its inhabitants towards a path of growth and understanding. He was not a tyrant but a shepherd, guiding his flock towards a future of harmony and enlightenment.

The Sanctuary of Echoes was not merely a place of reflection but a repository of knowledge, a testament to the journey he had undertaken. Within its ethereal walls, he preserved the memories of his struggles, the lessons he had learned, and the wisdom he had gained. This archive was not only for him; it was for all beings who would walk this world, a reminder of the constant striving for balance, a testament to the power of human potential, and a beacon of hope shining into the uncertain future.

He had faced cosmic horror, wrestled with his inner demons, and ultimately emerged victorious. But his victory wasn't an end but a beginning, the start of a new era, an era of growth, compassion, and unity. He had faced the abyss and emerged, not unscathed, but transformed, forged in the fires of his own internal conflicts. He understood now the full extent of the responsibility that came with his newfound godhood. His reign wasn't about control but about fostering growth, about ensuring that the balance of the cosmos was maintained. He had transcended not only the hell within himself but the very limitations of his mortality, achieving a profound and lasting peace.

The hum of the cosmos resonated within him, a constant reminder of his connection to all things. He was no longer just a man, a god, or even a cosmic entity. He was the embodiment of the universe's potential, a living testament to its infinite possibilities. His transformation wasn't an ending; it was an ongoing evolution, a constant journey of self-discovery within the boundless expanse of creation. The echoes of his journey, of his battles, and of his triumphs would resonate throughout the cosmos, a testament to the enduring strength of the human spirit and a testament to the unwavering hope for a better future. He stood, bathed in the ethereal glow of the Sanctuary, the transformation complete, ready to embrace the endless journey that lay ahead, a journey of cosmic proportions, a journey of infinite possibilities, a journey of enduring hope.

The resonant hum that had filled the Sanctuary of Echoes subsided, leaving behind a quietude that felt pregnant with potential. He looked down at his hands, the celestial light still shimmering within his skin, a gentle aurora borealis playing across his flesh. He was ready. The transformation was complete, not just his own, but the world's. He had remade the cosmos in his image, a reflection of the harmony he had finally achieved within himself. Now, it was time to share that harmony, to establish the new order, the new pantheon.

His family. The thought brought a warmth to his heart, a feeling as profound and encompassing as the cosmos itself. He reached out, and the ethereal fabric of the Sanctuary rippled, coalescing into the forms of his wife, Lyra, and their three children: Aella, Orion, and Zephyr. Lyra, always his anchor, his unwavering source of strength and compassion, now radiated a celestial grace that rivaled his own. Her eyes, once filled with a gentle sorrow, now sparkled with the light of a thousand stars, reflecting the infinite expanse of her newly granted power.

"My love," he said, his voice a soft resonance that carried the weight of eternity, "it is time."

Lyra smiled, a radiant expression that illuminated the Sanctuary. "I have been waiting, my beloved," she replied, her voice echoing his own, a harmonious blend of celestial power and unwavering devotion. "The time for our new dawn has come."

Their children stood beside them, each a testament to the union of cosmic power and mortal love. Aella, the eldest, had inherited his strength and her mother's compassion, her aura a vibrant blend of fiery energy and gentle nurturing. Orion, the middle child, possessed an innate wisdom beyond his years, his calm demeanor masking a potent intellect and the ability to perceive the subtle currents of causality that shaped the cosmos. Zephyr, the youngest, was a whirlwind of energy, her playful spirit radiating a joy that transcended the boundaries of time and space. Each possessed unique abilities reflecting their individual personalities and their connection to the cosmic forces.

Their new domains reflected their respective natures. Lyra's realm was the Vale of Serenity, a place of breathtaking beauty and profound peace, a sanctuary for all creatures weary of the harsh realities of the cosmos. It was a place where souls could find solace, where the wounds of the past could heal, and where the promise of a brighter future could take root. Aella's domain, the Fiery Peaks, was a land of untamed energy and untamed spirit, a place where ambition and innovation thrived, and where the sparks of creation constantly ignited. Orion's domain was the Whispering Library, a repository of knowledge beyond comprehension, where the secrets of the cosmos were preserved and the mysteries of the universe unveiled. Zephyr's domain, the Everbloom Meadow, was a vibrant garden of endless possibilities, a testament to the boundless creativity and untamed joy of existence, where all things flourished in harmony.

The creation of these realms was not merely a matter of cosmic manipulation; it was a reflection of their deepest selves, the embodiment of their individual essences. They didn't simply rule these domains; they were extensions of their beings, living embodiments of the power they wielded. Each realm was crafted with meticulous care, infused with the love and compassion that had shaped their family. The buildings, the flora, the fauna—all were imbued with a celestial grace that reflected the harmony of their familial bond.

Their roles as gods were not simply about power or dominion. They were shepherds of their respective realms, guiding their inhabitants toward a path of growth and enlightenment. They were teachers, protectors, and healers. They fostered creativity, nurtured ambition, and celebrated the diversity of life in all its forms. Their relationship as a family was not only a personal bond; it was a reflection of the interconnectedness of all things, a testament to the power of unity in the face of cosmic chaos.

Lyra's gentle guidance helped ease the transition of the mortal realm into the new era. Her influence calmed the anxieties of those still reeling from the past conflicts and helped them adapt to the changes brought about by their new godhood. She fostered a sense of community, reminding everyone of their interconnectedness and the importance of compassion.

Aella's fiery energy ignited a new wave of innovation and creativity across the realms. She inspired artists, scientists, and inventors to push the boundaries of their potential, driving progress and advancement with her bold leadership and unwavering belief in the capacity for growth. She encouraged ambition but tempered it with wisdom, reminding everyone that true power came not from domination but from collaborative innovation.

Orion's vast knowledge brought enlightenment to those seeking wisdom and understanding. He guided scholars and philosophers, helping them decipher the mysteries of the cosmos and understand their place within the grand design. He fostered a culture of learning and inquiry, encouraging everyone to seek knowledge and expand their understanding of the universe.

Zephyr's playful spirit spread joy and wonder across all realms. She inspired artists, musicians, and storytellers, fostering a vibrant culture of expression and celebration. Her irrepressible joy reminded everyone of the importance of play, the significance of laughter, and the beauty of simple pleasures in life. She championed spontaneity and embracing the unknown, fostering a sense of wonder and boundless curiosity in all those around her.

Their combined influence helped shape a new world, a world of harmony and balance, where the forces of creation and destruction were intertwined in a delicate dance. Their family dynamics, characterized by love, respect, and mutual support, formed the foundation of the new pantheon, a shining example of how disparate forces could coexist and complement each other, forming a whole greater than the sum of its parts. Their homes, their domains, were not mere residences but reflections of their very essence, each a unique testament to their individual personalities and their harmonious unity as a family. Their combined efforts served not only as a powerful force for good but also as a source of inspiration, shaping the very nature of the new cosmos they had created. They were a family united, their destinies intertwined, and their reign, one of enlightened stewardship and shared responsibility. Their collective power ensured a balanced future where creativity, compassion, and wisdom thrived in perfect harmony, a testament to the enduring strength of family, even amongst the gods. The era of chaos was over; the era of harmonious coexistence, of family, had begun. The echoes of their unified reign would resonate throughout eternity.

The initial euphoria of their ascension began to settle, replaced by a sobering awareness of the monumental task ahead. Maintaining the delicate balance between the mortal and celestial realms was not a simple matter of decree; it was a constant negotiation, a delicate dance between opposing forces. The very fabric of existence, once ravaged by the demonic incursion, now pulsed with a fragile harmony, a precarious equilibrium that required constant vigilance.

Lyra, in her Vale of Serenity, found herself grappling with the complexities of mortal grief. While the physical wounds of the past had healed, the emotional scars remained, a persistent reminder of the suffering endured. She established sanctuaries for the heartbroken, temples dedicated to remembrance and healing, where the souls of those lost could find solace. These were not simple memorials; they were active spaces, filled with therapists gifted with the ability to mend fractured minds and spirits, weaving threads of compassion through the lingering darkness. The air hummed with a gentle energy, a soothing balm for the wounded psyche, while murmuring waterfalls and whispering willows offered solace to the grieving. The Vale was not merely a place of peace; it was a crucible where sorrow was transmuted into strength, a testament to the resilience of the human spirit.

Meanwhile, Aella, in her Fiery Peaks, faced the challenge of channeling untamed ambition. The raw energy that fueled her domain threatened to consume it, a potent force that could easily spiral out of control. She established rigorous training grounds, where aspiring innovators learned to harness their power responsibly. They weren't simply taught to create; they were taught the ethical implications of their creations, the potential consequences of unchecked ambition. Giant forges glowed with celestial fire, creating tools and technologies designed to benefit all creation, not just a select few. Aella fostered a culture of collaboration, emphasizing the importance of shared goals and mutual respect. She instilled in them a deep appreciation for the delicate balance between progress and preservation. She saw to it that innovation complemented and supported the balance she and her family strove to maintain across the realms.

Orion, within the Whispering Library, confronted the weight of universal knowledge. The vast archives contained secrets that could shatter the fragile harmony, truths that, if misused, could plunge the cosmos back into chaos. He established a rigorous system of access, ensuring that only those with the maturity and wisdom to handle such knowledge could delve into the library's depths. He trained guardians, beings of immense intellect and unwavering integrity, capable of guiding seekers through the labyrinthine corridors, ensuring the preservation of knowledge without unleashing its destructive potential. The library itself was a marvel of celestial architecture, its shelves seemingly stretching into infinity, holding countless volumes bound in starlight and written in the language of the cosmos. The whispers within its walls offered enlightenment to those prepared to listen and guidance to those seeking answers.

Zephyr, in the Everbloom Meadow, found joy threatened by the very abundance of its existence. The meadow's boundless creativity, if left unchecked, could lead to chaos and imbalance. She established festivals of creation and celebration, events that channeled the meadow's exuberance into constructive endeavors.

Artists and musicians from all realms converged in the Everbloom Meadow, their creativity intertwining in a vibrant tapestry of expression. Zephyr's laughter echoed through the vibrant landscape, a joyful reminder that creativity, like life itself, must be embraced with an open heart. Her governance wasn't simply about managing the chaos but understanding and guiding its creative energy, transforming its exuberance into a powerful catalyst for growth and positive expression.

Their individual efforts, however, were only one part of the equation. The true challenge lay in their collective harmony. They held regular family councils, celestial gatherings where they shared their experiences, addressed emerging challenges, and fine-tuned their governance of the realms. These weren't simply meetings; they were deeply personal exchanges, reflecting the love, trust, and mutual respect that formed the bedrock of their family. They debated strategies, resolved conflicts, and learned from each other's strengths and weaknesses, refining their approach to governing the cosmos.

Their collaborative efforts extended beyond their individual domains. Lyra's compassionate influence helped to alleviate the anxieties that rippled through the mortal realm, ensuring a smooth transition into the new era. Aella's fiery drive for innovation prompted creative solutions to problems arising from the shift in cosmic energies. Orion's wisdom guided them through the complex ethical dilemmas inherent in remaking the cosmos, creating a system of laws that ensured fairness and justice. Zephyr's joyful spirit inspired a culture of harmony and mutual respect, ensuring that the newly established balance was not rigid but dynamic, adaptive to the ever-changing needs of the cosmos.

The balance, however, was not static. It required constant adjustments, a perpetual dance of adaptation. Unexpected challenges arose, testing their abilities and their unity. There were moments of doubt, moments where the weight of their responsibility threatened to crush them. But they persevered, their love and commitment to each other and to the cosmos they ruled, proving to be their most potent weapon. They learned to rely on each other's strengths to compensate for each other's weaknesses, transforming their individual vulnerabilities into a collective strength.

Their reign wasn't marked by absolute power but by shared responsibility. They empowered others, fostering a culture of participation and collaboration throughout their domains. They established councils of advisors, bringing diverse perspectives to their decision-making process. They listened to the voices of their subjects, acknowledging their concerns and incorporating their feedback into their governance. This was not a tyranny but a partnership, a cooperative effort aimed at building a better future for all.

Years turned into centuries, and the new cosmos flourished. The fragile balance that they had so carefully constructed held. The once-scarred lands healed, a vibrant tapestry of life replacing the desolation. The threat of demonic incursion faded into legend, a distant memory replaced by the promise of a brighter future. The new pantheon, born from love and forged in the fires of tribulation, reigned not through dominance but through stewardship. They were not mere rulers, but guardians of a cosmos striving for a harmonious existence. Their story became a testament to the power of love, resilience, and the enduring strength of family, even among the gods. The afterglow of their triumph illuminated the cosmos, a beacon of hope that would guide the universe through the millennia to come, a promise of the balance maintained, the balance won, a balance that they would forever strive to protect.

The weight of the cosmos pressed down on him, not as a physical burden, but as an unrelenting pressure on his mind, a constant hum of responsibility that vibrated through his very being. The initial euphoria of victory, the intoxicating rush of power that had accompanied his ascension, had long since faded, replaced by a sobering awareness of the enormity of his task. He was no longer just a man; he was a god, the supreme god, the architect of a new reality, and the fate of countless beings rested on his shoulders.

The grand council hall, a breathtaking edifice of shimmering obsidian and celestial silver, felt less like a seat of power and more like a cage of his own making. The air thrummed with the energy of a thousand unseen forces, a symphony of anxieties and hopes echoing in the vast chamber. Around him sat his family, each radiating the weight of their own domains, their faces etched with a mixture of exhaustion and determination. Lyra, her eyes reflecting the sorrow and resilience of the mortal realm, sat beside him, her hand resting gently on his. Aella, her fiery spirit tempered by the wisdom of her years, observed the proceedings with a keen gaze. Orion, his gaze distant yet perceptive, seemed to hold the wisdom of the ages within his very being. And Zephyr, her radiant smile a beacon of hope in the otherwise somber assembly, offered a silent reassurance.

Their first major conflict arose over the restructuring of the celestial bureaucracy. Aella, ever the innovator, championed a radical overhaul of the system, advocating for a more meritocratic approach, replacing the ancient hierarchies with a system based on competence and skill. Orion, steeped in the traditions of the old order, cautioned against such drastic change, emphasizing the importance of preserving order and stability. The debate raged for days, the council hall echoing with impassioned arguments, the very air crackling with celestial energy. Lyra, ever the mediator, sought to find a compromise, suggesting a gradual transition, blending the best elements of the old and new systems. Zephyr, in her own way, provided a crucial counterpoint, offering insights into the human element of the process, reminding them of the importance of considering the impact on the mortals they governed.

The discussions were often fraught with tension. The sheer volume of administrative tasks, the complexities of governing multiple realms, the constant need for arbitration among competing interests—it was a burden that tested their limits. Each decision held profound consequences, each misstep potentially jeopardizing the fragile harmony they had established. The administrative center, a dazzling network of shimmering pathways and interconnected spheres, pulsed with information, constantly updating them on the state of the cosmos. Reports streamed in from across the realms, each one highlighting the challenges and opportunities that presented themselves. They reviewed the progress of Lyra's healing sanctuaries, assessing their impact on the mortal population; the efficiency of Aella's innovative programs; the efficacy of Orion's safeguards on the Whispering Library; and the impact of Zephyr's festivals on the overall balance of the Everbloom Meadow.

One particularly thorny issue revolved around the allocation of resources. Aella's ambitious projects demanded significant investments, straining the already limited resources. Lyra's sanctuaries, vital to the healing of the mortal realm, also required substantial funding. Orion's protection of the Whispering Library also needed careful resource allocation, as did Zephyr's projects to ensure the continued balance of her realm. The debates were often heated, with each member passionately advocating for their respective domains. It was a crucible of compromise, a testing ground for their newly acquired leadership skills. He found himself mediating disputes, balancing the needs of different realms, and striving to ensure a just and equitable distribution of resources. It was a delicate act of political maneuvering, requiring diplomacy, tact, and a deep understanding of the needs and desires of all parties involved.

The management of the inter-realm relationships also presented significant challenges. The seven reptilian tribes, though initially welcoming of the new order, began to express grievances about their perceived lack of representation. Their concerns, though valid, threatened to destabilize the balance that had been painstakingly established. He convened a series of meetings with the tribal leaders, engaging in dialogues that lasted for weeks. He had to address their fears, alleviate their anxieties, and demonstrate his commitment to their well-being. It was a complex process, requiring empathy, understanding, and a willingness to compromise. The negotiations extended well into the night, and although he was physically exhausted, his mind still raced with the complexities of these inter-realm interactions.

Beyond the political complexities, there was the ever-present threat of residual demonic influence. Despite their victory, pockets of darkness still lingered, remnants of the chaos that had once consumed the world. These weren't organized forces, but insidious whispers, subtle corruptions that sought to undermine the delicate balance. Orion, with his vast knowledge, was responsible for detecting and neutralizing these threats, but the task was never-ending, a constant vigilance against the insidious creeping darkness.

These were just some of the challenges that weighed heavily upon him. His responsibility encompassed everything, from the allocation of resources to the maintenance of inter-realm harmony, from the detection of demonic influences to the overall well-being of all creatures. The weight of the cosmos was not merely metaphorical; it was a tangible pressure, a crushing burden that tested his resilience.

Yet, amidst the immense pressures, there were moments of quiet reflection, moments where he could appreciate the progress made, the triumphs achieved. He looked upon the flourishing realms, the thriving mortal populations, the vibrant tapestry of life that had sprung forth from the ashes of destruction, and felt a sense of profound satisfaction. It was a testament to their collective effort, a manifestation of their shared vision. The journey had been arduous, the challenges seemingly insurmountable, but their perseverance, their unwavering commitment to their shared destiny, had brought them to this point.

His reign was far from over; the journey was far from complete. The challenges would continue to arise, the threats would continue to emerge, and the responsibilities would continue to weigh heavily upon him. But he had his family, his allies, his unwavering love for them, and his commitment to the cosmos he now ruled to guide him through the dark times. This was not a simple victory but a continuous struggle for balance, a perpetual dance between order and chaos, a testament to the enduring power of love, resilience, and the unwavering strength of family, even amongst the gods. The afterglow of their triumph was not just a radiant light; it was a constant reminder of the immense responsibility that lay ahead, a task that would shape the future of the cosmos for eons to come.

The obsidian towers of the celestial city, once symbols of oppressive power, now gleamed with a soft, ethereal light, reflecting the newly established harmony of the cosmos. The shimmering pathways that connected the various realms pulsed with a gentle rhythm, a tranquil counterpoint to the frenetic energy that had defined the previous era. Below, the mortal world unfolded like a vibrant tapestry, its diverse landscapes teeming with life, its cities radiating an unprecedented energy of peace and prosperity. The scars of the demonic invasion were slowly fading, replaced by lush vegetation and thriving communities. Lyra's healing sanctuaries, beacons of hope across the land, were overflowing with patients recovering from physical and spiritual wounds, their laughter echoing through the valleys.

The administrative center, once a source of constant stress, now hummed with a sense of efficient order. Aella's innovative systems, initially met with resistance, had proven remarkably effective, streamlining the bureaucracy and ensuring a fair distribution of resources. Orion's safeguards, a complex network of celestial wards and protective spells, silently guarded against the lingering vestiges of demonic influence. Zephyr's festivals, celebrations of life and renewal, spread joy and hope throughout the mortal realm, uniting diverse cultures in a shared spirit of optimism.

Even the seven reptilian tribes, once a source of potential conflict, had integrated smoothly into the new order. Their unique perspectives and skills had become invaluable assets, enriching the fabric of the cosmos with their distinct traditions and customs. He had learned to listen, truly listen, to their concerns, respecting their ancient wisdom and acknowledging their rightful place within the celestial governance. The long negotiations, the countless dialogues, had borne fruit, transforming mistrust into mutual respect and cooperation. Their integration was a testament to the power of diplomacy and empathy, a symbol of truly inclusive governance.

The weight of his responsibility, however, had not lessened. It had, in fact, grown more profound. He carried the weight of an entire cosmos in his heart. Every decision held immense consequences, each action reverberating through countless realms. He was acutely aware that the balance he had worked so hard to achieve could be shattered at any moment, but he also knew that the resilience of the cosmos, fostered by their shared struggle, was a force to be reckoned with.

One evening, as the celestial sunset painted the sky in hues of amethyst and gold, he sat with his family on the balcony of the grand council hall. Lyra rested her head on his shoulder, her breath a gentle rhythm against his chest. Aella, her fiery spirit now tempered by a profound sense of purpose, pointed out a constellation that resembled a dragon, a reminder of their past struggles. Orion, ever observant, silently traced patterns on the surface of a celestial orb. Zephyr, her eyes sparkling with mirth, recounted stories of the festivals celebrated in the Everbloom Meadow, the laughter of mortals filling the air.

The conversation drifted, touching on the intricacies of the cosmos, the beauty of its diverse ecosystems, and the potential yet unexplored. They spoke of challenges that still lay ahead, the ever-present threat of unforeseen disturbances. This was not an ending but a mere chapter break in an ongoing saga. They discussed the future of the cosmos, the next steps of their grand plan. They needed to address the long-term implications of the changes that had occurred, ensuring the continued prosperity and stability of their realms. Aella proposed a new initiative focusing on technological advancements, a responsible exploration of the cosmos to further understand its intricacies and leverage its resources for the benefit of all. Orion advocated for the continued study of the ancient texts, believing that wisdom from the past could provide solutions for the future. Lyra focused on expanding the healing sanctuaries across all realms, working towards universal physical and mental well-being. Zephyr emphasized the importance of cultural exchange and artistic expression, aiming to foster a sense of unity among the diverse populations of the cosmos.

Their shared commitment, their bond as a family, had forged an unbreakable unity. Their differences, once sources of conflict, had become catalysts for creativity and innovation. They were not simply gods ruling from on high but a family working together, their combined strength transcending individual ambitions and fostering a collaborative effort to improve the lives of those under their care. This was a government built not on fear or intimidation, but on love, trust, and mutual respect.

As the stars blazed across the night sky, he felt a profound sense of hope and anticipation. The new beginning was not without its challenges; the path ahead would inevitably be fraught with difficulties, and he knew he could not control every outcome. But he also understood that within the cosmos' inherent chaos, order could emerge, and it was their responsibility as its guardians to ensure its continued flourishing. The wounds of the past were slowly healing, the scars a reminder of their journey and an inspiration for their future.

The mortals, once victims, now held the future in their hands. His role wasn't to dictate their path but to guide them, to protect them from the looming dangers of the cosmos. He felt a deep sense of responsibility to ensure that this new dawn would not be overshadowed by the darkness that had threatened to consume their world. The challenges would persist—the lingering demonic influence, the complexities of inter-realm diplomacy, the constant need for resource allocation—but they had overcome similar challenges before, and they would face these new trials with renewed courage and wisdom.

The celestial realms, once places of harsh hierarchies and oppressive power, were now slowly transforming into beacons of hope and prosperity. The changes would take time, and the full impact of the new era would unfold gradually over generations. But they were ready, together, to meet the future with strength, resolve, and unwavering love.

He looked at Lyra, at Aella, at Orion, and at Zephyr, each radiating their own unique strengths and their shared commitment to their new order. Their collective strength exceeded the sum of their individual parts. It was a family bond forged in the crucible of cosmic struggle, a testament to their resilience. The universe was vast and unknowable, filled with both wonder and peril, yet they had a new chance to build a better world. He saw this not as the culmination of a journey but as the start of a new chapter. A new beginning, promising a future brighter than any they could have imagined, a future shaped not by fear and darkness, but by the unwavering light of love, family, and hope. This was a future, he knew, that would require constant vigilance, relentless effort, and an unwavering faith in the resilience of the cosmos.

8

Echoes of Xalzar

The obsidian towers of the celestial city, now beacons of ethereal light, still held whispers of a darker age. While the surface shimmered with peace, a subtle unease permeated the air, a chilling reminder of the battles fought and won. Even in the restored harmony, the echoes of Xalzar, the fallen god of shadows, persisted, a faint tremor in the cosmic symphony. It wasn't a blatant assault, not a resurgence of demonic hordes, but a subtle, insidious influence, a persistent hum of malevolence lurking beneath the surface of the newly established peace.

This lingering influence manifested in unexpected ways. In the dreams of the celestial beings, fragmented visions of twisted landscapes and tormented souls flickered, fleeting glimpses into a reality that refused to fully relinquish its hold. Orion, ever vigilant in his celestial observatory, detected erratic fluctuations in the cosmic energies, anomalies that defied explanation, hinting at an unseen force subtly manipulating the very fabric of reality. Aella, despite her technological prowess, found her most advanced systems exhibiting unpredictable glitches, their sophisticated algorithms faltering under the weight of an unseen interference. Even Lyra, with her unparalleled healing abilities, encountered patients whose wounds defied her touch, their suffering rooted in a darkness that transcended the physical realm.

The most palpable evidence of Xalzar's lingering influence was concentrated in the Whispering Woods, a once-sacred grove that had borne the brunt of the demonic invasion. Even after the restoration, a palpable sense of dread clung to the ancient trees, their gnarled branches reaching out like skeletal fingers, their leaves whispering secrets only the wind could understand. The air itself crackled with an unsettling energy, a tangible presence that chilled the very marrow of those who dared to enter. The soil, enriched by the blood of countless battles, remained stubbornly resistant to Lyra's healing magic, its darkness seemingly intertwined with the very essence of the land.

Zephyr, with her innate connection to the natural world, felt this influence most keenly. The vibrant festivals she had orchestrated throughout the cosmos failed to touch the Whispering Woods. The joy and hope that radiated from the other realms seemed to falter at its edge, replaced by a silence that was heavy with unspoken sorrow. Attempts to cleanse the grove with potent spells and rituals proved futile; the darkness resisted, clinging stubbornly to the land, refusing to relinquish its hold. Zephyr, her usual radiant spirit dimmed, dedicated herself to studying the anomalies within the Whispering Woods, desperate to understand and ultimately neutralize the lingering malignancy.

One day, while exploring the deepest recesses of the Whispering Woods, Zephyr stumbled upon a hidden cavern, its entrance obscured by a curtain of shimmering, obsidian vines. Hesitantly, she stepped inside, her heart pounding in her chest. The air within the cavern was thick with the stench of decay and the whispers of forgotten horrors. The walls were adorned with strange symbols, glyphs that seemed to writhe and shift before her eyes, their meaning both alien and terrifyingly familiar. At the center of the cavern, she found a pulsating black orb, radiating an aura of profound darkness that seemed to suck the very light from the surrounding space. This orb, she sensed, was the nexus of Xalzar's lingering influence, the heart of the darkness that threatened to engulf the newly restored cosmos.

The orb pulsed with a rhythm that mirrored the erratic fluctuations Orion had detected in the cosmic energies. Zephyr reached out tentatively, her fingers brushing the cool, smooth surface. A surge of dark energy coursed through her body, leaving her reeling, momentarily incapacitated by the sheer power of the artifact. She understood now. Xalzar's defeat had not been absolute. A fragment of his essence, a shard of his dark soul, remained, anchored to this world through the orb. This wasn't merely a lingering influence; it was a dormant seed of chaos, waiting for the right moment to blossom into something far more destructive.

She retreated from the cavern, her body trembling, but her mind ablaze with newfound understanding. This was not a problem to be solved through brute force; it required a more subtle, more strategic approach. She shared her discovery with her family, describing the pulsating orb and the sinister power it held. Orion proposed setting up a powerful warding system to contain the orb's influence, preventing its dark energy from spreading further. Aella suggested exploring the possibility of technologically neutralizing the orb, perhaps by harnessing its energy for beneficial purposes. Lyra offered to create a powerful healing spell, aiming to purify the corrupted energy within the orb itself.

However, the most crucial insight came from Lyra. While studying ancient texts, she discovered a prophecy hinting at the existence of an ancient artifact, a celestial amulet capable of absorbing and neutralizing the power of any dark entity. The amulet, lost centuries ago, was rumored to be hidden somewhere within the Whispering Woods. The quest for this amulet became their immediate priority, a race against time to prevent Xalzar's lingering influence from growing into a cataclysmic threat. The challenge was immense, fraught with dangers both known and unknown, but the future of the cosmos hung in the balance. Their newly established peace, their hard-won victory, rested on the success of this perilous quest.

The search for the amulet took them deep into the heart of the Whispering Woods, a place where reality seemed to warp and twist around them, where the boundaries between the mortal and celestial realms blurred. They faced trials that tested their strength, their resolve, and their faith in one another. They encountered creatures twisted by Xalzar's influence, guardians of the darkness that resisted their every step. Orion's wards faltered against the concentrated malevolence, Aella's technology malfunctioned under the weight of the unnatural energies, and Lyra's healing magic struggled against the deep-seated corruption.

Throughout their arduous journey, Zephyr's understanding of the Whispering Woods proved invaluable. She navigated them through the labyrinthine paths, interpreting the cryptic messages whispered by the wind and the ancient trees. Her connection to the natural world allowed her to sense the subtle shifts in the energy, guiding them towards their elusive goal.

Finally, after weeks of relentless pursuit, they found it—a hidden chamber nestled deep within the earth, guarded by a grotesque creature made of twisted branches and shadows. Inside, nestled on a pedestal of petrified wood, lay the celestial amulet, radiating a warmth that dispelled the surrounding darkness. It pulsed with a gentle light, its energy pure and potent, a beacon of hope in the heart of despair.

Their task, however, was not yet complete. The amulet's power was immense, its use requiring careful consideration. They had to find a way to channel its energy precisely to neutralize the orb's malignant influence, to sever the last vestiges of Xalzar's presence, without causing further disruption to the delicate balance of the cosmos. The future of the realms rested on their ability to wield this incredible power with wisdom and precision. The next steps, they knew, would be as critical as any they had faced so far. The subtle whispers of Xalzar remained, a stark reminder that their struggle was far from over. The cosmos, despite its newfound peace, held many more secrets and many more threats yet to be unveiled.

The wind, once a gentle caress across the restored landscapes, now carried a chilling undercurrent. It wasn't the howl of a storm nor the mournful sigh of a dying star, but a whisper, a sibilant hiss that slithered into the ears of those who listened closely enough. It spoke of Xalzar, not in the thunderous pronouncements of his former power, but in a subtle, insidious murmur that insinuated itself into the fabric of reality. Zephyr, her connection to nature heightened by the recent cosmic upheaval, was the first to truly hear it—a haunting melody woven into the rustling leaves of the resurrected forests, the crashing waves of the rejuvenated oceans, and the very heartbeat of the cosmos itself.

These whispers weren't geographically confined. They echoed across the celestial city, a discordant note in the otherwise harmonious symphony of its revitalized architecture. The obsidian towers, now shimmering with a celestial luminescence, seemed to hum with the whispers, their polished surfaces reflecting not only starlight but also the shadowed essence of Xalzar's lingering presence. The whispers were felt in the hushed reverence of the newly consecrated temples, an unsettling tremor beneath the prayers offered to the newly established pantheon. They even permeated the vibrant, bustling marketplaces, an undercurrent of unease woven into the joyous chatter of the resurrected populace.

The whispers spoke not of immediate threat, but of potential. A potential for chaos, for a return to the age of shadows, for a resurgence of the darkness that had nearly consumed the cosmos. They painted fragmented images in Zephyr's mind—visions of a twisted, nightmarish landscape, eerily similar to the infernal realms

Xalzar had once commanded. In these visions, she saw remnants of tortured souls, trapped in an eternal twilight, their anguished cries echoing silently in the spaces between the whispers.

Orion, within his celestial observatory, detected corresponding anomalies. The cosmic energies, once stabilized after the final battle, now exhibited subtle fluctuations, almost imperceptible ripples in the grand cosmic ocean. These fluctuations mirrored the rhythm of the whispers, a synchronized dance between the physical and ethereal realms, hinting at an unseen force manipulating the very threads of existence. His advanced instruments, normally flawless in their precision, began recording data that defied rational explanation. The data suggested a subtle warping of spacetime, a minute distortion in the very fabric of reality itself—a distortion that seemed to emanate from the Whispering Woods.

Aella, despite her technological prowess, found her newly created devices—marvels of celestial engineering—malfunctioning under the influence of this subtle perturbation. The intricate algorithms she had painstakingly crafted faltered, their sophisticated functions corrupted by a subtle interference, a phantom signal that she couldn't trace or identify. Her advanced sensors detected bursts of energy that were both profoundly powerful and completely invisible to the naked eye. The patterns were strangely familiar, though maddeningly elusive, possessing a rhythm that resonated unnervingly with the whispers.

Even Lyra, the healer, whose touch could mend the most grievous wounds, found herself facing limitations. She encountered patients whose ailments defied her healing magic, their suffering rooted in a profound darkness that seemed to transcend physical injury. Their wounds pulsed with an unnatural energy, reminiscent of the demonic taint that had once plagued the cosmos. Lyra, ever perceptive, understood these ailments were not purely physical. They were manifestations of the whispers, a manifestation of Xalzar's lingering influence upon the mortal plane.

The Whispering Woods, however, remained the epicenter of this unsettling phenomenon. The whispers there were not simply audible; they were felt—a palpable presence that clung to the ancient trees, the twisted branches, and the gnarled roots. The very soil seemed to resonate with an oppressive weight, a resistance to the healing energies of the cosmos. Zephyr, deeply connected to the natural world, felt an intense surge of sorrow emanating from the woods, a mournful lament that resonated with the whispers. It was as if the land itself was weeping for the losses suffered during the war, a silent testament to the enduring impact of Xalzar's reign of terror.

The whispers, however, held a perverse sort of intelligence. They weren't random noises; they formed patterns, creating a cryptic language that only Zephyr, with her deep connection to the natural world, could begin to understand. She heard not just the lament of the woods but also a subtle warning, a hint of a potential resurgence. The whispers hinted at a power source, a hidden nexus within the woods, a point of origin for this malevolent influence. It was a dark energy subtly warping reality, subtly influencing the minds and actions of even the most steadfast celestial beings.

Driven by a mixture of fear and determination, Zephyr ventured deeper into the Whispering Woods, her intuition guiding her through the labyrinthine paths. She sought the source of the whispers, the heart of Xalzar's lingering influence, a potential focal point for a devastating counterattack. She carried with her an intricate set of runes, ancient symbols that, according to Lyra, held the power to disrupt or perhaps even absorb the dark energy. But as Zephyr ventured further into the heart of the woods, a chilling realization dawned on her.

The whispers weren't just trying to communicate; they were attempting to manipulate. They played upon her deepest fears and her most vulnerable emotions, attempting to sway her towards a path of despair and hopelessness. They spoke of her failures, her losses, and her doubts. They twisted her memories and her dreams and made her question her very purpose.

As she pressed further, the whispers intensified, weaving themselves into horrifying visions. She saw the fallen god, Xalzar, not as a defeated entity, but as a malevolent consciousness, lurking in the shadows, his eyes burning with an unholy light. He spoke to her directly, not through words, but through raw emotion, a torrent of hate, despair, and hopelessness. He offered her power, darkness, and revenge, whispering promises of dominion and control.

Yet, amidst the terror, Zephyr held firm. She called upon the strength of her family, her newfound faith, and the power of her connection to the living world. She pushed through the torment, her resolve strengthening with every step, until she reached the heart of the darkness—a twisted, ancient oak, its branches reaching towards the heavens like skeletal fingers, pulsating with a dark energy. From the gnarled heart of the oak, she heard the whispers most clearly—a final, desperate attempt to break her will.

But Zephyr resisted. She channeled her own strength, her connection to the light, and her unwavering belief in her destiny. She unleashed the runes, their ancient power exploding in a blinding wave of light, pushing back the darkness, silencing the whispers. The dark energy of the oak recoiled, then suddenly extinguished, plunging the area into complete, terrifying silence. The silence, however, was far more terrifying than the whispers had ever been, for it signified not peace, but the ominous anticipation of something yet to come. The fight against Xalzar was far from over. The whispers had been silenced, but the echoes, the memories of the darkness that had nearly consumed the cosmos, remained... And with those echoes, the ominous possibility that one day they might return, even stronger than before.

The silence following the silencing of the whispers was deafening. It wasn't the peaceful quiet of a sun-drenched meadow but the oppressive stillness of a tomb, a void pregnant with unspoken dread. Zephyr, despite her victory, felt a chilling emptiness settle over her, a profound loneliness that mirrored the desolate landscape surrounding the now-dormant ancient oak. The runes, having performed their task, lay scattered on the ground, their luminescence fading, leaving behind only the lingering scent of ozone and a palpable sense of unease.

The triumph felt hollow. The victory, pyrrhic. The darkness had been banished, yes, but the absence of its malevolent whispers left a void that felt far more unsettling than the cacophony it had replaced. The echoes of Xalzar, though subdued, still resonated within her, a faint tremor in the depths of her soul. It was as if the war had ended, but the battle within herself had just begun.

The journey back to the celestial city was silent, the celebratory atmosphere of the previous days replaced by a palpable tension. The others, Orion, Aella, and Lyra, sensed the shift in her demeanor, the subtle change in the vibrant energy that usually surrounded her. They didn't press her, understanding the weight she carried, the invisible burden of a victory that didn't feel like a victory at all. They knew the whispers had left scars, not just on the landscape, but on Zephyr's soul.

In the quiet solitude of her chambers within the celestial city, the doubts intensified. The meticulously crafted architecture, the shimmering obsidian towers that once had filled her with awe, now seemed to mock her with their cold, unyielding perfection. The celestial luminescence seemed to cast long, menacing shadows, distorting familiar objects into grotesque parodies of their former selves. Sleep offered no respite; instead, her dreams were haunted by fragmented images, flickering visions of the twisted, nightmarish landscape she'd glimpsed within the Whispering Woods.

The whispers, though silenced externally, continued their insidious work within the confines of her own mind. They were no longer audible, but they manifested as a relentless barrage of self-doubt, a chorus of insidious questions that gnawed at her confidence. Had she truly vanquished Xalzar? Or had she merely pushed back a tide that would inevitably return, stronger and more vengeful than before? Had she sacrificed too much? Had the cost of her victory been too great?

The doubts weren't mere anxieties; they were subtly crafted narratives, woven from her deepest fears and insecurities. They twisted memories, painting past events in a new, darker light, questioning her motives and her decisions. The love she shared with Orion, once a beacon of hope, now felt fragile, tinged with the suspicion that it might be an illusion, a fleeting moment of happiness before a return to the abyss. The joy she experienced in the company of Aella and Lyra, once a source of strength, now seemed tainted with a lurking sense of inadequacy, a constant fear of falling short of their expectations.

Even her newfound divinity, the godhood she had embraced, felt precarious, a mantle she wore uneasily, constantly haunted by the fear that she was unworthy of such power. She questioned her ability to rule justly, to guide her people towards a brighter future. The weight of her responsibilities, once a source of pride, now felt like an unbearable burden, a crushing weight that threatened to drag her down into the same darkness she had fought so hard to overcome.

The doubts extended beyond her personal life. They questioned the very nature of her victory. Had she truly transformed the hell within her into a heavenly paradise? Or had she merely masked the darkness, concealing it beneath a veneer of celestial beauty? Had she created a fragile utopia, a deceptive façade that masked a deeper, more profound corruption? The seemingly harmonious symphony of the restored cosmos felt discordant now, a deceptive melody masking an underlying dissonance. The bustling marketplaces, the vibrant temples, the joyous celebrations—they all felt like hollow, theatrical performances masking a profound unease.

The very act of creation itself seemed suspect. Had she truly remade the world or merely rearranged the pieces of a broken reality, leaving the underlying fault lines intact, waiting for the inevitable collapse? The beauty she had crafted seemed to exist only on the surface, concealing a deeper, more fundamental flaw—a flaw that mirrored the darkness she carried within.

These doubts weren't born of weakness; they were the seeds of a deeper, more profound understanding. They were the echoes of Xalzar, not in his raw, brutal form, but in his insidious, manipulative essence. They were the subtle whispers of cosmic doubt, a pervasive uncertainty that questioned the very fabric of existence. They questioned the meaning of creation, the nature of good and evil, and the ultimate purpose of her own existence.

The struggle became internal, a battle waged not against a demonic entity but against the insidious whispers of self-doubt, a war fought within the confines of her own mind. Zephyr found herself increasingly isolated, retreating further into her own thoughts, seeking answers in the solitude of her chambers. The celestial observatory, once a place of scientific inquiry and wonder, now felt like a tomb, a reminder of the vastness of the cosmos and the infinitesimal nature of her own achievements.

Her family, ever vigilant, noticed her distress. Orion, with his profound understanding of the cosmos, sensed the subtle shifts in the cosmic energies, the faint ripples of discord that mirrored the turmoil within her. Aella, ever practical, saw the subtle signs of physical exhaustion and mental strain; her sophisticated diagnostic tools revealed a pattern of erratic energy fluctuations within Zephyr's own being, a subtle imbalance that hinted at the depth of her internal struggle. Lyra, with her innate empathy, understood the pain that lay beneath Zephyr's stoic façade; she saw the shadows lurking beneath the surface of her serene countenance, the subtle hints of despair hidden beneath the mask of divine composure.

They rallied around her, offering support, reassurance, and love. They understood that the fight against Xalzar was far from over; the battle had merely shifted from the external to the internal. The whispers had been silenced, but the seeds of doubt they had planted continued to sprout, their roots penetrating deeply into the fertile ground of her mind. The struggle to overcome these doubts, to find faith amidst the uncertainty, would be a long and arduous one. But Zephyr, bolstered by the unwavering love of her family and her unyielding belief in her own strength, vowed to confront these doubts head-on, to find the truth within herself, and to ensure that the victory she had won would not be undone by the insidious whispers of despair. The fight for her own soul, a fight more complex and challenging than any battle against a fallen god, had just begun.

The revelation came not in a dramatic flash of lightning or a booming voice from the heavens, but in the hushed whispers of a forgotten language, etched onto crumbling tablets within the Sunken Library of Xylos. This library, a labyrinthine city submerged beneath a crystalline lake high in the celestial mountains, was a repository of forgotten lore, a place where the echoes of ages past resonated with chilling clarity. Orion, with his innate understanding of celestial languages, deciphered the ancient script, his brow furrowed in concentration as he traced the faded glyphs with a trembling finger.

The prophecy spoke of Xalzar, not as a vanquished foe, but as a force of nature, an inevitability woven into the very fabric of existence. It didn't speak of a simple return, a resurrection from ashes, but of a cyclical resurgence, a relentless tide that would ebb and flow throughout eternity. The tablets described Xalzar not as a singular entity, but as an archetype, a primordial darkness that could manifest in countless forms, adapting to each new era, each new threat, ever-evolving, ever-learning.

The ambiguity of the prophecy was its most unsettling aspect. It didn't offer a clear timeline, no precise date or event to mark Xalzar's return. Instead, it spoke in metaphors, riddles wrapped in layers of cryptic symbolism. It alluded to celestial alignments, to shifts in the cosmic currents, and to subtle changes in the very essence of reality itself. These were not signs that could be readily observed; they were subtle tremors, barely perceptible shifts in the fundamental forces that governed the universe.

The prophecy hinted at a catalyst, a spark that would ignite Xalzar's resurgence—a weakness within the newly established order, a crack in the celestial armor, a point of vulnerability that would allow the darkness to seep back in. It spoke of a "broken heart," a fractured unity, and a discord within the newly formed pantheon as the potential catalyst for Xalzar's return. This was deeply unsettling, for the newly established harmony between Zephyr and her family, the foundation of their newly built celestial order, was precisely what held the cosmos together.

The tablets also mentioned a method of prevention, a ritual of unimaginable complexity and potential danger. It involved manipulating the very currents of creation, a dangerous dance with the fundamental forces that underpinned reality itself. The cost of this ritual, the prophecy warned, would be immense—a sacrifice so profound it could shake the very foundations of existence. The potential consequences included the loss of memories, the severing of connections to loved ones, or even the annihilation of entire worlds, potentially creating a much greater void than Xalzar's influence. The choice between prevention and acceptance seemed a terrifying one, a paradox that tested the very limits of their power and wisdom.

The revelation cast a pall over the celestial city. The joyous celebrations that had marked Zephyr's victory were replaced by a grim silence, a palpable sense of foreboding. Even the radiant celestial glow seemed dimmer, its brightness dulled by the impending shadow of the prophecy. The weight of this knowledge was heavy, a crushing burden that pressed down on every soul, a reminder of their precarious position in the grand cosmic tapestry.

Zephyr, despite her newfound godhood, felt a profound sense of helplessness. The power she wielded, the authority she commanded, felt insignificant in the face of this ancient, immutable prophecy. The victory over Xalzar felt like a temporary reprieve, a mere postponement of an inevitable reckoning. The whispers of doubt, which had once haunted her, returned with renewed intensity, amplified by the chilling certainty of Xalzar's eventual return.

Orion, ever the pragmatist, began meticulously researching the prophecy's cryptic details, poring over ancient texts and consulting with scholars from across the cosmos. He sought to unravel the prophecy's ambiguities, hoping to find a way to avert the impending catastrophe. He delved deeper into the mechanics of the cosmos, searching for clues amidst the intricate dance of celestial bodies and the subtle fluctuations of cosmic energy. His work was arduous and perilous, a journey into the heart of cosmic uncertainty, pushing the boundaries of knowledge itself.

Aella, with her unwavering practical approach, focused on preparing for the inevitable. She initiated plans to strengthen the defenses of the celestial city, to bolster their magical reserves, and to train a new generation of warriors capable of confronting the darkness. Her actions were not fueled by despair but by a determined resolve—a refusal to succumb to fear or surrender to fate. Her efforts were a testament to the strength of their will to resist the darkness.

Lyra, with her profound empathy, worked to bolster the morale of the celestial citizens. She sought to ease their anxieties, to instill hope amidst despair. She spent tireless hours offering comfort and reassurance, reminding them of the resilience of the human spirit, the enduring strength of their collective will. Her compassion was a beacon of light, a source of inspiration during their darkest hour. Her soothing energy served as a vital counterpoint to the encroaching fear.

Zephyr, despite her inner turmoil, refused to surrender to despair. She found strength in her family's unwavering support, their shared determination to confront the challenge ahead. The prophecy, while daunting, had also revealed a path to possible prevention, a dangerous but necessary ritual that would need careful consideration. The ritual could potentially rewrite reality itself, making it a decision of immense responsibility.

The journey towards understanding the prophecy and preparing for Xalzar's return was a daunting task. The weight of their responsibility was immense; the fate of countless worlds rested on their shoulders. But Zephyr, with her family by her side, vowed to face this challenge head-on, to fight for their existence, to ensure that even if the darkness returns, it would not extinguish the light that they had so painstakingly kindled. The battle for their world was far from over; the most crucial battle yet lay ahead. The whispers of Xalzar had been silenced, but their echoes continued to reverberate in the hearts of all who had felt his wrath and knew his potential to destroy.

The immediate aftermath of the prophecy's revelation was a whirlwind of activity. Aella, ever the pragmatist, took charge of the logistical preparations. Her first order of business was strengthening the celestial city's defenses. This wasn't simply a matter of reinforcing walls or bolstering magical wards; it was about creating a fortress capable of withstanding an assault from a cosmic entity capable of warping reality itself. Teams of celestial engineers, guided by Aella's meticulous plans, began weaving intricate networks of enchantments into the city's very fabric. These enchantments weren't mere defenses; they were dynamic, self-adjusting systems, capable of adapting to Xalzar's ever-shifting tactics. Ancient, forgotten runes, unearthed from the deepest archives of the Sunken Library, were etched onto colossal crystal structures that now formed the city's outer walls. These runes pulsed with an ethereal energy, resonating with the fundamental forces of creation, forming a barrier capable of deflecting even the most potent dark magic.

Beyond the city walls, Aella oversaw the construction of a vast network of interconnected defensive platforms. These platforms, strategically positioned across the celestial landscapes, were equipped with powerful magical cannons, capable of unleashing devastating blasts of pure celestial energy. Each cannon was manned by teams of highly trained celestial warriors, their skills honed through years of rigorous training. Aella also initiated a comprehensive training program for a new generation of defenders. This program wasn't limited to physical combat; it encompassed advanced magical techniques, strategic thinking, and the ability to adapt to unpredictable situations. The recruits were carefully selected, their potential for both power and resilience rigorously assessed. Aella's preparation was multifaceted; she aimed to fortify not only the physical defenses but also the collective strength and spirit of their celestial army.

Orion, meanwhile, delved deeper into the heart of the cosmos, seeking to understand the mechanics of Xalzar's resurgence. His research took him to the furthest reaches of known space, to desolate nebulae and shimmering galaxies teeming with untold wonders and potential threats. He consulted with ancient, wise beings, celestial librarians guarding knowledge older than time itself. He spent countless hours poring over cosmic charts, deciphering ancient star maps that revealed patterns in the movements of celestial bodies, patterns that might hold the key to predicting Xalzar's return. He ventured into the swirling vortexes of cosmic energy, using delicate instruments to measure the subtle fluctuations of the universe's fundamental forces. His work was fraught with danger; a single misstep could unravel the fabric of reality itself, yet Orion pressed on, driven by an unwavering determination to understand the enemy and find a way to combat it. He also worked to refine his understanding of the preventative ritual mentioned in the prophecy, painstakingly analyzing its complex steps and potential consequences.

Lyra, ever compassionate, focused her efforts on the hearts and minds of the celestial citizens. She traveled across the realms, visiting cities and villages, offering solace and encouragement. She organized community gatherings, using her soothing magic to calm anxieties and inspire hope. She created beautiful works of art, imbuing them with powerful messages of resilience and unity. Lyra established centers for meditation and spiritual guidance, helping people to find inner peace and strength. She worked tirelessly to keep the spirits of the people high, recognizing that a strong, united population was just as vital a defense as any magical fortification. Her actions were subtle, yet incredibly powerful, reminding everyone that even in the face of cosmic horror, the human spirit could prevail. She helped bridge the gaps between different celestial communities, fostering collaboration and mutual support in their preparations for the inevitable.

Zephyr, though burdened by the weight of her newfound godhood and the terrifying prophecy, remained focused. She oversaw the overall strategy, coordinating the efforts of Aella, Orion, and Lyra. She held regular meetings, engaging in thoughtful discussions about the best course of action, the potential risks, and the best strategies for preventing disaster. Her leadership was characterized by a profound understanding of both the cosmic threats and the delicate balance of power within her family and amongst her allies. She worked tirelessly to ensure that everyone felt empowered to contribute to the common goal. She also devoted considerable time to contemplating the preventative ritual, aware of its potential to alter the fabric of reality itself. This was not merely a defensive measure; it was a gamble with the very essence of creation. The implications of failure were so horrific that the decision required intense reflection and careful consideration.

The preparations were vast in scale, spanning the breadth and depth of their cosmos. Fortifications were erected on celestial plains, sprawling cities were built on asteroids, and defensive networks were established throughout the seven reptilian tribes' kingdoms. The work required a collaborative effort across different races and cultures, a testament to the unifying power of shared fear and the urgent need for survival. The logistical complexities were staggering, requiring the mobilization of resources and manpower across vast distances. Each world is prepared in its own way, tailoring its defenses to its unique geography and capabilities. This was a total war preparation; they were mobilizing the whole cosmos against a threat that would shake the very foundations of existence.

The sheer scale of the undertaking was immense, a testament to the magnitude of the threat. Yet, despite the daunting task ahead, there was a renewed sense of purpose, a collective resolve to confront the inevitable. The impending return of Xalzar was no longer just a prophecy; it was a rallying cry, a call to arms that united disparate factions and pushed them towards a common goal: survival. The preparations were not merely defensive; they were a testament to their resilience, their refusal to be swept away by the cosmic tides of fate. The struggle would be long and hard, the cost potentially immeasurable, but their determination remained unwavering. The echoes of Xalzar might loom large, but so too did the combined will of a cosmos united against the encroaching darkness. The celestial lights shone brighter, not with the naive joy of victory, but with the steely resolve of those preparing for the ultimate test.

9

The Shadow's Return

The first sign wasn't a cataclysmic event, not a shattering of worlds or a rending of the heavens. It was subtler, a discordant note in the celestial symphony, a tremor in the fabric of reality itself. A subtle shift in the constellations, a whisper of cold that snaked through the warmest nebulae, a feeling of...wrongness. Then, the whispers began. Not audible whispers, but a creeping dread, a sense of impending doom that settled over the hearts of even the most stalwart celestial beings. It started as a low hum, a resonant vibration felt deep within the bones, a premonition of unimaginable horror. This was Xalzar's return, heralded not by trumpets and fire, but by the chilling silence before the storm.

The silence was shattered. A rift tore open in the very fabric of spacetime, a jagged wound in the cosmos spewing forth a torrent of chaotic energy. From its depths emerged Xalzar, not as the legend described him—a towering figure of immense power—but as a shifting, amorphous entity, a storm of shadows and cosmic dread. His form was fluid, constantly changing, a nightmare given flesh, or perhaps, the absence of flesh. He was a void where existence should have been, a negation of all that was good and holy. His arrival was an assault on the senses, a cacophony of discordant sounds, blinding flashes of corrupted light, and a stench that carried the weight of eons of despair.

The celestial city, so meticulously fortified, shuddered under the onslaught. The runes etched into its crystalline walls pulsed frantically, struggling to contain the encroaching darkness. Magical cannons unleashed their celestial fury, blasts of pure energy impacting against Xalzar's form, yet only causing ripples in the swirling chaos. The attacks seemed to have little effect, the being simply absorbing the energy and becoming even more potent, growing stronger with every assault. It was a terrifying sight: the might of a celestial army, reduced to impotent frustration before an enemy that mocked their efforts.

The landscape itself was warped and contorted by Xalzar's presence. Mountains crumbled into dust, rivers reversed their flow, and stars themselves seemed to falter and dim, their light extinguished by the encroaching darkness. The vibrant colors of the celestial realm were replaced by a sickly green hue, a testament to the insidious corruption spreading across the cosmos. Trees twisted into grotesque shapes, their leaves replaced by sharp, obsidian spikes. Flowers wilted and died, their vibrant colors leaching away into the pervading gloom. The very air crackled with malevolent energy, a tangible manifestation of Xalzar's malevolent intent.

The battle raged across the celestial plains. Celestial warriors fought with the courage of desperation, their blades clashing against ethereal tendrils of shadow, their magic deflecting waves of corrupted energy. But even their most powerful assaults proved futile against Xalzar's ever-shifting form and his ability to absorb and redirect their attacks. The ground beneath their feet trembled, the very fabric of reality threatening to unravel under the weight of the conflict. The sounds of battle were horrific—the screams of the dying, the clash of steel against shadow, the thunderous roar of celestial cannons, all interwoven with Xalzar's chilling laughter, a sound that echoed across the cosmos, freezing the blood in the veins of those who heard it.

Aella, despite her meticulous preparations, found herself overwhelmed. Her defenses, though formidable, were proving inadequate against an enemy who seemed to defy the laws of physics, the very structure of reality. She witnessed the fall of her warriors, the destruction of her meticulously crafted defenses, and felt the chilling touch of despair. Yet, even in the face of such overwhelming odds, she refused to yield. She ordered a strategic retreat, regrouping her forces, focusing on containment rather than outright defeat. She knew that complete annihilation wasn't possible; the goal was to minimize the damage and buy time, hoping that Orion's research or Lyra's influence might provide a solution.

Orion, observing the battle from a remote observatory, was horrified. His calculations, his predictions, had been off. Xalzar's return was far more devastating than he'd anticipated. He pored over his data, searching for any clue, any weakness in the being's chaotic form. The ancient texts offered little solace; the prophecies were vague, the descriptions incomplete. He realized he was dealing with something far older, far more powerful than he had ever imagined. The lines of cosmic energy he had been painstakingly studying now pulsed wildly, mirroring the chaos unfolding before him. The universe itself seemed to be screaming in agony, a silent testament to the horror of Xalzar's return. His focus narrowed. He needed to find a way, any way, to disrupt the being's connection to the cosmic currents, to weaken it, to make it vulnerable. He worked tirelessly, driven by a desperate hope that he could still find a way to save his world.

Lyra, witnessing the devastation, felt the weight of her compassion magnified a thousandfold. She moved through the ravaged landscape, using her healing magic to soothe the wounded and offering comfort to the dying. Her art became a desperate attempt to preserve beauty in the face of encroaching chaos, her music a beacon of hope in the encroaching darkness. But the scale of the destruction was beyond comprehension; the wounds inflicted by Xalzar ran deep, cutting to the very core of existence. She found herself powerless against this cosmic horror, her healing magic barely able to make a dent against the pervasive destruction. Her compassionate nature was tested to its limits as she struggled with the immense suffering around her. Her hope was beginning to dwindle, replaced by a chilling despair.

Zephyr, witnessing the chaos from the celestial council chamber, felt the crushing weight of her responsibilities. Her calm demeanor fractured, replaced by a storm of emotions. The strategy she'd meticulously crafted was falling apart. The careful balance of power she'd worked so hard to maintain was threatened. The future of her family, her world, indeed the entire cosmos, felt poised on the edge of oblivion. Her gaze fell on the celestial orb holding the preventative ritual, its intricate design now a stark reminder of the desperate gamble they were facing. The sheer scale of the disaster forced her to confront the stark reality that their meticulous preparations were inadequate. She needed a new strategy, a radical solution, or all was lost. The fate of countless lives rested on her shoulders, a burden she felt pressing down with unbearable weight. The question that haunted her, chilling her to the bone, was whether they had even the slightest chance of winning this war. The weight of the cosmos was too much for even a goddess to bear. She needed a miracle, and quickly.

The wind howled a mournful dirge across the Obsidian Peaks, a chilling counterpoint to the frantic activity at their base. Here, amidst the jagged, black crags that scraped at the bruised twilight sky, the armies of light were gathering. Not just the celestial legions, arrayed in their shimmering, ethereal armor, but a tapestry of beings from every corner of existence—humans, elves, dwarves, sprites, even representatives from the seven reptilian tribes, their scaled bodies gleaming under the spectral light. They were united not by shared blood or creed, but by a common enemy, the encroaching shadow of Xalzar.

The air crackled with the potent energy of a thousand different magics, a chaotic symphony of power that nonetheless held a strange, unifying harmony. Healers tended to the wounded, their hands glowing with emerald light, while mages chanted ancient incantations, weaving shields of shimmering energy around the assembled forces. The very ground beneath their feet seemed to vibrate with the potent magic, a tangible manifestation of the collective will to resist. This wasn't simply an army; it was a testament to the resilience of life, a defiant stand against the encroaching void.

At the heart of this gathering stood Orion, his eyes glowing with an almost feverish intensity. Weeks of relentless work had etched deep lines onto his face, yet his gaze held an unwavering resolve. He'd deciphered enough of the ancient texts to understand Xalzar's weakness: his dependence on the cosmic currents, the lifeblood of the universe itself. Severing that connection, even momentarily, was their only hope. He'd devised a complex array of runes, etched onto colossal obsidian monoliths, designed to disrupt the flow of cosmic energy, creating a localized void that would weaken Xalzar. It was a gamble, a desperate act of defiance against the inevitable, but it was all they had.

Beside Orion stood Aella, her celestial armor gleaming with an otherworldly light. The battle had left its mark, but her resolve remained unbroken. The strategic retreat had been agonizing, the sight of her fallen warriors a wound that festered in her heart. Yet, she'd used the time wisely, consolidating the remaining forces, instilling hope and strategy where despair had threatened to consume them. She moved among her troops, her presence a calming force in the storm of anxiety, her voice a clarion call to courage. She'd discovered an unexpected alliance with the reptilian tribes, their ancient wisdom and powerful magic a crucial asset in the upcoming battle. The pact, however, was fragile; based on mutual necessity rather than genuine trust, the potential for betrayal loomed large.

Lyra, her face pale with exhaustion but her spirit undimmed, moved silently through the ranks, her healing magic a balm to the wounded. Her music, though subdued compared to her earlier, defiant performances, now served a different purpose. It wasn't a rallying cry; it was a lullaby of courage, a soothing balm to frayed nerves and broken hearts. It was a silent testament to her unwavering compassion, a beacon of hope amidst the gathering storm. She had established a temporary sanctuary, a place of respite away from the frenetic activity, where the dying could find peace and the wounded could find solace. Her compassion, a force as powerful as any spell, was an essential part of their collective strength.

Nearby, Zephyr, her goddess-like grace somehow amplified by her evident worry, oversaw the logistical preparations. Her celestial council was in constant session, strategizing, coordinating, and planning for every contingency. She'd delegated tasks efficiently, channeling the collective energy into focused action. The weight of the cosmos still burdened her, but she wore it with quiet dignity, her gaze firm, her determination unwavering. She had reached out to ancient entities, powerful beings whose aid was crucial, their involvement adding another layer of complexity to the already precarious situation. The ancient entities were not easily swayed, their motives often enigmatic and their requests baffling, but their power was undeniable.

And then there was the protagonist, the seemingly ordinary man who had become the unlikely focal point of this cosmic conflict. He stood silently, observing the preparations, his face etched with a grim determination. The ritual that had unleashed the demonic forces within him had irrevocably changed him, but it had also granted him a power he hadn't anticipated, a connection to the very fabric of reality. He was no longer the ordinary man from the mundane world; he was a nexus of power, a living embodiment of the struggle between light and darkness, poised to become the pivotal figure in the battle to come. He could feel the weight of expectations, the hope of countless beings resting on his shoulders. The demons within him were dormant, but not defeated. Their potential for resurgence was a constant reminder of the precariousness of his newfound power, a subtle undercurrent to his resolve.

The setting sun cast long, ominous shadows across the Obsidian Peaks, mirroring the encroaching darkness that threatened to consume their world. But in the heart of this gathering, there was a light that burned brighter than any star, a fire forged in the crucible of despair, a determination that refused to yield. It wasn't just an army gathering; it was hope coalescing, a desperate but powerful defiance against the cosmic horror that threatened to engulf them all. The air thrummed with a mixture of fear and determination, a palpable energy that promised a battle unlike any the cosmos had ever witnessed.

The final preparations were frantic yet methodical. The obsidian monoliths, glowing with runes of immense power, were carefully positioned according to Orion's calculations. The celestial cannons were primed, their celestial energy humming like a thousand caged suns. Healers moved amongst the warriors, their hands glowing with restorative energy. Mages chanted ancient spells, their voices weaving a tapestry of protection. Lyra's music, now a blend of sorrow and hope, played softly in the background, a constant undercurrent of resilience.

But even amidst this organized chaos, a sense of unease hung heavy in the air. This wasn't merely a battle against a powerful foe; it was a struggle against the very fabric of reality, a conflict that threatened to unravel existence itself. The weight of this understanding pressed down on the assembled forces, a silent acknowledgment of the colossal stakes. This was a fight for survival, not just for themselves, but for the entirety of their world, and potentially, for the cosmos.

The protagonist felt the weight of this responsibility, the gravity of the situation pressing down upon him. The demons within him stirred, sensing the approaching battle, and he felt a cold fear grip his heart, a stark reminder of the treacherous path he was treading. Yet, he knew he could not afford to falter. His gaze swept across the assembled multitude, their faces etched with a mixture of hope and fear. This was their last stand, a desperate gamble against impossible odds. He drew strength from their collective resolve, their unwavering determination to fight against the encroaching darkness. He was no longer just a man; he was a symbol of hope, a beacon of defiance against the encroaching void.

The final preparations concluded, and a tense silence descended upon the Obsidian Peaks. The air crackled with anticipation, a silence so profound it felt almost deafening. Then, a low hum resonated from the heart of the assembled forces, a collective breath held in suspense. The clash of cosmic horrors was about to begin. In the distance, a ripple of darkness distorted the fabric of the sky, a harbinger of Xalzar's approach. The battle for the cosmos was about to begin.

The ripple in the sky deepened, a chasm of inky blackness spreading across the twilight, swallowing stars and distorting the very fabric of reality. From its depths emerged Xalzar, a being of pure shadow and malevolent energy, his form shifting and swirling like a vortex of cosmic dread. He was vast, his true size immeasurable, a terrifying embodiment of the void itself, his presence suffocating, a crushing weight on the very soul. Tendrils of shadow snaked out from his form, reaching towards the assembled armies, corrupting the land and twisting the very air into a weapon.

Orion, at the forefront of the celestial legions, raised his hands, his body radiating a blinding light that momentarily pushed back the encroaching darkness. He unleashed a torrent of celestial energy, a wave of pure light that crashed against Xalzar's shadow-form. The impact was earth-shattering, a collision of cosmic forces that shook the Obsidian Peaks to their very foundations. The air crackled with raw energy, a deafening roar echoing across the desolate landscape. But Xalzar remained unscathed, his shadow-form absorbing the attack, growing even darker, even more terrifying.

The battle commenced in earnest. Celestial legions clashed with shadow creatures, the air filled with the clang of weapons and the screams of the dying. Mages unleashed spells of unimaginable power, weaving intricate patterns of light and energy, desperate attempts to pierce the impenetrable darkness that surrounded Xalzar. The reptilian tribes unleashed their ancient magic, their scaled bodies glowing with arcane power, their attacks vicious and precise. But Xalzar's power was overwhelming, his shadow creatures multiplying exponentially, their attacks relentless and devastating.

Aella led the charge, her celestial blade cutting through shadow creatures with brutal efficiency. She fought with a fury born of grief and determination, her every strike fueled by the memory of her fallen comrades. But even her unmatched skill was tested to its limits. Xalzar's shadow creatures were not merely mindless beasts; they were extensions of his will, adapting and evolving to counter every attack.

Lyra, though surrounded by chaos, continued her healing song. Her music was a lifeline, a source of strength and resilience for the wounded, a beacon of hope amidst the despair. Her compassion, a force as powerful as any weapon, kept the army fighting. Her song, though faint in the maelstrom of the battle, resonated with an almost divine power, mitigating the worst damage.

Zephyr, despite the chaotic scene, maintained a calm command. Her celestial council swiftly adapted their strategy, redirecting forces and bolstering defenses. She worked tirelessly, organizing the defense and channeling the energy of the remaining fighters. With calm determination, she oversaw the activation of the runes etched onto the obsidian monoliths. The monoliths pulsed with power, disrupting the flow of cosmic energy, creating a localized void that began to weaken Xalzar. The effect was subtle at first, a slight dimming of his power, but it was enough to give their forces a crucial advantage.

The protagonist, meanwhile, stood apart from the main fighting, his eyes burning with an unnatural light. He knew he could not engage Xalzar directly; his power was too vast, his darkness too overwhelming. He focused his energies instead on amplifying the runes' power, channeling his own connection to the fabric of reality to enhance their effect. He felt the demonic forces within him stir, their power a potent weapon, but one that required careful control. The risk of unleashing them was ever-present, a constant threat that loomed over his actions.

He drew upon the ancient knowledge he had gleaned from the texts, focusing on a specific frequency, a point of vulnerability that Orion had identified. He sent forth a concentrated burst of energy, a wave of pure willpower that resonated with the runes, amplifying their effect exponentially. Xalzar roared, a sound that tore at the very fabric of reality, as his power faltered. The localized void widened, its influence spreading. His shadow creatures weakened, their movements sluggish, their attacks less potent.

Seeing their opportunity, the armies of light pressed their attack, their renewed vigor fueled by Xalzar's weakening power. The balance of power began to shift, the tide of the battle turning in their favor. Aella, empowered by the weakening of the enemy, unleashed her celestial fury, severing Xalzar's connection to the shadow creatures, freeing countless warriors from his grasp. But Xalzar was far from defeated. He rallied his remaining forces, his power flickering but still immense, in a last desperate attempt to reclaim the upper hand.

The protagonist, realizing the full extent of Xalzar's power, knew that the time had come for a final confrontation. He unleashed the full power of his demonic essence, a force of raw chaos that balanced the celestial energy coursing through his veins. The ensuing explosion of energy was blinding, a clash of absolute power that threatened to tear apart the very fabric of existence. The landscape trembled, the heavens themselves groaning under the strain.

In the heart of the maelstrom, the protagonist and Xalzar clashed. The battle was a dance of cosmic horror, a struggle between light and darkness, between order and chaos. The air was saturated with raw energy, a maelstrom of power that threatened to consume everything in its path. They exchanged devastating blows, each strike shattering mountains and tearing apart the very fabric of reality.

Finally, with a last, desperate surge of power, the protagonist channeled the combined energy of the runes, the monoliths, and his own inner chaos. He unleashed an attack of unimaginable power, a wave of pure energy that shattered Xalzar's shadow-form, severing his connection to the cosmic currents. Xalzar screamed, a sound of pure agony that echoed across the cosmos, before dissolving into nothingness, his malevolent energy dissipating into the void from which he had come.

A profound silence descended upon the Obsidian Peaks, a silence broken only by the gentle hum of the recovering cosmos. The shadow had retreated, its malevolent influence extinguished. The battle was won, but at a great cost. Many had fallen, their sacrifice a testament to the indomitable spirit of those who had fought against the encroaching darkness. The victory was bittersweet, but it was a victory nonetheless. The world had been saved from the brink of annihilation. The protagonist, exhausted but victorious, gazed upon the scene before him. The weight of his burden still rested on him, but the victory was undeniable. The road to recovery was long, but they had survived. And in that survival, they found hope. A new era had begun, an era forged in the fires of a cosmic conflict, an era of hope, and perhaps, a new pantheon.

The silence that followed Xalzar's annihilation was deafening, a stark contrast to the cacophony of the battle that had just concluded. The Obsidian Peaks, once majestic and imposing, were now scarred and broken, a testament to the cosmic struggle that had unfolded. Mountains lay shattered, their peaks cleaved in two, the earth itself cracked, and bleeding fissures of molten rock. The air hung heavy with the scent of ozone and the lingering taint of shadow, a grim reminder of the darkness that had nearly consumed the world.

Orion, his celestial armor dimmed and tarnished, descended from the sky, his usually radiant form bearing the marks of battle. His eyes, usually filled with celestial fire, held a weary sadness, reflecting the heavy toll the conflict had taken. He approached the protagonist, who stood amidst the wreckage, his form flickering with an unstable energy, the remnants of the demonic power he had unleashed.

The protagonist, once a seemingly ordinary man, was now a being of immense power, a conduit of both celestial and demonic energy. The victory had come at an exorbitant price. He was drained, his body aching, his spirit weary. The demonic forces within him, though subdued, still pulsed with a restless energy, a constant reminder of the chaos he held within. His eyes, once reflecting the gentle light of his soul, now held a haunting depth, the reflection of the abyss he had faced and conquered. The weight of the world, quite literally, rested upon his shoulders.

Aella, her celestial blade dripping with shadow-matter, approached slowly. Her face, usually radiant with beauty and courage, was etched with exhaustion and grief. The battle had claimed many of her comrades, friends she had fought alongside for centuries. The loss was palpable, a heavy weight on her heart, a constant reminder of the fragility of life. She offered a hand to the protagonist, her eyes filled with admiration and a hint of concern.

Lyra, her healing song now a faint whisper, moved amongst the wounded, her touch mending broken bodies and soothing shattered souls. Her music, though weaker than it had been during the height of the battle, still held an almost divine power, a balm for the ravaged landscape and the wounded spirits of the warriors. The song was laced with grief and determination, a testament to her indomitable spirit. Yet, even her healing magic was stretched to its limits by the scale of devastation.

Zephyr, her face grim but determined, surveyed the battlefield with a practiced eye. Her celestial council worked tirelessly, coordinating rescue efforts, tending to the wounded, and assessing the damage. The victory was undeniable, but the path to recovery would be long and arduous. The reptilian tribes, weakened but not broken, began to tend to their injured, their ancient magic weaving intricate patterns of healing.

The landscape was a testament to the ferocity of the battle. The air itself hummed with residual energy, a chaotic symphony of celestial and demonic forces. The Obsidian Peaks, once a symbol of strength and resilience, were now fractured and scarred, a somber reminder of the battle's intensity. The very ground beneath their feet trembled occasionally, as if the earth itself was still reeling from the shockwaves of the cosmic clash. Even the sky remained unsettled, streaked with remnants of shadow and celestial light, a poignant reminder of the conflict that had ravaged the land.

The protagonist, despite his victory, felt a deep sense of emptiness, a hollow ache in his soul. The demonic forces within him, though quelled, were far from eradicated. He knew that the shadow's defeat was not a final end, but a mere pause in an endless struggle. The battle had been won, but the war, it seemed, was far from over. He had glimpsed the depths of cosmic horror, and the vision continued to haunt him.

Days turned into weeks, and weeks into months. The land slowly began to heal, the earth mending its wounds, the sky clearing of its lingering darkness. Yet, the scars remained, a constant reminder of the battle that had tested the world to its limits. The protagonist, though hailed as a hero, carried the burden of his victory. The weight of his power, the darkness within him, and the knowledge of the cosmic horrors that lurked beyond the veil remained heavy upon his soul.

He spent his days amongst the survivors, his time divided between healing the wounded, assisting in the reconstruction of their world, and battling the lingering shadows that clung to the edges of reality. He discovered that victory did not bring peace, only a different kind of struggle. The demons within him needed constant vigilance, a testament to the difficult task of forging balance within himself. He found solace in his interactions with Aella, Lyra, and Zephyr. Their friendship, forged in the crucible of battle, was a source of comfort, though it could not completely eradicate the haunting weight of his past.

The physical toll of his battle with Xalzar was immense. His body was weakened, marked by scars that were not merely physical but resonated with the cosmic energy that coursed through his veins. He was still powerful, but his strength was brittle, prone to sudden ebbs and surges, making him vulnerable. He learned to rely on his connection to the celestial and demonic energies that resided within him; his mastery of magic deepened through necessity. He was no longer the ordinary man from the past, but neither was he fully a god. He existed somewhere in between, a fragile balance of light and shadow, a testament to his profound and harrowing victory.

The celebration that followed the defeat of Xalzar was subdued, a stark reflection of the great losses suffered during the war. The joy of victory was tempered by grief and the somber knowledge of the scars that would never fade. Though they had triumphed over a cosmic horror, the world was irrevocably changed. The landscape, the people, and even the protagonist himself bore the marks of the war.

The cost of the victory went far beyond the physical. The emotional and psychological toll was immeasurable. The protagonist found himself isolated, haunted by visions and the echo of Xalzar's malevolent energy. He wrestled with the duality of his nature, the constant pull between the light and the darkness that resided within him. His relationship with his companions, once a source of strength, grew complex. The changes within him were hard for them to comprehend, creating a rift that threatened their carefully constructed bonds.

But despite the pain and uncertainty, the protagonist pressed forward. He knew he could not afford to falter. The shadow was vanquished, but the battle for his own soul, and for the future of his world, had just begun. The path ahead remained uncertain, fraught with peril, but in the silence of the aftermath, he found a new determination, a resolve forged in the fires of cosmic conflict. The rebuilding was a slow and painstaking process, but as the land slowly healed, so too did the protagonist begin to find a semblance of peace within himself. The victory, though pyrrhic, was a testament to the resilience of the human spirit and the indomitable will to survive. The new era, however, carried with it the weight of sacrifice, a reminder that even in the grand victories, there is always a price to be paid.

The Obsidian Peaks, once jagged teeth tearing at the celestial canvas, were now a shattered panorama of fractured stone and smoking chasms. Rivers of molten rock, cooled to obsidian veins, snaked across the ravaged landscape, carving new paths through the earth. Where towering spires had once scraped the heavens, only jagged stumps remained, stark reminders of the cataclysmic battle. The air, thick with the lingering scent of ozone and shadow, vibrated with a low hum, a phantom echo of the cosmic energies unleashed. The very ground beneath one's feet trembled with a faint, persistent tremor, as if the planet itself was still shuddering from the impact.

Beyond the immediate vicinity of the Obsidian Peaks, the devastation spread in concentric circles. Forests were reduced to charcoal skeletons, their ancient trees twisted and broken like brittle twigs. Fields, once verdant and teeming with life, were now barren wastelands, the fertile earth poisoned by the clash of celestial and demonic energies. Villages and cities lay in ruins, their structures reduced to rubble, the lives they once held extinguished like candles in a hurricane. Even the seemingly untouched areas bore the marks of the conflict—a subtle shift in the landscape, an unusual silence where birdsong once echoed, a lingering chill in the air that spoke of the shadow's lingering presence.

The toll on the populace was equally devastating. Reports trickled in from across the land, detailing the extent of the destruction and the immense loss of life. The reptilian tribes, though they had fought with fierce loyalty alongside the celestial forces, suffered grievously. Their ancient cities, built into the very fabric of the earth, were breached and ravaged. Their intricate, symbiotic relationship with the land was fractured, leaving them vulnerable and deeply wounded. The healing magic of their shamans, normally capable of incredible feats of restoration, was strained to its limits by the scale of the catastrophe. The air was heavy with mourning.

The protagonist, despite his victory, felt none of the triumph typically associated with such a momentous achievement. The weight of the world pressed heavily on his shoulders, a crushing burden that intensified with each passing day. His body, once strong and capable, was a tapestry of scars, a physical manifestation of the cosmic energies he'd wielded. These were not simple wounds; they were resonating nodes of power, pulsing with celestial and demonic energies, often causing unpredictable surges and ebbs in his strength. His usually clear mind was clouded with fragments of visions, nightmares of the abyss he had momentarily glimpsed—a cosmic horror beyond human comprehension, a reality that threatened to unravel the very fabric of existence.

Aella, despite her unwavering courage, was profoundly affected. The loss of her comrades was a wound that refused to heal, a constant ache in her heart. Her celestial blade, usually a symbol of unwavering resolve, now felt heavy and useless in her hands. She found solace in tending to the injured, her touch still capable of remarkable feats of healing, but even her skill felt insufficient in the face of such widespread devastation. Her radiant smile was muted, replaced by a weary stoicism that masked the depth of her sorrow.

Lyra, the celestial songstress, found her healing melodies laced with a profound grief. Her music, once a beacon of hope and resilience, now carried a haunting undertone, a lament for the fallen. Though she tirelessly continued her work, her voice was weaker, strained by the immense task of soothing shattered souls and mending broken bodies. The echoes of the battle reverberated in her music, a constant reminder of the cost of victory.

Zephyr, the pragmatic strategist, faced the daunting task of coordinating the relief efforts and rebuilding a shattered world. The scale of the damage was almost unimaginable, requiring unprecedented levels of coordination and resources. The celestial council worked tirelessly, but even their combined efforts felt inadequate in the face of such widespread devastation. The burden of responsibility weighed heavily upon her, the future uncertain and fraught with challenges. The victory over Xalzar had bought them time, but the path to true recovery remained long and arduous.

The physical and emotional scars of the war were not limited to the immediate aftermath. Months turned into years. While the land slowly healed, leaving behind a transformed but not unrecognizable landscape, the scars on the people's souls remained deeper and more intractable. The memory of Xalzar's reign of terror haunted the survivors, manifesting as pervasive anxieties and a collective sense of unease. Nightmares plagued the populace, and the once vibrant communities suffered from a pervasive lethargy and lack of collective spirit.

The protagonist, despite his immense power, found himself increasingly isolated. His companions, though they remained loyal, struggled to comprehend the profound changes that had taken place within him. The demonic energies that still pulsed within him created a distance between him and those he loved, a palpable tension that threatened to fracture their carefully constructed bonds. He found himself yearning for a connection that seemed increasingly impossible to attain. His victory had been a personal sacrifice, and his isolation deepened the emotional wounds of his ordeal.

He began to understand that the shadow was not merely a physical entity but a manifestation of a deep cosmic darkness, one that had touched every aspect of his being. The battle he had won was merely a prelude to a far more protracted and personal struggle—a lifelong battle against the lingering shadow that threatened to consume him from within. His transformation into a being of immense power was only a part of his burden. The responsibility for his world's destiny became more acute, a duty that only grew heavier with each passing day.

The weight of the war affected every aspect of his existence. His dreams were filled with the swirling chaos of the cosmic conflict, the faces of the fallen, and the chilling visage of Xalzar. The silence of his waking moments was haunted by the echoes of the battle, a constant reminder of the destructive power that resided not only in the external world but also within himself. He sought solace in solitude, but even in his solitude, the echoes of war continued to reverberate, reminding him of the price of his victory. The scars of war, both visible and invisible, were etched into the very fabric of his being. The path ahead was uncertain, fraught with peril, but he knew that he must press on, not for glory or recognition but for the sake of his world and for his own salvation. The true battle, he realized, had only just begun.

10

A New Equilibrium

The first rays of dawn, fractured and weak, struggled to pierce the perpetual twilight that clung to the Obsidian Peaks. Dust, fine as powdered bone, drifted on the wind, a constant reminder of the cataclysm. Yet, even in this desolation, the seeds of hope began to sprout. Aella, her face smudged with soot and grime, oversaw the painstaking work of clearing rubble from what remained of a village nestled in a valley sheltered from the worst of the destruction. Her celestial blade, though dulled, served as a surprisingly effective lever, prying apart shattered stones and freeing trapped timbers. Around her, reptilian tribesmen, their scales scarred but their spirits unbroken, worked with a quiet intensity, their powerful limbs moving with surprising grace. Humans, their faces etched with grief but their eyes resolute, lent their strength to the effort. The air hummed with a low, almost imperceptible thrum, a combination of the lingering chaos energy and the concerted effort of countless beings working towards a common goal.

This wasn't mere rebuilding; it was a tapestry woven from sorrow, resilience, and a shared determination to defy the void. The old methods failed here; the land was poisoned, the very essence of the earth tainted by Xalzar's demonic influence. Lyra's music, though still laced with grief, now included notes of restoration, melodies that sought to coax life back into the blighted earth. Her songs weren't just for the ears but for the land itself, weaving harmonies that resonated with the earth's wounded spirit, encouraging the regeneration of flora and fauna. Zephyr, ever practical, had established a complex network of supply lines, coordinating the distribution of resources across the ravaged land. Caravans of winged beasts, their burden heavy with supplies, traversed the skies, their movements choreographed to avoid the still-unstable pockets of shadow energy.

The protagonist, despite his physical and spiritual weariness, found a new purpose in this arduous task. His celestial power, tempered by his ordeal, allowed him to accelerate the healing process, coaxing life from the poisoned earth and purifying the air with currents of celestial energy. His touch, once capable of unleashing devastating power, now gently caressed the land, mending the wounds inflicted by the war. He didn't work alone; he guided, encouraged, and shared his power with those willing to learn, teaching them to harness the renewed energies flowing through the land. The reptilian shamans, their own powers augmented by the protagonist's instruction, performed intricate rituals, weaving their ancient magic with the celestial energies to restore the balance of nature.

The rebuilding extended beyond the physical realm. The psychological scars of the war ran deep, leaving the survivors haunted by nightmares and consumed by anxieties. Lyra's music, along with the protagonist's quiet encouragement, helped alleviate some of the pervasive psychological trauma. He shared his experiences, not to boast of his victory, but to offer a shared sense of catharsis. He spoke of the darkness he had faced, of the struggle within, to instill in the survivors a sense of shared understanding. The shared trauma, though a bitter burden, became a unifying force, forging bonds of empathy and understanding.

The process of rebuilding varied from region to region. In the sun-drenched plains, the focus was on restoring the fertile lands, coaxing life back into the poisoned soil. Teams of celestial beings worked tirelessly, using their healing powers to purify the earth, while humans and reptilians worked together to replant crops and revitalize the ecosystems. In the once verdant forests, now reduced to charcoal skeletons, the focus shifted to reforestation, a monumental task that required patience and skill. The celestial beings, with their mastery over nature, guided the growth of new trees, while reptilian tribesmen, with their deep understanding of the symbiotic relationships within the ecosystem, ensured that the new forests flourished.

The cities, once symbols of human achievement, presented a different kind of challenge. The task of rebuilding wasn't merely about restoring the structures but about rebuilding the communities. Here, the role of the protagonist was pivotal. He used his power to create spaces for dialogue, facilitating reconciliation between the different factions. He encouraged the creation of collaborative projects, fostering a sense of community and shared purpose. He taught them to build not just homes, but sanctuaries that reflected their resilience and capacity for hope. The architecture became a testament to their collective healing, a physical manifestation of their shared resilience.

The rebuilding of the reptilian cities presented unique challenges. Their intricate, subterranean structures, built in harmony with the earth, were deeply intertwined with the landscape and the earth's magic. The protagonist, with the aid of the reptilian shamans, worked to restore the balance, carefully mending the damaged subterranean networks and coaxing the life force back into the earth. The reptilian tribes, despite their losses, played a vital role in the restoration process; their understanding of the earth's rhythms and their deep connection with nature proved indispensable. The synergy between the celestial beings and the reptilian tribes fostered a new respect and understanding, a new level of cooperation unprecedented in their history.

As months turned into years, the landscape began to transform. The charred earth regained its verdant hue, the forests slowly re-emerged, and the cities rose from the rubble. Yet, the process wasn't solely physical. The emotional wounds of the past demanded an equally profound healing. The protagonist, his own wounds still raw, took the lead in this intricate process. He organized festivals of remembrance and reconciliation, where the collective trauma of the war was acknowledged and shared. He fostered a culture of mutual support and compassion, ensuring that no one felt isolated in their grief. The healing was not a swift process but a gradual, painstaking work that transformed the very fabric of their societies.

The process of rebuilding the realms was not simply a physical reconstruction but a deeply spiritual and emotional journey. It required cooperation not just between different species but between different aspects of existence—the physical, spiritual, and emotional. The protagonist, in his role as the new supreme god, didn't simply command but served as a catalyst, a facilitator of this collective healing. His power was not wielded to dominate but to empower; his role was not that of a ruler but of a guide, leading his people towards a new equilibrium, a new understanding of their shared reality. The scars of the past remained, but they served as reminders of their resilience, a testament to their capacity to overcome even the darkest of times. A new era was dawning, an era forged not in the fires of destruction but in the crucible of shared sorrow, resilience, and an unwavering commitment to building a better future. The rebuilding of the realms was a testament to the enduring power of hope and the unwavering spirit of life itself.

The air, once thick with the stench of decay and shadow, now carried the faint, sweet scent of wildflowers. In the heart of the ravaged land, a sanctuary of healing had been established—a sprawling complex of shimmering crystal structures, pulsating with gentle celestial energy. Here, the focus was not on rebuilding the old but on forging something new, something stronger and more resilient. Within the crystal structures, specialized chambers cater to various needs. One chamber hummed with the restorative power of Lyra's music, its ethereal melodies washing over the injured, soothing their physical and emotional wounds. The melodies weren't just sounds; they were intricate patterns of energy, carefully crafted to repair damaged cells, mend broken bones, and calm frayed nerves. Patients, both human and reptilian, lay on beds of shimmering moss, their bodies bathed in the healing light, their faces serene in slumber.

Another chamber, bathed in the warm glow of amethyst crystals, served as a place of spiritual healing. Here, the protagonist, aided by the reptilian shamans, conducted intricate rituals, weaving celestial energy with ancient magic to cleanse the lingering darkness from the survivors' souls. These rituals involved intricate chants, hypnotic movements, and the careful manipulation of energy flows, designed to unravel the trauma etched deep within their minds and spirits. The shamans, their ancient knowledge augmented by the protagonist's celestial power, acted as conduits, channeling the energy to heal the deepest wounds of the war. The air thrummed with power, a palpable testament to the intricate interplay of celestial and earthly magic.

Outside the crystal structures, sprawling gardens flourished. These weren't ordinary gardens; they were living testaments to the power of restoration. The soil, once barren and poisoned, had been carefully nurtured, its essence purified by the protagonist's celestial energy and the unwavering efforts of countless beings. Flowers of impossible hues bloomed in abundance, their petals shimmering with iridescent light. Trees, their branches reaching towards the heavens, bore fruits of unparalleled sweetness and vitality. This wasn't merely landscaping; it was a conscious effort to re-establish a symbiotic relationship between the land and its inhabitants, a tangible representation of healing and rebirth.

The protagonist, despite his newly acquired godhood, didn't stand aloof, directing the efforts from a distant pedestal. He worked alongside everyone, his hands calloused from tending the gardens, his voice hoarse from singing Lyra's songs of healing with the villagers. He understood that true healing wasn't just about mending physical and spiritual wounds; it was about mending the fractured fabric of their society. He encouraged collaborative efforts, fostering a sense of community and shared purpose. He taught the villagers to weave their grief and resilience into the very fabric of their lives, transforming their pain into a source of strength and creativity.

The healing process extended beyond the physical and spiritual. It involved the meticulous rebuilding of shattered communities, the mending of broken trust, and the fostering of a new culture of empathy and understanding. He instituted programs focused on trauma healing, utilizing innovative techniques combining ancient rituals with celestial energy manipulation. These programs were designed not just to alleviate the immediate symptoms of trauma but to empower individuals to process their experiences, to find meaning in their suffering, and to integrate their past into a hopeful future. Support groups were established where survivors could share their stories, offer comfort, and find strength in shared experience. Art therapy became a powerful tool, allowing individuals to express their pain and trauma through creative outlets.

The protagonist, drawing on his own harrowing journey, shared his story, not to boast, but to emphasize the importance of vulnerability and the possibility of transformation. He highlighted the power of facing one's inner demons, the importance of embracing imperfection, and the profound capacity for healing that resides within every being. His vulnerability resonated deeply with the people, fostering a sense of shared experience and creating a space for empathy and understanding. He acknowledged the collective trauma, validating their pain and offering a path towards healing and reconciliation.

The physical rebuilding of the cities was interwoven with the emotional and spiritual healing. The architecture itself reflected the healing process. Buildings were constructed not just as dwellings but as sanctuaries. Spaces are designed to foster peace, tranquility, and a sense of belonging. Public spaces were meticulously crafted to facilitate interaction, promote social cohesion, and encourage community engagement. Memorials were created to honor the victims of the war, not as monuments to suffering, but as reminders of resilience and the enduring power of hope. Each structure, each garden, each public space became a living testament to the journey of healing, a tangible embodiment of their collective resilience.

The healing wasn't just about repairing the damage inflicted by Xalzar; it was about creating a better world, a world built on empathy, understanding, and cooperation. The protagonist, guided by wisdom gained from his ordeals, encouraged a shift in societal values. He championed policies that emphasized equality, cooperation, and mutual respect among the various races and species. He encouraged a re-evaluation of social structures, advocating for systems that prioritized well-being, justice, and sustainability.

Years passed. The landscape, once scarred and desolate, was transformed into a paradise of vibrant life. The cities, once symbols of division and conflict, now pulsed with a renewed energy, their inhabitants united by a shared commitment to building a better future. The scars of the war remained, etched into the land and the hearts of the people, but they served as reminders of their resilience, a testament to their ability to overcome adversity and build something beautiful from the ashes of destruction. A new equilibrium had been established, not a simple return to the old order, but a harmonious balance born from pain, loss, and an unwavering commitment to healing and rebuilding. This new world, forged in the crucible of darkness and despair, now shone with the light of hope, a testament to the enduring power of the human and reptilian spirit. The healing was not complete; it was an ongoing process, but the path towards a brighter future was clear, illuminated by the unwavering light of hope and the shared commitment to a new equilibrium.

The air, still carrying the faint scent of wildflowers, now held a sharper edge, a tangible tension that spoke of unresolved conflicts. The healing, while profound, hadn't erased the deep divisions that had scarred the land for centuries. The seven reptilian tribes, though cooperating in the rebuilding efforts, still carried ancient grudges and mistrust towards each other, their scaled skins reflecting the shadows of their past conflicts. The humans, too, bore the weight of their own internal divisions, fractured by years of war and societal inequalities. Reconciliation, the protagonist understood, wouldn't be a single act, but a painstaking process requiring empathy, understanding, and a willingness to confront the painful truths of their shared history.

The first step involved creating spaces for dialogue and understanding. The protagonist, guided by the wisdom of the ancient reptilian shamans and the ethereal guidance of Lyra, designed a series of interconnected meeting halls, nestled within the heart of the newly established crystal city. These weren't mere structures; they were carefully crafted spaces designed to foster communication and reconciliation. The architecture itself was symbolic, blending elements of human and reptilian aesthetics, reflecting the shared effort to forge a new identity. Natural light streamed through stained-glass windows depicting scenes of unity and cooperation, scenes crafted by artists from all factions, their collaborative efforts weaving together threads of a shared future.

The walls were adorned with murals, depicting the history of the seven tribes and the humans, not as a glorification of conflict, but as an honest representation of their past. These weren't biased narratives; they were the result of extensive collaborative efforts, ensuring that the stories of all parties were accurately and respectfully represented. The murals depicted the battles, the betrayals, the losses, but also the moments of unexpected alliance, the small acts of kindness, and the shared struggles that had ultimately bound them together. The protagonist encouraged open discussions around these murals, leading facilitated dialogues that helped unpack years of misrepresentation, misinformation, and ingrained biases. These discussions weren't always easy; tempers flared, old wounds reopened, but the structured setting, guided by trained facilitators, ensured that the conversations remained productive, focused on bridging gaps rather than deepening divisions.

One particular mural depicted the legendary Serpent's Coil, a sacred place held dear by the Xylos tribe, a site that had been desecrated during the war. The depiction wasn't just an image; it was a meticulously crafted three-dimensional relief, created using Xylos's traditional craftsmanship, augmented by celestial energy to imbue it with a subtle, calming aura. The act of creating this mural together, with the protagonist leading the effort, was a powerful symbol of reconciliation, a physical manifestation of their shared commitment to healing the wounds of the past. The discussion surrounding this mural was particularly poignant, with elders from the Xylos tribe sharing the deep emotional pain of losing their sacred site, and members from the other tribes expressing remorse and taking collective responsibility for the past atrocities. The process was arduous, filled with tears and moments of intense emotional release, but it also fostered a deeper level of mutual understanding and empathy.

Beyond the meeting halls, the reconciliation extended to the rebuilding of their cities. The protagonist, understanding the importance of shared spaces, commissioned the construction of a series of interconnected bridges, spanning the chasms that had long separated the various settlements. These weren't just functional structures; they were majestic works of art, incorporating elements of all seven reptilian tribes' architectural styles, interwoven with human architectural designs. Each bridge represented a commitment to unity, a tangible symbol of the bridges being built between the races. Along the bridges, gardens were established, flourishing with flowers and plants from all regions, representing the diverse flora of the land, previously fragmented by conflict.

These public spaces weren't just aesthetically pleasing; they were meticulously designed to facilitate interaction and foster a sense of shared community. The layout encouraged spontaneous encounters, promoting cross-cultural exchange and reducing the physical and psychological barriers that had long kept the communities isolated. Markets sprang up along the bridges, filled with vendors from all factions, offering their unique goods and creating opportunities for economic collaboration and cultural exchange. Performances, festivals, and communal gatherings were organized, fostering a sense of shared identity and collective purpose. The protagonist actively participated in these events, his presence reassuring and encouraging.

Beyond the physical structures, the reconciliation involved a profound spiritual transformation. The protagonist, drawing on his newly acquired celestial powers, facilitated rituals and ceremonies designed to heal the deep-seated trauma that affected all factions. These weren't simple religious events; they were carefully designed therapeutic experiences, weaving together elements of ancient reptilian shamanistic practices, human spiritual traditions, and celestial energy manipulation. The rituals focused on forgiveness, letting go of past grievances, and embracing a new future built on peace and harmony. Many participated, finding solace and healing through shared rituals, their collective energy forming a powerful force for transformation. This spiritual healing played a crucial role in softening hearts, bridging gaps, and creating a sense of shared purpose.

The process of reconciliation was far from seamless. Old prejudices resurfaced, disagreements arose, and moments of tension were unavoidable. But through perseverance, understanding, and the shared commitment to a better future, these conflicts were resolved through open dialogue and mutual respect. The protagonist didn't impose solutions; he facilitated the process, ensuring that all parties had a voice and were empowered to actively participate in shaping their shared future. He acted as a catalyst, igniting the flame of hope, fueling the desire for change. The transformation was gradual, requiring patience, persistence, and the unwavering belief in the possibility of reconciliation.

As years passed, the visible scars of the war began to fade, replaced by the blossoming of a new era. The once-fractured alliances were mended, the seven reptilian tribes and the humans stood together, united by their shared resilience and their shared commitment to building a world founded on peace, understanding, and mutual respect. The new equilibrium wasn't a mere restoration of the old order; it was a profound transformation, a testament to the enduring power of reconciliation and the boundless capacity of diverse beings to forge a harmonious existence. The world, once fractured, was now healed; not without scars, but strengthened by them, standing as a beacon of hope and a testament to the resilience of life itself. The path towards true unity was still long, but the journey, once fraught with peril and uncertainty, was now illuminated by the radiant glow of hope and a shared commitment to a brighter future.

The crystalline spires of the newly built city, Aethelgard, shimmered under the twin suns, a testament to the collaborative spirit that had risen from the ashes of war. No longer were the settlements of humans and the seven reptilian tribes segregated; instead, they intertwined, forming a vibrant tapestry of architecture and culture. The Xylos, with their penchant for intricate, bioluminescent structures, contributed shimmering, organic-looking buildings that pulsed with soft, internal light, seamlessly integrated with the humans' more geometric, earth-toned constructions. The towering obsidian structures of the Drakon, once symbols of isolation and power, now stood as sentinels, guarding the city's perimeter, their dark surfaces reflecting the starlight like polished mirrors. The vibrant, coral-like buildings of the Hydros, previously hidden beneath the ocean's depths, now graced the canals that snaked through the city, their shimmering surfaces alive with the ebb and flow of the water. Each tribe's unique architectural style, once a source of division, now contributes to the city's breathtaking beauty, a visual manifestation of the newfound unity.

The social fabric mirrored this architectural harmony. The old caste systems, which had perpetuated inequality and strife, were dismantled. A council of representatives from each tribe and the human settlements was established, ensuring that every voice was heard, every perspective considered. This council, far from a simple governing body, became a vibrant forum for debate, collaboration, and the ongoing evolution of their shared society. The laws were rewritten, emphasizing equality, justice, and environmental stewardship. Education was prioritized, with schools established across the land, teaching a curriculum that celebrated the diverse histories and cultures of all inhabitants, fostering mutual respect and understanding.

The economic structure underwent a radical transformation. The old system, based on exploitation and competition, was replaced by a collaborative model that prioritized sustainability and equitable distribution of resources. Trade flourished, facilitated by the interconnected network of bridges and canals. The once-isolated tribes now exchanged goods, knowledge, and cultural practices, enriching the lives of all. Artisans from different tribes collaborated, creating breathtaking works of art that reflected their shared heritage and their collective vision for the future. The creative energy released by this collaboration was remarkable, leading to an artistic renaissance, with music, dance, and theater flourishing across the land.

However, the path towards this new equilibrium wasn't devoid of challenges. The scars of the past ran deep, and old prejudices occasionally resurfaced. Disagreements arose, particularly regarding the allocation of resources and the interpretation of the new laws. But the conflict resolution mechanisms established during the reconciliation process proved remarkably effective.

Instead of resorting to violence, disputes were addressed through open dialogue, mediation, and compromise. The council served as a crucial platform for airing grievances and finding solutions through mutual understanding and respect. The experience had taught them that compromise wasn't a sign of weakness but a testament to strength, a demonstration of the ability to transcend their differences for the common good.

Beyond the material improvements, a deeper spiritual transformation took place. The protagonist, utilizing his newfound celestial powers, continued to facilitate healing rituals and ceremonies, addressing the lingering trauma of the past. These ceremonies, drawing upon the combined wisdom of different spiritual traditions, fostered a sense of shared identity and purpose. The focus shifted from individual grievances to collective healing, from personal suffering to collective well-being. The protagonist didn't simply act as a healer; he guided his people towards self-healing, empowering them to find their own path to peace and reconciliation. The collective energy generated through these rituals was palpable, contributing to the overall sense of harmony and well-being.

The relationship between humans and the reptilian tribes, once characterized by mutual fear and distrust, has now evolved into a complex network of interdependence and cooperation. They discovered unexpected commonalities, shared values, and a surprising capacity for empathy. They learned to appreciate the unique contributions of each tribe to their society, recognizing the strength that lay in their diversity. The old narratives of superiority and inferiority were replaced by a more nuanced understanding of their shared humanity, transcending the differences in their physical forms. This newfound respect was reflected in the everyday interactions between the different groups, in the way they collaborated on projects, in the celebrations they shared, and in the stories they told about their shared history.

Aethelgard wasn't merely a city; it was a microcosm of the new world order, reflecting the principles of equality, cooperation, and sustainability that underpinned their new society. It was a vibrant, ever-evolving entity, a place where innovation flourished, where creativity blossomed, and where the future held limitless possibilities. The gardens, meticulously designed and tended, were havens of tranquility and beauty, offering spaces for reflection and rejuvenation. The canals, pulsating with life, served not just as transportation routes but also as venues for communal activities, artistic performances, and celebrations. The architecture itself was a living testament to their shared past and their hopeful future.

The protagonist, now revered as a god among his people, continued to play a pivotal role in guiding the nascent civilization. However, he was no longer the sole decision-maker; he acted as a mentor, a guide, a facilitator, empowering others to take ownership of their destiny. His influence was subtle but profound, inspiring others to aspire to greater heights, to embrace the responsibility of shaping their future. He understood that true leadership lay not in control but in empowerment, in fostering the growth and development of all individuals. He taught them that the greatest power lay not in domination but in compassion, not in conquest but in collaboration.

Years passed, and Aethelgard grew into a magnificent metropolis, a beacon of hope for the entire world. The principles of harmony and sustainability, once abstract ideals, had been translated into tangible realities, shaping every aspect of their society. The once-fractured land had been healed, the wounds of war slowly fading into the past. The seven reptilian tribes and the humans, once locked in a bitter conflict, now stood together, a unified people, their shared history forging an unbreakable bond. Their journey had been long and arduous, fraught with challenges and setbacks, but it had ultimately led them to a new equilibrium, a new dawn, a new world order built upon the foundations of peace, understanding, and a shared commitment to a brighter future. The future remained unwritten, full of uncertainties and challenges, but they faced them together, united by their shared hope and their unwavering belief in a world where harmony was not just a dream but a reality.

The whispers of Aethelgard's prosperity rippled outwards, carried on the winds that swept across the rejuvenated land. The once-scarred earth, healed by the protagonist's celestial energies, now teemed with life, its vibrant ecosystems restored to a breathtaking balance. Forests, once ravaged by war, flourished anew, their ancient trees reaching towards the twin suns, their canopies sheltering a multitude of creatures, both familiar and fantastical. Rivers, once choked with pollution and strife, flowed freely, their waters teeming with fish, their banks lined with lush vegetation. The very air hummed with a revitalized energy, a palpable sense of harmony that permeated the land.

This harmony extended beyond the physical realm. The spiritual healing initiated by the protagonist continued, its influence spreading across the land like wildfire. Temples, dedicated to the new pantheon established by him and his family, rose in every settlement, not as symbols of dominance but as centers of community, places of learning, meditation, and spiritual growth. These temples were not mere structures of stone and wood; they were living entities, pulsing with the combined energy of their worshippers, their architecture designed to facilitate healing and spiritual enlightenment. The ceremonies performed within their hallowed halls were not rituals of supplication but acts of shared communion, strengthening the bond between the people and the divine, and fostering a sense of collective identity and purpose.

The protagonist, though revered as a god, consciously avoided the trappings of power. He understood the dangers of absolute authority, the insidious nature of unchecked influence. He chose instead to act as a guide, a mentor, a facilitator, empowering others to shape their own destinies. He established academies across the land, dedicated to the study of magic, science, and philosophy, fostering a spirit of intellectual curiosity and critical thinking. These academies were not hierarchical institutions but collaborative spaces, where students from all backgrounds, humans and reptilians alike, learned side-by-side, challenging each other's assumptions and expanding their horizons. The curriculum emphasized not just the acquisition of knowledge but the development of critical thinking skills, problem-solving abilities, and a commitment to ethical decision-making. The aim was not to create obedient followers but independent thinkers, capable of shaping their own lives and contributing to the betterment of society.

His influence extended even further, reaching into the realm of art and creativity. He inspired a new era of artistic expression, where the diverse cultures of the seven reptilian tribes and humanity blended seamlessly, resulting in a vibrant tapestry of creative works. Musicians composed symphonies that echoed the harmony of the restored world, poets penned verses that captured the beauty of the rejuvenated landscape, and painters created masterpieces that reflected the spirit of the new era. The arts served not merely as entertainment but as a means of expressing shared values, celebrating their diverse heritages, and fostering a sense of collective identity. The protagonist's influence was not forceful; it was inspirational, an intangible force that shaped the creative impulses of the land, guiding them towards a vision of peace and harmony.

The economic system, too, bore the imprint of his legacy. The principles of sustainability and equitable distribution of resources, once abstract ideals, were translated into tangible realities. Trade flourished, not as a zero-sum game but as a means of mutual benefit, fostering cooperation and interdependence between different communities. The old notion of scarcity was replaced by a new understanding of abundance, a recognition that the planet's resources were sufficient to meet the needs of all its inhabitants, provided they were managed wisely and shared equitably. Innovative technologies, developed within the academies, made it possible to harvest renewable energy sources, reduce pollution, and conserve natural resources, ensuring the long-term sustainability of their civilization. The economic prosperity that followed was not based on exploitation but on collaboration, on a shared commitment to the well-being of all.

Generations passed. Aethelgard, once a humble city, grew into a sprawling metropolis, a testament to the power of unity and cooperation. Its magnificent architecture, a fusion of human and reptilian styles, reflected the harmony between the different cultures. Its thriving markets buzzed with activity, its schools and academies teemed with eager learners, and its temples resonated with the collective spirituality of its inhabitants. The protagonist's influence continued to be felt, not through direct intervention but through the principles he had instilled, the values he had championed, the systems he had helped to build. His legacy was not a monument of stone but a living, breathing entity, reflected in the vibrant culture, the flourishing economy, and the enduring peace of the world he had helped to create.

The story of his life, passed down through generations, became a legend, a testament to the power of individual action, the transformative potential of human (and reptilian) spirit, and the possibility of overcoming even the darkest of challenges to achieve a state of lasting peace and harmony. It wasn't a story of a single hero conquering insurmountable odds; it was a narrative of collective effort, of shared responsibility, of the collaborative spirit that ultimately forged a brighter future for all. The memory of the conflict, the pain, the loss – these were not erased, but integrated into the collective consciousness as lessons learned, as a reminder of the fragility of peace and the importance of constant vigilance.

Even the celestial entities, those cosmic beings with whom the protagonist had forged an alliance, continued to observe the flourishing world he had helped to create. Their presence was subtle, a background hum in the cosmic symphony, a gentle guidance rather than direct intervention. They understood the importance of allowing this new civilization to evolve organically, to find its own path towards its destiny. They recognized that true progress was not imposed but achieved, that lasting peace and harmony could not be gifted but had to be earned through constant effort, through a commitment to justice, equality, and sustainable living. The protagonist's triumph was not merely a personal achievement; it was a beacon of hope, a demonstration of the potential for transformative change, a testament to the enduring power of the human, and reptilian, spirit to overcome seemingly insurmountable odds. The new equilibrium, so hard-won, was not just a state of being; it was a dynamic process, an ongoing journey towards a future that remained unwritten, yet brimming with the potential for limitless growth, exploration, and harmony. The legacy continues, woven into the very fabric of the world, a testament to a future where hope triumphs over despair, and where the harmonious coexistence of different cultures is not just a dream but a vibrant reality. The whispers of Aethelgard's success carried on the winds, a promise of peace and prosperity for generations to come, a testament to the enduring power of unity, compassion, and the enduring human (and reptilian) spirit.

11

The Mortal Coil

The celestial choir faded, the echoes of their praise dissolving into the gentle rustle of leaves. The weight of godhood, once a comforting mantle, now felt like a suffocating shroud. He had reshaped Aethelgard, forged a new pantheon, and woven a tapestry of peace from the threads of war and hatred. Yet, a gnawing emptiness remained, a void that even the adoration of countless beings couldn't fill. He missed the sting of mortality, the sharp tang of fear, the visceral joy of simple pleasures. He missed being human.

The decision, whispered initially to the cosmic entities who had become his closest confidants, hung heavy in the still air. To relinquish godhood, to shed the mantle of immortality, to return to the fragile, fleeting embrace of mortality – it was a choice that defied logic, that challenged the very foundations of his new reality. The cosmic entities, ancient and wise, neither approved nor disapproved. They understood the inherent paradox of his desire, the yearning for an experience that he had so painstakingly escaped. They saw in his choice not a weakness, but a strength, a testament to the unwavering curiosity that had driven him to reshape the world in the first place.

He sought not a retreat, but a deeper understanding. His reign as a god had been a grand experiment, a symphony of creation and governance, but it lacked a certain… resonance. He had guided the seven reptilian tribes and humanity towards peace and prosperity, but he hadn't truly felt their struggles, their joys, their petty squabbles, their profound loves. He had observed humanity from a distance, a benevolent observer crafting a perfect world, but he yearned to be a participant, to feel the pulse of life beat within his mortal frame once more.

The transformation was subtle, a slow unraveling of celestial energies, a gentle shedding of divine light. It wasn't a dramatic fall from grace, but a conscious, deliberate choice. He didn't descend from the heavens in a fiery spectacle, but rather faded away, his presence thinning like morning mist, leaving behind only the faintest echo of his divine power. The transition was as profound as it was quiet, a silent withdrawal from a realm he had mastered, a quiet return to the world he had once known.

He chose not to reappear in Aethelgard, the magnificent city he had helped build. Instead, he sought out a humble village nestled deep within a verdant valley, far from the towering spires and bustling markets of his creation. Oakhaven, it was called, a place untouched by the grand scale of his ambitions, a village where life moved at a slower, more deliberate pace. The villagers, oblivious to his true identity, greeted him with simple smiles and quiet curiosity. He was just another traveler, weathered and weary, seeking shelter and respite. He didn't reveal his divine origins, for it was precisely the anonymity, the ordinariness of life, that he craved.

He took up residence in a small cottage on the outskirts of the village, its walls adorned with faded tapestries and its hearth filled with the warmth of a crackling fire. He traded his celestial robes for simple homespun clothing, his divine radiance for the gentle glow of a hearth fire. He worked alongside the villagers, his hands calloused and stained with earth, his back aching from the labor. He helped tend the fields, planting seeds and harvesting crops, experiencing the cycle of life and death in a way he had never done before. He learned to bake bread, the aroma filling the cottage with a warmth that transcended the simple act of sustenance. He learned to mend clothes, the rhythmic stitch of needle and thread a soothing balm to his soul. He learned to laugh, a sound he had almost forgotten, amidst the simple joys and shared struggles of daily life.

He fell in love again, a love that was rooted in shared experiences, in the simple act of being present in each other's lives. It was not the grand, cosmic love he had shared with his divine family, but a love that was grounded in the earthy reality of shared laughter, whispered secrets, and the comfort of holding hands. He felt the bittersweet sting of loss, the profound emptiness of absence, when a loved one passed away, a reminder of the precious fragility of life. He felt the intense joy of watching life bloom anew, from the first tentative sprouts in the spring to the bountiful harvest in the autumn.

He experienced illness, the weary ache in his bones, the rasping cough, the fever that burned with an intensity he had only observed from afar. He experienced the helplessness of being vulnerable, the terrifying realization of his mortality. He felt the fear of death, not the grand, cosmic fear of annihilation, but the intimate, human fear of oblivion, the loss of connection, the end of a life lived.

He delved into the complexities of human relationships, the intricacies of love and hate, the tangled web of ambition and betrayal, and the profound capacity for both good and evil. He witnessed kindness and cruelty, generosity and greed, empathy and indifference. He saw the light and darkness within humanity, a duality that he had only grasped intellectually, not viscerally. He learned that the world wasn't simply black and white, good and evil, but a kaleidoscope of shades and hues, a tapestry woven from countless individual threads.

He walked amongst the villagers, not as a god but as one of them, sharing their stories, their laughter, and their sorrows. He understood, with a clarity that transcended divine wisdom, the profound beauty and heartbreaking fragility of human existence. He learned that true understanding wasn't found in the grand cosmic tapestry of creation, but in the seemingly insignificant details of daily life, in the simple acts of kindness, in the shared moments of joy and sorrow.

His time in Oakhaven was not a retreat from responsibility, but a recalibration, a recalibration of his understanding of humanity, of his place in the cosmos. He hadn't abandoned his responsibilities, but rather redefined them. His presence in Aethelgard was still felt, an invisible hand guiding the evolution of his creation, but his heart now resided in the humble village, beating in sync with the rhythms of a simple life. He had traded the weight of godhood for the weight of humanity, and in doing so, had discovered a profound truth: that the greatest wonders were not found in the heavens but in the hearts of men and women, in the shared experiences of a simple life. The lessons of mortality, he realized, were far more profound than any celestial knowledge he had previously possessed. His new divinity wasn't about cosmic power, but about the quiet, persistent, ever-growing power of understanding and compassion. And that, he realized, was a far more fulfilling kind of immortality.

The first snowfall of the year dusted Oakhaven in a pristine layer of white. He watched from his cottage window, a mug of steaming tea warming his hands, as the villagers moved about their daily tasks, their breaths puffing out white clouds in the crisp air. The idyllic scene, so utterly ordinary, held a profound beauty that resonated deep within him. He had witnessed the breathtaking grandeur of celestial landscapes, the dazzling spectacle of cosmic events, but nothing compared to the quiet elegance of a snow-covered village.

He had experienced the human capacity for love in its many forms. The fierce protective love of a mother for her child, the tender affection between siblings, the passionate embrace of lovers, the quiet companionship of old friends. He had also witnessed the darker side of love—the jealousy that gnawed at hearts, the possessiveness that strangled relationships, the betrayal that shattered trust. These experiences, so intensely human, added layers to his understanding of the complexities of existence, complexities far beyond the binary oppositions he had encountered in the celestial realms.

Illness struck him hard that winter. A simple cold, at first, but it quickly escalated into a debilitating pneumonia. He lay in bed, his body wracked with coughs, his lungs burning, the world outside fading into a blurry haze. The fear, raw and visceral, surprised him. It wasn't the fear of annihilation, but the fear of fading away, of being lost in the quiet oblivion of death. He felt the fragility of his existence, the tenuous thread that connected him to life, more acutely than he ever had during his celestial reign. The village healer, a kind old woman with gnarled hands and wise eyes, tended to him with unwavering patience and skill, her touch a comforting reassurance in the midst of his suffering. He realized then that even in the face of death, there was comfort to be found in human connection, in the simple act of being cared for.

He recovered slowly, the experience leaving an indelible mark on his soul. He looked at the world with different eyes, his perception sharpened by his brush with mortality. The vibrant colors of the spring blossoms, the sweet taste of freshly picked berries, the warmth of the summer sun—these simple pleasures now held an intensity, a depth of meaning that he had never before recognized.

Spring brought new life to Oakhaven, but it also brought sorrow. Old Elara, the village baker, passed away peacefully in her sleep. He attended her funeral, standing amongst the mourners, feeling the collective grief like a tangible presence in the air. The simplicity of the ceremony, the heartfelt words of remembrance, and the quiet dignity of the villagers as they laid her to rest spoke volumes about the human capacity for love and loss, a capacity that was both beautiful and heartbreaking. Elara's absence left a hole in the fabric of the village, a reminder that life, like the seasons, was a cycle of birth, growth, decay, and renewal.

He continued his life in Oakhaven, working alongside the villagers, sharing their joys and sorrows, learning from their experiences, and contributing to the community. He learned to appreciate the slow rhythm of rural life, the changing seasons, the cycles of sowing and reaping, and the quiet beauty of the natural world. He discovered a profound satisfaction in the simple act of creating something tangible, something that would outlast his own fleeting existence. He crafted furniture, his hands shaping the rough wood into elegant pieces, each piece imbued with his love for the craft and his appreciation for the beauty of simple things.

He witnessed the complexities of human relationships unfold around him. He saw friendships flourish and fray, loves blossom and wither, rivalries ignite and subside. He learned that human relationships were not simple equations, but intricate tapestries woven from threads of joy and sorrow, hope and disappointment, loyalty and betrayal. He saw the capacity for both profound generosity and shocking cruelty, coexisting within the same individual, a duality that surprised him even after his cosmic journeys. He realized the complexity wasn't a flaw, but rather, the very essence of being human.

He watched children grow, their laughter echoing through the village, their boundless energy a constant source of amusement and wonder. He saw the quiet dignity of aging, the wisdom that comes with years, the acceptance of mortality that accompanies the waning of life. He experienced the joys of celebration and the pains of loss, the exhilaration of success and the sting of failure. He learned that life was a complex, multifaceted experience, full of unexpected twists and turns, joys and sorrows, triumphs and defeats. He learned that there was beauty in both the light and darkness, the triumphs and failures, the highs and lows, all part of the richly woven fabric of existence.

He began to understand the true meaning of immortality. It wasn't about endless life, but about leaving a legacy, about the impact one had on the lives of others, about the difference one made in the world. He found a different kind of immortality in the memories he created, in the relationships he nurtured, and in the contributions he made to the community. His immortality resided not in a celestial throne, but in the hearts of the people of Oakhaven, in the quiet corners of the village that held traces of his life.

One evening, as he sat by the fire, watching the flames dance, he felt a profound sense of peace. He had journeyed from the heights of godhood to the depths of mortality, and in doing so, had found a deeper understanding of himself, of humanity, and of the universe. He had traded celestial power for human connection, cosmic understanding for earthly empathy, and found that the second exchange was far more rewarding. He was no longer a god, but he was complete. He was home.

The following summer, he decided to build a schoolhouse. The village children, currently educated in haphazard shifts by various willing adults, deserved better. He spent weeks poring over ancient texts, rediscovering forgotten architectural techniques, and adapting them to the resources available in Oakhaven. The villagers rallied around him, their collective effort a testament to their communal spirit. Men felled trees, women hauled stones, children carried water, their shared purpose knitting them together in a tapestry of cooperation. The air buzzed with the sounds of hammers, saws, and laughter, a symphony of human endeavor that resonated deeply within him. The simple act of building, he realized, was a profound expression of hope, a tangible manifestation of faith in the future.

He taught the children not only reading and writing but also the history of Oakhaven, weaving tales of their ancestors into the fabric of their education. He spoke of the hardships they had overcome, the triumphs they had celebrated, and the lessons they had learned. He instilled in them a sense of pride in their heritage, a sense of belonging to a community, and a sense of responsibility towards their future. He told them stories, not of celestial battles and cosmic horrors, but of everyday heroism, of kindness shown, of sacrifices made, of resilience in the face of adversity. He taught them to value not only intellect but also empathy, compassion, and courage.

Autumn arrived, painting the landscape in hues of gold, crimson, and russet. The new schoolhouse stood proudly on a small hill overlooking the village, a beacon of hope and learning. The children's laughter echoed within its walls, a sound he found more melodious than any celestial choir he had ever heard. He watched them from afar, a warmth spreading through his chest, a feeling of profound satisfaction washing over him. He had found a purpose, a connection to the mortal realm that transcended his past life, a fulfillment he had never experienced in his celestial reign.

The winter that followed was harsh, but the villagers endured it with remarkable fortitude. He spent his evenings by the fire, reading, writing, and sharing stories with the villagers. He learned their songs, their customs, and their folklore, and woven himself into the rich tapestry of their lives. He found solace in their company, in their shared experiences, in their unwavering belief in the human spirit. He saw their resilience in the face of hardship, their capacity for joy amidst sorrow, and their unwavering commitment to each other. This quiet strength, born of shared experience and mutual reliance, humbled him.

One particularly cold evening, as a blizzard raged outside, a young boy named Thomas came to his cottage, shivering and lost. He had wandered away from his family during a snowstorm. He was frightened, cold, and alone. He wrapped the boy in warm blankets, fed him hot soup, and reassured him that everything would be alright. As he held the child, feeling his small, fragile body trembling in his arms, a wave of profound empathy washed over him. He understood the vulnerability of human life, the fragility of existence, and the immense responsibility that came with caring for another being.

The following spring, he witnessed the miracle of rebirth firsthand. He helped plant the seeds, tend the crops, and harvest the bounty of the land. He learned the intricate dance between humans and nature, the delicate balance between taking and giving. He learned the importance of sustainability, the necessity of living in harmony with the earth. He realized that the connection between humans and their environment was not merely transactional but deeply spiritual, a relationship forged in mutual respect and interdependence.

He participated in the village festivals, celebrating the harvest, the solstices, and the equinoxes. He learned the ancient rituals, the songs, and the dances, immersing himself in the cultural heritage of Oakhaven. He felt the vibrant energy of the community, the collective joy and shared experience. The vibrant energy wasn't a magic born of celestial power, but something far more grounded and resonant—the collective spirit of a community.

He discovered the beauty of human creativity, the expression of the human spirit through art, music, and storytelling. He helped the villagers restore the old village well, its stones worn smooth by time, a testament to generations of human endeavor. He assisted in building a new community hall, where villagers could gather, celebrate, and share their stories. He helped restore the village's ancient library, breathing new life into forgotten tales and rediscovered knowledge.

He learned the value of patience, the importance of listening, and the significance of presence. He saw the beauty in imperfections, the elegance in simplicity. He learned that humanity's strength lay not in its ability to conquer but in its capacity for empathy, resilience, and compassion. He saw the profound interconnectedness of all living things, the delicate balance of the ecosystem, and the importance of respecting nature. He witnessed the transformative power of love, both in its capacity to heal and to destroy.

He helped mend fractured relationships, offering reconciliation and forgiveness. He saw the complexities of human relationships, their beauty and their pain, their strength and their fragility. He helped foster a spirit of cooperation and understanding within the community. He worked with the village elder to establish a system of conflict resolution based on empathy and understanding. He assisted in creating a support network for the elderly and the vulnerable.

He learned to appreciate the nuances of human emotions, their depth, and their intensity. He experienced the full spectrum of human experience—joy, sorrow, love, loss, hope, despair—and came to appreciate their complexity and their beauty. He came to understand that humanity's strength lay not in its ability to transcend its limitations but in its ability to embrace them, to learn from them, and to grow from them. His life wasn't a conquest, but a conversation, a participation in the continuous narrative of humanity.

He found that true power didn't lie in celestial authority or cosmic manipulation but in the quiet acts of kindness, in the strength of community, and in the enduring spirit of humanity. He had exchanged the weight of a god's responsibility for the warmth of human connection, and in that exchange, found something far more profound than immortality. He found belonging. He found peace. He found home. The cosmos held wonders, but Oakhaven held his heart. His journey wasn't over, not by a long shot, but its destination was finally clear: not some distant celestial throne, but the quiet, beating heart of humanity itself.

The following spring brought not only the thaw but a revelation. He'd spent the winter immersed in the lives of Oakhaven's people, learning their rhythms, their resilience, their quiet strength. He'd witnessed their capacity for both immense joy and crushing sorrow, their ability to find solace in community, and their unwavering belief in the face of adversity. And it had changed him, profoundly. The celestial battles, the cosmic horrors, the manipulations of the mortal plane – they all seemed distant, almost unreal, compared to the tangible reality of human experience. He'd felt the weight of a god's responsibility, the burden of celestial power, but now, he felt something else: humility.

His perspective shifted. His understanding of power, of influence, of divinity itself, underwent a transformation. He'd once wielded power with the detached authority of a celestial being, manipulating events from afar, orchestrating destinies with a casual disregard for the consequences. Now, he saw the intricate web of human interaction, the delicate balance of cause and effect, the unforeseen ripples that even the smallest action could create. The power he now sought wasn't the power to control, but the power to understand, to connect, to participate.

He travelled beyond Oakhaven, drawn by a newfound curiosity. He visited bustling cities, their streets teeming with life, their markets overflowing with goods from distant lands. He witnessed the soaring ambition of architects, the meticulous craftsmanship of artisans, and the passionate performances of musicians. He saw the vibrant tapestry of human culture in all its diversity, its contradictions, and its complexities.

He journeyed to isolated mountain villages, where people lived in harmony with nature, their lives deeply intertwined with the rhythms of the seasons. He learned their ancient traditions, their reverence for the land, and their intimate connection to the spiritual world. He learned that divinity wasn't confined to celestial realms; it resided in the beating heart of the earth, in the rustling leaves, in the whispering wind, in the unwavering strength of the human spirit. He understood that true power lay not in manipulating these forces but in respecting them, in living in harmony with them.

He ventured into vast, untamed forests, where he encountered ancient beings, creatures of myth and legend. He listened to their wisdom, their tales of a world beyond human comprehension, a world where the boundaries between reality and dream were blurred, where the lines between life and death were fluid. He learned the interconnectedness of all things, the intricate dance of life and death, and the delicate balance of the ecosystem. He realised that the destruction he'd witnessed in his previous existence, the chaos he'd unleashed, stemmed from a fundamental disregard for this delicate balance.

He spent time in bustling ports, witnessing the arrival and departure of ships from across the seven seas, each carrying stories of distant lands, of different cultures, of diverse perspectives. He learned the universality of the human experience, the common threads that bound humanity together despite its differences. He learned that while each culture held unique customs and traditions, the fundamental human emotions – love, loss, joy, sorrow, hope, despair – were universal. These were the fundamental building blocks of humanity, irrespective of language, geography, or culture.

He journeyed to desolate wastelands, remnants of ancient battles, where he encountered survivors, clinging to life in the harsh environment, their resilience a testament to the indomitable spirit of humankind. He saw the raw power of human endurance, the capacity to survive even in the face of overwhelming odds. It wasn't a passive survival; it was an active striving, a fierce clinging to life and hope. He learned that true strength wasn't about conquering or controlling, but about enduring, adapting, and preserving.

In each place, he sought not to impose his will, but to learn, to observe, to understand. He listened to the stories of ordinary people, their triumphs and their failures, their joys and their sorrows. He learned to see the world through their eyes, to feel their emotions, to share their experiences. He learned that the most profound magic wasn't about manipulating the elements or summoning celestial beings; it was about connecting with the human heart, about fostering empathy, about inspiring hope.

He helped people heal from past traumas, both physical and emotional. He witnessed the transformative power of forgiveness, of reconciliation, of finding solace in community. He helped rebuild shattered communities, fostering a sense of hope and shared purpose. He learned that healing wasn't about erasing the past, but about acknowledging it, learning from it, and moving forward. His celestial powers became tools for healing, not weapons of control. He used his ability to manipulate the elements not to inflict destruction, but to restore balance, to mend the wounds of the earth, and to rebuild what had been broken.

His newfound understanding deeply influenced his decisions as a god. He no longer saw humanity as a pawn in a cosmic game, but as a vibrant, resilient, and complex tapestry of individual lives, each one precious and unique. He understood the folly of imposing his will upon them; his power was now a force for guiding, assisting, and protecting. He had learned that true power resided not in control but in service, not in dominance but in partnership. He realised that true divinity lay not in celestial authority but in empathetic understanding. He had seen the human heart, its capacity for both great darkness and radiant light, and he understood that his role was not to judge, but to nurture, to guide, and to protect.

He continued his work, not as a supreme god ruling from a distant throne, but as a participant in the ongoing narrative of humanity. His celestial realm became less a place of power and more a sanctuary, a place of reflection and learning, a place where he could draw upon the wisdom gained from his experiences among mortals. He forged alliances with cosmic entities, not through coercion, but through understanding, through respect, and through a shared vision of a world where both the celestial and the mortal realms could coexist in harmony. He led by example, showing through his actions the importance of compassion, understanding, and respect for all life, irrespective of its form or origin.

His journey was far from over. His understanding was continuously evolving, his perspective deepening with every experience. But the lessons he learned in the mortal coil—the beauty of human connection, the resilience of the human spirit, the transformative power of empathy—had irrevocably changed him. He had found not just a new purpose, but a new definition of divinity, one grounded not in celestial authority, but in the quiet, beating heart of humanity itself.

The celestial courts shimmered with an unfamiliar light, a gentle luminescence that reflected not the harsh brilliance of absolute power, but the soft glow of understanding. He stood before the assembled pantheon, his family gathered close, their presence a comforting anchor in the swirling vortex of divine energy. His gaze swept across the assembled gods and goddesses, their faces a mixture of curiosity and apprehension. His transformation, subtle yet profound, was palpable. The rigid authority, the detached aloofness that had once characterized his demeanor, had softened, replaced by a quiet strength born of empathy and experience.

He began to speak, his voice resonating with a newfound resonance, carrying the weight not of celestial decree, but of shared experience. He recounted his journey through the mortal coil, not as a tale of conquest, but as a pilgrimage of discovery. He spoke of the bustling cities, the quiet villages, the untamed forests, the desolate wastelands—each a chapter in a grand narrative of human resilience, creativity, and unwavering hope. He described the laughter of children, the quiet wisdom of elders, and the unyielding spirit of those who clung to life in the face of adversity. He spoke of the intricate tapestry of human experience, of the common threads that bound humanity together, despite its diverse cultures and traditions. He painted a picture not of weakness, but of profound strength, a strength that lay not in the wielding of celestial power, but in the quiet endurance of the human spirit.

His words resonated deeply within the assembled deities. Many had viewed mortals as insignificant pawns, their lives mere threads in the grand cosmic tapestry. But his words revealed a different perspective, a vision of humanity's inherent worth, its capacity for both immense darkness and breathtaking light. His descriptions of the quiet acts of kindness, the selfless sacrifices, and the unwavering hope that he had witnessed among mortals had chipped away at their ingrained prejudices, revealing a deeper appreciation for the mortal realm.

His leadership style underwent a profound transformation. Gone were the arbitrary decrees and the forceful impositions of his will. His governance now emphasized collaboration, negotiation, and mutual respect. He established councils composed of representatives from each of the seven reptilian tribes, granting them a voice in the governance of the celestial realms. He fostered dialogue between the various factions, encouraging mutual understanding and compromise. He championed initiatives aimed at promoting peace and prosperity throughout the cosmos, focusing on fostering cooperation and shared progress rather than asserting dominance. His celestial powers were now directed towards nurturing growth, healing wounds, and restoring balance, rather than inflicting destruction.

He frequently descended to the mortal plane, not to impose his will, but to observe, to learn, and to offer assistance. He worked alongside mortal healers, collaborating on innovative methods of treating disease and alleviating suffering. He helped rebuild shattered communities, using his celestial powers to restore damaged ecosystems and infrastructure. He aided those affected by natural disasters, offering not only material assistance but also spiritual solace and emotional support. He actively sought the wisdom of mortals, recognizing that their experience and perspectives enriched his own understanding of the cosmos. He listened to their stories, their fears, their hopes, and their dreams, allowing them to shape his decisions and influence the direction of his governance.

One day, he found himself in a small village nestled within a valley, where he encountered a group of artisans crafting intricate tapestries. He didn't command them to change their methods or dictate their designs; instead, he sat with them, learning their techniques, sharing stories, and offering gentle suggestions. He marvelled at their creativity, their patience, and their dedication to their craft. Through them, he learned that even the simplest acts of creation could hold profound beauty and meaning.

Later, in a bustling city, he visited a hospital, where he observed the tireless efforts of healers tending to the sick and injured. He offered his assistance, using his powers to heal the most critically injured, not with a wave of divine power that minimized the effort of mortal healers, but by working alongside them, augmenting their skills and empowering them to do more than they thought possible. He showed his appreciation for their dedication and their unwavering commitment to compassion, reminding him of the resilience of the human spirit.

In the celestial realms, his interactions with other deities changed as well. He engaged in debates, not with an air of superiority, but with a genuine desire to find common ground. He listened to dissenting opinions, acknowledging their validity and incorporating them into his decision-making process. He fostered a sense of community and shared purpose, transforming the celestial courts into a place of collaboration and mutual respect. He demonstrated that true power lay not in controlling others but in fostering growth, understanding, and harmony.

He even revisited the sites of ancient battles, the desolate wastelands where the echoes of past conflicts still lingered. He didn't seek to erase the past, but to learn from it, using his powers to heal the scars upon the land and to foster reconciliation among the surviving factions. He worked to establish memorials, not to celebrate victory, but to honor the sacrifices made and to encourage lasting peace. He showed that true strength lay not in conquest, but in reconciliation, in healing, and in remembering the past to prevent its repetition.

His actions spoke louder than any decree. His leadership was not a matter of commanding, but of guiding, inspiring, and nurturing. He continued to learn, to grow, to evolve, ever mindful of the lessons he'd learned in the mortal coil. He had discovered that true divinity lay not in wielding cosmic power, but in fostering empathy, compassion, and understanding – in recognizing the inherent worth of every being, celestial or mortal, and in striving to create a universe where all could flourish. His journey was far from over, but he had found a path, a way to balance the cosmic and mortal realms, to weave a tapestry of existence where the threads of both were intertwined, strong and beautiful. His reign was not one of absolute power, but of collaborative guidance, a testament to the transformative power of a renewed perspective.

12

The Celestial Council

The air in the Celestial Council hall hummed with a low, resonant thrum, a symphony of celestial energies subtly shifting and swirling. Rows upon rows of deities, their forms shimmering with an ethereal light, occupied the polished obsidian seats, their expressions ranging from bored indifference to rapt attention. The seven reptilian tribes, their scaled bodies gleaming under the soft, diffused light, were represented by their chosen councilors—imposing figures, each radiating power and ancient wisdom, seated amongst the more traditionally humanoid gods. My family sat beside me, their presence a silent reassurance, a constant source of strength. My mother, her eyes twinkling with amusement and pride, offered a slight nod. My siblings, their faces etched with a mixture of awe and concern, watched me with unwavering support.

The initial debates were predictable. The Goddess of Storms, her normally tempestuous nature seemingly subdued by the gravity of the occasion, argued for a renewed campaign against the encroaching shadows from the Outer Void, a threat that had plagued the cosmos for eons. Her words were sharp, her arguments forceful, backed by centuries of experience battling the cosmic horror that threatened to unravel all of creation. She presented detailed reports and intricate charts depicting the encroaching darkness and pleaded for immediate action. Her voice resonated with a primal urgency, a warning against complacency.

Opposing her was the God of Abundance, a jovial deity whose domain encompassed the fertile lands and bountiful harvests of the mortal realms. He argued against immediate conflict, suggesting a more diplomatic approach, emphasizing the need to understand the nature of the shadows before resorting to violence. He spoke of fostering understanding, of finding common ground instead of resorting to war. He proposed a research initiative, a study to understand the motivations and nature of these encroaching forces, a quest for knowledge rather than conflict. His words, though gentle, carried the weight of his considerable power and influence, calming the tempestuous energy in the hall.

The ensuing debate was passionate, a clash of ideologies mirroring the eternal struggle between order and chaos, defense and diplomacy. Arguments flew back and forth, crackling with divine energy. Each deity voiced their concerns, their perspectives shaped by their unique domains and experiences. I watched and listened, observing the interplay of power, the intricate dance of influence and persuasion. My perspective, shaped by my journey through the mortal realm, allowed me to see beyond the polarized viewpoints, to perceive the nuances of the situation that eluded many of the assembled deities.

My intervention, when it came, was not one of forceful decree but a gentle suggestion, a proposal for a balanced approach. I argued for a combination of both defense and diplomacy, for a strategy that embraced both the need for preparedness and the potential for understanding. I proposed a three-pronged approach: strengthening our defenses against the shadows while simultaneously engaging in diplomatic efforts to establish communication and committing significant resources to researching their nature and origins. My words, born of experience, carried a weight of authority, not from my inherited power but from the wisdom I gained during my transformation.

The ensuing discussions revolved around the logistics of this three-pronged approach. The allocation of resources, the selection of diplomatic envoys, and the design of the research initiative were debated in detail, each point discussed with careful consideration. The reptilian councilors, with their centuries of experience in navigating complex political landscapes, played crucial roles in mediating the debate, ensuring all voices were heard and all concerns addressed.

The debate spilled over into a second session. This time, the focus shifted to internal matters—the allocation of celestial resources to the mortal realms. The Goddess of Justice argued for a strict system of meritocracy, based on the progress and righteousness of each mortal nation. Her logic was undeniable—reward those who acted justly and prospered, and punish those who did not. However, the God of Mercy countered this proposal, pointing out the inherent inequalities in the mortal world, factors outside of any individual nation's control that led to hardship and suffering. He proposed a system of assistance for struggling nations and regions, aid that was neither a reward nor a punishment but a gesture of compassion.

The God of Knowledge proposed a different angle altogether, suggesting a focus on assisting the advancement of knowledge and technology in the mortal realms, creating a self-sustaining cycle of improvement. He argued that by providing the tools for self-reliance and progress, the celestial beings could have a longer-term positive impact on humanity than simply handing out gifts based on arbitrary judgment.

This debate highlighted the complexities of governing across vastly different scales and cultural values. The discussion revealed the inherent tension between universal laws and localized needs, between the pursuit of justice and the practice of mercy, and between the ideals of self-reliance and the obligations of compassion.

My input again sought a balance, proposing a tiered system that combined elements of all three perspectives. A core amount of resources would be allocated based on merit and progress, a significant portion would be directed towards assisting those in need, and a substantial investment would be directed towards fostering knowledge and education across all mortal nations. It was a complex, multi-faceted plan, requiring careful coordination and ongoing assessment. But it was also a plan that reflected a deep understanding of the mortal realm, a recognition of its complexity, and a commitment to fostering progress and prosperity for all, regardless of their societal standing or current circumstances.

The final session of the council addressed a matter of cosmic significance—the fate of a dying star, a celestial body whose demise threatened to destabilize a vast region of the cosmos. Several deities proposed to simply let it die, arguing that such events were inevitable and that interfering might cause more harm than good. Others suggested an intervention, perhaps utilizing celestial energy to prolong the star's life or to mitigate the damage from its eventual collapse. The risks were substantial, the potential consequences immeasurable.

After a long and careful deliberation, we decided on a strategy that combined both caution and proactive intervention. We would not attempt to prevent the star's death, but we would deploy celestial energies to guide its collapse, minimizing the potential disruption to surrounding systems and stellar bodies. This required a complex maneuver involving a coordinated effort of several powerful deities, a delicate dance of celestial energies, and a collaboration across traditional divisions and conflicting viewpoints.

The Celestial Council adjourned with a sense of accomplishment, a weary acceptance that even in the celestial realms, the paths towards harmony and progress were complex and frequently fraught with difficulty. But the atmosphere was one of unity, collaboration, and shared purpose. The decisions made were not simply decrees but carefully considered outcomes of extensive discussion, reflecting not only the wisdom of the assembled deities but also the profound influence of the mortal journey I had undergone. The very nature of governance in the celestial realms had shifted—from a system of rigid authority to one of collaborative governance. It was a testament to the transformative power of empathy, understanding, and the integration of both celestial power and mortal wisdom. My journey was far from over, yet the subtle shift in the celestial fabric, the quiet revolution in governance, spoke of a future far brighter than anyone had dared to imagine.

The adjournment of the Celestial Council did not signal the end of my responsibilities. Maintaining balance, I quickly discovered, was a ceaseless endeavor, a constant dance across the precarious fault lines of the cosmos. My first task was to oversee the implementation of the three-pronged approach to the encroaching shadows from the Outer Void. Strengthening defenses involved bolstering the celestial wards protecting the mortal realms, a process that required intricate manipulations of magical energies and the careful weaving of protective spells across vast distances. This was not simply a matter of reinforcing existing barriers; it involved adapting the defenses to the evolving nature of the shadow threat, a constant arms race against an unknown enemy. I spent days consulting with specialists in celestial engineering and arcane warfare, poring over ancient texts, and drawing on my own unique experiences to devise new strategies and techniques.

The diplomatic initiative proved equally challenging. Establishing contact with the shadowy entities was fraught with peril. We had to select envoys carefully, individuals who possessed both immense power and remarkable diplomatic skills. The chosen representatives were a diverse group—a serene, ancient oracle known for her uncanny ability to perceive hidden truths; a cunning, quick-witted trickster god capable of navigating even the most treacherous negotiations; and a seasoned warrior goddess known for her unwavering resolve and surprising capacity for empathy. Their mission was fraught with uncertainty; they were venturing into the unknown, into a realm of cosmic horror where even the slightest miscalculation could have devastating consequences. I provided them with enchanted artifacts and protective amulets designed to shield them from the corruptive influence of the shadows and to aid them in their communication efforts. Their journey was meticulously tracked, and their progress was reported back to me on a daily basis.

The research initiative proved the most intellectually stimulating, yet equally challenging. We assembled a team of the cosmos' most brilliant minds—mathematicians, physicists, historians, theologians, and even philosophers. Their task was nothing less than to unravel the mysteries of the Outer Void, to understand the origin, nature, and motives of the encroaching shadows. This required a multidisciplinary approach, combining rigorous scientific inquiry with the mystical insights of ancient prophecies and forgotten lore. The research team established observatories in the far reaches of space, deploying celestial probes to collect data on the shadows' composition and behavior. They delved into ancient texts, seeking clues to their origins, interpreting cryptic prophecies, and deciphering the enigmatic language of the stars. They debated their findings, argued over interpretations, and challenged one another's theories, their collective intellect forging a path towards understanding, a journey of discovery that was as perilous as it was rewarding.

My efforts to maintain balance extended far beyond the immediate threat from the Outer Void. The mortal realms were a cauldron of conflict and change, demanding my constant attention. I mediated disputes between warring nations, using my influence to foster diplomacy and peaceful resolutions. I intervened in natural disasters, using my power to mitigate the damage and alleviate suffering. I inspired acts of heroism and courage in times of great need. I encouraged the pursuit of knowledge and innovation, fostering technological advancements and cultural exchanges. My interactions with the mortal realms were not limited to resolving crises; I also spent time observing the rise and fall of empires, witnessing the evolution of human societies, and experiencing the full spectrum of human emotions.

My journey took me to a myriad of diverse settings—from the bustling marketplaces of vibrant cities to the serene tranquility of hidden monasteries. I witnessed the beauty of untouched nature in the vast wilderness areas and the cold, harsh landscapes of forgotten ruins, haunted by echoes of ancient civilizations. I interacted with mortals from all walks of life—rulers and peasants, scholars and artisans, warriors and healers. I learned from their experiences, their struggles, and their triumphs, gaining a profound understanding of the human condition.

One such journey brought me to the edge of the Whispering Woods, a vast and ancient forest shrouded in mist and mystery, where ancient spirits and forgotten deities roamed. Here, I encountered a conflict between the woodland spirits and a group of human settlers who were encroaching upon their sacred grounds. The woodland spirits, guardians of the forest's balance, were enraged by the destruction of their habitat, while the settlers believed they had a right to the land for their survival. I spent several days mediating between them, seeking a compromise that would ensure the coexistence of both humans and spirits. Ultimately, I managed to negotiate an agreement, designating a portion of the forest as a protected sanctuary for the spirits while ensuring that the settlers had access to the resources they needed. This required a delicate balancing act, a testament to the importance of understanding the perspectives of all parties involved.

Another critical aspect of maintaining balance lay in overseeing the distribution of celestial resources. The allocation system I had proposed was complex and required constant monitoring and adjustment. Inevitably, disputes arose over the fairness of the system and conflicts over resource allocation between various mortal nations and regions. The most challenging case involved two neighboring kingdoms locked in a centuries-old feud, each claiming rightful ownership over a vital river system. My solution involved a complex arrangement of water rights, the construction of irrigation systems, and the implementation of conflict-resolution mechanisms. It was a long and arduous process, requiring not only my intervention but also the assistance of numerous celestial beings and the cooperation of the kingdoms' leadership. However, the success of this endeavor resulted in the establishment of a peaceful treaty and set an example for others.

The constant pressure of maintaining balance often left me exhausted, but the rewards were immense. I witnessed the growth of civilizations, the flourishing of art and culture, and the advancement of knowledge. I saw the positive impact of celestial intervention, both on a grand scale and in individual lives. I felt a profound satisfaction in witnessing the harmony that emerged from the resolution of conflict, the peace that resulted from my efforts. The very fabric of reality was shifting, becoming more harmonious under my guidance, a subtle shift that was both rewarding and terrifying in its implications. The responsibility was immense, the task seemingly endless, yet I pressed on, driven by a sense of purpose, a conviction that my work was essential for the continued flourishing of the cosmos. For the balance, once lost, would not be easily recovered. My work, then, was not merely to rule, but to ensure the ceaseless rhythm of existence continued its harmonious dance, a dance I would strive to lead for as long as it would take.

The whispers of discord, faint at first, soon swelled into a cacophony. My role as mediator, a seemingly simple task initially, morphed into a relentless juggling act, each ball a complex conflict threatening to unravel the delicate tapestry of existence. The Celestial Council, despite its pronouncements, could not resolve every issue; the intricacies of mortal affairs, the tangled threads of ambition, resentment, and ancient grudges, demanded a more hands-on approach.

My first intervention involved the warring factions of the Sylvani, a race of arboreal beings whose ancient forests spanned vast swathes of the eastern continent. For centuries, the Sunwood and Shadowwood clans had battled for dominance, their conflict fueled by a rivalry as old as their shared history. The dispute centered on a mystical spring, the source of both life-giving water and potent magic, its control vital to the survival and power of each clan. The battlefield was a shattered landscape, a testament to their protracted war, the air thick with the scent of decay and the lingering echoes of magical blasts.

To reach a resolution, I didn't simply descend from the heavens with pronouncements of peace. Instead, I spent weeks immersed in their culture, learning their history, and understanding the root of their animosity. It was a deeply personal journey, far removed from the sterile debates of the Celestial Council. I walked among the Sylvani, attending their ceremonies, observing their customs, and even partaking in their rituals. I sought to understand their perspectives, to feel the weight of their history, and to connect with their emotions on a level deeper than mere observation. It was a process that required patience, empathy, and a deep understanding of their unique sensibilities.

The heart of the conflict lay not in any current grievance, but in a long-forgotten prophecy foretelling the dominance of one clan over the other. This prophecy, interpreted differently by each side, fueled their unending conflict, turning even the slightest disagreement into a renewed battle. My solution was not to disregard the prophecy but to reinterpret it. I showed them, through careful analysis of the ancient texts and a subtle manipulation of the very magic that fueled their conflict, that the prophecy was not a prophecy of conquest, but of unity, of a harmonious merging of their cultures and powers, a symbiosis that would amplify their strength rather than diminish it. The process was painstaking, requiring numerous private meetings, emotional appeals, and displays of my own power, subtly nudging them towards a different interpretation of their shared destiny.

The transformation was slow but noticeable. The once-fierce warriors began to collaborate, sharing their knowledge of ancient magic and forestry. The once-hostile borderlands began to heal, the scarred earth slowly recovering under the combined efforts of both clans. The mystical spring, once a source of conflict, became a symbol of unity, its waters shared equally between Sunwood and Shadowwood, its magic utilized for the betterment of their combined society. The ultimate success wasn't simply the cessation of hostilities but the forging of a new identity, a unified Sylvani culture stronger and more vibrant than ever before.

Another challenge arose in the vast, shimmering expanse of the Aethel, a realm governed by the capricious and powerful Elementals. These beings, manifestations of pure elemental energy, frequently clashed over their respective territories, their conflicts causing earthquakes, volcanic eruptions, and catastrophic weather events. Their power was immense, exceeding even the combined strength of many of the celestial beings. Their temperament, however, was unpredictable and often irrational. Diplomacy alone would be useless; a more assertive, even forceful, intervention was required.

The issue arose from a territorial dispute, a clash between the fiery Salamanders and the watery Undines. Their battleground was a massive volcanic island, an area of immense geological instability, where their conflicting energies caused violent tremors and eruptions. The devastation threatened neighboring mortal lands, causing widespread suffering and displacement. I could not simply ignore their conflict; the consequences would be disastrous.

My approach involved a combination of strategic manipulation and raw power. I didn't directly engage in battle, instead using my influence to subtly alter the flow of elemental energies, creating a buffer zone between the two factions. I employed a complex array of enchantments, diverting some of their power into less destructive channels, subtly guiding their energies towards more productive endeavors. This wasn't a suppression of their power but a redirection, a channeling of their chaotic forces into a more balanced state.

The process involved arduous negotiations, requiring me to understand the elemental language, interpreting their subtle shifts in energy as a form of communication. It was a dance of wills, a delicate balancing act between firmness and diplomacy. The Salamanders, fiery and impulsive, needed a demonstration of my power, a subtle reminder of my authority. The Undines, fluid and enigmatic, required a deeper understanding of their emotional state, a soothing influence to calm their turbulent energies.

This involved a significant risk. Miscalculating, even slightly, could unleash an unimaginable catastrophe. But through careful manipulation and skillful negotiation, I managed to establish a fragile truce. The volcanic activity subsided, the tremors ceased, and the warring factions withdrew, albeit reluctantly, into separate territories. The success, however, was fragile. It required continued monitoring and subtle adjustments, a constant vigilance to prevent any future conflicts. The resolution, therefore, was not an end, but a beginning—a constant and ongoing management of elemental energies, a testament to the challenges inherent in maintaining equilibrium in such a turbulent realm. The long-term solution demanded a thorough understanding of the elemental forces and a commitment to continued monitoring and subtle interventions. This was a far cry from the simple meditation I'd initially envisioned. The cosmos, I was learning, was far more complex, far more challenging, and far more demanding than I had initially imagined.

The weight of governance pressed down upon me, a tangible burden that dwarfed even the celestial authority I wielded. The Celestial Council, a body I'd once viewed with detached reverence, now felt like a distant echo, a faint murmur in the maelstrom of daily concerns. The ethereal debates, the carefully worded decrees—they were insufficient, mere drops in the ocean of mortal affairs. The true work lay in the mundane, the intricate, the agonizingly slow process of mediating conflicts, resolving disputes, and guiding disparate populations towards a semblance of harmony.

My next significant challenge arose within the shimmering expanse of the Azure Sea, a vast, unpredictable realm teeming with aquatic life of unimaginable variety and power. The Merfolk, a race of sentient beings inhabiting sprawling coral cities and deep-sea trenches, were locked in a protracted conflict with the Kryll, a civilization of intelligent cephalopods residing in the abyssal plains. Their conflict wasn't one of simple territorial disputes; it was a clash of civilizations, a philosophical war over control of the ocean's resources, the very essence of their existence.

The Merfolk, with their humanoid forms and advanced magical abilities, relied on sunlight filtering through the upper waters, cultivating kelp forests and harnessing the power of ocean currents. The Kryll, possessing a collective consciousness and sophisticated bioluminescent technology, thrived in the perpetual darkness of the deep, extracting rare minerals and harnessing the geothermal vents for energy. Their conflict was not merely a battle for territory but a fundamental disagreement over the very definition of resource management, a clash between surface-dwelling sustainability and deep-sea exploitation.

The Celestial Council had, as usual, attempted mediation. Their pronouncements of peace, however, fell on deaf ears. The Merfolk, resentful of Kryll encroachment on their traditional fishing grounds, saw the deep-sea mining as a sacrilegious violation of the ocean's sanctity. The Kryll, in turn, viewed the Merfolk's reliance on surface level resources as inefficient and unsustainable, arguing that their methods were depleting the ocean's resources for a small portion of its inhabitants. The issue lay not in resolving a single point of contention, but in bridging a fundamental philosophical chasm.

My approach differed significantly from the Celestial Council's detached pronouncements. I delved into the depths, spending months immersed in the vastly different cultures of both societies. I learned their languages, their histories, their traditions—the intricate tapestry of their belief systems and social structures. I discovered that the conflict was rooted in a misunderstanding of each other's needs, fueled by ancient myths and cultural biases. The Merfolk's perception of the Kryll as mindless destroyers was a misunderstanding of the Kryll's sophisticated resource management techniques, while the Kryll's view of the Merfolk as wasteful and short-sighted stemmed from a lack of understanding of surface-level ecosystems.

The solution involved more than just mediating a treaty; it involved fostering mutual understanding and respect. I helped create channels of communication, establishing a system of exchange and collaboration. The Merfolk learned from the Kryll's resource management techniques, understanding the potential for sustainable deep-sea mining. The Kryll, in turn, discovered the delicate balance of surface-level ecosystems and the potential for collaboration in preserving biodiversity. The result was a remarkable transformation. Rather than conflict, a symbiotic relationship emerged, where the two societies leveraged each other's strengths, leading to a more sustainable and prosperous existence for both. The challenge lay not just in resolving the immediate conflict but in building lasting bridges of understanding between two vastly different civilizations.

Another crisis arose in the vast, desolate plains known as the Whispering Wastes, a land ravaged by centuries of conflict between the nomadic tribes of the Sandwalkers and the technologically advanced city-state of Aethelgard. The Sandwalkers, fierce warriors living in harmony with the harsh desert environment, were fiercely independent, their culture built on freedom and self-reliance. Aethelgard, on the other hand, was a burgeoning metropolis, its advanced technology and sophisticated weaponry posing a significant threat to the nomadic tribes' traditional way of life. Their conflict was rooted in differing views of land ownership and resource allocation; Aethelgard saw the Wastes as an untapped resource, while the Sandwalkers viewed the land as sacred, a heritage passed down through generations.

The attempts of the Celestial Council to broker peace had failed spectacularly, resulting in increased hostility and escalated conflict. I understood that a simple diplomatic solution would prove insufficient. This required a deeper understanding of the cultural nuances and a strategic approach that balanced negotiation and diplomacy with a display of power.

My strategy involved a long-term engagement, building trust with both the Sandwalkers and the leaders of Aethelgard. I spent months traveling with the Sandwalkers, participating in their rituals, learning their customs, and sharing their hardships, earning their respect and establishing a bond of mutual understanding. Simultaneously, I engaged in diplomatic talks with Aethelgard's ruling council, explaining the Sandwalkers' perspective and demonstrating the potential for collaborative development rather than exploitative conquest.

The solution involved a novel approach—the creation of a mutually beneficial partnership. I facilitated the development of technologies that allowed Aethelgard to extract resources sustainably while respecting the Sandwalkers' ancestral lands. In exchange for access to specific resources, Aethelgard provided the Sandwalkers with advanced technologies and medical care, improving their quality of life without compromising their traditional way of life. This partnership fostered mutual respect and interdependence, shifting the dynamic from conflict to cooperation. It was a testament to the power of understanding, negotiation, and a commitment to finding solutions that respected the diverse perspectives and needs of all involved. The resulting harmony between the Sandwalkers and Aethelgard wasn't simply the absence of conflict but the birth of a new era of cooperation, a symbiotic relationship forged through mutual understanding and respect.

The challenges continued, each more complex, more demanding than the last. The weight of governance was not simply a burden but a crucible, forging my understanding of diplomacy, strategy, and the intricacies of cosmic influence. The success of each intervention wasn't solely due to my powers but to the understanding, compromise, and adaptability of the diverse beings I governed. It was a constant learning process, an unending journey of negotiation, adaptation, and the unwavering pursuit of peace, a path often far removed from the detached pronouncements of the Celestial Council. The cosmos, in all its chaotic glory, demanded more than pronouncements—it demanded understanding, empathy, and a relentless commitment to balance.

From my vantage point atop the Obsidian Spire, the world stretched out before me like a breathtaking tapestry woven from starlight and shadow. Below, the sprawling cities pulsed with life, their lights twinkling like fallen stars against the velvet night. The Azure Sea shimmered, its surface a mirror reflecting the celestial bodies, a testament to the fragile peace I had brokered between the Merfolk and the Kryll. Even the Whispering Wastes, once a desolate expanse scarred by conflict, showed signs of rejuvenation, the nomadic tribes of the Sandwalkers and the citizens of Aethelgard coexisting in a tentative yet promising harmony.

Yet, the tranquility was deceptive. The cosmos, in its infinite wisdom or capricious cruelty, had a penchant for unsettling the balance. New challenges, as intricate and demanding as those I had already overcome, loomed on the horizon. The whispers of discontent, faint at first, were growing louder, hinting at brewing conflicts that threatened to unravel the carefully constructed peace.

The most pressing concern stemmed from the shadowed corners of the world, places untouched by the light of my governance. The seven reptilian tribes, ruled by their winged overlords, stirred restlessly. Their ancient rivalries, simmering for millennia, threatened to boil over, dragging the entire world into a maelstrom of chaos. The winged beings, once content with their secluded dominion, now seemed to harbor ambitions that extended far beyond their ancestral lands. Their whispers of forgotten prophecies and the stirring of slumbering cosmic entities sent shivers down my spine. The very fabric of reality seemed to be fraying at the edges, the delicate balance I had so painstakingly established trembling under the weight of looming threats.

Their ambitions, however, were not merely territorial. The winged beings, through their intricate rituals and dark magic, sought to manipulate the very currents of time and space, to unravel the fabric of reality itself and reshape it according to their own twisted desires. Their ancient texts, filled with cryptic prophecies and diagrams of forbidden knowledge, spoke of a cosmic entity, a primordial being of unimaginable power, trapped within the heart of a dying star. They believed that by releasing this entity, they could reshape the world in their image, ushering in an era of absolute dominance.

Their plans, however, were fraught with peril. The primordial entity was not a mere servant; it was a force of nature, a being of pure chaos, whose release could unravel the very fabric of existence. The risk was immeasurable, the consequences potentially catastrophic. I knew that I had to act decisively, but my intervention would require a delicate balance of power and diplomacy. The Celestial Council, while helpful in small-scale conflicts, was ill-equipped to handle a cosmic threat of this magnitude. Their methods of detached pronouncements were useless here; this was a battle for the very soul of reality.

Beyond the immediate threat posed by the reptilian tribes, a deeper, more insidious danger lurked in the shadows. The very fabric of reality itself seemed to be fraying at the edges, threatened by the incursion of entities from realms beyond human comprehension. These were not mere creatures of myth or legend; they were forces of pure cosmic horror, their motivations as inscrutable as their power was terrifying. Their influence was subtle at first, barely perceptible, but its presence was undeniable. Dreams became nightmares, reality warped and twisted, and sanity itself was a fragile thing, easily shattered under their gaze.

These entities, unlike the reptilian tribes, were not motivated by ambition or conquest, but by an incomprehensible hunger, a cosmic appetite for destruction and annihilation. They existed outside the laws of cause and effect, their actions unpredictable and their motives unknown. Combating them was not simply a matter of force or strategy; it required a profound understanding of the cosmos itself, a knowledge that extended far beyond the grasp of even the most powerful mages.

My journey forward was not merely a quest for peace and stability, but a confrontation with the very limits of my being, a test of my understanding and mastery of the cosmic forces that shaped my reality. The path ahead was fraught with peril, a maelstrom of cosmic horror and ancient prophecies, a battle for the very soul of existence.

Yet, I was not alone. My family, my loyal companions, stood by my side, their unwavering support a beacon in the encroaching darkness. We were a beacon of hope amidst the encroaching chaos, a symbol of resistance against the cosmic horror that threatened to engulf our world.

The Celestial Council, despite their limitations, remained a valuable ally. Their knowledge of celestial laws and cosmic entities, though often theoretical, provided invaluable insights into the looming threats. Their wisdom, though somewhat detached, proved invaluable in navigating the treacherous currents of cosmic politics. Their pronouncements, while often insufficient, provided a foundation upon which I could build my strategies.

My strategy involved multiple fronts. First, I would need to address the immediate threat posed by the reptilian tribes and their winged overlords. This would involve a combination of diplomacy, strategic alliances, and the calculated use of power. It would require not just military prowess but a deep understanding of their culture, their motivations, and their fears.

Simultaneously, I would need to address the insidious incursion of cosmic entities. This would require a different approach altogether, one that involved exploring the realms beyond our own, seeking alliances with entities that could potentially assist us in combating the encroaching horror. This was a perilous undertaking, as it risked exposing our world to even greater dangers, but it was a risk I was willing to take.

The path forward was long and arduous, filled with unpredictable challenges and the constant threat of failure. But the stakes were too high, the consequences of inaction too dire, to consider anything less than a total commitment. The future of our world, the fate of countless beings, rested upon my shoulders, a weight that dwarfed even the celestial authority I wielded. Yet, I stood resolute, my resolve unwavering, prepared to face whatever challenges lay ahead, knowing that the fight for the future was a fight worth fighting, a fight that would determine the very destiny of our world.

The Obsidian Spire, once a symbol of my own ascension, now stood as a watchtower, a vantage point from which I could survey the unfolding cosmic drama. The journey ahead was uncertain, fraught with peril, but my spirit remained unbroken. For I was not merely a god; I was a protector, a guardian, a shepherd guiding his flock through the darkest nights of the cosmos. The path forward was not merely a path of conquest or control, but a path of understanding, compassion, and the unwavering pursuit of a future where harmony and balance reigned supreme, even in the face of cosmic horror. The challenge lay not in the power I wielded, but in the wisdom I could muster, the empathy I could extend, and the alliances I could forge to protect the delicate balance of existence in this vibrant, yet constantly threatened, world. The future, although uncertain, held both the promise of a brighter dawn and the threat of an unimaginable darkness. The choice, the burden, and the ultimate responsibility rested solely on me, the supreme god of gods.

13

The Tapestry of Fate

The air hummed with a low, resonant thrum, a vibration that resonated not just in my ears but deep within my very bones. Before me, the Hall of Whispers stretched into an impossible infinity, its walls shimmering with an ethereal luminescence. This was no ordinary place; this was the nexus of fate, a mystical realm where the threads of time intertwined, where the past, present, and future were not linear progressions but a vibrant, interconnected tapestry.

Each thread, shimmering with its own unique light, represented a life, a moment, or a decision. Some glowed brightly, vibrant and strong, while others were faint, almost extinguished, whispers of lives lived and lost. The sheer complexity of it was breathtaking, overwhelming. To comprehend it all would be to grasp the entirety of existence, a task beyond even my divine abilities.

Yet, I had come seeking answers. The recent unrest, the subtle shifts in cosmic energies, the growing whispers of impending doom—all pointed towards a convergence, a point in time where the threads of fate would intertwine in a way that threatened to unravel the very fabric of reality. My investigation began not with a grand gesture, but with a single, seemingly insignificant thread.

It pulsed with a faint, crimson light, a thread that belonged to a young woman named Lyra. I'd known Lyra only briefly—a kind soul working in the gardens of the Obsidian Spire, whose gentle touch brought new life to the barren wastes. Her thread, however, was entangled with others—a warrior, a mage, and a winged being from the reptilian tribes. Each of them had their own separate threads, but all weaved in and out of Lyra's, creating a complex pattern that extended across centuries.

Following the crimson thread, I journeyed through time, witnessing moments both grand and minute. I saw Lyra as a child, playing amongst the wildflowers near the whispering wastes; I saw her as a young woman, her gentle soul illuminated by love; and then I witnessed the abrupt and violent severing of her thread—a sacrifice in an ancient ritual to appease a forgotten god, a god whose very existence I had only dimly understood.

Lyra's sacrifice, it turned out, was not an isolated event. Her thread was connected to other sacrifices—a continuous stream of lives offered to the same dark entity over thousands of years, each life feeding the entity's power, strengthening its influence in the mortal realm. This entity, it seemed, was feeding on the life force of the chosen ones, their very essence fueling its power. The sacrifices weren't random, chosen for their inherent purity or piety; it was a systematic design, a carefully orchestrated plan to drain life energy.

The warrior's thread, intertwined with Lyra's, revealed a lineage of protectors—champions who had fought against the entity for millennia, their battles documented in ancient texts, hidden in forgotten libraries. They were warriors trained in an ancient style of fighting, using energy from the very earth. These battles had never truly ended, merely paused, a stalemate caused by a delicate balance of power.

The mage's thread revealed a hidden order, a secret society of scholars who had long studied the entity, its origins, and its plans. Their knowledge, vast and intricate, was locked away in a series of cryptic texts and hidden rituals, only now, centuries later, being revealed through the unraveling of Lyra's thread.

And finally, the winged being's thread revealed a sinister plot—a calculated move by the reptilian tribes, a desperate attempt to gain power by manipulating the entity. They were unaware of the complete picture; their plans were partially successful in weakening the entity's barriers. This was a pivotal detail; their attempts to control the entity seemed to be unintentionally feeding it power. Their ancient texts, filled with cryptic prophecies and diagrams of forbidden knowledge, detailed this strategy, indicating that their ambition had blinded them to the catastrophic consequences.

As I traced the threads, I started to grasp the grand design. The entity's power was tied directly to the very fabric of fate itself. It existed in the gaps and crevices, in the spaces between moments, between lives. The more lives it consumed, the greater its control over the currents of time. It fed on chaos, on sorrow, on the very essence of loss.

The entity was not merely a creature of cosmic horror but a manifestation of entropy, a force that sought to unravel the tapestry of existence, to reduce everything to nothingness. The sacrifices weren't merely fuel; they were points of influence, anchoring the entity in the mortal plane, making it stronger with every sacrifice.

This was not simply a conflict between good and evil. It was a battle for the very nature of reality, a fight to prevent the complete collapse of existence. The tapestry of fate, once a thing of beauty and wonder, now threatened to unravel, leaving behind a void of nothingness. My intervention wasn't just about saving Lyra or stopping the reptilian tribes; it was about safeguarding existence itself, about preserving the delicate balance between creation and destruction.

My understanding of the situation was evolving, leading me down a path of unprecedented complexity. The task before me was not merely to defeat a cosmic entity but to understand the intricate mechanisms of fate, to manipulate the very threads of time itself. The path forward was treacherous, fraught with paradoxes and unimaginable dangers. Yet, I felt a sense of grim determination; the fate of existence rested upon my shoulders, a burden I was prepared to bear. The whispers of impending doom were growing louder, the threads of fate vibrating with an ever-increasing intensity. The time to act was now.

The crimson thread of Lyra, I now understood, was but a single strand in a vast, cosmic net. Following it had led me to a chilling revelation: every life, every event, however seemingly insignificant, was inextricably linked to every other. The death of a humble gardener in a remote village could ripple outwards, causing a chain reaction that reshaped empires and altered the course of history. This interconnectedness, this intricate web of cause and effect, was far more profound than I had ever imagined.

My journey through the Hall of Whispers continued, the shimmering threads guiding me through the labyrinthine corridors of time and space. I witnessed the birth of stars, the rise and fall of civilizations, and the fleeting lives of countless beings, all woven together in an intricate tapestry of existence. One thread, shimmering with a deep indigo light, led me to the forging of a legendary sword, a weapon said to possess the power to cleave through even the fabric of reality. The sword, I discovered, was not simply a physical object but a nexus of energies, a conduit for cosmic forces. Its creation was intertwined with the lives of several individuals: a master blacksmith, whose skill was unmatched; a mystic, who imbued the sword with magical properties; and a king, who commissioned its creation and whose ultimate fate became entwined with it. The king, a cruel and ambitious ruler, used the sword to conquer many lands, but his ruthless ambition ultimately brought about his downfall, his thread ending in a desperate, bloody battle, his life force cruelly consumed.

Another thread, this one shimmering with emerald green, transported me to the heart of a flourishing forest, a place of ancient magic and primordial power. Here, I witnessed the evolution of a species of sentient trees, their slow, deliberate growth mirroring the unfolding of time itself. Their very existence was intricately connected to the life force of the planet, their roots drawing strength from the earth's core, their leaves nourishing the sky's vibrant energies. Their growth, their struggles, their eventual decay—all played a part in the delicate balance of nature, every leaf that fell, every branch that broke, contributing to the intricate cycle of life, death, and renewal. Their thread, despite its serene appearance, was tangled with the threads of many races. The sentient trees had warned many tribes through dreams and visions, guiding them through disasters, subtly shaping the evolution of their cultures, only to be largely ignored and gradually forgotten as the cultures flourished without understanding the source of their seemingly arbitrary good luck. Their extinction caused an unforeseen climate change and had ripple effects of societal collapse that were only evident centuries later.

Yet another thread, glowing with an unsettling obsidian black, drew me to a desolate wasteland, a place scarred by ancient battles and forgotten conflicts. Here, I witnessed the desperate struggle of a group of nomadic people, forced to wander the harsh landscape, seeking sustenance amidst the ruins of a long-vanished civilization. Their resilience, their adaptability, their capacity for love and hope in the face of unimaginable hardship—these qualities were woven into the very fabric of their existence. Their thread revealed a stark but beautiful truth: even in the face of overwhelming adversity, the human spirit could endure and even find a way to thrive. Their sacrifices, born not out of ritual but from desperation, served as a subtle beacon of hope that sparked the rebirth of a new age.

These glimpses, these fragments of existence, revealed a deeper truth: the universe is not a collection of isolated events but a seamless, interconnected whole. Every action, every decision, has consequences that ripple outwards, touching the lives of countless others, spanning epochs and universes. The concept of linear time, of a fixed past and a predetermined future, crumbled before the awe-inspiring complexity of this cosmic tapestry.

The Hall of Whispers was not merely a place of observation but a place of participation. I could not simply observe the threads; I could influence them. I could guide them, redirect them, even sever them—but such an act would come with unforeseen consequences. The act of severing one thread would cause others to unravel, the repercussions rippling across time and space in ways that were impossible to predict. Each touch, each alteration, created new branches, altered destinies, and added to the infinite complexity of existence.

My journey led me across centuries and millennia. I walked among the dinosaurs in a world of vibrant green, saw the rise and fall of civilizations born of cosmic dust, and witnessed the creation and destruction of entire galaxies. The scale of interconnectedness was breathtaking. The choices of a single individual in one era affected entire ecosystems and societal structures in another. A moment of kindness in a forgotten age echoed across epochs, influencing the very shape of future civilizations and even the course of cosmic events. Similarly, a single act of cruelty could trigger wars and catastrophes across multiple universes, creating rifts and paradoxes that threatened to unravel reality itself.

I saw empires crumble due to a misplaced word spoken centuries ago, a decision made out of spite, a love lost causing the fall of a kingdom, a misplaced belief leading to generations of suffering, and a single act of defiance changing the course of history.

This journey through the tapestry of fate was not merely an intellectual exercise; it was a visceral experience, a profound immersion into the very essence of existence. It challenged my understanding of causality, of free will, and of the nature of reality itself. The line between observer and participant blurred; my very presence in the Hall of Whispers was changing the tapestry, adding new threads to the intricate design.

The whispers of impending doom grew stronger. The threads, once vibrant and steady, now throbbed with an almost frantic energy, warning of an impending cataclysm. The entity, its power amplified by the countless sacrifices, was drawing closer, its influence spreading like a malignant shadow across the cosmos. The time for contemplation was over. The time for action had arrived. The weight of countless destinies rested on my shoulders, and the fate of all existence lay in the balance. The path forward, however, remained shrouded in mystery, a labyrinth of infinite possibilities, where every decision held the potential for both salvation and annihilation.

The crimson threads of Lyra, once a singular focus, now seemed to branch into a thousand shimmering tributaries, each representing a potential future. The Hall of Whispers, once a silent observer, now pulsed with a chaotic energy, a symphony of possibilities playing out before me. I saw futures where I succeeded, futures where I failed, and futures where the very fabric of reality unraveled.

One thread, a vibrant emerald green, showed a world bathed in the golden light of a new dawn. Humanity, unified under a banner of peace and understanding, flourished. The seven reptilian tribes, once locked in endless conflict, now collaborated, their collective wisdom guiding the world toward an era of unprecedented prosperity. Magic flowed freely, a benevolent force shaping the landscape and enriching lives. My family, my wife, Elara, and our children ruled not as tyrannical gods but as benevolent guardians, their reign marked by compassion and justice. The demonic forces, once a consuming torment, were transmuted into a source of creative energy, powering the very heart of this utopian world. The air hummed with a harmonious energy, a testament to the balance achieved between the mortal and divine realms. This future, though idyllic, felt...incomplete. It lacked the grit, the struggle, and the hard-won victories that forged true strength and resilience.

Another thread, a deep sapphire blue, depicted a world plunged into an unending twilight. The entity, its malevolent influence unchecked, had cast a pall of despair across the cosmos. Humanity, fragmented and demoralized, struggled to survive amidst the encroaching darkness. The seven reptilian tribes, consumed by internal strife, had fallen prey to the entity's insidious whispers, turning upon each other in a desperate, self-destructive war. Magic, twisted and corrupted, served only to fuel the entity's power. The landscape was scarred by battles, the air thick with the stench of decay. This future, grim and desolate, was a stark warning, a testament to the catastrophic consequences of inaction. Yet, even amidst this ruin, sparks of resistance flickered, tiny embers of hope refusing to be extinguished. The thread suggested a possibility, a slim chance for redemption, but the cost seemed insurmountable.

A third thread, shimmering with an unsettling obsidian black, showed a reality fractured into countless dimensions, a chaotic kaleidoscope of fragmented realities. The entity, in its pursuit of ultimate power, had shattered the very fabric of existence, creating rifts and paradoxes that threatened to unravel all of creation. Humanity, along with all other life forms, was scattered across these disparate realms, desperately trying to maintain their existence amidst the swirling chaos. Each shard of reality was a universe unto itself, governed by different laws of physics, different magical systems, and different versions of me. In some, I was a benevolent ruler; in others, a tyrannical god; in still others, a tormented prisoner of the entity itself. This reality was the most terrifying, a testament to the absolute destruction that could result from my failure. Yet, even here, amidst the fragmented realities, threads of connection remained, subtle echoes of hope whispering across the fractured dimensions. A distant harmony, a beacon of unity that hinted at the possibility of restoring order from chaos.

Each thread I examined revealed a different aspect of my destiny, a different path I could choose. But the choice was not simply a matter of choosing between good and evil; it was a labyrinth of infinite possibilities, where even the seemingly best choices contained the seeds of their own destruction. The weight of countless destinies, countless realities, rested on my shoulders. The whispers in the Hall of Whispers grew louder, urging me to choose, to act, to shape the tapestry of fate according to my will.

I focused on the emerald thread, the utopian future. But as I reached out, I felt a resistance, a subtle pushback from the other threads. The sapphire thread, the dark future, pulsed with a foreboding energy, pulling me towards its grim embrace. The obsidian thread, the fractured reality, vibrated with a chaotic energy that threatened to consume me. The tapestry of fate was not merely a passive observer; it was a dynamic, responsive entity, influencing my choices and shaping my destiny.

I realized that the future was not predetermined, not a fixed path laid out before me. It was a fluid, ever-changing landscape, a mosaic of possibilities that shifted and rearranged themselves according to my actions. Each choice I made would ripple outwards, affecting not only my own destiny but the destinies of countless others. The threads were not separate entities; they were interconnected, their fates intertwined, their energies interwoven. To influence one was to influence them all.

The concept of free will, once clear and defined, now felt blurred, nuanced. Was I truly free to choose my own destiny, or was I merely a pawn in a larger cosmic game, a puppet dancing to the tune of fate? The question haunted me, a chilling reminder of my own limitations. Yet, within those limitations lay the very essence of my power. The ability to choose, even amidst the constraints of fate, was a power in itself, a testament to the human spirit's capacity for resilience and agency.

I spent what felt like eons navigating this labyrinth of possibilities, observing, contemplating, and eventually, acting. I found myself moving away from the purely utopian visions, as those futures felt almost sterile. The cost of absolute peace was seemingly a dulling of the human spirit, a sacrifice of individuality for the sake of unity. The dark futures, however, were not to be embraced. The total annihilation of life was a cost too high.

My focus shifted to the fractured reality, the chaotic kaleidoscope of dimensions. This, I sensed, held the key. The entity's ultimate ambition was not merely destruction but control, to mold all of creation according to its will. But in the fragmentation of reality, in the infinite diversity of possibilities, lay the seeds of resistance. By embracing the chaos, by working within the fragmented dimensions, I could potentially weaken the entity's power, sow the seeds of rebellion, and ultimately, restore balance to the cosmos.

The journey through these potential futures was not merely a passive observation; it was a crucible, forging my will, sharpening my resolve, and preparing me for the trials that lay ahead. Each glimpse into the future, however terrifying or alluring, strengthened my understanding of the stakes, the complexities, and the weight of my responsibilities. The time for contemplation was over. The time for action had arrived. The tapestry of fate awaited my touch, and I knew, with a certainty that went beyond mere intuition, that the path to salvation would not be easy. It would be a path forged in fire, a dance with fate itself, a battle not just for my own survival but for the survival of all existence. The whispers of the cosmos urged me onward, towards a future that was both unknown and yet, inexplicably, within my grasp.

The obsidian threads, representing the fractured realities, pulsed with a chaotic energy that resonated deep within my bones. I reached out, not with the intention of choosing this reality, but of understanding it, of feeling its intricate weave. It was a tapestry woven from paradox, a symphony of discordant notes that somehow, inexplicably, held a faint undercurrent of harmony.

Within this fractured landscape, I saw countless versions of myself, each a reflection of a different choice, a different path not taken. In one reality, I had succumbed to the entity's influence, becoming a puppet of its will, a tyrannical god ruling over a desolate wasteland. In another, I had embraced the darkness, wielding its power for my own ends, a ruthless conqueror who had achieved dominion over the fragmented realms. These realities, though terrifying, served as cautionary tales, highlighting the dangers of unchecked ambition and the corrosive nature of power.

But amidst the darkness, I also saw glimpses of light, flickering embers of resistance in the most unexpected places. In one fractured reality, a small group of humans, empowered by a forgotten magic, had rallied together, creating a sanctuary amidst the chaos. They weren't fighting to conquer but to survive, to preserve the remnants of hope in a world teetering on the brink of oblivion. Their resilience, their unwavering spirit, inspired me. Their struggle underscored the enduring strength of the human spirit, even in the face of unimaginable adversity.

In another fragmented reality, one of the seven reptilian tribes, having escaped the entity's manipulative grasp, had forged a fragile alliance with a group of fairies, their combined magical prowess creating a bulwark against the encroaching darkness. This unexpected alliance, a testament to the power of cooperation and the unexpected bonds of unity, provided a glimmer of hope in a world fractured by conflict and despair. It demonstrated the potential for change, the possibility of forging new alliances, and breaking down the barriers of ancient grudges.

I realized that my influence on destiny wasn't about imposing my will on the multiverse but about subtly nudging the probabilities, about amplifying the forces of hope and resilience, and about subtly weakening the entity's influence. It wasn't about creating a perfect, utopian world but about fostering a cosmos where resilience could flourish, where hope could take root, and where the human spirit could not be extinguished.

My approach shifted. I started by focusing on the small acts of defiance, the subtle moments of resistance that flickered within the fragmented realities. I amplified these acts, not through direct intervention, but through subtle manipulations of probabilities. A chance encounter, a whispered word of encouragement, a seemingly insignificant event—each action, however small, had the potential to create a ripple effect, altering the course of events in unexpected ways.

In one reality, a young human, destined to succumb to despair, stumbled upon an ancient text that unlocked a hidden potential within them. The probability of this encounter had been incredibly low, almost negligible. But by subtly influencing the circumstances, by guiding the young human towards the text, I increased the likelihood of this event occurring. The change wasn't immediate, but it was palpable. The young human, now empowered, became a beacon of hope, inspiring others to join their cause, slowly chipping away at the entity's control.

In another reality, I nudged two warring reptilian tribes toward a tentative truce, capitalizing on a shared enemy—a particularly virulent strain of demonic influence. I didn't force them together, but I created the conditions that made cooperation more likely, subtly amplifying their shared desire for survival over their ancient hatred. The truce was fragile and temporary, but it represented a significant shift in the balance of power, weakening the entity's ability to manipulate the conflicts between the tribes.

The act of influencing destiny, I discovered, was a delicate dance, a balancing act between intervention and non-interference. It wasn't about imposing my will but about gently guiding events towards a more positive outcome, respecting the free will of all beings while simultaneously nudging them towards paths that would benefit the greater good. It was about working *with* the chaos, harnessing its energy to fuel hope and resistance.

The setting itself became fluid, shifting and reforming as I influenced the flow of probabilities. The fragmented realities began to coalesce in subtle ways, their edges blurring as the forces of hope and resistance grew stronger. The obsidian threads, once chaotic and terrifying, started to gleam with a faint light, the darkness giving way to a nascent dawn.

The process was exhausting, demanding a level of focus and precision that pushed my abilities to their limits. Each subtle change, each influenced event, required careful calculation, a deep understanding of the interconnectedness of the fractured realities. One wrong move, one misplaced intervention, could have catastrophic consequences, undoing all the progress I had made.

Yet, the sense of purpose, the knowledge that I was making a difference, fueled my efforts. The whispers of the cosmos, once a source of confusion and uncertainty, became a guiding voice, providing subtle clues and hints as I navigated the labyrinth of probabilities. I felt a growing connection to the fragmented realities, an empathy that transcended space and time, allowing me to intuitively understand the needs and desires of those who inhabited these fractured worlds.

As I continued to subtly influence destiny, the tapestry of fate began to shift. The fragmented realities, though still chaotic, started to exhibit a greater degree of coherence. The forces of resistance grew stronger, fueled by a renewed sense of hope. The entity's grip, once absolute, began to weaken, its malevolent influence gradually diminishing. The transformation wasn't instantaneous, but it was undeniable, a slow, gradual shift towards a more balanced and harmonious cosmos.

The journey was far from over. The entity remained a formidable threat, its influence lingering in the shadows. But the seeds of hope had been sown, the forces of resistance had been strengthened, and the future, once bleak and uncertain, now held the promise of a brighter dawn. The tapestry of fate, once a terrifying labyrinth of infinite possibilities, was now slowly transforming, its threads weaving together to form a pattern of resilience, hope, and, perhaps, even redemption. The weight of countless destinies remained, but now, I carried it with a newfound confidence, knowing that even amidst the chaos, even within the constraints of fate, the human spirit, amplified by subtle interventions, possessed the power to shape its own destiny. The cosmos whispered its approval, a faint hum of harmony echoing through the newly forming realities. The path ahead remained long and arduous, but the journey had become one of collaboration, of gentle guidance, and of the subtle art of influencing the very fabric of destiny itself.

The obsidian threads of the tapestry shimmered, no longer solely a chaotic storm of fractured realities but now possessing a subtle, almost imperceptible luminescence at their edges. My understanding of the multiverse had deepened, transforming from a horrifying spectacle of infinite possibilities to a complex, interconnected system, a delicate ecosystem of choice and consequence. The weight of countless destinies, once a crushing burden, now felt more akin to a responsibility, a profound understanding of the intricate dance between fate and free will.

I had initially approached the task with a naive sense of omnipotence, believing I could simply rearrange the threads of fate to my liking, molding the multiverse into a perfect utopia. But I had learned a harsh lesson: the universe resists such blatant manipulation. The more forcefully I attempted to impose my will, the more violently the tapestry resisted, throwing up new obstacles and creating unforeseen consequences. My earlier, more heavy-handed interventions had inadvertently caused more harm than good, creating rippling effects that exacerbated existing problems.

The key, I realized, lay not in control, but in influence. Not in imposing a predetermined outcome, but in subtly nudging probabilities, in empowering the inhabitants of these fractured realities to choose their own paths, to forge their own destinies. It was a profound shift in perspective, a transition from a tyrannical god-king to a subtler, more nuanced architect of possibilities. My role wasn't to dictate the future but to cultivate it, to nurture the seeds of hope and resilience that already existed within the chaos.

This new approach required a profound level of empathy, an ability to connect with the myriad beings inhabiting these fractured realities, to understand their hopes, their fears, and their aspirations. I had to learn to listen to the whispers of the cosmos, not as a commanding voice dictating my actions, but as a subtle guide, offering insights and suggestions rather than directives. This required a different kind of magic, a magic not of brute force, but of subtle influence, of gentle persuasion, of empowering others to shape their own futures.

The setting itself reflected this shift. The obsidian threads, still representing the fractured realities, no longer pulsed with a furious, chaotic energy. The landscape, previously a maelstrom of clashing realities, now possessed a strange, paradoxical serenity. Fractured landscapes still existed, but they were interspersed with pockets of unexpected peace, oases of hope amidst the chaos. I saw entire civilizations rise and fall, not as predetermined events, but as a consequence of countless choices, each a ripple in the ocean of probabilities.

I witnessed a reptilian tribe, once locked in a brutal war with another, forge a tentative alliance, their shared hatred for a newly emergent demonic entity overriding their ancient rivalries. This wasn't a forced union but a natural consequence of altered probabilities—a subtle shift in the wind, a chance encounter that led to a grudging truce. The outcome was fragile, vulnerable to collapse at any moment, but it represented a profound shift in the balance of power, a testament to the power of cooperation and the unexpected alliances that can arise in times of crisis.

In another reality, a young woman, initially destined for a life of servitude and despair, discovered a hidden talent for healing. This magical ability allowed her to mend not only physical wounds but also the fractured spirits of her people. This wasn't a magical intervention on my part, but a subtle nudge, a chance encounter with a forgotten text, a whispered word of encouragement at a critical moment—small actions that amplified the existing potential within her. She became a beacon of hope, inspiring others to embrace their own abilities and defy the encroaching darkness.

The process of guiding these realities towards a more positive outcome was incredibly demanding. It required an almost infinite capacity for empathy, a profound understanding of cause and effect, and a level of patience that defied description. One misplaced intervention, one subtle nudge in the wrong direction, could unravel everything, unleashing a chain of unintended consequences that could shatter entire realities.

But with each successful intervention, with each subtle shift in probability, I felt a growing connection to the multiverse, a sense of purpose that transcended my own existence. The whispered harmonies of the cosmos, once a source of fear and confusion, now resonated with a gentle, reassuring rhythm, a symphony of infinite possibilities tempered by the subtle influence of choice. I was no longer a mere observer, a passive witness to the unfolding of fate; I had become an active participant, a collaborator in the grand tapestry of existence.

The tapestry of fate, once a terrifying labyrinth of infinite possibilities, was slowly transforming, its threads weaving together to form a pattern of resilience, hope, and, perhaps, even redemption. The weight of countless destinies remained, but I carried it with a newfound confidence, knowing that even amidst the chaos, even within the constraints of fate, choice, amplified by subtle interventions, possessed the power to shape its own destiny. The journey was far from over; the path ahead remained long and arduous, but it was a path I now walked with a deeper understanding of the delicate balance between fate and free will, a balance I had learned to respect, to nurture, and to carefully cultivate. The cosmos hummed its approval, a testament to the subtle art of influencing destiny itself. The balance, once a source of fear, now represented a profound, almost sacred responsibility— the responsibility to guide, to encourage, and to empower the choices that would shape the future of all realities. My power, I realized, lay not in control, but in fostering the capacity for choice, in nurturing the seeds of hope and resilience within the intricate, ever-shifting tapestry of fate. The future, once a terrifying unknown, now held the promise of a brighter dawn, a dawn born not of absolute power but of delicate balance, a symphony of fate and free will playing out on the ever-shifting threads of existence.

14

Legacy of Paradise

The obsidian threads of the multiverse, once a terrifying maelstrom of fractured realities, now shimmered with a gentle, ethereal light. The chaos had not vanished; it remained, a subtle undercurrent beneath the surface of a newly forged paradise. But the discordant notes had been muted, harmonized into a symphony of breathtaking beauty. The landscape itself had undergone a profound transformation. Jagged, obsidian spires, once symbols of the fractured realities, now stood softened, their sharp edges smoothed by a gentle, iridescent glow. They were no longer monuments to chaos but majestic pillars supporting a breathtaking celestial dome, painted with constellations unknown to the mortal realm before. Rivers of liquid starlight snaked their way through valleys once scarred by conflict, their waters reflecting the myriad colors of a sky ablaze with otherworldly aurorae.

Cities, once ravaged by war and despair, had risen again, rebuilt not with stone and mortar, but with shimmering, self-replenishing materials born of the transformed magic that permeated this new world. Buildings pulsed with a soft, internal luminescence, their architecture echoing the fluid, organic shapes of the natural world. They were not simply structures; they were living entities, breathing, growing, and evolving in harmony with their inhabitants. Gardens of impossible flora bloomed across the landscape, their vibrant hues a stark contrast to the bleakness that had once prevailed. Flowers that glowed with internal light, trees that bore fruit of pure energy, and creatures of unimaginable beauty roamed freely, their very existence a testament to the profound change that had swept across the multiverse.

The reptilian tribes, once locked in endless conflict, now coexisted in a fragile but surprisingly harmonious alliance. Their scales, once dull and scarred by countless battles, now shimmered with vibrant, iridescent patterns, reflecting the peace that had settled over their ancient lands. They had learned to harness the new, gentler magic, using it not for conquest, but for creation, for building magnificent cities that blended seamlessly with the natural world. Their ancient rivalries had not been erased, but they had been transformed, channeled into a collaborative spirit focused on building a future worthy of their shared heritage. Their cities, once fortresses built for defense, were now open and welcoming, showcasing a remarkable blend of their unique cultural identities. Elaborate temples, dedicated not to war gods but to the spirits of nature and harmony, stood as symbols of their renewed commitment to peace.

Even the demons, those terrifying entities born from the depths of my own tormented past, had undergone a metamorphosis. They had not vanished, but their malevolent energy had been redirected, transmuted into a powerful creative force. They now served not as instruments of destruction but as architects of paradise, their dark magic harnessed to shape and mold the landscape, their immense power tempered by a newfound sense of purpose. They worked alongside the other races, their unique abilities crucial in shaping the new world, their terrifying strength channeled into feats of creation rather than annihilation. Their imposing forms still held an air of mystery and power, but their eyes, once burning with malevolent hatred, now held a strange, almost melancholic sadness, a reflection of their past transgressions and their newfound commitment to redemption.

The human civilizations, once clinging precariously to survival, flourished in this new Eden. They had learned to harness the transformative power of the paradise, their minds expanding in tandem with the magic that surrounded them. They had moved beyond the limitations of their past, developing new technologies and creating vibrant art forms that celebrated the beauty and wonder of their newfound world. Their cities were marvels of engineering and aesthetics, each reflecting the unique cultures and traditions of their respective regions. Education and innovation thrived, fostering a society of creativity, cooperation, and mutual respect. Gone were the days of strife and conflict; this was a world where compassion and empathy reigned supreme.

But the paradise was not static; it was a dynamic entity, constantly evolving, growing, and adapting to the needs of its inhabitants. New landscapes were born, new creatures emerged, and new challenges arose, constantly testing the resilience and adaptability of the people who called it home. This was not a utopia in the simplistic sense of the word; it was a world of complex challenges and profound opportunities, a world where progress required constant effort, where the inhabitants were not passive recipients of paradise but active participants in its ongoing creation.

The celestial dome, shimmering with countless stars and nebulae, was not merely a backdrop but an integral part of this living world. It pulsed with energy, its patterns shifting and changing, reflecting the ongoing transformation of the multiverse. The constellations themselves were not fixed; they shifted and rearranged, each movement reflecting a profound cosmic event, a testament to the continuous creation and evolution that permeated every aspect of this new reality. This dynamic celestial landscape served as a constant reminder of the power of change, the beauty of constant renewal, and the unending potential for growth and transformation.

My own role had also shifted. I was no longer simply the architect of this paradise but a facilitator, a guide, a humble servant of its inhabitants. I had learned that true power lay not in control, but in empowering others to shape their own destinies. My family, once mere mortals, now stood beside me, sharing in the responsibility of guiding this new world. We were not gods in the traditional sense, but custodians, protectors, and collaborators in the grand tapestry of existence. We understood the delicate balance between order and chaos, between intervention and non-intervention. We had learned to listen to the whispers of the cosmos, to understand its subtle rhythms, and to harmonize our actions with its ongoing symphony of creation.

The paradise was a testament to the power of transformation, a reflection of the endless potential for change, growth, and redemption. It was a world forged not from absolute power, but from a deep understanding of the interconnectedness of all things, a world born from the ashes of chaos and tempered by the gentle hand of compassion and empathy. It was a world where the echoes of past horrors served as a constant reminder of the importance of peace, a world where the lessons of suffering had been transformed into seeds of hope, resilience, and unwavering faith in the capacity for good, even in the darkest of times. The paradise was a living testament to the power of choice, the enduring strength of hope, and the endless possibilities that reside within the heart of even the most broken souls. And as I looked upon this magnificent world, I knew that the journey was far from over, that the paradise, like life itself, was a continuous process of creation, evolution, and endless, wondrous transformation.

The newfound peace wasn't merely the absence of war; it was a positive, vibrant force that pulsed through every fiber of existence. The air itself hummed with a gentle energy, a subtle vibration that resonated with the harmonious symphony of the cosmos. Children, born under the benevolent gaze of the newly formed pantheon, played freely in gardens where flowers bloomed in impossible colors, their petals shimmering with an inner light. These weren't merely beautiful; they were imbued with a gentle magic, capable of soothing ailments and lifting spirits. The very air tasted sweeter, cleaner, imbued with the essence of a world reborn.

The seven reptilian tribes, once locked in bitter conflict, now collaborated on magnificent projects that showcased the unique strengths of each culture. Their cities, once isolated fortresses, are now connected through shimmering pathways of solidified starlight, allowing for easy and safe travel between their diverse realms. Architects from different tribes worked together, blending their styles into breathtaking structures that seamlessly integrated nature and technology. Giant, crystal-clear domes protected sprawling gardens, where exotic fruits and vegetables grew in abundance, providing nourishment for all. Massive hydroponic farms, powered by the gentle energy of the transformed landscape, produced food with unprecedented nutritional value, eliminating famine from the land entirely.

The once-scarred battlefields were now transformed into vast, fertile plains, teeming with life. Animals, long hunted to near extinction, roamed freely, their populations flourishing under the watchful eye of the newly established guardians of nature. These guardians weren't simply tasked with preservation; they were beings of immense power, capable of healing the land and nurturing its inhabitants. Their presence was a constant reminder of the delicate balance between nature and civilization, a balance that was now carefully maintained.

Humanity, too, experienced an unprecedented golden age. Art flourished, fueled by a newfound sense of hope and creativity. Masterpieces were born, capturing the beauty and wonder of the transformed world in breathtaking detail. Music filled the air, its melodies weaving together the diverse cultural traditions into a harmonious tapestry of sound. Literature explored the profound philosophical questions raised by the shift in the cosmic order, weaving tales of resilience, hope, and the endless potential for good. Scientific advancements surged forward, propelled by a spirit of collaboration and innovation. New technologies, born from a deep understanding of the underlying magic of the world, solved age-old problems, improving the quality of life in unprecedented ways. Healing arts reached new heights, capable of curing diseases that had plagued humanity for centuries. Life expectancy soared, and the concept of premature death became increasingly rare.

The transformation wasn't limited to the physical realm; it extended to the spiritual and intellectual spheres as well. Education was not a privilege but a right, readily accessible to everyone. Libraries, filled with scrolls and holographic archives of knowledge, stood as beacons of enlightenment, empowering individuals to shape their own destinies. Philosophical debates thrived in the open squares of cities, fueled by the boundless curiosity of a people liberated from the constraints of fear and conflict. The pursuit of knowledge became a driving force, pushing humanity to explore the boundaries of its understanding, to delve into the deepest mysteries of existence.

The demons, once symbols of fear and chaos, now served as architects of the paradise. Their immense power, channeled into creative endeavors, resulted in breathtaking feats of engineering and artistry. They sculpted mountains, carved valleys, and built magnificent structures that defied the laws of physics. Their dark, brooding presence was still palpable, a constant reminder of the dark past, but their actions reflected a newfound commitment to redemption. They built grand observatories that allowed humanity to peer into the furthest reaches of the cosmos, unraveling the mysteries of the universe and understanding their place within the grand scheme of things. They were the silent, powerful architects of a world that had been resurrected from the ashes of chaos.

The pantheon, my family and I weren't distant, unreachable deities. We were active participants in the daily life of our creations, guiding and supporting, but always striving to empower them to forge their own paths. We held regular councils, listening to the concerns and aspirations of our subjects, ensuring that the laws and structures of the paradise remained responsive to the needs of the people. We weren't dictators but facilitators, enabling the harmonious growth of all civilizations, ensuring that their unique cultures and identities were preserved and celebrated.

The prosperity wasn't merely material; it was spiritual and emotional as well. A sense of unity and shared purpose permeated the entire realm. People worked together, collaborating on projects that benefited the entire populace. Competition existed, but it was healthy, focused on innovation and progress rather than domination and conquest. Empathy and compassion reigned supreme, creating a society where everyone felt valued and respected. The concept of "other" was fading, replaced by a shared identity as inhabitants of this newly forged paradise.

The paradise was not static; it continued to evolve and grow, responding to the needs and desires of its inhabitants. New challenges arose, testing the resilience and adaptability of the people, but these challenges were met with collaboration and innovation. The cosmos itself seemed to respond to the newfound harmony, gifting the world with new wonders and possibilities. New constellations appeared in the night sky, new creatures emerged from the transformed landscapes, and new magical arts were discovered.

The obsidian threads of the multiverse, once a symbol of chaos and fracture, now shimmered with a gentle, iridescent glow. They were not erased but transformed, integrated into the very fabric of existence, serving as a constant reminder of the transformative power of hope and resilience. The darkness remained, a subtle undercurrent beneath the surface of the paradise, but it was no longer a threat; it was a reminder of the past, a source of strength, a testament to the capacity for good even in the face of unimaginable evil. It was a constant reminder that peace is not the absence of struggle but the triumph of hope over despair. The paradise wasn't just a place; it was a living testament to the potential for change, a symbol of the enduring power of the human spirit, a beacon of hope in the vast expanse of the cosmos. And in the heart of this paradise, the legacy of a man who had wrestled with his demons and emerged victorious continued to inspire and shape a world reborn.

The celestial choirs, once a distant, ethereal echo, now sang in harmony with the mortal world. Their voices, woven into the very fabric of existence, carried messages of peace, understanding, and shared purpose. The gods and goddesses, no longer aloof and distant, walked among their creations, their presence a source of comfort and inspiration rather than fear and awe. Regular gatherings, held in shimmering celestial meadows bathed in the light of a thousand suns, brought together representatives from all realms—human, reptilian, fae, and even the reformed demons—to discuss matters of mutual concern and to celebrate the shared triumphs of their collaborative efforts.

The celestial bodies themselves seemed to respond to the newfound harmony. Constellations shifted and rearranged, painting new and breathtaking patterns across the night sky. Meteors, once harbingers of destruction, now blazed with vibrant colors, showering the land with blessings of fertility and abundance. The stars themselves seemed to pulse with a gentle energy, their light a tangible expression of the cosmic concordance. The very fabric of space and time seemed to soften, allowing for easier communication and travel between different realms. Journeys that once took years now took mere moments, fostering a sense of interconnectedness and shared destiny.

The reptilian tribes, masters of architecture and engineering, collaborated with the fae, artisans of unparalleled skill and creativity, to build breathtaking cities that blended seamlessly into the natural landscape. Crystalline structures, imbued with intricate enchantments, towered over verdant valleys, their spires reaching towards the heavens. Waterfalls cascaded down their sides, their waters purified and infused with magical energy. Within these cities, humans and reptilians worked side-by-side, their differences celebrated as strengths, their collaborations resulting in breathtaking works of art and innovative technologies.

The fae, keepers of ancient wisdom and keepers of the balance of nature, played a vital role in nurturing the harmony between the celestial and mortal realms. Their intricate dances and enchanting melodies wove a spell of peace and understanding, calming conflicts and diffusing tensions. They established a network of enchanted pathways through the forests, connecting all the realms and allowing for safe and efficient travel. Their delicate touch healed the scars of the past, restoring balance to ecosystems that had been ravaged by war. They were the guardians of the world's natural wonders, ensuring that their beauty and biodiversity were protected for generations to come.

The demons, once agents of chaos and destruction, were now actively engaged in the task of rebuilding and restoring the ravaged lands. Their immense power, channeled towards constructive ends, resulted in miraculous transformations. They reshaped mountains, created fertile valleys, and built monumental structures that defied the laws of physics. Their dark energy, once a source of terror, now fueled the creation of intricate energy grids that powered the entire realm, providing clean, limitless energy for all inhabitants. Their mastery of earth and stone allowed them to construct magnificent underground cities that served as hubs for the development of new technologies and scientific advancements.

Humanity, too, contributed significantly to the harmony. Their scientific advancements, fueled by collaboration and a deep understanding of the underlying magic of the world, led to breakthroughs in medicine, agriculture, and sustainable living. They developed ingenious methods of harnessing solar and geothermal energy, creating a society that thrived without exploiting the earth's resources. They established global networks for the exchange of ideas and knowledge, fostering a spirit of cooperation and shared purpose.

This wasn't merely a fragile peace; it was a deep, abiding harmony that resonated at every level of existence—from the smallest atom to the vast expanse of the cosmos. The once-fractured multiverse, now unified, hummed with a gentle energy that pulsated through every being, every object, every particle of existence. The obsidian threads that once symbolized chaos and division now shimmered with an iridescent light, woven together into a beautiful tapestry of interconnectedness.

The celestial and mortal realms were not separate entities; they were intertwined, inseparable parts of a greater whole. The gods and goddesses were not distant rulers but active participants in the daily lives of their creations. They held regular councils where all inhabitants, regardless of their origin or station, had the opportunity to express their concerns and aspirations. Their decisions were guided by compassion, wisdom, and a deep understanding of the delicate balance that needed to be maintained.

This unity extended beyond politics and governance. It permeated every aspect of life—art, music, literature, philosophy, science, and technology. Human creativity flourished, empowered by the newfound sense of unity and shared purpose. Masterpieces of art and literature celebrated the beauty and wonder of the transformed world, capturing the spirit of collaboration and mutual respect. Music resonated with the harmony of the cosmos, its melodies weaving together the diverse cultural traditions of all realms.

The very air hummed with the energy of this harmony. The sun shone brighter, the stars twinkled with renewed intensity, and the earth pulsed with life. The forests were lush and vibrant, the oceans teemed with life, and the mountains stood tall and majestic. The harmony was not just a condition; it was a state of being, a way of life, a testament to the power of cooperation, understanding, and mutual respect.

This newfound paradise, however, wasn't static or immutable. It continued to evolve, to adapt, to grow, constantly responding to the challenges and opportunities presented by the ever-changing cosmos. New threats might emerge, new discoveries made, and new challenges to overcome. But the essence of the harmony—the unwavering commitment to collaboration, understanding, and shared purpose—would remain, ensuring that the paradise would endure, a testament to the enduring strength of the human spirit and the boundless potential for good that exists within every being, whether mortal or celestial. The legacy of the man who had once wrestled with his inner demons and emerged victorious served as an eternal reminder of the power of hope, resilience, and the transformative power of unity. The journey wasn't over, but the path forward was illuminated by the radiant glow of a harmonious universe.

The reptilian cities, shimmering metropolises of obsidian and crystal, pulsed with a life unlike any other. Each of the seven tribes—the Scaled Ones, the Obsidian Claws, the Azure Breath, the Crimson Fang, the Emerald Eye, the Golden Scale, and the Shadow Stalkers—maintained their distinct architectural styles, reflecting their unique histories and cultural practices. The Scaled Ones, known for their pragmatic approach and advanced engineering, constructed towering structures that harnessed geothermal energy, their buildings seamlessly integrated with the landscape, appearing as if grown from the earth itself. Their cities were characterized by intricate networks of tunnels and underground chambers, where they cultivated rare and exotic plants, utilizing their unique bioluminescent properties to illuminate their subterranean world. Their social structure, while hierarchical, was underpinned by a strong emphasis on meritocracy, with individuals rising through the ranks based on their skills and contributions to the community. Art flourished in the form of intricate carvings on obsidian walls, depicting scenes of their rich history and mythology, and elaborate metalwork crafted from rare and precious metals mined from deep within the earth.

In stark contrast, the Obsidian Claws, renowned for their artistic prowess and mastery of shadow magic, created cities that seemed to blend seamlessly with the twilight. Their architecture utilized obsidian in myriad ways, shaping the very shadows into living sculptures, creating a city that felt both mysterious and captivating. Their art was an expression of their deep connection to the night, focusing on themes of transformation, illusion, and the hidden depths of reality. They were masters of illusion, creating captivating performances that blurred the line between reality and dream, their rituals and ceremonies designed to tap into the power of the unseen world. Their social structure was less hierarchical than the Scaled Ones, with a strong emphasis on individual expression and creativity.

The Azure Breath, dwelling in coastal cities constructed from shimmering, iridescent seashells and coral, possessed a deep reverence for the ocean. Their architecture mirrored the fluid, ever-changing nature of the sea, with structures that appeared to sway and shift with the tide. Their art was deeply spiritual, reflecting their profound connection to the natural world, expressed through intricate mosaics created from seashells and songs that captured the rhythms and mysteries of the ocean. They were skilled navigators and explorers, charting unexplored waters and uncovering the secrets of the deep. Their society was communal, with a strong emphasis on cooperation and shared resources.

The Crimson Fang, inhabiting mountainous regions, carved their homes into the very rock face, their cities blending seamlessly with the rugged terrain. Masters of fire and earth magic, they shaped volcanoes and caverns into magnificent living spaces. Their art was powerful and visceral, expressing their connection to the raw, untamed power of nature. Their intricate metalwork, forged in the fires of active volcanoes, was imbued with magical properties, and their songs echoed the roar of the mountains. Their society was organized around clans, each led by a powerful chieftain, with their warrior culture deeply ingrained in their very being.

The Emerald Eye, inhabiting vast forests, constructed cities that seemed to grow organically from the trees themselves, their architecture intertwined with the natural world. Masters of botany and healing, they possessed a profound understanding of the interconnectedness of all life. Their art reflected their respect for nature, characterized by intricate wood carvings, delicate flower arrangements, and healing potions. They were guardians of the forest, ensuring the preservation of its biodiversity. Their social structure was largely egalitarian, with decision-making processes guided by consensus and respect for the elders.

The Golden Scale, dwellers of sun-drenched plains, created cities that shimmered under the sun, utilizing gold and other precious metals to adorn their magnificent structures. Their culture was characterized by extravagance and opulence, reflecting their love for beauty and their mastery of light magic. Their art was opulent and luxurious, showcasing their skill in goldsmithing, jewelry making, and textiles. Their sophisticated social structure relied on trade and diplomacy, forging alliances with other civilizations.

Finally, the Shadow Stalkers, inhabiting dark, mysterious caverns, created cities that seemed to exist in the twilight between worlds, their architectural style blending seamlessly with the shadows. Their mastery of stealth and subterfuge was unparalleled, and their art was characterized by hidden meaning, riddles, and cryptic symbols. Their society was intensely private and secretive, their social structure based on loyalty and trust. Their culture valued knowledge and secrecy, mastering the art of espionage and deception.

Beyond the reptilian tribes, the fae civilization thrived in a realm of ethereal beauty and breathtaking wonder. Their cities, built amidst ancient forests and sparkling streams, were breathtaking architectural feats. Their homes, carved from living trees or woven from starlight, were works of art themselves, reflecting their profound connection to the natural world. They were skilled artisans, crafting exquisite jewelry and intricate tapestries from flowers, leaves, and moonlight. Their music was enchanting, weaving spells of peace and harmony, and their dances were captivating, reflecting the grace and elegance of their civilization. Their society was governed by a council of elders, their wisdom guiding the fae community with compassion and foresight. They valued knowledge, balance, and the preservation of the magical equilibrium of the world. Their artistic expression extended beyond mere aesthetics, encompassing powerful enchantments and subtle magics woven into the fabric of their daily lives.

Humanity, too, had flourished in this new paradise, creating cities that reflected their own unique blend of technology and magic. Great metropolises, characterized by a harmonious blend of futuristic architecture and natural elements, dotted the landscape. Sustainable energy sources, harnessed through ingenious, magical engineering, powered their societies. Art reflected a newfound unity, expressing a profound appreciation for both the natural world and the technological marvels that had risen from human ingenuity. Human culture drew inspiration from all the other civilizations, blending traditions and ideas into a new, vibrant tapestry. They valued innovation, cooperation, and the pursuit of knowledge, driving advancements in all aspects of their lives, from medicine and agriculture to scientific exploration and technological innovation.

This rich tapestry of cultures, each distinct and unique, yet bound together by a shared commitment to peace and harmony, created a world of unprecedented vibrancy and diversity. The legacy of paradise wasn't simply a single narrative but a kaleidoscope of stories, each reflecting the unique voice and identity of its people. The air itself seemed to hum with the energy of creativity and innovation, a testament to the power of unity and the enduring strength of the human spirit. This new era was one of shared progress and mutual respect, a paradise built not on conquest or domination, but on collaboration and understanding—a testament to the transformative power of a shared vision and the triumph of unity over the darkness that had once threatened to consume their world. The future was bright, promising continued growth and prosperity for all the inhabitants of this newly forged paradise, a vibrant mosaic of cultures living in harmonious coexistence, an endless source of wonder and inspiration for generations to come.

The obsidian pathways of the Scaled Ones' city, once gleaming under the geothermal light, now pulsed with a softer, gentler luminescence. The energy, once harnessed for sheer power, now flowed into intricate systems that nurtured the city's vast underground gardens, providing sustenance and beauty in equal measure. New structures, built with a grace and fluidity previously unseen, rose alongside the older buildings, incorporating elements of the fae's ethereal architecture and the humans' innovative technological marvels. The Scaled Ones, ever practical, had embraced the spirit of collaboration, their engineering prowess now focused on creating symbiotic relationships between their city and its environment. The intricate carvings on the obsidian walls now included images of the protagonist, depicted not as a conquering hero but as a wise teacher, guiding the seven tribes towards unity. His lessons, etched in the very stone, served as a constant reminder of the principles of cooperation and mutual respect.

The Obsidian Claws' city, once shrouded in twilight mysteries, now shimmered with a newfound brilliance. The shadows, once manipulated for illusion and deception, now danced with light, creating breathtaking displays of artistry and wonder. Their mastery of shadow magic, combined with the Golden Scale's understanding of light, led to the creation of breathtaking spectacles of light and shadow, performances that enchanted and uplifted the entire realm. The city itself became a living artwork, constantly evolving and transforming, a testament to the power of creative expression. Their artistic endeavors now focus on celebrating the diversity of the realm, portraying the unique cultures and histories of all beings. The once-secret rituals of the Obsidian Claws were now shared with the world, revealing the beauty and power of their ancient traditions.

The Azure Breath's coastal cities, always a reflection of the ocean's fluidity, now incorporate intricate, sustainable coral farms, their shimmering structures seamlessly integrated with the ocean's life. Their mastery of ocean currents, enhanced by human engineering, allowed them to create efficient, environmentally conscious systems that harvested the ocean's energy without harming its delicate ecosystem. The Azure Breath's songs, once limited to their own community, now echoed across the seas, spreading messages of harmony and understanding throughout the realm. Their navigation skills expanded, leading to the discovery of new and vibrant underwater ecosystems, bringing forth wonders previously unknown. The seas themselves seemed to respond to their harmony, their waters calmer and clearer than ever before.

The Crimson Fang's mountainous cities, once symbols of untamed power, now showcased the fusion of volcanic energy and sustainable energy sources. Their mastery of fire and earth magic, combined with human ingenuity, allowed them to create a stable, clean energy source that fueled their cities, powering the intricate networks of underground tunnels and caverns that crisscrossed the mountains. Their art, once focused on the raw power of nature, now celebrated the delicate balance between nature's untamed energy and human ingenuity. The clans remained, but their warrior culture had evolved, their skills now devoted to protecting the environment and ensuring the safety of all inhabitants.

The Emerald Eye's forest cities, once deeply secluded, have now become centers of learning and healing, their botanical knowledge shared with the entire realm. Their deep understanding of the interconnectedness of all life allowed them to develop revolutionary medicines and agricultural practices, leading to an unprecedented era of prosperity and health. The forests themselves flourished under their care, their biodiversity richer and more resilient than ever before. Their egalitarian society continued to thrive, their wisdom and compassion shaping the future of the paradise.

The Golden Scale's sun-drenched cities, always characterized by opulence, now embraced sustainable practices, their mastery of light magic used to create efficient energy systems and ingenious methods of water conservation. Their love for beauty led to breathtaking displays of artistry and design, reflecting the unity and harmony of the diverse cultures in the realm. Their skills in goldsmithing and jewelry-making were now combined with the artistic talents of other civilizations, creating truly unique and breathtaking works of art. Their diplomacy, always a strength, continued to foster cooperation and understanding throughout the realms.

The Shadow Stalkers' cities, once cloaked in mystery, now emerged from the shadows, their knowledge of subterfuge and stealth used for the benefit of the entire realm, their skills devoted to ensuring the safety and security of all inhabitants. Their cryptic symbols and hidden meanings, once secrets guarded closely, were slowly revealed, enriching the overall cultural tapestry. Their wisdom, once guarded closely, was gradually revealed, enriching the understanding of other cultures and shaping the world's future.

Humanity, having overcome its inner darkness, thrived in this era of unity. Their cities, a blend of futuristic design and nature's beauty, showcased the power of human ingenuity and collaboration. Their technological advancements continued, focused on sustainability and the betterment of life for all beings. Humanity's art and culture reflected the richness and diversity of the realm, representing a harmonious blend of all the civilizations. They served as a bridge between all the different societies, encouraging communication and cooperation. Their commitment to learning and progress drove innovation in medicine, technology, and understanding of the cosmos. Their history was now a story of resilience, creativity, and unity—a reminder of their ability to overcome any darkness and build a paradise.

The legacy of the protagonist wasn't confined to the physical realm. The very fabric of magic itself had shifted. The demonic energies that had once threatened to consume the world were now channeled into creative forces, fueling the art, the innovation, and the prosperity of the new paradise. The gods and goddesses, once distant and aloof, now actively participated in the world's affairs, their power intertwined with the very essence of life itself. The balance between the mortal and the cosmic realms had been restored, a testament to the protagonist's triumph over the darkness within and without.

Generations passed, and the world continued to flourish. The story of the protagonist became legend, a beacon of hope and inspiration. His children and grandchildren, empowered by his legacy, continued to guide and protect this newly forged paradise, ensuring the continued peace and prosperity of all its inhabitants. His influence extended far beyond his own lifespan, his legacy shaping the very soul of the world, inspiring countless acts of courage, creativity, and compassion. The paradise he had created was not merely a physical place but a state of being, a reflection of the transformative power of unity and the enduring strength of the human spirit—a testament to the lasting impact of a single individual's journey from darkness to light, from despair to hope, from chaos to paradise. The world continued to evolve, to grow, and to thrive, its future secured by the lasting legacy of a man who once battled demons within and without, ultimately forging a new heaven on earth. The tapestry of civilizations continued to weave its intricate pattern, a testament to the enduring strength of unity and collaboration in a world once teetering on the brink of destruction, now radiant with the promise of a brighter future, a future forged in the crucible of darkness and brought forth into the light by the lasting legacy of a single, extraordinary man.

15

Epilogue: A New Dawn

The sun, a benevolent eye in the cerulean sky, cast its golden gaze upon the sprawling city of Aethelgard, a metropolis born from the ashes of old conflicts and forged in the crucible of a new dawn. This wasn't merely a city of stone and mortar; it was a testament to the symbiotic relationship between humanity and the seven reptilian tribes, a living tapestry woven with threads of magic, technology, and shared dreams. Here, amidst the soaring spires of human architecture and the organically flowing structures of the Scaled Ones, lived Lyra, the protagonist's eldest daughter. She possessed her father's unwavering resolve but tempered it with a wisdom born of centuries spent observing the delicate balance of the world he had remade. Lyra, a prodigy of both magic and diplomacy, spent her days mediating between the different cultures, ensuring the continued harmony that her father had established. Her court, a vibrant mosaic of representatives from each tribe, reflected the era of unprecedented unity.

Across the shimmering ocean, in the coastal city of Aquamarina, resided Theron, Lyra's younger brother. Unlike his sister's diplomatic nature, Theron possessed a restless spirit, a thirst for exploration reminiscent of his father's early adventures. He commanded the Azure Breath's fleet of magnificent seafaring vessels, each crafted with a blend of human technology and the Azure Breath's mastery of aquatic magic. His explorations weren't merely for conquest or discovery; Theron sought to uncover new ecosystems, to understand the deeper mysteries of the ocean, and to expand the realm's knowledge and understanding of the natural world. He often returned with tales of undiscovered underwater cities, vibrant coral reefs teeming with life, and the songs of ancient, sentient creatures, enriching the already rich tapestry of the realm's knowledge and inspiring awe across all cultures.

In the heart of the Crimson Fang's mountainous realm, nestled amidst volcanic peaks and geothermal vents, lived Elara, the protagonist's niece. She inherited her father's strength and her uncle's ingenuity, combining them into a unique form of earth and fire magic. Unlike the Crimson Fang's previous reliance on raw power, Elara channeled her abilities into harnessing sustainable energy sources, creating a network of interconnected geothermal power plants that provided clean, efficient energy across the mountainous region. Elara oversaw the meticulous crafting of intricate tunnels and caverns, expanding the Crimson Fang's infrastructure while preserving the unique geological beauty of their homeland. Her work was a powerful symbol of progress, demonstrating that even the fiercest tribes could adapt and embrace change without compromising their cultural identity.

Deep within the Emerald Eye's sprawling forests, nestled amongst towering ancient trees and whispering brooks, lived Faelar, the protagonist's granddaughter. She inherited the gentle compassion and deep wisdom of her grandmother, a renowned healer of both the mortal and fae realms. Faelar, a visionary botanist, led the Emerald Eye in creating magnificent botanical gardens and arboreta, preserving and studying the unique flora and fauna of their land while developing new medicinal treatments and agricultural practices that spread prosperity across the realm. Her empathy extended beyond her own people, nurturing a network of healers and scholars who traveled across the land, sharing their knowledge and assisting the less fortunate.

The Golden Scale's sun-drenched cities, always a beacon of artistry and innovation, saw the rise of Orion, the protagonist's grandson. He possessed his grandfather's diplomatic skill and added to it his own unique understanding of light magic, using it to enhance both the aesthetics and functionality of the Golden Scale's cities. Orion's projects ranged from creating breathtaking displays of light and shadow that celebrated the cultural diversity of the realm to devising efficient solar energy systems and ingenious water conservation methods. He saw beauty not only in extravagance but also in sustainability and harmony, proving that luxury and environmental responsibility were not mutually exclusive concepts.

Even in the shadowed cities of the Shadow Stalkers, a new generation emerged. Silas, a young Shadow Stalker trained in the ancient arts of stealth and deception, found a new purpose in protecting the realm. Instead of employing his skills for secretive purposes, he used his mastery of shadows and illusion to safeguard the realm's vulnerable populations, acting as a silent guardian against any lurking threats. Silas's leadership fostered a new era of transparency within the Shadow Stalkers' society, sharing their knowledge and wisdom while maintaining the privacy and discretion that were essential to their existence. Their skills, once used for subterfuge, now served as the unseen shield that protected the realm's fragile peace.

Humanity, the bridge between all these disparate cultures, continued to flourish. Their cities became living testaments to their adaptability and inventiveness, blending futuristic technology with the organic beauty of nature. The human scientists, engineers, and artists worked in tandem with the reptilian tribes and the fae, creating marvels of technology and art that showcased their collective creativity. Their advancements in medicine extended lifespan and improved overall health across all species. They didn't just invent; they collaborated and shared, ensuring that every culture had access to the fruits of collective ingenuity.

The legacy of the protagonist extended beyond these individual achievements. His children, grandchildren, and the many individuals inspired by his actions ensured the harmony he had fought so hard to achieve. The demonic energies he had once wrestled with were now harnessed for constructive purposes, fueling the magical innovations that shaped the realm. The new generation of deities, born from a union of the old pantheon and the power he had attained, actively participated in the world's affairs, their influence weaving its way through the very fabric of existence. The cosmic entities, once distant observers, now interacted with the mortal realm in ways that fostered growth, understanding, and a deeper connection between all of existence.

Centuries passed, and the world continued to evolve, yet the memories of the protagonist remained. His story became a central pillar of the realm's culture, a tale recounted in countless forms—epic poems, vibrant murals, intricate tapestries, and the whispered secrets of elders. His journey from darkness to light served as an ongoing inspiration, a testament to the resilience of the human spirit and the power of hope to conquer even the deepest despair. The paradise he created was not simply a geographical location but a state of being, a reflection of the enduring power of unity and the endless potential for growth and transformation. The world he had forged was a testament to his actions, a living monument to the man who had battled demons within and without, bringing forth a dawn of peace and understanding that echoed across the ages. The new generation carried the torch, ensuring that the world would forever remember and strive to maintain the paradise he had created.

Yet, even in this idyllic paradise, the echoes of the ancient cycles resonated. The very nature of existence, it seemed, was a continuous dance between creation and destruction, a cosmic waltz played out across eons. Lyra, in her wisdom, understood this: the peace they enjoyed wasn't a static endpoint, but a fleeting moment in an endless stream of time. She saw the subtle shifts in the magical currents, the slow, almost imperceptible changes in the climate, and the whispers of discontent that occasionally arose even in the most harmonious communities. These were not signs of impending doom, but rather the natural rhythms of a world perpetually in flux.

The ocean, once a source of wonder and exploration under Theron's watchful eye, began to subtly alter. New currents emerged, previously unknown species appeared from the abyssal depths, and ancient, slumbering volcanoes beneath the waves stirred from their millennial sleep. Theron, ever the explorer, embraced these changes, viewing them not as threats but as opportunities for further understanding. His expeditions became increasingly daring, venturing into regions previously deemed too hazardous, seeking to unravel the mysteries that the shifting ocean revealed. He charted new underwater landscapes, discovering lost civilizations and forgotten technologies, adding to the realm's ever-growing body of knowledge. He learned to interpret the language of the deep, deciphering the cryptic warnings and ancient prophecies whispered on the currents by the ocean's sentient beings. His work became crucial in mitigating the potential hazards of the evolving underwater world, ensuring that the harmony extended even to the unexplored depths.

Elara, in her mountain kingdom, witnessed the awakening of ancient geothermal energies. The volcanoes, once dormant, exhibited renewed activity, their fiery breath shaping the very landscape. She didn't resist these changes but, instead, adapted her engineering marvels to harness the increased power, expanding the geothermal network to unprecedented scales. Her creations became more resilient, capable of withstanding the increased seismic activity and the unpredictable nature of the awakening volcanoes.

She discovered new, more potent sources of geothermal energy, hidden deep within the Earth's core, leading to groundbreaking advancements in energy production and technological innovation. Her work, once focused on sustainability, became a testament to resilience, a dance with the unpredictable power of nature.

Faelar, in the emerald forests, observed the subtle changes in the flora and fauna. New species emerged, while others adapted to the shifting environment, a testament to the constant evolution of life. Her botanical gardens became not merely repositories of knowledge but living laboratories, where she studied the interplay between species and the ever-changing ecosystem. She developed new agricultural techniques, enhancing the resilience of crops and ensuring food security in the face of environmental shifts. Her understanding of the intricate web of life allowed her to anticipate and mitigate potential ecological imbalances, ensuring that the balance of nature remained undisturbed, even amidst the constant changes. Her gentle hand guided the evolution, preventing any catastrophic ecological shifts.

Orion, in the Golden Scale cities, witnessed a renaissance of art and architecture inspired by the changing world. The interplay of light and shadow, once a source of aesthetic delight, became a tool for adapting to the fluctuating sunlight caused by the shifts in the celestial bodies. He developed new building techniques that responded to the changing light patterns, optimizing energy efficiency and enhancing the beauty of his creations. His innovative designs mirrored the dynamism of the world, creating structures that were not merely functional but deeply connected to the rhythm of the natural world. His creations reflected both the elegance of nature's constant change and the inherent beauty of adapting to it.

Silas, the silent guardian of the Shadow Stalkers, found that his skills were needed more than ever. The changing world brought new challenges and new threats, both from the natural world and from the shifting magical currents. His mastery of stealth and illusion became essential in safeguarding the realm against unforeseen dangers. He trained a new generation of Shadow Stalkers, instilling in them the wisdom of their ancestors while adapting their techniques to suit the challenges of a world in constant flux. He ensured that their skills, once cloaked in secrecy, were now used openly as protectors of the fragile balance of the world.

Humanity, too, adapted, their ingenuity fueled by the constant challenges posed by the ever-changing world. Their scientists worked tirelessly to understand and predict the shifts in the magical currents and the environmental changes. Their engineers created structures that could withstand natural disasters and adapt to the changing landscape. Their artists channeled the dynamism of the world into breathtaking creations, capturing the essence of change and transformation. Their collective wisdom ensured that humanity remained a bridge, connecting all cultures and enabling them to navigate the changing landscape together.

The cycle of creation and destruction, therefore, was not a threat to the paradise that had been created, but rather its very essence. It was a constant reminder that even in moments of profound peace, the forces of change are always at play. The new pantheon, a blend of old gods and the cosmic entities, understood this. They guided the changes, preventing chaos and ensuring that the realm continued to evolve in a harmonious way. They were not static rulers but active participants in the ongoing cosmic dance, ensuring that the world remained vibrant, dynamic, and alive.

The story of the protagonist, once a tale of personal triumph, has now transcended into a cosmic narrative. His legacy became a reminder that even amidst the grand cycles of creation and destruction, the human spirit, fueled by hope and resilience, could create moments of enduring beauty and harmony. His story was not just a story of a man who overcame his inner demons, but a testament to the resilience of the human spirit in the face of the relentless, ever-evolving cosmos. His world, a testament to his victory, would continue to change, to evolve, to dance to the rhythms of creation and destruction, but it would do so in harmony, reflecting the enduring power of his legacy. The cycle continues, but within its embrace lies the enduring promise of a new dawn, forever renewed, forever evolving, but always striving towards a harmonious balance between the forces that shape existence itself. The new dawn, though perpetually re-emerging from the ashes of the past, ensured that the paradise endured, a testament to the constant striving towards a balance between chaos and order, destruction and creation. The cycle was not an end, but a beginning, a continuation of the story, a testament to the endless dance of creation and destruction, constantly shaping and reshaping the world. The journey was endless, a testament to the constant and ever-changing nature of existence itself.

The centuries that followed Theron's ascension saw the slow, deliberate unfolding of a new era. His wisdom, once a personal triumph over inner demons, became the bedrock of a burgeoning civilization. The knowledge he had gleaned from his journey, from the whispers of cosmic entities to the secrets held within the depths of the ocean, was meticulously documented and disseminated throughout the realm. In the shimmering city of Aethel, built upon the foundations of his former battleground, a grand academy was erected – the Citadel of Celestial Wisdom. Here, scholars from every corner of the world gathered, poring over ancient texts, interpreting the cryptic prophecies whispered on the winds, and deciphering the intricate patterns of the magical currents.

The Citadel wasn't merely a repository of knowledge; it was a living, breathing organism, constantly evolving and adapting to the changing world. Its curriculum was not rigid, but rather fluid, adjusting to the discoveries and challenges that each new generation faced. The wisdom of Theron, passed down through countless generations, remained at its core, but it was constantly enriched and expanded upon, incorporating the insights of brilliant minds across the ages. The lessons weren't simply theoretical; students embarked on expeditions, mirroring Theron's own journeys, exploring the depths of the ocean, charting uncharted territories, and delving into the mysteries of the ancient ruins that peppered the landscape.

The influence of Theron's legacy extended beyond the Citadel of Celestial Wisdom. In Elara's mountain kingdom, his teachings on resilience and adaptation were incorporated into the curriculum of the engineering schools. The next generation of engineers learned not only to build magnificent structures but also to anticipate and mitigate the effects of natural disasters, ensuring the continued prosperity of the mountain communities. They built structures that danced with the rhythm of the earth, incorporating seismic dampeners and geothermal energy sources, transforming the landscape into a marvel of harmonious engineering.

In Faelar's sprawling emerald forests, the botanical gardens became centers of ecological stewardship, guided by Theron's lessons on the delicate balance of nature. Scholars studied the intricate interactions between species, developing new techniques to protect endangered species and ensure the sustainability of the ecosystem. They didn't simply observe nature; they actively participated in its evolution, guiding it gently towards a state of harmonious coexistence. The forests flourished, their beauty a testament to the harmonious interplay between nature and human intervention.

Orion's city, once a dazzling spectacle of art and architecture, became a hub of innovation and creative expression. The principles of adaptation, honed during Theron's journey, were applied to the design of new buildings and urban infrastructure. Structures responded to light patterns, changing with the seasons, optimizing energy efficiency and creating breathtaking aesthetic displays. The vibrant culture of Aethel thrived, a beacon of creativity and expression, inspired by Theron's legacy.

Silas's Shadow Stalkers, once guardians of secrets, became the protectors of the realm, their skills refined and expanded to meet the evolving challenges of a dynamic world. Their training incorporated not only physical prowess and mastery of illusion but also a profound understanding of the magical currents and the intricate workings of the cosmos. They served as guardians, not in secrecy, but as visible protectors, their presence a symbol of harmony and security.

The influence of Theron's legacy reached even the most remote corners of the world. In the seven reptilian cities, his wisdom was translated and adapted to their unique culture. His teachings on understanding the inner demons and forging harmony became a key part of their spiritual development. The reptilian tribes, once warring factions, found common ground in his philosophy of balance and adaptation. They developed a deeper understanding of the interconnectedness of all life and created collaborative projects, working together to preserve their unique ecosystems.

Humanity, under the guidance of Theron's teachings, embraced a new golden age. Their scientists, inspired by his journeys into the unknown, pressed ever further, exploring the intricacies of the cosmos and the very fabric of reality. Their engineers, building upon the foundations laid by Elara, constructed sustainable cities that seamlessly integrated with the natural world. Their artists, drawing inspiration from Orion's innovative designs, created works of art that captured the very essence of change and transformation.

The new pantheon, a council of gods representing the blend of old and new cosmic entities, ensured the wisdom of Theron's legacy was not confined to specific locations or cultures. They commissioned grand libraries across the land, filled with scrolls, tablets, and holographic archives detailing Theron's journey, his triumphs, and the lessons learned. These libraries were not static institutions but dynamic centers of learning, constantly updated with new discoveries and insights.

Furthermore, the pantheon established a system of traveling scholars and itinerant teachers, who carried the wisdom of Theron across the realm. They visited villages, cities, and secluded communities, sharing their knowledge and engaging in dialogues, ensuring that Theron's legacy was accessible to everyone. They weren't just educators; they were storytellers, weaving tales of Theron's journey, inspiring hope and instilling in the hearts of the people a deep understanding of the interconnectedness of all things.

The passage of time did not diminish the impact of Theron's wisdom; rather, it amplified it. Each generation built upon the foundations laid by their predecessors, adding their own insights and experiences to the ever-growing tapestry of knowledge. The stories of Theron became myths, legends imbued with philosophical depth, reminding each generation of the importance of self-discovery, resilience, and the enduring power of the human spirit. His legacy wasn't a fixed point in history, but a vibrant, ever-evolving force, shaping the destiny of the realm for centuries to come. His journey, once a struggle against inner demons, became a beacon of hope and inspiration for all who followed.

The wisdom of Theron transcended cultural boundaries and time itself. The reptilian tribes, with their unique perspective and ancient traditions, integrated his teachings into their own cosmology, enriching their understanding of the cosmic dance. The fairies, with their intimate connection to nature, adapted his lessons on ecological balance into their intricate magical systems. Each culture interpreted and applied his wisdom in its own way, resulting in a richer, more diverse, and harmonious world. The common thread linking them all was the acknowledgment of the cyclical nature of existence, the understanding that change was inevitable, and the importance of adapting and evolving to meet the challenges of an ever-changing cosmos.

The legacy was not merely a collection of teachings; it was a way of life. It emphasized the importance of constant learning, continuous self-improvement, and the pursuit of knowledge for its own sake. It promoted understanding, cooperation, and respect for all forms of life. It fostered innovation, creativity, and a deep appreciation for the beauty of the natural world. This legacy lived not just in grand academies and libraries but in the daily lives of the people, in their interactions with each other, their relationship with the environment, and their collective pursuit of a better future. It was a testament to the enduring power of hope, resilience, and the ability of the human spirit to overcome seemingly insurmountable challenges. The new dawn, far from being a static state of utopia, became a perpetual cycle of renewal, a constant striving towards balance, a reflection of the ongoing cosmic dance between creation and destruction. The journey of Theron and the wisdom he shared were not just a story of the past; they were a roadmap for the future, a guiding light illuminating the path towards a harmonious existence for all.

Yet, even in this seemingly perfect world, sculpted from the crucible of Theron's trials, shadows lingered. The very act of remaking reality, of forging a new pantheon from the ashes of the old, left unanswered questions echoing through the ages. The whispers of the cosmic entities, once a source of profound knowledge, now seemed to hold a deeper, more unsettling mystery. Their pronouncements, though benevolent in their intent, carried an undercurrent of ambiguity, leaving room for interpretations that shifted like sands on a windswept dune.

For instance, the nature of the demonic forces that Theron had conquered remained a source of endless debate within the Citadel of Celestial Wisdom. Was it truly vanquished, or merely contained, slumbering beneath the surface of the new paradise? Some scholars hypothesized that the very act of transmuting hell into heaven had created a paradoxical entity, a powerful force neither wholly good nor wholly evil, existing in a perpetual state of flux. Others suggested that the demons were merely a manifestation of the inherent duality of existence, a necessary counterpoint to the divine. This duality, they argued, was not to be eradicated, but understood and managed, an integral part of the cosmic dance.

The very act of creation itself, the miraculous remaking of the world, generated its own set of enigmas. The new pantheon, while seemingly harmonious, comprised entities from vastly different cosmic realms. Their motivations, though ostensibly aligned with Theron's vision, remained largely inscrutable. Did they fully embrace Theron's principles of harmony and balance, or were their own agendas subtly at play, veiled beneath a facade of benevolent cooperation? Their silence on certain matters, their cryptic pronouncements, fuelled speculation and endless debate.

The integration of the seven reptilian tribes, once fierce rivals, into the unified world order posed another challenge. While their collaborative efforts in preserving their ecosystems were remarkable, their inherent cultural differences presented ongoing tensions. The deep-rooted suspicion and mistrust, inherited from centuries of conflict, could not be erased overnight. The possibility of future conflicts, fueled by subtle power struggles and conflicting interpretations of Theron's legacy, remained a potential threat.

The nature of Theron's own immortality also raised troubling questions. His ascension to godhood had been a triumphant culmination of his journey, yet it also presented a new set of vulnerabilities. Did his newfound immortality come with unforeseen limitations? Was he susceptible to forms of influence or manipulation previously unknown? The very concept of immortality, once a symbol of ultimate power, now seemed tinged with an existential dread. The possibility of eternal stagnation, of becoming a passive observer in the ever-evolving cosmic dance, haunted some of the more philosophical minds of the Citadel.

Then there was the question of the future. Theron's legacy had laid the foundations for a golden age, but could this utopia endure? The very act of creating paradise could, paradoxically, breed complacency and stagnation. The absence of struggle, of challenge, might weaken the very spirit that Theron had sought to cultivate. Would future generations, born into a world without conflict, be equipped to face unforeseen threats or navigate the inevitable changes that time would bring?

The potential for unforeseen cosmic events, for disruptions in the fabric of reality, remained a significant concern. The cosmic entities, while benevolent in their interactions with Theron, had hinted at larger forces, at powers beyond human comprehension. These forces, though largely dormant, could awaken at any moment, presenting challenges that even Theron's wisdom might not fully prepare humanity for. The very stability of the new world, therefore, seemed to depend on a fragile balance, susceptible to events beyond anyone's control.

The unanswered questions extended even to the nature of magic itself. Theron's mastery had been extraordinary, but the precise mechanisms of magic, the underlying principles that governed its manifestations, remained elusive. His teachings provided a framework, a practical understanding, but a complete theoretical explanation eluded even the most brilliant minds. Was magic a fundamental force of the universe, an integral part of its fabric, or was it something else entirely, something more akin to a complex, self-organizing system, governed by rules yet to be fully understood?

Furthermore, the relationship between the mortal and immortal realms continued to be a source of both wonder and uncertainty. Theron's journey had bridged the gap between these realms, but the precise nature of this connection remained poorly understood. Were there further gateways between the worlds, undiscovered pathways that could lead to either unimaginable opportunities or catastrophic consequences? The very fact that these pathways existed posed a profound challenge, necessitating constant vigilance and a deeper understanding of the cosmic tapestry.

The question of free will versus destiny was perhaps the most profound of all the unanswered questions. Theron's journey had been one of self-discovery, a testament to the power of individual choice. Yet, his destiny, his eventual ascent to godhood, seemed predetermined, guided by the whispers of the cosmic entities. This paradox raised fundamental questions about the nature of free will, about the extent to which human actions are truly free, or merely a part of a larger cosmic design. Was the triumph over inner demons an act of individual agency or a preordained part of a larger cosmic narrative?

In the final analysis, the epilogue was not a definitive conclusion, but a new beginning. The new dawn, though promising, was not without its shadows. The unanswered questions served not as flaws, but as opportunities – opportunities for further exploration, for deeper understanding, and for future narratives. The world Theron had created, while a testament to his triumph, was a dynamic, ever-evolving entity, its future unwritten, its potential limitless. The reader, having witnessed Theron's incredible journey, was left to ponder these mysteries, to contemplate the ongoing dance of creation and destruction, and to imagine the possibilities that lay ahead. The story of Theron, far from ending, had only just begun its next chapter. The cosmic dance continued, its rhythms both familiar and strangely new, leaving the fate of the newly reborn world hanging in a delicate and intriguing balance. The very fabric of reality, it seemed, remained woven with threads of both hope and uncertainty, a testament to the ever-present duality at the heart of existence.

The newly formed pantheon, a dazzling constellation of beings from disparate cosmic realms, convened in the celestial court. Theron, now the Supreme God, observed them with a mixture of pride and apprehension. Their unity, forged in the crucible of his victory, felt fragile, a delicate balance poised on the edge of a knife. The whispers of the cosmic entities, once a source of guidance, now felt more like cryptic riddles, their pronouncements laced with an unsettling ambiguity. The very act of creation, the breathtaking transformation of hell into a paradise, had birthed unforeseen complexities.

The integration of the seven reptilian tribes presented a unique challenge. Their long history of conflict had left deep-seated scars, a legacy of suspicion and mistrust that refused to yield easily to Theron's utopian vision. Despite their remarkable collaboration in ecological restoration, undercurrents of rivalry persisted. Subtle power struggles simmered beneath the surface, fueled by divergent interpretations of Theron's legacy and the distribution of resources in the newly created world. The whispers of old grievances, like the rustle of leaves in a forgotten forest, carried the potential for future conflicts. Their unique physiology and cultural nuances, previously sources of conflict, now presented an opportunity for a rich tapestry of societal development, but careful stewardship would be needed to navigate the complexities of such a diverse population. The creation of a common language, a unifying culture that respected individual identities, became a crucial undertaking for the new world order.

The nature of magic itself remained a profound enigma. Theron's mastery had been unprecedented, but the underlying principles governing its manifestations remained elusive. The Celestial Academy, a hub of learning and research within the Citadel of Celestial Wisdom, was abuzz with debates on the theoretical underpinnings of magic. Some scholars posited that magic was a fundamental force of the universe, a fabric woven into the very cosmos. Others argued that it was a complex, self-organizing system, perhaps even a form of advanced technology developed by ancient, forgotten civilizations. This debate had significant implications for the advancement of magic and its application in various aspects of life. The potential for both immense progress and catastrophic misuse depended on a thorough understanding of this elusive force.

The delicate balance between the mortal and immortal realms was another significant area of concern. Theron's ascension had bridged the gap between these realms, yet the precise nature of this connection remained poorly understood. Scholars warned of the potential for unforeseen consequences should this connection be mishandled. The possibility of unintended gateways opening, leading to both opportunities and catastrophic events, demanded careful monitoring and rigorous research. The creation of a sophisticated network of celestial sentinels became crucial to ensure the stability of this newly forged link between worlds.

Even Theron's immortality, a triumphant culmination of his arduous journey, carried with it unforeseen complexities. While his power was undeniable, it was not without its limitations. The constant pressure of maintaining the delicate balance of his created world weighed heavily on him. He became more acutely aware of the ever-present duality of existence, the constant interplay between creation and destruction, order and chaos. His existence became a paradox: the holder of ultimate power, yet simultaneously burdened by the weight of its responsibility. He found solace only in the subtle beauty of his new paradise, in the quiet moments of contemplation under the eternally twilight sky.

The very fabric of reality, Theron discovered, was not static; it was dynamic, ever-evolving. The cosmic entities, though benevolent, hinted at forces far beyond human comprehension, potent entities that slumbered beneath the surface of the universe, capable of disrupting its delicate balance. The possibility of a cataclysmic event, something that could unravel the very fabric of reality, loomed large in the minds of the pantheon. It was this possibility, more than any other, that tested Theron's resolve. The stability of the new world depended on the ability of its inhabitants, both mortal and immortal, to adapt to the ever-changing realities of the cosmos. The delicate balance between the known and unknown, the order and chaos, the light and darkness, would continuously be challenged.

The question of free will versus destiny loomed large. Theron's journey had been a testament to the power of individual choice, but his destiny, his ascension to godhood, seemed predetermined, shaped by forces beyond his immediate comprehension. This paradox, the interplay between individual agency and cosmic design, fueled countless debates within the Citadel of Celestial Wisdom. Were human actions truly free, or were they merely threads in a larger cosmic tapestry, woven by forces unseen? This question continued to haunt Theron, a lingering echo of his own trials and triumphs. He knew, however, that the future of his world depended not only on his wisdom but on the choices of his people, their capacity for both compassion and courage, their ability to make decisions in the face of uncertainty.

The seeds of future stories were planted in this newly reborn world. The integration of disparate cultures, the exploration of the mysteries of magic, the delicate balance between mortality and immortality, the potential for unforeseen cosmic events – these were not just challenges; they were opportunities, fertile ground for future adventures. The story of Theron, the man who transmuted hell into heaven, was not an ending but a beginning, a springboard for countless new narratives, each one a testament to the enduring power of hope, resilience, and the eternal dance between creation and destruction.

The final image, lingering in the reader's mind, was not one of perfect utopia, but a dynamic world, ever-evolving, its future unwritten, its potential limitless. A world where the echoes of past conflicts mingled with the promise of a brighter tomorrow. A world where the gods and mortals, the reptilian tribes and the fairies, co-existed in a fragile yet resilient harmony. A world filled with the potential for both unimaginable beauty and unspeakable terror, a world where the seeds of both hope and despair were sown, side-by-side, in the fertile ground of an ever-evolving reality. This newly formed paradise, like the cosmos itself, was a vast canvas, waiting to be painted with the strokes of countless futures, each brushstroke a testament to the enduring power of choice, the unending dance of creation and destruction, the endless mysteries of existence. The story of Theron, therefore, was not a conclusion, but a prologue, the prelude to countless tales yet to be told, each echoing with the rhythms of the cosmic dance, each carrying the weight of hope and uncertainty, each reflecting the delicate balance of a world ever teetering on the precipice of the unknown. The future, like the cosmos itself, remained unwritten, a vast and mysterious expanse, waiting to be explored.